THE ROYAL LIBRARIAN

Daisy Wood worked as an editor in children's publishing before she started writing her own books. She has a degree in English Literature and an MA in Creative Writing from City University, London. This is her third published novel for adults. She divides her time between London and Dorset, and when not lurking in the London Library, can often be found chasing a rescue Pointer through various parks with a Basset Hound in tow.

By the same author:

The Clockmaker's Wife
The Forgotten Bookshop in Paris

Under the name of Jennie Walters:

What We Did in the War

The
Royal
Librarian

DAISY WOOD

Published by AVON
A division of HarperCollins*Publishers* Ltd
1 London Bridge Street
London SE1 9GF

www.harpercollins.co.uk

HarperCollins*Publishers*
Macken House, 39/40 Mayor Street Upper,
Dublin 1 D01 C9W8, Ireland

A Paperback Original 2024
24 25 26 27 28 LBC 6 5 4 3 2
First published in Great Britain by HarperCollins*Publishers* 2024

ISBN (PB): 978-0-00-863692-0
ISBN (TPB): 978-0-00-863997-6

Typeset in Sabon LT Std by Palimpsest Book Production Limited,
Falkirk, Stirlingshire

Printed and bound in the United States

For Molly Walker-Sharp

Author's note

This novel is a work of fiction. The plot described in the following pages has no basis in reality, and there's no suggestion that the Royal Librarian at Windsor Castle during the Second World War handed over any of his responsibilities. Yet it's undoubtedly true that the Royal Family would have been in great danger had Britain been invaded by Nazi Germany, which seemed likely during the summer of 1940. Hitler apparently believed King George VI would abdicate during the relentless bombing of London during the Blitz, which began that September, and there's evidence that he was planning to reinstate the Duke of Windsor on the throne with a puppet government carrying out Nazi orders, similar to the Vichy regime in France.

The princesses, Elizabeth and Margaret, stayed at Windsor from May 1940 until the end of the war, and Princess Elizabeth enlisted in the ATS when she turned eighteen in 1945. Plans were prepared for the Royal Family to be secretly evacuated to a house in the country – and possibly from there to Canada – but they were never put into effect. I've tried to convey something of the atmosphere of the castle in those times: the chilly stone corridors, gloomy dungeons and weapons mounted on every wall. And something of the princesses' characters, too: Elizabeth aware of her responsibilities from a young age, and Margaret charming but naughty, clamouring for attention.

For obvious reasons, it's been difficult to find out much about life at Windsor Castle both then and now. I was directed to a fascinating file in the Royal Archives at Windsor, giving details of ration cards, fuel restrictions, the need to salvage string – and even a letter from one of the secretaries living in the north terrace, requesting permission to continue using their wireless sets, which I wove into the story. And Marion Crawford, the princesses' nanny, recounts in her book *The Little Princesses* being taken to the vaults by the Royal Librarian and shown the Crown Jewels, stuffed into a biscuit tin.

I was also inspired to create the character of George Sinclair by reading about Thomas Kendrick and his MI6 secretaries at the British Passport Office in Vienna; he and his staff worked long hours granting visas that enabled hundreds of Austrian Jews to escape the country. Helen Fry's books, *The Walls Have Ears* and *Spymaster: The Man Who Saved MI6*, give a fascinating insight into this extraordinary man. And that dreadful incident in the Prater park in Vienna on 23 April 1938, which I describe in the book, is also true.

In short, I've taken a few facts and a lot of imagination to launch a giant 'what if?' I hope readers will forgive my temerity, and enjoy the ride.

Prologue

Windsor Castle, July 1940

Sophie is taken away through St George's Gate for the last time. She knows in her heart she won't be coming back. Her wrists are handcuffed behind her back, and she's escorted by two policemen, one on each side, as though she were the most dangerous criminal in Britain. 'I'm not the enemy,' she wants to shout, but no one will believe her. Heads turned as she marched along the corridors from the Superintendent's office, past footmen in battle-dress livery and housemaids appearing from nowhere to gawp. She could guess what they were thinking: 'We never trusted that girl, and look how right we were.'

I am the Royal Librarian, she reminds herself, straightening her shoulders, and I have done nothing wrong. Is that true, though? Even now, she has no idea.

She catches sight of the Long Walk rolling away through the park, and the memory of the times she has found sanctuary there, mourning her parents, pierces her like a knife. What would they say if they could see her, paraded in all her shame? But they are both gone, and she is alone

1

in a strange country. She has been playing for high stakes and lost the game, and there is no one to speak up for her anymore.

Chapter One

Vienna, March 1938

Sophie and her father listened in silence to the noise outside their apartment: car horns blaring, people cheering, a bicycle bell trilling over and over like a demented bird and, far in the distance, the alarming beat of drums. The wireless was only playing German military music, so they'd switched it off.

Sophie went to the window and stared out for the hundredth time at the people milling about below, many clutching swastika flags that matched the banners hanging from balconies and pasted over hoardings. A few days before, the Chancellor had announced his resignation on the radio and let the Nazis take control of the government. He'd asked God to bless Austria at the end of the broadcast, but without much hope. 'God save us all,' Sophie's mother Ingrid had muttered, and her father had had tears in his eyes. And now Adolf Hitler was back in the country of his birth, being driven in triumph at that very moment through the streets he'd once swept. Ingrid had gone to her cake shop, not far from the Ringstrasse, to make sure it wasn't looted; there was a febrile atmosphere in the city that they all knew could soon lead to violence. The schools were closed, and so was the library where Sophie worked. Today, anything could happen – and her little sister Hanna still wasn't home. Sophie reproached herself for letting Hanna out to play at her best friend's house. The Blumenthals lived several streets away and Gretel's older brother had recently joined the Hitler Youth brigade. What if Frau Blumenthal had taken Hanna and Gretel out into the streets to join in the celebrations?

She turned away from the window, sighing.

'Try not to worry,' her father said, looking up from his book. 'Hanna's with Gretel and she's a sensible girl – I'm sure they'll stick together.'

Yet Sophie couldn't bear to be confined a minute longer in the dark, cramped apartment. 'I'll go round to the Blumenthals',' she told him. 'I shouldn't have let her visit them today. The least I can do is bring her back.'

'You'd be better off staying here,' Otto replied. 'They might have gone out somewhere and you have no idea where.'

'That's exactly what I'm afraid of,' Sophie said. 'We should be together at a time like this and it's bad enough Mutti's not home. I need to find my sister.'

Her father shifted uneasily in his chair. He didn't want to be left alone, Sophie realised, with a pang of sympathy mixed with irritation and fear. What would happen to the family if Otto were no longer in charge?

'Well, if there's any sign of trouble,' he warned, 'come straight home.'

Not so long ago, he would have been out looking for his daughter himself, but since losing his job at the National

Library the week before, he hadn't left the apartment. Sophie would find him sitting in a chair, staring into space. Her father's only crime was to have Jewish parents: a fact she and her sister had hardly been aware of until recently. Now everyone seemed to know Herr Klein's guilty secret. Sophie could only assume that somehow the Blumenthals hadn't heard; as soon as they did, the invitations to play with Gretel would dry up. Her quietly confident father had become timid and hesitant, unable to make the smallest decision. The day before, a neighbour from the floor above – a minor government official – had rapped on their door and virtually pushed his way in, demanding the keys to the family car.

'You won't be needing it anymore,' the man had said, and laughed. 'It's not as though you can go anywhere.'

Otto had made some half-hearted protest but given in embarrassingly quickly when the neighbour threatened to come back with his friends. 'What could I do?' he'd said to the family. 'He'd have taken the car anyway.' But he couldn't look any of them in the face and spent the afternoon shut in his bedroom.

Sophie took her coat from the hall stand, tied a headscarf low over her brow and ran down the stairs of their apartment building. Neither she nor Hanna conformed to the dark-haired Jewish stereotype. Sophie was a blend of her parents' colouring, with olive skin that turned nut-brown in summer, honey-coloured hair and light green eyes, while Hanna's blonde curls and blue eyes came directly from their mother. No one would think she had a drop of Jewish blood in her. Hanna had probably simply lost track of the time, parading about Gretel's apartment in Frau Blumenthal's high-heeled shoes or chatting with her friend on the swings in the park nearby. There was no answer when Sophie rang the bell of the Blumenthals' apartment, however, and the park was empty save for an elderly man, marooned on a bench with his dog. Everyone was out in the streets.

Sophie's heart quickened as she stepped into the crowded street, scanning the various groups of people for a glimpse of Hanna's red beret and blue coat. It was a bright spring afternoon, the tightly furled buds of the magnolia trees about to burst into flower.

'*Achtung!*' shouted a teenage boy, wobbling past on his bicycle with a girl balanced on the crossbar who shrieked with laughter. Sophie stepped back, colliding with a family dressed in their best clothes, their faces alight with excitement and the children clutching swastika flags. 'Hurry up, Grandpa,' a small boy urged. 'We'll never catch up with the Führer at this rate!'

And then walking down the middle of the road came a gang of the Hitler Youth, arms linked, chests puffed out in white shirts and red swastika armbands. There must have been about ten of them, pink-cheeked and proud in their moment of glory. Sophie took shelter in the doorway of an apartment building and turned her face away as they marched by. The little boy who'd urged his grandfather to hurry shouted, '*Sieg Heil!*' in a squeaky voice and raised his right arm in the Nazi salute, which they ignored.

'What are you doing, sucking up to those thugs?' Sophie felt like asking the kid, but the shameful truth was, she was frightened of the boys, even though they couldn't have been older than fourteen or fifteen. She had once seen a pair of them kick away the stick of an elderly rabbi and beat him with it when he fell in the gutter. When she'd tried to intervene, one had twisted her arm behind her back until she'd cried out in pain. They did as they pleased because no one dared stop them, and now their leader had arrived, they would be bolder and nastier than ever.

Sophie waited until the Hitler Youth were a safe distance away before joining the stream of people heading for the city centre. She would go as far as the canal, she decided, and hope to meet Hanna and Gretel on their way home. Approaching the bridge, she found barriers in place along the main road as ranks of soldiers in grey-green uniform with rifles over their shoulders marched in time with the military band towards the centre of the old town, while SS stormtroopers linked arms to hold back the spectators. Following behind the troops were teams of horses pulling wheeled guns, jeeps crammed with military personnel and then a long line of grey Mercedes gliding past with darkened windows. Swastikas were everywhere she looked: on the flags waved by children, on the soldier's armbands, rippling on banners hung from balconies. And all around her, people were cheering at the tops of their voices, craning to catch a glimpse of the German troops who had come to occupy their country.

'*Sieg Heil!*' screamed a middle-aged woman next to Sophie, raising her right arm in the Nazi salute and practically toppling over in her excitement. Children were hoisted on their parents' shoulders, boys perched on lampposts and the stormtroopers watched with grim satisfaction.

'I saw him, the Führer,' shouted a man pushing his way through. 'Half an hour ago. He was standing in a Jeep. You might as well leave; he won't come this way again.' But nobody took any notice.

Sophie's heart was hammering against her chest as she fumbled to retie her headscarf, dislodged in the melee. She couldn't bear to think of her little sister lost in this scrum

7

but there was no hope of finding Hanna here and being surrounded a second longer by these idiotic, grinning faces was intolerable.

'Let me through,' she called, raising her arms in front of her face. 'I have to get home.'

'Watch it,' a man growled, and a shove in the back sent her stumbling forward into the side of a large woman in a fur coat who tutted and thrust her away, so vigorously that she fell on her hands and knees. I could die here, she thought; these people could trample me underfoot and no one would do anything to help. They could sense she was afraid and would turn on her like a pack of wild animals.

Yet just at that moment, she heard a voice ask, 'Sophie? Is that you?' and someone was lifting her up.

Her rescuer was Wilhelm Fischer: a boy she'd known in junior school who lived not far from the Kleins, and whom she still occasionally bumped into. He'd been the cleverest boy in the class and she the cleverest girl, and they'd always been rivals rather than friends. She found him arrogant and he, she suspected, thought her a prig. Still, she was relieved to see him now.

'Let's get out of here,' he said, taking her by the arm and managing to clear a path through the crowd. He was broad-shouldered with sharp elbows and a menacing air, and he was blond, too: as fair as any Aryan youth leader could have wanted. People got out of his way.

Wilhelm steered her towards a quieter side street and then into the shelter of an arched doorway, where they took stock of each other. He looked much older than the last time she'd seen him, the year before, skating with his friends around the outdoor ice rink. He'd lost weight since then and needed a shave.

'Come to celebrate our glorious leader?' he asked, scrutinising her. 'Where's your flag?'

'I'm just trying to find my little sister,' she replied. 'Where's yours?'

'I must have left it at home.' He glanced warily up and down the street before adding, 'You know I'm a Communist, don't you?'

'The news must have passed me by.' Her attempt at a joke fell flat. 'Though I suppose you're keeping it quiet.' The party had been banned since a Fascist government had come to power in Austria five years before.

'I was, but they've rumbled me. I've been in jail for the past couple of months.'

'I'm sorry,' Sophie said awkwardly. She wasn't sure how to act around the cocky schoolboy who seemed to have suddenly turned into a man.

'Don't be. It was fine; I met some interesting people.' He took another look around and then said in a lower voice, 'We can fight back, you know. That bastard Hitler won't have it all his own way.'

Sophie let out her breath. 'I hate him as much as you. My father's Jewish.'

Wilhelm whistled, and looked at her for a few seconds without speaking. 'So what are you going to do?'

'I'm not sure. We'll try to leave, I suppose, but it might be too late.' She swallowed a rising sense of panic. 'My mother didn't want to abandon her shop, you see, and she's not Jewish – she never converted. We have passports but we need a sponsor before we can get visas for another country.'

'Aren't there organisations that can help you?'

'Perhaps.' But the Kleins weren't part of the Jewish

9

community. Her father didn't go to synagogue or observe the religious holidays, they didn't live in a Jewish area or eat kosher food at home, and her parents' friends came from many different backgrounds. The family opened Christmas presents under a candle-lit tree and celebrated Easter with decorated eggs. When it was time for religious education at school, first Sophie and then Hanna had stayed in their seats when the Jewish children were taken out for separate instruction, learning about the Christian faith instead. They had sensed the danger of their Jewishness, such as it was, even then. Otto's family had cut him off for marrying outside the faith, so Hanna and Sophie didn't see their Klein relatives. They were Mischlinge: half Jews with a foot in each camp, belonging properly to neither.

'Well, let me know if I can help,' Wilhelm said. 'You remember where we live?'

Sophie nodded. 'Thanks. That's kind of you.'

'See you, then.' He sauntered off down the street, his hands in his pockets. 'Wait!' she shouted, running after him. He turned, shading his eyes against the sun.

'Why are *you* here today?' she asked.

He grinned and for a moment they might have been twelve, listening to Herr Meyer droning on about the unification of Germany. 'Sizing up the enemy.' He pointed his fingers in the shape of a gun. 'One day I might get lucky.'

'Be careful,' she said, and he put a hand to his forehead in a mock salute, which turned into a wave. She watched until he'd disappeared from view, wanting to call him back again but unable to think of a reason.

Chapter Two

Vienna, March 1938

It was another hour before Sophie caught sight of Hanna from her vantage point at the end of the Blumenthals' street. Her sister was walking hand in hand with Frau Blumenthal while Gretel skipped along on her mother's other side. Both girls were holding swastika flags and chattering at the tops of their voices.

Sophie was flooded with such sweet relief, she thought for a moment her legs might give way. 'There you are,' she said in a bright, false voice, approaching the trio. 'Goodness, we were beginning to get worried. You're very late, Hanna.'

'We saw the Führer!' Hanna's eyes were shining. 'He was standing in a tank.'

'That was one of the generals, silly,' Gretel put in. 'But there were horses, too, and so many soldiers.' She swung her arms and legs stiffly, imitating the goose step, and both girls collapsed into giggles. Perhaps it wouldn't be such a bad thing if the Blumenthals dropped Hanna; Sophie had always disliked the way her sister behaved when she was with Gretel.

'I told the girls, one day they'll tell their children they were here today.' Frau Blumenthal was as jubilant as her daughter. 'You just wait and see; now the Führer's in charge, things will start looking up.'

Sophie took Hanna by the hand, extracting the swastika flag at the same time. 'What do you say to Frau Blumenthal?' she asked.

'Thank you for having me,' Hanna parroted, then stuck her tongue out at Gretel.

Sophie forced herself to smile at the woman before she took her sister away.

'What's the matter?' Hanna asked warily, once they were alone. 'Are you cross about something?'

Sophie knelt beside her. 'I've been worried, that's all, not knowing where you were. And this is not a day to be celebrating, whatever Frau Blumenthal says.' She lowered her voice. 'Listen to me, *Liebchen*. Hitler is a horrible man: he hates Jews, including Papa and you and me. He doesn't want people like us in this country.'

Hanna pulled her hand from Sophie's grip. 'But Papa isn't really Jewish and nor are we. That's why Opa and Oma Klein don't want to see us.'

'We're Jewish enough, believe me,' Sophie said grimly, hiding the swastika flag in her pocket to dispose of later. She couldn't bring herself to carry it openly, not even for protection. A few streets away from home, they passed a group of Jews on their hands and knees, scrubbing at the pro-independence slogans that had been daubed on pavements and walls. A Hitler Youth brigade stood over them: children humiliating grown men and women before an audience of Vienna's finest citizens in search of entertainment.

'Why are the boys making those people do the cleaning?'

12

Hanna whispered. 'They didn't write on the pavements, did they?'

'That doesn't make any difference,' Sophie said, squeezing her sister's hand. 'It's just an excuse to pick on them.'

'But that wouldn't happen to Papa, would it?' Hanna asked.

Sophie was torn between an instinct to protect her sister and the need to tell her the truth. Hanna was the golden child, who'd arrived by some miracle ten years after her sister and been adored ever since – especially by Sophie, who'd become like a second mother to her while Ingrid was busy at work. Hanna used to cry each morning when Sophie set off for school and would be waiting at the window to catch sight of her when she came home in the afternoon. Sophie was the only person who could soothe Hanna's tantrums, the one she'd cry out for if she fell over.

'Probably not,' she told Hanna now, 'but you never know.'

Their mother must have spotted them coming down the street because she was waiting in the doorway of their apartment building by the time they approached. 'Thank God,' she said, hugging them both. 'Now run upstairs, Hanna – the door's open.'

They watched her go, skipping into the gloomy foyer like a small blonde sprite. Ingrid turned to Sophie. 'Things are bad. It's worse than I feared.'

'Did something happen at the shop?' Sophie asked.

'Some thugs burst in, looking for Tamara and wanting to know if I was Jewish. Somebody must have denounced us.' Tamara Grossman was her mother's assistant, a wonderful pastry chef and a committed, practising Jew.

'And did they find her?' Sophie looked into her mother's worried face, noticing the shadows under her eyes, the tic

13

when she was tired that made her left eyelid droop and the perpetual frown creasing her forehead these days. Frau Klein had always seemed young for her age, with her girlish figure and unlined skin, but today anyone would have thought she was ten years older.

'I told her not to come in today, thank God. In the end, they smashed up a cabinet and went away.' Ingrid took Sophie by the shoulders. 'You've been out in the streets, you've seen how people are behaving. I have to take care of Papa, but you must keep Hanna safe. Do you understand?'

'Of course, always. We'll all look after each other.'

'That's not what I mean. You girls have to leave Vienna, as soon as you can.'

A cold hand had squeezed Sophie's heart. 'But what about you and Papa?' she stammered, willing herself to have misunderstood.

'We'll try to follow, but you must go now. I have to stay with Otto, and it may be more difficult for him to escape.'

'How can we get away, though?' Sophie asked. 'I mean, we have passports but not the proper visas. And where would we go?'

'We'll think of something.' Ingrid rubbed her forehead. 'Maybe you could have a word with Judith Dichter? I heard a rumour they were off soon.'

The Dichters were a Jewish family who lived on the ground floor. Sophie used to play with Judith Dichter when she was younger, but their mothers had had some kind of falling out; she could remember only raised voices and slammed doors, and then Judith had gone to a Jewish school, and the two girls had gradually lost touch. Sophie wondered now whether the Dichters' faith and the Kleins' lack of it might have caused the argument.

'We'd better go upstairs,' her mother said, 'or Papa will wonder what we're talking about. Not a word to him yet – he'll only worry.'

Sophie followed her mother, head reeling. She'd stepped from solid ground into thin air and the rush of vertigo made her heart race. Managing by herself would be hard enough but to cope with Hanna, too, in a foreign country where they knew no one – it was a terrifying prospect. Why couldn't her parents come with them? Were they simply too frightened to leave Vienna?

Early that evening, Sophie steeled herself to call on the Dichters. It had been a long time since she'd set foot in their apartment, and she wasn't sure of her welcome. It seemed an age before Frau Dichter opened the door a crack, and only after Sophie had identified herself.

'You were lucky to catch us,' she said. 'We're off tomorrow, *baruch Hashem*, which I'm guessing is why you're here. Do you want to say goodbye to Judith?'

'Yes, thank you,' Sophie said, 'I should like that. Where are you going? And how did you manage it?'

Frau Dichter smiled grimly. 'So now you want our help, and your mother's too proud to ask for it. Well, suppose I can't blame her for that. You'll need to work hard and pray for a good helping of luck. Do you have passports?' Sophie nodded. 'That's something. You have to get exit visas to leave Austria, which will cost you plenty, and then entry visas for whichever country is willing to let you in. You all speak English, don't you? That should help.'

Sophie nodded again. Frau Klein's mother had been born in England and lived there until she was sixteen, so she had made sure Ingrid could speak the language fluently, and

Ingrid had followed that example in turn with her own daughters. She'd talk in English to them so frequently that it became second nature, and had read each of them bedtime stories from Beatrix Potter to Charles Dickens. Just as well, as things turned out.

'And where are you going?' she asked.

Apparently the Dichters had spent hours in the library, looking through British and American telephone directories and firing off letters to random strangers, begging for help and employment.

'We had two replies,' Frau Dichter said. 'One from New York and one from a place called Liverpool. It's a city in northern England, and that's where we're heading. It's impossible to get a visa for America. Go to the British Embassy and queue up there – you're young and they might take pity on you. The officials are very helpful.'

'And you're all going? Herr Dichter, too?'

'My husband is already in Paris.' A shadow crossed Frau Dichter's face. 'He was there on business so he's staying where he is. But wait, I'll call Judith.'

Judith appeared: a wraith of a girl with dark, deep-set eyes. She and Sophie had drifted so far apart that they had little to say to each other, especially on such a momentous day.

'I hope everything goes well for you.' Sophie wished she could come up with something a little more original. 'Good luck.'

'Thank you. You, too.'

Desperately, Sophie searched for some parting memory. 'Do you remember that time we climbed a tree in the park and got stuck, and your brother had to talk us down?'

'Of course. How could I forget?' Judith smiled but her lip trembled. On an impulse, Sophie hugged her.

16

Judith pulled back, resisting the embrace. 'Get out of Vienna as fast as you can,' she said quietly in Sophie's ear. 'There's nothing for us here.'

The next day, Adolf Hitler gave a speech from the balcony of the Hofburg Palace to the hundreds of thousands of townspeople crammed into Heroes' Square, announcing Austria was now part of the German Reich. The Kleins stayed at home – the schools being still closed – except for Ingrid, who had decided to reopen her shop, despite the risks, rather than mope around the apartment. The wireless played nothing but Nazi anthems so the girls and their father sat quietly, reading or absorbed in their own thoughts.

Later that evening, after Hanna had gone to bed and Sophie was doing the washing up after supper, she said to her mother, 'I really think we should all stay together. You can cook, Papa can drive, and we speak English – surely someone will want to employ us and let Hanna carry on at school. If we can find jobs in England, then we'll be able to get visas.'

Ingrid laid down the tea towel. 'It'll be so much harder for the four of us to find work, and there's no time to waste. You girls must be the priority. Don't worry about Papa and me; he'll stay quietly at home while I run the shop – no one will bother us if we lie low. And then maybe we can follow you. This is for the best, I promise. You'll soon find a job in an English or American library while Hanna goes to school. Can you look after her? I know it's a lot to ask.'

'I suppose so,' Sophie replied, dazed. The future that lay before her was changing by the day. She'd been working at the local library since she'd left school at sixteen, learning the fundamentals of cataloguing and stock acquisition, while her father taught her the finer principles of curatorship at evenings and weekends. Otto was a conservator and curator at the magnificent National Library of Vienna, and Sophie was determined to work there herself one day. She loved the calm regularity of librarianship; each book a treasure trove of information or experience that would be categorised, labelled and stored in its rightful place. And she could think of nothing more magical than spending her days surrounded by stories.

'You're such a clever girl, Sophie,' Ingrid said, clearly willing her daughter not to make things any more difficult than they already were. 'You can do anything if you put your mind to it.'

For the next few weeks, Sophie spent every waking moment thinking about one thing alone: escape. As well as placing advertisements in two British newspapers, she was also writing letters to strangers every day and standing in endless queues at various government buildings, trying to find out what documentation was required to leave the country. They would need a lot of money to pay the Austrian authorities, that much was clear, as well as funds to take with them, so she and her mother set about selling as much of the family's jewellery and furniture as could be spared. By tacit agreement, they didn't consult Otto in these arrangements; his position as head of the family no longer seemed relevant. They said nothing to Hanna either, not wanting to worry her until the last moment, but Sophie and her mother had urgent, whispered conversations every evening after supper.

'You and Papa could come abroad with us,' Sophie pleaded yet again. 'At least let me try.'

Frau Klein only shook her head. 'Your father can't start

again, not in this state, and I won't leave him. He's a good man and he needs me.'

But we need you too, Sophie longed to say, though she knew that was unfair. Her parents were devoted to each other. In the early days when her father was so happy in his work at the library, her mother had just opened the cake shop and Hanna was an adorable, curly-haired toddler, their apartment had been full of sunshine and laughter. Now it was a dark, dreary place and Otto Klein a morose stranger dressed in her father's clothes.

'You have to understand,' her mother said, 'I'm Papa's only protection: they'll arrest him immediately if I leave. As long as I'm here, he's safe.'

Ingrid had changed since the Germans had arrived in Vienna. She had always been practical and hard-working, but now there was a hardness in her eyes and a note of determination in her voice that Sophie hadn't heard before. 'Now let me get on,' she said, putting on her apron. 'I need to make a cake for Hanna.'

Hanna would be nine in a couple of days. None of them could have had any idea that her birthday would mark a turning point in their family history: a day so unimaginably awful, it would haunt Sophie for the rest of her life.

Chapter Three

Lacey waited for the lights to change at the corner of the street, stamping her feet to keep the circulation going and shifting her groceries from one hand to the other. She could see her apartment building from here, which was reassuring; in another five minutes, she'd be home. Stepping back to avoid a spray of slush from a passing car, she collided with a woman behind her who growled some inaudible curse. Lacey apologised, clutching her grocery sacks against her chest, although what she could have said was, 'Why do you have to stand so close?' Why was everyone in the store and on the sidewalk – and in fact the whole of Philly – determined to shuffle right up to her with their germs and smells and hostile eyes? Especially those who weren't wearing masks and probably weren't vaccinated either, not even once? She turned and headed towards a side street where there weren't so many people around, which meant she lost sight of her home for a few minutes. But that was OK; she knew it was there.

To calm down, she pictured herself entering the keypad

code, pushing open the outer door, walking the fifteen paces across the lobby with its tired pot plants and taking the three flights of stairs to her apartment – she never used the elevator anymore – then unlocking her very own door, dumping her bags in the hall and closing it behind her. Not much further to go. Across the road and along the sidewalk, where all she had to navigate was a mean-looking dog on the end of an extending leash whose owner wasn't paying attention, and a delivery guy weaving past on a bicycle, then turn the corner and she could see her building again. Breathing in to a count of three and out to a count of five, keeping her eyes fixed on the reassuring brownstone, her heart rate spiked only momentarily when an ambulance swerved past with its siren blaring. At last the outer door was open and she was inside. She paused for a moment with her eyes shut, steadying herself before tackling the stairs. See, that wasn't so bad.

'Oh, hi, Lacey!' called a voice from the floor above. 'How's it going?'

She experienced the usual flash of panic before realising it was the good-looking guy from the apartment opposite hers: Rick, whom she'd had once had a crush on, a lifetime ago. Now she couldn't bear to look him in the face.

'Fine,' she said, trying to sound casual. 'Just popped out for some groceries, you know how it is.'

'Still writing?' He was leaning against the wall with his arms folded, watching with a patronising smile as she made it to the landing. (And not offering to help, incidentally.)

'Yup. Just finishing a script.' She pushed past, willing him to stand aside. 'Better get back to it.'

'Sure. But I was meaning to ask, is there any chance you could feed Rosa this weekend?'

22

'Um, let me think.' She paused on the threshold of her apartment and felt in her pocket for the key, a bag of apples threatening to fall from the top of the sack. 'Yeah, should be OK.'

'Thanks, you're a star. We'll be back Sunday.' He flashed the smile again before retreating into his minimalist lair.

Ugh, Lacey thought, slamming the door with one foot behind her. Why couldn't she just say no? This guy had strung her along for months, getting her to feed his cat and take in his packages, inviting her for the occasional coffee to keep her interested and then casually introducing her to his boyfriend when she happened to bump into them early one morning. She'd heard him whisper as she walked away, and they'd both laughed. He'd known exactly what he was doing; he'd taken her for a fool, and she was still behaving like one.

'You have to realise, some guys are just deeply disappointing,' her sister Jess had said. 'That's your problem, Lacey. Your imagination is in overdrive and your bullshit detector isn't switched on.' Jess often made sweeping pronouncements like that; sometimes she would follow them with a laugh, which was even more irritating. Being four years older didn't give her the right to lay down the law about everything. She was a research scientist, involved in some mysterious project to do with gene therapy, and didn't set much store by imagination.

How did other people fall into relationships so easily, and then maintain them? Lacey wondered, walking through to the kitchen. Jess had had three long-term boyfriends before finally settling down with Chris and having children; Lacey had had a thousand ridiculous crushes but never managed to stay with anyone for longer than a couple of months.

Her timing was all wrong: as soon as she began to fall in love with whichever guy she was dating, he disappeared faster than a rat up a drainpipe.

'You try too hard,' Jess had told her. 'You're super intense and that puts men off.'

But now Lacey wasn't trying at all; any sort of male attention these days made her feel sick. She'd been glad of the chance to hide away during lockdown and lick her wounds in private, thankful to have a job that allowed her to spend hours alone instead of having to pretend to be normal in a busy office. After a few years trying to make a living as a journalist, she'd fallen into ghostwriting. She'd been interviewing a wheelchair basketball athlete, a young woman who'd been paralysed after a car accident, and they'd got on so well and the girl had been so inspiring that when she'd asked Lacey for her help in writing a memoir, Lacey had agreed without thinking twice. The book had found a publisher and sold well, Lacey had found an agent, and that was the start of her new career.

Most of the time, people asked her to shape their life stories for self-publication, but occasionally publishers commissioned her to work with a celebrity, which could be challenging. She'd learned early on not to think of herself as these people's friend, no matter how close they became during the process; they lived in a different universe and although she might share it for a while, she'd never be welcome there on a permanent basis. Sometimes a star who'd shared too much would threaten her with injunctions the next day, implying she'd somehow tricked them into giving their secrets away. Yet Lacey still got a thrill from writing, despite the hassles with ridiculous schedules and an occasional difficult client, and the joy of holding a printed book that she'd created from nothing never grew stale. It was just a pity she was turning into a crazy hermit in the process. She'd only just recovered from Thanksgiving in Manhattan with her mom, and in two weeks, Christmas was coming.

She was unpacking her groceries when her phone rang: Jess. 'Bad news,' her sister said. 'The kids have Covid and Chris tested positive this morning.'

'Oh no!' Lacey stopped with a box of crackers in her hand. 'How are they? And what about you?'

'Pauly has a cough and Emma's running a fever but they're not too bad. I'm fine so far, but I guess I'll be coming down with it soon. Chris, on the other hand, is practically dying.'

'Jeez, really?'

Jess snorted down the phone. 'Well, you'd think so from the fuss he's making.'

'Don't say things like that!' Lacey said. 'Not in this situation: it isn't funny.'

'Sorry, but he has me waiting on him hand and foot and you know I'm not much of a nurse. Anyway, I'm afraid we won't be making it over for Christmas.'

'I guess you won't.' That terrible realisation had just dawned on Lacey. 'So it'll be me and Mom and Cedric at Gubby's this year? Plus Crazy Sue?'

Their grandmother, known to the family as Gubby since the girls were small, always invited a handful of guests with nowhere else to go at these kinds of celebrations. That year, most of them had cried off because of Covid – all except Crazy Sue, Gubby's walking partner.

'Cheer up – Cedric can't come,' Jess said. 'I've just got off the phone with Mom. He has the flu, or so they're claiming, but I think he just wants to chill in the apartment eating lentils and watching the history channel. So you and

Mom can have quality time with Gubby, once Crazy Sue's gone. I'm actually quite jealous.'

'And how's Mom?' Lacey asked carefully.

'In good spirits. Still into yoga but the interior design business seems to have fizzled out.'

Their mother had wild enthusiasms, which she pursued energetically for a few months and then abandoned, leaving behind boxes of equipment that she'd ask Lacey to sell on eBay. The periods between crazes were hard.

'The honeymoon phase with Cedric isn't over,' Jess added. 'I reckon you've had a lucky escape. They'd have kept you awake all night in Bethlehem.'

Ugh, Lacey thought for the second time that morning. Cedric was their mother's current partner and an enigmatic presence: after four years, Lacey still felt as though she hardly knew him. He was tall and lugubrious with sparse sandy hair and a melancholy Scandinavian face, very careful with himself and usually suffering from some sort of ailment. He would never go anywhere without checking the weather forecast and traffic updates, and he was particularly fussy about food.

'With my digestion, I can't afford to take any risks,' he would say, examining the plate of whatever he'd been offered and prodding it tentatively with a fork. He was vegetarian, teetotal, gluten intolerant and afraid of mushrooms.

How does she put up with him? the sisters had wondered after they'd first met Cedric – although they had to admit that Adele, their glamorous, impulsive mother, was more stable now than she had been for years.

'He must balance her out,' Jess had said, and they'd decided Cedric was worth putting up with for that reason alone. Adele was quite a responsibility.

26

'I miss you guys,' Lacey said now. 'I haven't seen the kids for so long, I probably wouldn't recognise them.' Chris was Canadian, and he and Jess had been living in Vancouver for the past four years.

'I know, we miss you too,' Jess said. 'Why don't you come over and see us when you've finished the book?'

'I'd love that.' And she would, although the prospect of getting the subway and then sitting on a plane for six hours or more was daunting. It wasn't so much Covid she was dreading – she'd had the virus and although it wasn't pleasant, she didn't feel that bad – but contact with other people. She no longer had the energy for all those minor interactions she never used to think twice about; it was easier to stay home and live online. Even talking to a real live person on the phone these days was an effort. Damn it, though! She couldn't hide from the world forever. She'd made the trip to Manhattan for Thanksgiving with her mom and Cedric, and now she would handle Christmas; it could be a dress rehearsal for further challenges to come.

She practised deep breathing and meditation and visualised herself at each stage of the trip, dealing with whatever minor disasters might occur: picking up the rental car, filling it with gas if necessary, driving on the freeway, finding somewhere to park at the other end. Her beloved grandma was waiting, and Crazy Sue was easy company: all she'd have to do was sit back and let the chat roll over her. And of course, her mom would be there, too. This time, Lacey wouldn't rise to the bait if (when) Adele asked about her love life. Instead, she would smile serenely and change the subject. That was the plan, anyway.

She didn't sleep much the night before she was due to travel but apart from minor palpitations when she took a wrong turning downtown, the journey went smoothly. Her spirits rose when she took the exit and drove along snowy streets she'd known all her life. Bethlehem: the Christmas City, where the light displays and porch decorations grew more elaborate each year and passers-by said hello even if they didn't know you. Gubby was rooted in the community; it took hours to walk with her down Main Street, she was stopped so many times, and the neighbourhood kids still knocked on her door at Hallowe'en.

The Pennsylvanian town was full of history: it had been founded by members of the Moravian Church on the banks of the Lehigh River, and some of the early colonial buildings still remained. The old steelworks which flourished in the twentieth century had been preserved and turned into an arts and music venue, and there was a music festival every year that brought a million people to the town – except for the previous year, when Covid had sent Musikfest online. There were plenty worse places to live, Lacey thought, wondering whether the time had come to leave Philly, whether here she might feel safe.

And there was Gubby, standing on the porch of the white clapboard house and waving, the biggest smile lighting up her face. No one would have guessed she was well into her nineties, yet Lacey was struck by how tiny she seemed nowadays. A wreath hung on the front door and there were candles in every window, which Lacey knew would be lit when dusk fell, as usual. The 'Santa, please stop here' sign had been stuck in the cement boot and the sinister Christmas gnome that had terrified the girls when they were little leered from the top step. Inside, the same dented baubles and glass ornaments would be draped over the wonky fake tree ('I swear you can't tell it from real, apart from the smell') and

Gubby would have heated up a vat of the mulled wine that nobody wanted to drink, not even Crazy Sue. Christmas could begin.

'Come here, darling,' Gubby said, reaching up for a hug. Her silvery hair was sticking up in tufts so that she looked more like a fledgling than ever. She was wearing one of her trademark bright silk scarves and a purple dress that Lacey happened to know had come from the children's department of Macy's. Nothing gave Gubby greater glee than buying kids' clothes at half the price.

Lacey swallowed the lump in her throat. Her grandmother held her at arm's length for a proper look. 'Why, whatever's the matter?'

'Ignore me.' Lacey smiled through the tears that had sprung to her eyes. 'Just so glad to be here, that's all.'

'Well, I'm glad, too.' Gubby took her by the hand and towed her into the house. 'Now, your mom called and she's not coming till tomorrow, so we have plenty of time to talk. Come and tell me all your news.'

If only she could, Lacey thought. It would be such a relief to unburden herself to the one person she knew would be on her side, no matter what, but Gubby would be so horrified if she found out what had happened all those months ago – coming up for two years now – that telling her was unthinkable. She couldn't expose her gentle, innocent grandmother to the brutal modern world; it wouldn't be fair. Besides, Lacey herself didn't want to remember, couldn't imagine relating the sordid details and reliving the horror and shame all over again. She hadn't shared the story with anyone, not even her sister. She was dealing with the trauma in her own way and eventually she would heal. Time and patience, that was all she needed.

Chapter Four

Bethlehem, Christmas Day, 2021

'So how's the love life?' Adele said, reaching for the wine bottle to refill her glass and hooking one elegant leg over the other. 'Leave the clearing up and come tell me all about it.'

Her ash-blonde hair had been cropped short and she was wearing a black satin skirt that clung to her narrow hips, teamed with a crimson mohair sweater. It was tough, Lacey reflected, being upstaged by your own mother.

'There's not much to say, really.' She didn't trust herself to turn around. 'I've been pretty busy with work.'

'Oh, work!' Adele snorted. 'There'll be time for that later. You're in your prime, girl. Don't waste the good years hunched over a computer – it ruins your posture. I can show you some asanas to help with that. Cow Face pose is especially good.'

Lacey couldn't help laughing. 'Cow Face pose? Mom, are you for real?'

'Seriously. We can get up early tomorrow morning and practise together before I leave. And you're getting quite deep frown lines, incidentally. Do you think you should get your eyes tested?'

Lacey flicked a brushful of soap suds at her mother. 'Anyone else would be proud their daughter was a published author. Do you know, I went to the Moravian Bookshop the other day and they had two of my titles in there? Two!'

'It's a shame you don't get your name on the cover.' But the next thing Lacey knew, her mom's arms were around her waist and she was being pulled away from the sink. 'I am proud of my clever daughter,' Adele said in her ear. 'I just don't want her to get too big for her boots. Now sit, have a drink and chat to your darling mama while we have the chance.'

Lacey let herself be guided to a chair. 'OK,' she began, 'I think we do need to talk about Gubby. Where is she, by the way?'

'Saying goodbye to Crazy Sue – she'll be a while yet. What about her, though?'

'Well, don't you think entertaining at Christmas is getting too much? I mean, today was fine in the end, but no one could say things ran according to plan.' Gubby was meant to have been in charge of cooking the vegetables, while Adele had promised to bring the turkey on Christmas Eve so she could put it in the oven first thing on Christmas Day. Lacey had contributed a ham glazed with molasses: her speciality.

Adele frowned. 'OK, so I should have got here last night and started cooking the turkey at dawn. I've already apologised for that. When do you think it'll be ready, by the way?'

Lacey glanced at Gubby's ancient stove. 'I reckon it should be done by tomorrow morning – we can eat it for breakfast.'

'Then you and your grandmother can have Christmas lunch all over again.' Adele stretched her arms above her head and yawned. 'Oh, I'm exhausted. The traffic this morning was awful.'

'Mom, I think next year we should go out to eat in a restaurant, as long as they're open by then. Sure, Grandma loves to entertain, and we've tried to share the load, but it's not really working, is it?'

Lacey had discovered too late to buy any more that there were no potatoes, only a thirty-pound sack of carrots her grandmother wouldn't get through in a year and some enormous beets no one could face boiling and peeling. None of them liked beets, anyway. Gubby had been embarrassed and it was sad to see proof that hosting a family dinner was getting too much for her. In the end, they'd eaten Lacey's ham with cranberry sauce, rice and frozen sweetcorn, and reassured Gubby that it made a lovely change.

'Such a shame, though,' Sue had said with a sigh. 'Are you sure the bird won't be cooked in time? I never get to eat turkey these days. No point cooking a roast dinner for one, is there?' Still, she had managed to eat three helpings of ham, and there was Gubby's wonderful chocolate cake for dessert.

'Mom would never eat restaurant food at Christmas,' Adele said. 'She loves putting up the decorations, you know that, and making cranberry sauce, and having a crowd of people sitting around her table. The holidays mean everything to her.'

'Well, maybe we should ask her if it's time for a change,' Lacey replied. 'You might be surprised.'

'Tell me about the current book,' Adele said brightly. 'Anyone I might have heard of?'

Lacey clenched her jaw, irritated as usual by her mother's refusal to consider a point of view that might be inconvenient, or differed from her own. 'Nobody famous,' she replied, after a short pause. 'It's a great read, though.'

Her latest project had been rewarding but exhausting. She'd been approached by Frances, a woman who'd lived with an aggressive, controlling husband for years before finding the strength to break free. She wanted to help other women in the same position by sharing her story, and raise funds for the women's refuge that had rescued her and her children in the process. Listening to what Frances had been through, Lacey had at first felt too angry and upset to focus on shaping the narrative, but she'd managed to find a way of channelling that emotion into a passionate, powerful memoir. Frances had found the process cathartic: recounting the abuse she'd suffered and then seeing it laid out on the page had made her realise how difficult it had been to stand up to her husband and forgive herself for not having tried to leave earlier.

Adele listened to Lacey explaining all this for a couple of minutes before interrupting. 'Hey, I forgot to tell you: I have a new job. On reception in the yoga studio a couple of blocks away. Isn't that cool? And five free classes a week. Cedric thinks—'

But Lacey didn't get the benefit of Cedric's opinion because Gubby came through the door, staggering slightly. 'Gracious,' she said. 'Did you know Sue's ex-husband hired a hitman to kill her and she had to climb out of a fourth-floor window to escape? She never told me that before. I wonder what the neighbours thought?'

She laughed, clapping a hand over her mouth like a naughty little girl, which made Lacey and Adele laugh, too.

It was a strange thing that the older Gubby grew, the more youthful she seemed. She had to walk with a stick outdoors these days, yet her sense of mischief was stronger than ever. Some kind of inhibition had gone, which could be embarrassing: she would stare at people in restaurants with unabashed interest and comment on their appearance more loudly than was polite.

'At my age, haven't I got the right to say what I think?' she would demand, and what she thought was often so funny that it was hard to disapprove.

'Just keep your voice down,' Lacey would hiss, 'or tell me later.'

'But later I'll have forgotten.' And Gubby would swivel her whole body around for another look. 'Now, someone should tell that poor unfortunate girl she should never wear pink – not with her hair. Whatever was she thinking?'

'Sit down, Grandma,' Lacey said now, pulling out a chair. 'You must be exhausted. Sue's enough to wear anyone out.'

Gubby was looking suddenly frail; her wrists were like twigs and the skin on her hands was stretched tight over painfully swollen knuckles. Lacey wanted to tuck her up in a quilt on the couch and spoil her, just like Gubby had done when she, Lacey, was off sick from school with mono and her grandmother had looked after her for a month.

Gubby collapsed into the seat. 'Well, Sue sure has lived an interesting life.'

'In her dreams,' Adele remarked, pouring herself another glass of wine. 'The last I heard, he threw her out of a moving car on the freeway. She's the original cat with nine lives.'

'Anyone for coffee?' Lacey asked, but her mother pushed her back down.

'Hold your horses,' she said. 'Now we're all together, it's

35

time for your Christmas gifts. Did you think I'd forgotten?' Her eyes were shining and a smile twitched at the corner of her mouth.

Lacey prepared herself: Adele's choices could be surprising. One year she'd presented them each with a framed photograph of herself in different alluring poses. She'd been hurt when Jess had burst out laughing. This time, however, Lacey and her grandmother each received a white envelope with an A4 sheet of printed paper inside.

'Plane tickets!' Adele announced, hugging herself, though they could see that for themselves. 'Mom, you can celebrate your birthday in Vancouver this spring! Since Jess can't come to us, we'll go to her. As long as we take Covid tests, we can travel.'

Lacey stared down at the printout in her hands. I can't do it, she thought. Gubby's birthday was in April, which was too soon, and Vancouver was too far away. Besides, Gubby hated a fuss being made of her birthday and she hadn't flown for years. Of course it was an incredibly generous present and a thoughtful idea, but Adele should have checked with them all first. Had she even consulted Jess?

'What do you think?' she asked her grandmother. 'Are you up for flying?'

'Don't worry, Mom.' Adele reached over to take her mother's hands. 'We'll be with you and everything'll be fine. They drive old people around airports in buggies these days.'

'I'm not being stuck with a bunch of old people!' Gubby retorted. 'And you wouldn't catch me in a buggy. I'll walk with everybody else, thank you very much.'

'So you'll come?' Lacey asked.

'Sure. Why not?' Her grandmother laughed, as though

36

surprised by her own daring. 'Those little munchkins are growing up fast and besides, who knows how many more birthdays I'll have? Might as well seize the moment.'

'And don't tell Jess,' Adele added. 'I've got it all worked out – I'm going to call her and then ring on the bell so she opens the door while she's still on the phone and we all yell, "Surprise!" I saw someone do that on Instagram and it looked so cool. You can film us, Lacey.'

'But you know Jess is a control freak,' Lacey said. 'She hates anything unexpected.'

Her mother waved an airy hand. 'Trust you to put a dampener on things. It'll be fine! Jess'll be so happy to see us and this way, she can't over-prepare. She has to learn to be more spontaneous. Come on, don't you want to see your sister?'

Lacey forced a smile. Of course she did, more than anything else in the world. It was time to step up.

Chapter Five

Bethlehem, December 2021

Adele slept late the next morning and there was no mention of yoga when she finally appeared downstairs, much to Lacey's relief.

'Do you want to come for a walk round the neighbourhood with me?' she asked her mother. They hadn't had much of a chance to talk the day before and she felt guilty, as always, that she and her mom weren't closer.

'Ugh, no thank you.' Adele poured herself a cup of coffee. 'I can't turn the corner without bumping into some guy I hooked up with in tenth grade.'

She'd been brought up in Bethlehem but couldn't wait to get away, going to college in upstate New York, marrying young and then moving to Pittsburgh where her daughters had been born. Their father, Jake, had left when Lacey was a year old and Adele took a variety of jobs so the family could get by, usually two or three at a time: waitressing, working in a deli and as a receptionist in an art gallery, selling Tupperware and mysterious products the girls weren't allowed to see which had her customers (strictly women only) shrieking with laughter over cheap wine in the evenings. They would sit on the stairs in their pyjamas, trying to work out the joke. When Lacey was six, Uncle Tony appeared on the scene. He had a lot of dark shiny hair and small, discoloured teeth. Jess had never liked him, but Lacey could remember happy times when he had taken them to the movies and bought the kind of food Adele disapproved of: hot dogs with fried onions and vinegary ketchup, popcorn in giant buckets, lurid candies that turned their tongues purple. There might have been only one happy time, in fact, but that was something, wasn't it? Then one weekend the girls went to stay with Gubby; when they got back, their mother told them that she and Tony were married and they had a new father now. Lacey had looked at Jess, uncertain what to think. Jess had turned away without speaking, gone to their bedroom and refused to come down for supper.

'Leave her,' Tony had ordered Adele. 'I'm not having a spoilt brat ruling my house.'

The happy times were over. Lacey would creep into her sister's bed and Jess would hold her as they listened to their mother and new father screaming at each other. After a couple of years, things got so bad that one terrifying, exciting night, Adele made the girls pack a suitcase each and go to sleep in their clothes, then smuggled them out of the house at dawn and drove to Bethlehem. It was going to be just the three of them again – and Gubby, of course. Tony had parked up outside her house the next day but Gubby's next-door neighbour, who was a firefighter and seven foot tall, bent down at the driver's window and said something that made him drive off in a cloud of exhaust fumes.

'What happens if he comes back?' Lacey asked.

'He won't dare show his sorry face,' Gubby replied. 'But

if he does, well, maybe I'll just have to shoot him. I'm old, I don't mind going to prison.'

The girls and their mother had stayed with Gubby for a year or so, and then Adele had packed them up and taken off again; they washed up in New Haven, Connecticut, where she'd got an office job at Yale University. Gradually they found their feet in the windy seaside city, its wide streets thronged with cycling students. Jess went to Yale in her turn – staying around to keep an eye on her mom and sister, Lacey later realised. They never saw Tony again but one day she came home from school to find a stranger sitting at the table who turned out to be her original father, Jake. He didn't look in great shape: his hair was long and greasy and he needed a shave, and his attempts to win her over were embarrassing. Tony had taught her to be wary of men arriving out of the blue, so she said she had basketball practice when Jake suggested taking her and her mom out for a meal. He was gone by the time she came home from her friend's house, and Adele was singing as she cooked spaghetti, barefoot on the sandy kitchen floor with sunshine streaming through the window.

'It's OK,' she said. 'Nothing's going to change around here.'

And Lacey could breathe for the first time in what seemed an age. Adele stayed where she was and it was her daughters' turn to leave: Lacey went off to college in Philadelphia, majoring in journalism, and Jess married Chris and moved to Vancouver. Lacey had stayed on in Philly after graduating; she loved the city, and being close enough to crash at Gubby's for chocolate cake and a good night's sleep at the weekend was a definite advantage. And then Adele had met Cedric online and stayed with him, to her daughters' surprise, eventually moving into his apartment in the Meatpacking district of Manhattan – which still made the girls laugh, as it was the least appropriate area in which he could possibly have lived.

'Will you have some French toast?' Gubby asked now, turning around from the stove.

'Thanks, Mom, but you know I never eat breakfast,' Adele replied, checking her phone. 'Time to hit the road or Cedric will be wondering what's happened to me. Sorry to dash but we'll have such fun hanging out with Jess. Can't wait!'

They were always looking ahead to the next time, Lacey thought. Maybe Christmas had been too much of a rush but in Vancouver they could cook together, go for long walks along the beach and talk about things that really mattered. Except, of course, they wouldn't. Her mother would be too tired, or have a headache, or drink too much, or be dealing with some crisis that meant she had to spend hours on the phone, and they would part saying how great it had been to see each other with all those conversations postponed yet again, all those opportunities wasted.

Adele finally left for New York in a flurry of kisses and instructions. 'You should take turmeric pills or drink the tea,' she told Lacey. 'A juice cleanse would help, too. And try to get out in the fresh air, Lace, anyone would think you lived under a rock. Oh, and by the way—' She beckoned her closer and whispered, 'Can you check Gubby's passport? I've asked her whether it needs renewing but she's not sure and she's bound to forget. She keeps telling me not to fuss so don't let her catch you. Bye, sweetheart. Come see us again soon! Cedric was so sorry to miss you.'

Gubby was washing up by the sink when Lacey came

back to the kitchen. 'Sit down,' Lacey said, taking the brush out of her hands. 'You must be exhausted.'

'Only if you sit, too,' Gubby said. 'Tell me what's wrong, honey. I'm worried about you.'

'About me? How do you mean?' Lacey attempted a laugh, though every nerve in her body was on high alert.

'You haven't been yourself for a while,' Gubby said, patting the chair next to her. 'And I can see you're concerned about this trip to Canada in April.'

'I think it might be too much for you, that's all.'

'Really?' Gubby took Lacey's hand and squeezed it. 'And is it going to be too much for you, too?'

Lacey's protestations were half-hearted and she could tell Gubby didn't find them convincing. 'I've found the past couple of years really difficult,' she admitted eventually. 'I've got no business complaining, I know that. It's been worse for people who've gotten really sick or lost loved ones, or been shut up with their kids all day in a tiny apartment, or who haven't been able to work. Or for seniors, like you.'

Gubby snorted dismissively. 'Oh, I've been fine. I have such wonderful neighbours and spending time indoors on my own is no hardship at my time of life. No, it's you kids I feel sorry for. Just when you should be out in the world, making mistakes and learning from them, doing your courting and getting to know who you really are, you've had to live like hermits. No wonder you feel out of sorts. But you'll get back on your feet, Lacey. You just need to be kind to yourself.'

'Thanks.' Lacey laid her head on Gubby's shoulder and let her grandmother stroke her hair, wishing she could stay like that for ever. All too soon, though, Gubby said she

43

might pop upstairs for a lie-down because actually, Christmas had been a little tiring.

Lacey's heart was full as she watched her grandmother walk unsteadily to the door. Darling Gubby: they were so lucky to have her. She finished the washing-up and then, seizing the chance, went to the bureau where important documents were kept and flipped through them until she found Gubby's passport. It had another couple of years to run and she was about to close it when two words jumped off the page. Her grandmother's place of birth was listed as Vienna, Austria.

Lacey looked again, sure she must have misread. There was a Vienna in Virginia, she knew that, but no – this was definitely Vienna, Austria. How come no one had ever mentioned this fact? The more Lacey thought about it, the stranger it seemed. As far as she knew, her grandmother had only been out of the States twice before: visiting Jess in Vancouver when each of her babies had been born. There had to be a rational explanation. Gubby's father had travelled for business; his wife must have accompanied him on a trip to Europe and had her baby over there early. Yet surely it was risky to go so far from home when you were heavily pregnant – especially in the days when air travel was more of a rarity. Gubby's face stared back at her from the photograph, both ancient and childlike in her innocence.

Lacey sat back on her heels, looking at the passport. Gubby seemed suddenly remote and unknowable. What was the story of her life? She'd had a younger brother, Jim, but he'd died of cancer a couple of years ago. Her father had been sales director of a company that made furniture and her mother a housewife, and she and Jim had been brought up in Santa Barbara. Had they been a happy family? It wasn't the sort of question you could ask out of the blue. Gubby had married her childhood sweetheart but he'd been killed a year later in a car crash, so she'd upped and left for the east coast: a brave thing for a young widow to do, all alone. She'd sat next to Bernard on the Greyhound bus and that was that: he was to become her second husband and Adele's father. It was a romantic story but Gubby didn't talk much about him; he'd died coming up for twenty-five years ago and now Lacey could hardly remember what he looked like.

Her grandmother lived in the present and she seemed content, although sometimes when she sat by the window, staring out, she looked so sad that Lacey wondered what she was thinking. It must be hard, growing old and losing your friends one by one. Maybe that was why Gubby loved to fill her house with people and feed them, keeping the darkness at bay.

Lacey's storyteller antennae were twitching. She put the passport back in its place and flicked through the rest of the papers in the cubbyhole in search of anything unusual. Tucked right at the back among tax certificates and insurance papers, she found an envelope slipped into the middle, stamped with a red crown and the words WINDSOR CASTLE. And now the hairs on the back of Lacey's neck were prickling because she was certain there was a mystery here, and maybe this letter held the key.

It was a couple of hours before Lacey heard her grandmother's tread on the stairs. 'Goodness, how long have I been asleep?' she said, yawning as she came into the kitchen. 'You should have woken me, sweetheart. I need to start fixing lunch.'

'There's no rush, Grandma,' she replied. 'I've carved some turkey and we can have sandwiches in a little while. In fact, you can probably eat turkey sandwiches the whole of next year.'

'Maybe we should give Sue a call,' Gubby suggested. 'She was so disappointed to miss the turkey yesterday.'

'Let's not,' Lacey said. 'I like it when it's just the two of us. Reminds me of when we used to live here.'

'That was a tough time for you girls.' Gubby patted her hand. 'But you came through it, all three of you, and look at you now. There's your sister working away in the science lab and your mom settled down with Cedric, who's a steady sort of man even if I don't much take to him, and you writing all these books.'

'I've been thinking, Gubby,' Lacey began, 'why don't you tell me your life story, so we have some record? You never talk about your family.'

'Oh, I don't hold with all this dwelling on the past. Not much to tell, anyway. Now you lay the table and I'll make a start on lunch.'

'I'm not even sure where you were born,' Lacey persisted (which was perfectly true).

Gubby shot her a look. 'Why would you care about that?'

Lacey shrugged. 'Oh, no reason, really.'

'I know when there's something on your mind,' her grandmother said. 'Come on, out with it.'

'OK, then.' Lacey took a breath and went on in a rush. 'It's just that Mom asked me to check your passport and I happened to see you were born in Vienna, which made me curious.'

A flush mottled Gubby's neck. 'You had no business poking around in my bureau,' she snapped. 'I might be old but I'm not senile. I can keep track of my own affairs, thank you very much.'

'I'm sorry,' Lacey said, 'I didn't mean to upset you.' This was awful; she'd never seen her grandmother so angry. 'But Vienna, Grandma! It sounds so glamorous.'

'I don't want to talk about it.' Gubby's lips were pursed in a thin line. 'You shouldn't have interfered.'

They ate an awkward, silent lunch and afterwards, Gubby said she was going upstairs to tidy her closets and sort out some clothes to take to the Goodwill. And no, she didn't need any help, thank you very much. Lacey sat in the living room, listening to the sound of her grandmother's footsteps overhead and fretting. Falling out with Gubby was a catastrophe. Lacey had once been mean to the girl nobody liked in grade school, and Gubby's disappointment when she heard was the most effective punishment possible. Her grandma was old, as she'd said: what if she had a heart attack and died before they could make up?

When she couldn't hold out any longer, Lacey crept upstairs to listen outside her grandmother's door. She could hear faint snuffling sounds inside, as though a small animal were building its nest, and her heart broke. Tapping quietly on the door, she opened it and went inside.

'Grandma, I'm so sorry.' She sat beside Gubby on the bed and gathered her in a hug. Gubby's cheek was damp and tears came to Lacey's own eyes. 'I feel awful. Please don't cry, I can't bear it.'

Gubby felt for a tissue in her pocket and blew her nose. 'Oh, it's not your fault,' she said. 'I'm just being silly. Things seem to be getting on top of me lately.' The bedroom looked like it had been burgled: mounds of clothing and books lay scattered over the floor, drawers were open and the laundry basket had been tipped over, spilling its contents.

47

'Leave this for the moment.' Lacey rubbed her grandma's back, feeling every knobbly vertebra. 'Come downstairs and I'll make you some coffee.'

'I'm in a muddle,' Gubby said, twisting the tissue in her fingers, 'and I can't seem to get out of it.'

'Talk to me. I'm sure we can sort this all out.'

Gubby gave a great despairing sigh. 'It's too late for that. I can't tell anyone, not now. You'd hate me if you knew.'

Lacey held her close again. 'You're the best grandma in the world. We all love you to pieces and nothing you could possibly say will ever change that. Something's upsetting you, Grandma, and you need to get it off your chest. Secrets are toxic.'

Gubby's fingers gripped her arm so tightly that she winced. 'Do you swear not to tell Adele? She can't know, not yet. Maybe after I'm gone.'

Lacey nodded. 'If that's what you want.'

Gubby took a deep breath. 'All right, perhaps it's for the best. I've lived with this for long enough.'

She talked haltingly at first, pausing to search for the right words and only gradually gaining confidence. Lacey daren't interrupt, although she had a thousand questions. She listened spellbound as the extraordinary story of her grandmother's childhood, thousands of miles away in another country, spilled out into the quiet room.

Chapter Six

Vienna, April 1938

'Why shouldn't we go to the amusement park?' Hanna kicked her feet against a chair under the table, sending the cat Felix running for safety. 'We always go to the Prater on my birthday.'

'This year is different,' her mother replied tartly. 'You can invite Gretel round for tea later and maybe Sophie will take you both for ice cream.'

'Gretel's not allowed to play with me anymore,' Hanna muttered. 'Why is everything so horrible now?' she burst out. 'And why must we stay home all the time? I hate this stupid apartment!'

Herr Klein stood up, clearing his throat. 'Hanna's right, a trip to the Prater is an important birthday tradition and one we should maintain. Ingrid, fetch your hat and coat.'

Sophie and her mother exchanged glances, startled by a tone in Otto's voice they hadn't heard for weeks.

Hanna's expression changed instantly. 'Hooray! Thank you, Papa.' She threw her arms around him and he lifted her high in the air.

'My goodness, such a big girl of nine. I shan't be able to do this next year.'

Next year, Sophie thought. Where will we be then?

'Are you sure, Otto?' Frau Klein asked, untying her apron. 'Then I must change into my best clothes.'

'Absolutely. Sophie, you must come, too. The whole family will go on an outing!'

So, in due course, off they went. This expedition felt very different from those of previous years: Sophie and her mother were tense, watchful, while Hanna chattered with an almost hysterical gaiety, swinging her father's hand. Otto walked with his head down and his hat pulled low. He must have noticed how much the city had changed in the last few weeks. The Austrian police now wore swastika armbands over their dark greatcoats, German soldiers stood guard outside official buildings and swastikas hung from every flagpole. The word *Jüde* had been daubed in crude letters on walls and pavements outside Jewish businesses – shuttered, or with their windows smashed, and 'soon to be reopened under new ownership', according to notices pasted on doors. Hitler had gone back to Berlin where he'd been greeted as a hero, according to the newspapers, and the country he'd left behind had adopted his ideas with enthusiasm. Antisemitism had become a mania.

Otto Klein paused for a moment to gaze down the wide streets towards the National Library. Sophie could remember the first time he'd taken her there to see the Bronze Age papyri and clay tablets. The library didn't merely contain books: it housed a collection of maps, globes, prints, medieval manuscripts and thousands of other extraordinary artefacts which showed mankind's earliest desire to record and communicate.

'Look, Sophie,' he'd said, lifting her up to the case. 'Can you imagine someone pressing a reed into wet clay to make those marks, over five thousand years ago?'

And Sophie had stared, mesmerised, as he talked to her about ancient civilisations that were in many ways as sophisticated as their own. The building itself was miraculous, too. She stood in the centre of the State Hall and gazed upward, past marble and mahogany pillars dripping with gold, statues of princes and painters and shelves of leatherbound books, up and up into the painted and gilded dome that soared far above her head like a vision of heaven itself. Surely her father must be some sort of hero to work in a place like this. He was certainly her hero. Hanna had a special bond with her mother, whereas Sophie had always been a daddy's girl. 'Heads in the clouds, the pair of you,' her mother used to grumble. 'If it wasn't for me, you'd forget to eat and put clothes on your back.'

Sophie loved her father's patience, his deep chuckle, the joy he took in simple pleasures like a walk through fresh snow or the perfect apple strudel, his appreciation of art, music and books. Books, above all. He'd been ill with rheumatic fever as a child, which had meant long hours convalescing by himself, reading and making up stories, and the habit had held. Most walls of the family's apartment were lined with bookshelves, and more volumes were stacked in boxes under every bed and table. Her mother often threatened to throw them out with the rubbish, and any new titles had to be added to the collection secretly when she was at work. 'Those wretched things are the bane of my life,' Ingrid would complain. 'All they do is gather dust and take up space.' Yet she was proud of her husband's knowledge and intellect, anyone could tell. They were the perfect match: clever Otto free to spend hours working and dreaming because of his practical, resourceful wife.

'I was a lonely little boy,' her father had told Sophie once, 'but look how lucky I am now. You see, it all came right in the end.'

Now Sophie slipped her arm through Otto's. 'Don't worry, Papa. They'll soon realise the library can't run without you.'

'I'm not so sure about that,' he replied. 'Perhaps I should learn to make pastry and ask for a job in your mother's shop.' He smiled and ruffled her hair and, just for a second, Sophie allowed herself to hope that things might somehow come right again.

They joined other families strolling towards the park entrance in the gusty spring sunshine. The giant Ferris wheel, the Riesenrad, turned so slowly it hardly appeared to move, its red carriages rocking a little in the breeze. From the top, you could see far over the city: across the canal to St Stephen's Cathedral, the Hofburg Palace and Heroes' Square, where Hitler had made his triumphant speech the month before. Sophie had been born in Vienna and couldn't imagine living anywhere else, but now its heartless beauty taunted her. She already felt like an outsider.

'Quick, there's not much of a queue!' Hanna broke away and began to run.

It must have been the noise that first alerted Sophie: a low, ominous rumble interspersed with small chirrups of excitement. She might also have sensed a change in the atmosphere, as though invisible violin strings were being tightened before the bow came flashing down.

'Hanna, get back here,' she called, her voice thin with fear.

Officers in SS uniforms armed with batons and whips

were moving through the crowd of Viennese in their weekend finery, searching for some unidentified quarry. They separated a few men from their families who stumbled together in a frightened herd towards the park lawns as the stormtroopers shouted and brandished their weapons. Mothers gathered their children and somebody gave a nervous laugh. '*Heil!*' shouted a spotty youth in the crowd, raising his arm in salute, and a straggly chorus of '*Heil! Heil!*' rose up, briefly gathering momentum before petering away into embarrassed silence. People were waiting to see what would happen next. There were maybe ten or twelve Nazis with one obvious ringleader: a strutting beast of a man, bull-necked and ginger-haired with a wet, roaring mouth and mean little eyes. He attracted everyone's attention and revelled in it, thwacking the baton against his meaty palm.

Otto hesitated, glancing behind; Sophie and her mother moved to stand one on each side of him, and Hanna ran up to take his hand. Their neighbours drew away, sensing trouble, and the Klein family found themselves isolated on the path.

'You!' The ginger-haired man approached and stood very close to Otto, staring into his face. '*Bist du Jüde?* Are you a Jew?'

Flecks of spittle landed on Otto's cheek but he didn't flinch. He stood very still, dropping Hanna's hand and clasping his own together. 'My name is Otto Klein,' he said calmly. 'I am an employee of the National Library of Vienna and fought for my country in the war.'

'That's not what I asked!' the German shouted. 'Are you a Jew? Don't bother lying – we'll take down your pants to find out.'

Another guffaw came from the circle of onlookers. A

woman holding a fat pug pushed to the front, craning to watch as she stroked the dog with varnished fingernails. Sophie was rooted to the spot, transfixed with fear and shame.

'I think there's been some mistake, Officer.' Ingrid Klein stepped forward. 'We are not a Jewish family. I am Catholic and my daughters have—'

'I don't care about you.' The SS officer prodded Herr Klein in the chest. 'For the third and last time, are you a Jew?'

Sophie held her breath. Her father looked across at her – why, she didn't know, and nor could she read his expression – then turned back to the German. She half-hoped he would lie, half-dreaded he might. 'Yes, I am,' he said calmly.

The man raised his baton and whacked Otto on the back: a casual blow. 'About time. Get over there with the others, and quick about it.'

'Why?' Frau Klein stood in his way. 'What are you going to do?'

'You'll see,' the German replied. Another SS officer approached, armed with a whip, and chivvied Otto Klein towards the small group of men standing on the grass.

'Now run, you miserable creatures!' yelled the red-headed man. 'Run as if your life depended on it.'

The Jewish men looked at him and then each other. 'But where are we to go?' one asked, spreading his hands with a shrug.

'Round the park!' And the officer slashed him across the face, leaving a bright trail of blood. 'Run till you drop, *Jüdenbrut*, and give us all a laugh.' And he set about striking as many of the men as he could reach, as though he were possessed.

Sophie stared in horror as the motley group set off, their

coats flapping. A few were Orthodox Jews with hats and side locks; most, like her father, were indistinguishable by their clothing from the people who watched so avidly. A couple of Nazis jogged alongside them, whipping the legs of those who fell behind.

'Did you ever see such a thing?' said a young woman, nudging her friend and giggling. 'They look like scarecrows come to life.'

The ginger-haired man smiled with satisfaction, thumping his baton into his hand again.

Ingrid Klein approached him. 'My husband has a weak heart. He shouldn't be made to run like this, it's dangerous.'

'Nonsense. The exercise will do him good.' The man smirked at his audience, drawing a smattering of applause. A couple of boys imitated the running men, their knees pressed together and feet splayed out, and people laughed and clapped for them, too. Spirits rose among the onlookers, who jeered and catcalled as they looked around for further victims. They soon found them. Other Jews were being rounded up, and emboldened by their success, the Nazis became more inventive in their schemes for humiliation. A group of Jewish men were stripped naked and forced to kneel on all fours and eat grass while the crowd bayed and howled. Sophie turned away from their thin, bare shanks and covered Hanna's eyes.

'Serve them right, the filthy animals,' shouted an elderly man, waving his walking stick in the air. 'Jews shouldn't be allowed in the Prater anyway.'

The red-headed stormtrooper prowled to and fro, grinning. A woman with her hair bundled up in a headscarf dropped to her knees in front of him. 'For pity's sake! My father can barely walk, let alone run.'

'He just needs a little encouragement.' The man dragged her up by the hair and sent her stumbling towards a nearby tree. 'Now climb up there and sing like a bird.'

'I-I beg your pardon?' she stammered.

'You heard me!' He slapped her across both cheeks. 'Get up that tree and pretend to be a crow, or a pigeon, or whatever else you fancy. Here, I'll get you started.'

And he thrust her into the lowermost branches, to the joy of his audience who began cawing and hooting themselves. More women were hoisted into trees and their thin, mortified voices brought shouts of delight from the onlookers. Forget the Riesenrad: here was better entertainment down on the ground. Meanwhile the men tottered and lurched over the grass, some clearly in distress, while children chased them, taunting.

Sophie gazed from one surreal scene to another, scarcely able to believe what she saw. Surely any minute now she'd wake up.

'Make them stop!' Hanna whispered, tugging her arm.

Sophie turned to the nearest officer and asked, 'Why are you doing this? What is the point of it all?' But he merely stared at her without bothering to reply, his eyes cold as frosted glass.

She had lost track of her father by now; the running men on their endless loop had been joined by others, with various groups intermingling and stragglers bringing up the rear. A tall figure who might have been Otto was staggering near the back, weaving as though he were drunk.

Her mother stepped forward. 'Please stop this charade, I beg you,' she said to the red-headed man, her voice clear and strong. 'People will die.'

'But we're having so much fun. You'd better pipe down

before I send you up a tree as well.' And he grinned, prodding her in the stomach with his baton.

'Mutti!' Sophie clutched her mother's arm and pointed. The tall man she now felt sure was her father had fallen and was lying still, while an SS officer struck him with a baton. Handing Hanna into her mother's care, Sophie took off, flying across the grass with her hair streaming out behind her. A man was kneeling to vomit and others she passed were wheezing and clutching their sides as they lurched along, but she couldn't stop to help. Drawing nearer, she saw the prone man was indeed Otto: lying on his back with his head to one side and his legs bent at a strange angle. The stormtrooper stood beside him, hands on his hips, breathing hard.

'Papa!' Dropping to the grass, Sophie put her arm under his neck to raise his head. 'Can you hear me? It's all right, I'm here.'

His face in the crook of her elbow was bruised and bloody, and his lips had a bluish tinge. His chest didn't seem to be moving. Should she feel for a pulse? Try to resuscitate him?

Suddenly her mother was beside her, scooping up Otto and pressing his cheek against hers as she rocked back and forth. 'Oh, my darling,' she cried. 'What have they done to you?' Hanna followed a few paces behind, wide-eyed with fear.

Sophie sprang to her feet and launched herself at the SS officer, who gave her such a clout with his truncheon that she fell back on the grass.

'Clear off, the lot of you,' he growled. 'Troublemakers!'

Frau Klein stood, her eyes glittering. 'My husband needs an ambulance immediately.'

'It's a bit late for that,' the man grunted. 'Wasn't in great shape, was he? I reckon we've done you a favour.'

Ingrid confronted him without the slightest trace of fear. 'You aren't fit to wipe the dirt off his shoes,' she said, then sucked in her cheeks and spat full in the German's face.

He stared at her, incredulous, wiping the spittle off his chin before twisting her arm behind her back and thrusting her ahead of him. 'Now you've done it, Jew lover. Say goodbye to your daughters – you won't be seeing them for a while.'

Frau Klein turned to the girls. Sophie had never seen her mother look so brave and beautiful in the white blouse and dirndl she wore for special occasions: as though she were a symbol of the old Austria, whose time had gone and would never come again. 'Look after Hanna for me,' she told Sophie calmly. 'And take care of yourself, my darling.'

Sophie couldn't reply for the lump in her throat and the crushing weight in her chest, so she merely nodded. Ingrid nodded in return and the Nazi led her off, shoving her along so that she stumbled and whacking the backs of her legs with his baton.

Sophie knelt beside her father, dashing away her tears. She kissed his clammy cheek and closed his beloved eyes, straightened his legs and crossed his hands over his chest. He looked noble now, like an effigy on a tomb. One of the running men slowed down as he tottered towards them, sweating under a fur-trimmed hat, then dropped to his knees and began to pray in a language she didn't understand.

'It's all right,' she said, 'he doesn't need you to do this. Please don't trouble yourself.'

The man ignored her and carried on chanting, so she struggled to her feet and grabbed Hanna by the hand, leaving him to it. What did it matter? Her father was dead so he wouldn't care. 'Come,' she told her sister. 'We'd better go home.'

Hanna pulled away. 'We can't leave Papa here!' She took a few steps towards his body.

'You should go,' said a nearby policeman; an Austrian, they could tell from his accent. 'No point hanging around. I'll see your father gets taken to the mortuary.' As though he were doing them a favour.

Why didn't you do something? Sophie felt like asking, but she hadn't the energy and anyway, there wasn't much point.

The afternoon's hysteria had now given way to a curious apathy. People had begun drifting away from the scene in twos and threes, apparently bored with this momentary diversion. Most of the Jewish men had collapsed but a few were still shuffling over the grass while the SS officers watched and chatted amongst themselves, occasionally shouting some half-hearted insult. Those who'd been stripped naked huddled together, their faces smeared with soil, and the bird women in the trees had fallen silent – apart from one, whose voice rose in a thin wail, her legs in button boots dangling down from the branches like wizened fruit.

Sophie took her sister's hand again and they walked out of the park for the last time.

'What are we going to do?' Hanna asked, her upturned face blank with shock.

'We'll make a plan,' Sophie replied, rubbing her sister's cold fingers. She hadn't the faintest idea what it could be.

Chapter Seven

Vienna, May 1938

'You will only get to Palestine now if you have relatives there or business interests in the country,' shouted a portly official from the steps of the British Embassy. 'There's no point attempting it otherwise.'

A groan rose up from the ranks of people standing shoulder to shoulder in the courtyard. 'What about America?' somebody called.

'Impossible. Jamaica or Grenada, maybe, but that's a slim chance.' He turned to go back inside, mopping his bald head with a handkerchief. It was eleven in the morning and unseasonally warm.

Sophie swayed for a moment, light-headed. She'd had nothing to eat or drink and had been standing in the sun for a couple of hours; it was just as well they were all packed in so tightly that falling over would have been difficult.

'Have some water.' The young woman beside her passed over a flask, which she accepted gratefully. 'Are you trying for a student visa? I've heard the British can give you one for three months and no one expects you to come back.'

Sophie wiped the lip of the flask and handed it back. 'Thanks. I'll take whatever I can get, frankly. I've been coming here for two days and I still haven't seen anyone.'

'On your own?' The girl had sharp hazel eyes, a tanned complexion and curly hair escaping from its pins. She wore a crimson silk shirt with the sleeves rolled up and a silver cuff around her wrist, and had a violin case slung across her back, as though she were an old-time troubadour. She looked energetic and resourceful, and Sophie was drawn to her immediately.

'I'm looking after my little sister,' she replied. 'My father died and my mother's . . . away for a while.' She still found it hard to believe those bald facts. 'I'm Sophie Klein, by the way.'

'And I'm Ruth Hoffman.' There was hardly room to shake hands so they smiled at each other instead. 'I have a cousin in South Africa,' the girl went on, 'or rather, I'm trying to rustle one up. I'm sure he or she will soon materialise. How old is your sister? Have you heard about the American couple who are taking kids back to the US with them?'

'What couple?' Sophie was dazed by this rush of information.

'I don't know their names but they're here in Vienna and somehow they've got permission to take fifty children home. I think you might be too late, though – they've been over for a few weeks. Still, you can always ask. The British know all about it. Hey! Stop pushing!' She turned to glare at the man behind her. 'Nobody's going anywhere.'

Yet a couple of people at the front of the queue had been admitted through the double doors and the line inched forward. Sophie was further behind than she had been the day before, though; at this rate, she wouldn't even get inside the building before it closed. She sighed, scanning the blank windows for a sign of life.

'Do you know, I met him once,' she told Ruth. 'The British passport officer. At a party in the National Library, where my father used to work.'

Ruth gripped her arm. 'Seriously? Why didn't you say? Can you remember his name?'

'Sure. It was George Sinclair. But—'

Ruth was propelling her forward. 'Let us through,' she called, jabbing with her elbows. 'We have an appointment.'

What did they have to lose? Sophie hardened her heart and put her head down so she wouldn't have to meet anyone's eye. When they'd reached the door, Ruth knocked until it eventually opened a crack and she was able to announce to the official inside, 'We have an appointment with Mr Sinclair.'

'Names?' the man asked, reaching for a clipboard.

'Sophie Klein,' Ruth replied. 'And sister.' She winked at Sophie.

'Not on the list,' he said eventually. 'I'm afraid you'll have to leave.'

Desperation made Sophie brave – or maybe it was Ruth's influence. She could do anything with this girl beside her. 'There must be some mistake,' she said. 'I spoke to his secretary yesterday and she promised me an appointment had been made. Please show us through.'

'We see Mr Sinclair,' Ruth chimed in. Her English was not good. 'If you do not let us in, he is angry.'

'Nice try, girls,' the man said, 'but you'll have to wait outside with the others.'

Sophie glanced around the entrance hall in which they were standing. Another line of applicants snaked towards a glass-fronted counter, at which two women sat on high stools.

The telephone rang constantly, and harassed officials emerged briefly from side doors to summon people through to unseen offices or ran up and down the stairs. Steeling herself, she stood in the middle of the hall and called as loudly as she could, 'Mr Sinclair? Are you there? It's Sophie Klein.'

Silence fell; everybody turned to stare. 'George Sinclair?' Sophie shouted again. There could be no turning back now. 'I must see you.'

'Now look here,' began the man with the clipboard, 'you can't just barge in and—'

Ruth took up the call. 'Where is George Sinclair?' She turned in a circle, looking about. 'We see him now.'

A buzz of outrage now rose from the waiting groups and a burly guard was making his way towards them when a man's head appeared, hanging over the staircase a couple of floors up. 'What on earth's going on?'

'Mr Sinclair?' Sophie hurried to the foot of the stairs. 'My name is Sophie Klein. We met in the National Library a few months ago, don't you remember?'

'And we have appointment.' Ruth was standing beside her. 'But there is mistake and not on list. We come up?' Without waiting for a reply, she took Sophie's arm and started bounding up the stairs.

'Just a minute!' shouted the guard, breaking into a run.

'Don't worry, Williams,' called the man above, a little wearily. 'I'll deal with this.'

It was George Sinclair and to Sophie's relief, he did recognise her. 'Oh yes. At the opening of some exhibition, wasn't it?'

'That's right – medieval illustrated manuscripts.' Sophie was breathless, still astonished by her own daring. 'I was a volunteer guide and we talked for a while. You complimented me on my English.'

'Which is excellent.'

'Thank you. And you met my father. He helped to curate the exhibition.' Sophie pressed on, despite her nerves. 'Please, Mr Sinclair, may we have five minutes of your time?'

He sighed. 'All right, then. You'd better come through.'

They were shown into a cramped office lined with bookshelves and filing cabinets, every surface (including the floor) stacked with boxes and folders, all stuffed with paper. The door to an interconnecting room was open and an elegant woman in her forties leaned against it, watching them with her arms folded.

'This is my assistant, Mrs Slater,' Mr Sinclair said. 'Esme, this is Miss Klein and Miss—?'

'Hoffman.' Ruth gave a dazzling smile. 'A friend.'

Mrs Slater looked sceptical but consented to shake hands. She was tall and slim, with a pale complexion and perfectly waved chestnut hair, and smelt of some expensive scent. An unlikely figure, somehow, to be working in the British Embassy.

'I'd invite you to take a seat but we only have two chairs, as you can see.' Mr Sinclair stood with his hands in his pockets, rocking back on his feet. His hair was rumpled and he looked as though he hadn't slept for a month. 'So, what can I do for you?'

'There are two things.' Sophie spoke quickly, aware she couldn't afford to waste words. 'My mother was arrested a few weeks ago and I don't know where she is. I wondered if you could find out and help her in some way. Her mother was British, if that makes a difference? Her name is Ingrid Klein and she is forty-five years old. She isn't Jewish, although my father is. I mean, he was.'

George Sinclair looked across at his assistant, who raised

65

her perfectly arched eyebrows with an unreadable expression. 'We can try,' he told Sophie. 'At least we may be able to locate her. And the other matter?'

'My sister and I are trying to leave the country. We have passports and exit visas and enough money to travel, but as yet we can't find anyone to sponsor us and have nowhere to go. Hanna is nine and I'm looking after her. My father died at the Prater, you see, the day my mother was arrested.'

He looked appalled. 'In that terrible incident? I'm so sorry. It was shameful.'

'And I also try to leave.' Ruth stepped forward. 'Maybe student visa? I play violin very good. Listen!' In a matter of seconds, she had taken the instrument and a bow out of the case and begun to play a swirling jig, tapping along with her foot as she watched to gauge their reaction. The music was loud and slightly alarming; Mrs Slater flinched.

Mr Sinclair held up his hand. 'All right, I'll take your word for it. But really, there's not much I can do. Everybody wants to leave and if you don't have the necessary documents, it's very difficult. I have to work within the law.'

'Miss Hoffman told me about an American couple who are rescuing Jewish children,' Sophie said. 'Could they take my sister?'

'Esme, I think you know about the Abrahams,' Mr Sinclair said. 'What's the current situation?'

Mrs Slater stepped forward. 'They leave in a couple of days' time and I'm afraid the children have all been selected and prepared, so there's no point trying to muscle in.'

'Then what shall we do?' Sophie asked, a tide of panic rising from the pit of her stomach. 'Please, you have to help us.'

'There's no "have to" about it,' Mrs Slater said sharply.

'You and your friend can give me your details and we'll make enquiries and get back to you. There's sometimes an opportunity for bilingual applicants, isn't there, Mr Sinclair?' And she gave him a meaningful glance.

'I suppose there might be.' George Sinclair looked at Sophie for longer than seemed necessary. 'Yes, give Mrs Slater your names and addresses and come back here in a few days' time. You may have the appointment which you seem to have taken anyway.'

Ruth had been following the conversation with interest, although she couldn't have understood much. 'You want I play violin?' she asked, sensing her last opportunity.

'No, thank you,' Mrs Slater said firmly, ushering the girls through to her office. 'I think we've got the general idea.'

'All right then, Sophie Klein. Tell me about yourself.' Ruth produced a paper bag from her pocket and took out a roll, which she broke in half and offered to Sophie. They were sitting in the railway station, watching an endless stream of passengers weighed down with luggage pour through ticket barriers and barge their way on to trains.

'Thanks.' Sophie sank her teeth into the soft bread, which was spread with butter and sugar and tasted delicious. 'Well, there's not really much to say. I worked in the library until a few weeks ago. My father was Jewish and my mother's Catholic, and we lived in an apartment near the Innere Stadt. Now my sister and I are staying with a friend.'

'You've been evicted?'

Sophie nodded. 'Soon after my father died.'

'So you lost everything?'

'Almost. The new people gave us five minutes to pack a few things.' Thank God she had planned ahead, sewing their papers, money and jewellery into the lining of her coat. They watched a woman in a fur coat hurrying past, followed by a porter pushing a trolley piled high with suitcases, topped by a shrouded birdcage in which a parrot was squawking like a banshee.

'That'll be us one day,' Ruth said, dusting off her hands on her skirt. 'We have to believe it will happen.'

Yet Sophie was losing hope. No one had responded to her enquiries and she was beginning to wonder whether the letters had even reached their destination. She and Hanna were living from day to day and all the emotional energy she could spare from fearing for her mother and mourning her father went to worrying about her sister. Hanna had hardly uttered a word since their father died. When Sophie spoke to her, she merely stared back as though she were in a stupor. Sophie was haunted by the feeling she was letting their mother down, not looking after her little sister half as well as Ingrid would have done, but Hanna had retreated to a place she couldn't follow.

They were sleeping on the Fischers' living-room sofa; it had been sobering to realise there was no one else to turn to for help. The Dichters had left and none of the other neighbours would open their doors. Sophie had appealed to her father's closest colleague at the library but he wouldn't even come down from his office to meet her, and her mother's cake shop was already shuttered with no sign of Tamara. Only Wilhelm and his mother had been prepared to take them in, and the girls couldn't stay there much longer.

'I can't leave without finding out about my mother,' Sophie told Ruth.

'You might have to,' she replied. 'Sorry to be brutal but

face facts: you may never know where she's gone or what's happened to her. Why was she arrested, anyway?'

'She spat at an SS officer,' Sophie replied.

Ruth laughed, clapping her hands. 'Yes! Good for her.'

That was all very well, but late at night when she couldn't sleep, Sophie sometimes wondered whether Ingrid had considered her daughters at all. Hadn't she felt the slightest need to protect them, rather than make some futile gesture that had been bound to end in her arrest? She had effectively handed Hanna over to Sophie even before that disastrous afternoon. And then in the morning Sophie would remember her mother's courage, her magnificent defiance, and long for her more desperately than ever.

'We have to be strong,' Ruth said. 'If you show them you're afraid, they'll destroy you. You have to think about your sister and yourself. That's the priority, and what your mother would want.'

'I suppose so,' Sophie replied, 'but it's hard. I'm not as brave as you.'

'You might be more like me than you think,' Ruth said. 'Making so much fuss in the embassy? That was brilliant. Don't be afraid to stick up for yourself because sure as hell, nobody else will.'

They sat in silence for a while, watching the passers-by. 'So what's your story?' Sophie asked.

'I was studying music at the Academy until last year. Now I live on my wits. I play in a restaurant some evenings, sometimes on the street.' Ruth glanced at the German soldiers patrolling the concourse in pairs, guns at the ready. 'I'd have a go now if there weren't so many Nazi scum about. My father's in a prison camp and my mother's in a sanatorium and I'm an only child so I'm fancy free. I've a room in a

69

tenement building in Leopoldstadt but it won't be for long; I'm getting out of Vienna one way or another, I'll tell you that for nothing. I've got permission to leave but nowhere to go, like you. Do you think George Sinclair is looking for a mistress?'

Sophie smiled. 'I didn't get that impression.'

'Nor me. I think the glamorous Mrs Slater might have filled that vacancy. Still, you could always have a try; I think he likes you and your English is excellent. Would you give me lessons?'

'Sure,' Sophie replied.

Ruth sighed with exasperation, shaking her head. 'You're far too soft. If you teach me English, what will I give you in return? Come on, think!' And she gave Sophie a poke in the ribs that made her gasp and straighten up.

'Hanna and I need somewhere to sleep,' she said, rubbing her side. 'Could we stay with you for a while?'

'Do you have money?'

'A little. We wouldn't expect you to feed us.'

'I should hope not.' Ruth considered the idea. 'All right, then, but you'll have to share a mattress on the floor. We'll try it for a week or so and see how things go. I hope your sister isn't a brat.'

'If she ever was, she's certainly not one now.' Sophie licked a sugar crystal from her lip. 'Wait a minute, though: you gave me half your roll without expecting anything back.'

'That's what you think,' Ruth said, and laughed.

Chapter Eight

Vienna, May 1938

George Sinclair wasn't present at their next meeting at the embassy so Sophie hadn't the chance to try out her seduction technique, even if she'd wanted to. She had brought Hanna along and Ruth came with them, even though it had been made clear that her lack of English was a disadvantage. Mrs Slater asked to speak to Sophie for a few minutes alone first, and her face was grave.

'Bad news, I'm afraid,' she said, straightening the blotter on her desk and aligning the stapler next to it. 'I'm sorry to have to tell you that your mother is dead.'

'What?' Sophie stared, incredulous. 'How can that be?'

'They say she fell out of a fifth-storey window.' Mrs Slater hesitated. 'It's possible she jumped.' She rearranged a pot of paperclips and a ruler before continuing, still not meeting Sophie's eye. 'Please accept my condolences. I thought you would like to break the news to your sister in your own time. It will come better from you than a stranger.'

'Thank you.' Sophie was dazed. Esme Slater was speaking again but she couldn't take in the words. Both her parents were gone; she and Hanna were orphans. 'Look after Hanna for me,' her mother had said. She must have known what might happen.

'Would you like a cigarette?' Mrs Slater held out a packet and Sophie took one, though she didn't usually smoke, and allowed it to be lit. 'Now, you must concentrate, Miss Klein, and listen carefully to what I have to say. Can you do that?' She was speaking in flawless German, without the hint of an accent.

'Yes, of course.' Sophie wouldn't cry. Later, there would be time to grieve.

'I've spoken to Mr Sinclair and we agree there might be opportunities for a girl with your abilities and background.'

What does that mean, exactly? Sophie wondered. Her ability to speak English, presumably, but how was her background relevant?

'Your sister, however, is a different matter,' Esme Slater went on. 'Are there any relatives or friends who could give her a home?'

'I'm afraid not.' Wilhelm's mother had needed some persuading to let the girls stay as long as they had, and Ruth had made it clear that the arrangement in her room in Leopoldstadt was only temporary. Besides, she couldn't bear to think of her darling Hanna being passed from hand to hand like a piece of unwanted luggage. 'Is there really no chance the American couple might take her?'

'None at all,' Mrs Slater said. 'They're leaving tomorrow morning. In the meantime, I should like you to keep in touch. Are you still at the address you gave me before?' She flipped through a rolodex.

'We're staying with Ruth Hoffman at the moment. I think you have her details.'

'Ah, yes. The impresario outside.' Mrs Slater raised her eyebrows. 'Keep this conversation private, would you? She's very determined but more difficult to place.' With that, she got up to open the door and call in the other two.

If she hadn't been numb, Sophie might have broken down when she saw Hanna trail into the office behind Ruth, her face pale and frightened. She held out her arm and Hanna ran towards her, shrinking against her sister's side and burying her face in her blouse. She has no one to turn to but me, Sophie thought, filled with such a fierce protective love that the last shred of weakness in her spirit burned away. She would have killed anyone who tried to hurt Hanna, torn them apart with her bare hands. Mrs Slater was talking and she caught the odd phrase – 'difficult present circumstances', 'regrettable state of affairs', 'not for the foreseeable future' – and then the three of them were being ushered outside.

'Well, that was a waste of time,' Ruth said, knitting her dark eyebrows. 'Why bother setting up a meeting if you don't have anything to offer?' She gave Sophie a suspicious stare. 'What did she talk to you about?'

'I'll tell you later.' Sophie glanced down at Hanna. 'When we're on our own.'

That afternoon, Ruth went to play her violin outside the opera house while Sophie took Hanna to St Stephen's Cathedral. Their mother would go to mass there at Easter and Christmas, and Sophie was planning to light a candle for her and explain to Hanna what had happened. She sat in the sacred hush, breathing the scent of incense and staring up at the richly patterned ceiling while Hanna dozed beside her. Neither of them were sleeping well on Ruth's floor in

Leopoldstadt; doors banged all night long and a baby cried astonishingly loudly every few hours in the apartment next door. Sophie settled Hanna's head more comfortably against her shoulder. Her sister's hair was tangled and her clothes smelt of the cabbage soup they had eaten at the Jewish refuge that morning. She looked shabby and unloved. What would their mother have said?

Hanna yawned and sat up. 'I don't want to sit in a church,' she said. 'I don't believe in God. If He exists, why does He let these terrible things happen?'

'I suppose He has to let us make our own mistakes,' Sophie replied, not even convincing herself. Now the moment had come, she couldn't bring herself to tell Hanna the awful truth. Surely her sister had suffered enough? She would break the news tomorrow, or in the next few days. Or maybe she would wait a couple of months until they were both feeling stronger. There was no rush, after all. Let Hanna accept one loss before being confronted with another.

'Come, let's walk back along the canal,' she said, taking her sister's hand. 'I think we can afford an ice cream.' As if that would make everything all right.

They rested some more in the sun on a bench beside the canal, wanting to postpone their return to the cluttered room in Leopoldstadt for as long as possible. Ruth's irritable sighs and sideways glances had quickly let them know their presence was a trial, and Sophie's attempts to teach her English were an ordeal for both parties. Ruth was a scatterbrain and Sophie too tired and worried to be patient. She had a feeling their trial period would soon be over and that it wouldn't be extended, which was disappointing; she'd thought she and Ruth might have become friends. The girls Sophie used to go around with at school had mostly dropped her over the past year, once the inconvenient truth about her Jewish father had emerged, and the women she worked with at the library were years older, with different interests and concerns. Sophie was lonely, and being with Ruth gave her some comfort.

Yet Ruth didn't seem to have the time or the inclination for anything so frivolous as friendship. That evening, however, they heard her singing as they climbed upstairs, and found her cooking noodles at the communal hotplate on the landing. She'd had a successful afternoon busking and was making supper for three. 'You can wash up, OK?' she told Sophie and Hanna.

They had just sat down on the floor with their plates on their laps when someone hammered on the door. There was nowhere to hide so they sat there, frozen, until Ruth got up to answer the summons. Their visitor was familiar: Esme Slater walked into the room, wearing a black cocktail frock and high heels with a fur coat slung over her shoulders, looking more out of place than ever.

'I'm sorry to call unannounced,' she began, not sounding sorry at all, 'but I have urgent news. Miss Klein, Sophie, would you mind stepping outside for a moment?'

The worst has already happened, Sophie reminded herself as she followed Mrs Slater into the dingy corridor; nothing anyone says can hurt you now. She was hollow inside, not daring to contemplate the enormity of her loss – or the hatred she felt for the Nazis, for that matter. It was safer to keep her mind empty or she would go mad.

'A chance has arisen for your sister,' Mrs Slater began, 'but we have to move quickly. You remember the American couple, the Abrahams?' Sophie nodded. 'Well, one of the children in their group has gone down with scarlet fever and can't travel. I thought of you straight away. The Abrahams have secured pre-arranged visas and it should be possible to substitute Hanna's name for that of the sick child. She's healthy, I presume?'

'Yes, but—'

Mrs Slater cut her off. 'You realise this is a miracle, don't you? Anyone would think your mother was looking out for Hanna.'

The old Sophie might have asked whether there were other children on the waiting list more deserving of a miracle than her sister. She considered that idea briefly before dismissing it. 'So what happens next?'

'Good girl,' Mrs Slater said briskly. 'You must both be at the train station tomorrow morning by eight. I'll meet you there and smooth over any last-minute hitches with the Abrahams. They and the children will be travelling to Berlin for physical examinations and final processing before catching the boat to New York a couple of days later. Hanna may bring one suitcase.'

'We don't have a suitcase,' Sophie replied.

'Then improvise.' Mrs Slater was already turning to leave.

'Just a minute.' Sophie caught her arm. 'This couple, the Abrahams: they're all right, aren't they? I mean, they'll look after the children on the journey, and once they get to America?' She hadn't even asked what would happen then.

'What an extraordinary question,' Mrs Slater remarked. 'These children are the lucky ones, believe you me. Everything's been arranged: they'll be fostered until their parents are in a position to join or send for them. In Hanna's case, of course, that doesn't apply.'

'She has me, though!' Sophie spoke more loudly than she'd intended. 'You understand this move isn't permanent?

When Hitler's no longer in power, I'll be coming to fetch my sister home.'

Mrs Slater looked at her for a few seconds without speaking. With her slanting, hooded eyes and beaky nose, she reminded Sophie of a bird of prey. 'Of course, my dear,' she said eventually, 'but a lot can happen before then. For now, you have to let Hanna go.'

She doesn't believe I'll make it, Sophie realised with a shock; either that, or she thinks the Germans will always be in charge of Austria. 'I understand,' she replied, icy calm. 'I'll be collecting my sister, though. She belongs here with me.'

'Why can't you come to America, too?' Hanna whispered, her eyes glistening in the dim light.

Sophie smoothed back her hair. It was strange, the need she felt to touch Hanna these days. They had never been a particularly tactile family but now she was always holding her sister's hand or putting an arm around her bony, sloping shoulders: as if to pack years' worth of caresses into a few days. Maybe she was trying to comfort herself as much as Hanna.

'I'm too old,' she said quietly. 'But we can write to each other and as soon as I can, I'll come for you.'

'But how will you and Mutti know where I am?' Hanna's voice had risen and Sophie put a finger to her lips; they were trying not to disturb Ruth, who was sleeping on the couch nearby.

'You mustn't worry about that,' she replied. 'The Abrahams will tell us where you are, I'll make sure of that. You won't simply disappear.' This was her greatest fear, almost too overwhelming to be spoken aloud.

'I don't want to go,' Hanna said. 'You can't force me. I want to stay here with you until Mutti comes back.'

'Listen to me, Liebchen.' Sophie propped herself up on one elbow. 'I know it seems daunting, travelling so far away on your own, but you're a brave, clever girl and the Abrahams are giving you the most wonderful chance. You'll be free! No one will hate you in America – other children will want to be your friend, and there'll be plenty to eat and parks where you'll be allowed to play, and the Nazis won't ever find you. Mutti would be so disappointed if you didn't go.'

'Does she know?'

'Yes,' Sophie said, without thinking twice. 'She wants what's best for you and she's so happy to hear you're going on this adventure. As soon as she can, she'll write. Mrs Slater's going to give me the address.'

Hanna traced the outline of Sophie's cheek with her finger. 'An adventure?' she repeated.

'Of course! Sailing across the ocean with lots of other children, and plenty of ice cream waiting for you in New York.' She settled Hanna's teddy in her arms as though she were a toddler and not a girl of nine. 'Now turn over and go to sleep and the morning will come before you know it.'

Hanna did as she was told. She cuddled her teddy and Sophie cuddled her, dozing fitfully as she waited for dawn to break and remembering the times Hanna had crawled into her big sister's bed when she couldn't sleep. Sophie had occasionally resented the time she'd had to spend looking after her little sister while her friends were out having fun; now she wished for those precious hours back so she could live them again. Hanna was part of her: letting her go would be like losing a limb, yet it was the right thing – the only thing – to do. At one point during that endless night, she sensed their mother's presence in the dark, telling her to be strong and unafraid and promising she would always be with them. The lightest of kisses touched her forehead, as though she had been brushed by angels' wings.

As soon as it was light, she slipped out of bed and took her skirt and blouse from the back of the chair. A creak of springs made her turn around to see Ruth sitting on the edge of the couch in men's pyjamas, watching her.

'All ready?' she asked.

'As ready as we'll ever be.' Her rucksack and a pillowcase sat waiting, packed with the few random things Sophie had grabbed from Hanna's bedroom before they left their home: a change of clothes, a couple of books and a framed photograph she had taken of Hanna with her parents one summer at Lake Achensee, with the mountains in the background. She had the same snapshot in her own bag.

'She's a lucky girl, your sister,' Ruth said. 'Don't you think it strange this chance should suddenly materialise in the nick of time?'

Sophie frowned. 'What are you implying?'

'I'm not sure.' Ruth yawned and scratched her arm. 'I can't work Mrs Slater out, that's all. She seems to be taking a personal interest in you and I'm not sure why.'

'Do you think I shouldn't let Hanna go to America?'

'Are you crazy? Of course you must!' Ruth peeled off her pyjama top and pulled an embroidered dress over her head. 'We have to survive and tell the world how these bastards are treating us. There'll be a day of reckoning; that's what I'm living for.' She emerged, scooping her curls into a topknot and tying it deftly with a shoelace. 'I'll come with you to the train station.'

'You don't have to,' Sophie said, though she was pleased by the offer. She couldn't let herself break down in front of Ruth, and maybe Hanna would stay strong, too.

'That's all right. I'm thinking of taking a journey myself.'

Sophie would have asked Ruth what she meant but now Hanna was awake so all her energy had to be concentrated on her. She tried to imagine what their mother would say in this situation, and failed: the whole scenario was too unlikely.

'Bags me the bathroom,' Ruth said, taking the key from its hook and making for the door. If it had been anyone else, Sophie might have thought they were being tactful.

She watched Hanna dress, her face giving nothing away. 'Shall I plait your hair?' she asked, though she was nowhere near as deft as Ingrid had been.

'I can manage,' Hanna said, so Sophie passed her the hairbrush. There was no point babying her sister any longer: she'd have to look after herself soon enough.

'Think of all the other children getting ready this morning and feeling just as nervous as you,' she said. 'Things are bound to be strange at first, but I bet you'll soon make friends.'

If only she'd had time to prepare for this sudden parting! She rifled through her rucksack, looking for any other reminder of home that Hanna could take with her. And then her fingers touched the knife and fork that some impulse had made her snatch from the kitchen table, under the nose of the couple who were throwing her and Hanna out of their apartment.

'Take these,' she said, putting the cutlery into her sister's pillowcase. 'Promise me you won't forget the meals we ate together.'

After an apple between the two of them and a glass of milk for breakfast, they caught the bus for the train station. Ruth took her violin; Sophie assumed she would be trying her luck busking later. Hanna didn't speak and she wouldn't rest her head on Sophie's shoulder; she sat with a straight back, staring out of the window with the pillowcase resting on her lap. Vienna sparkled in the early-morning light, but Sophie's heart had turned against it. What was the point of such beauty when people were behaving like brutes? The endless windows, terraces and statues of Schloss Belvedere beyond the window sickened her. This was her father's world of culture and history and it counted for nothing in the end; palaces and monuments were built out of vanity, offering only the illusion of civilisation. She wished she were leaving the city, too.

'It's for the best,' she muttered, almost to herself.

'I know that,' Hanna said, and Sophie caught a glimpse of the young woman she would become. She took her sister's hand and held it, and Hanna didn't pull away.

Although it was early in the morning, traffic was already thick and their bus was held up at a checkpoint for what seemed an age. Two German soldiers armed with rifles climbed on board, inspecting the passengers and checking their tickets. Sophie's hand shook as she held out hers and she kept her eyes lowered, but the man only glanced at her before smiling and patting her sister on the head. Blonde-haired, blue-eyed Hanna was a lucky charm. Sophie seized Ruth's wrist to look at her watch, her heart pounding; the minutes were ticking by and at this rate, they were in danger of missing the train. At last, however, the soldiers disembarked and the bus pulled slowly away. 'Come on, come on!' Sophie muttered to herself, digging her fingernails into her sweating palms.

By the time they'd reached the station, a crowd of children and their parents had already gathered on the concourse. Esme Slater broke away as soon as she spotted them.

'Thank goodness,' she said, hurrying forward. 'I was beginning to think you'd changed your mind. There isn't much time. Hanna, come and meet Mr and Mrs Abrahams.' She pulled her away, Sophie following on behind.

The Abrahams were instantly recognisable as foreign from the cut of their clothes, the whiteness of their teeth and some indefinable self-assurance that radiated from them. Mr Abrahams was a pleasant middle-aged man with regular features and broad shoulders; his wife a little younger in a straw hat and a blue frock splashed with crimson roses. She looked glamorous rather than motherly, and Sophie was suddenly ashamed of her own drab brown skirt and serviceable blouse. Sophie held her breath as Mrs Slater drew Mrs Abrahams aside to speak to her and push Hanna forward. The American woman smiled, bending down to raise Hanna's chin with her hand and look her in the face. Hanna smiled back, breaking Sophie's heart because she could tell the effort it cost her sister not to cry. Beside them, a small boy aged about five was clinging to his mother's leg with both arms while his father tried to prise him loose. It was agonising to watch; Sophie looked quickly away.

And now Mrs Slater was bringing Hanna back to her. 'Time to say your goodbyes,' she told them. 'Short and sweet would be my advice.'

Sophie gathered her wits, crouched beside her sister and hugged her close. 'Be happy and work hard,' she whispered. 'Stand up for yourself and don't forget me. I'll come for you, I promise. And in the meantime, I'll write as soon as I'm settled and let you know where I am.'

Hanna stared at her, mute. She'd turned pale but wasn't crying.

'Well done,' Mrs Slater said briskly. 'Now come with me, child. I've found a nice girl to sit next to you on the train. Her name is Lotti and I think you'll get along famously.' And then Hanna was led away, with one last look at Sophie over her shoulder.

And now I am quite alone, Sophie said to herself: a thought both terrifying and liberating. A blast of steam and the slamming of doors announced the train was ready for boarding; parents filed through the ticket barrier with their children and stood on the platform, craning to keep them in view until the very last minute. The youngest looked about four or five, clutching dolls and teddies, through to young teenagers: leggy girls and boys whose voices were beginning to break. A few of the children were excited, swinging their suitcases and hanging out of the train windows to call to their parents, but most simply looked bewildered.

Sophie had lost sight of Hanna and didn't want to risk upsetting her by pushing on to the platform and making a fuss. She turned around, looking for Ruth, and caught sight of the Abrahams walking towards the train.

'Thank you so much,' she said, hurrying towards Mrs Abrahams and in her agitation clutching her arm. 'God bless you.'

Mrs Abrahams looked startled, but she managed to smile. 'And you, too. Good luck, and don't give up.' She was younger than Sophie had first thought, yet composed and self-assured. She was clearly a formidable person: it must have taken some courage and imagination to have come here and spirited these children away.

'Tell everyone what the Nazis are doing to us,' Sophie said, tightening her grip. 'Please, Mrs Abrahams. The world has to know.'

'I'll do my best.' Mrs Abrahams disengaged her arm. 'But we can't force people to listen if they don't want to hear.'

Mrs Slater appeared from nowhere to glare at Sophie. 'I hope you're not making a nuisance of yourself.'

And now here was Ruth, running up to join them. 'I have ticket!' She waved it in the air – but it was the Abrahams she was addressing, rather than Sophie.

'Well done,' Mr Abrahams said. 'Just as far as Berlin, remember? I'm not making any promises after that.'

'Yes, thank you.' Ruth settled her violin case more comfortably on her back. 'I play very good music you like.'

Mrs Abrahams looked at her husband, shaking her head. 'Really, Seth? Another one?'

'Won't make much difference,' he replied, putting an arm around her shoulder and guiding her away.

'Ruth?' Sophie hissed, pulling her back. 'What are you doing?'

'I'm going with them to Berlin, to help look after the children,' she said. 'And bewitch them with my violin. They're musical, Mrs Slater told me. He's going to help me find a sponsor, though he doesn't know it yet.' She broke away. 'Now I must run. You can stay in my room for a few days but the rent's overdue so watch out.' Hurrying after the Abrahams, she turned back briefly to call, 'Remember what I said? Toughen up!' And then she was gone.

How dare she? If anyone was going with the Abrahams, it should have been Sophie. If Ruth had told her what she'd been planning, it might have been a little easier to bear, but the fact she'd kept the whole thing a secret felt like a betrayal.

'She won't get to America, you know,' Mrs Slater said, coming to stand beside Sophie. 'You'd only have been putting off the evil hour if you'd tried to go with them.'

She was right, Sophie realised. And Ruth was teaching her a final lesson: these days, you had to fight to survive and to hell with everyone else.

They stood watching as porters loaded luggage and the last few doors slammed while the engine hissed clouds of steam. Hanna is safe, Sophie reminded herself. Whatever happens now, she'll be free to lead some sort of life. Her own future looked bleak. She was entirely alone, with very little money and nowhere to stay. Unless she followed Ruth's example, there was no hope for her.

Chapter Nine

Point Grey, Vancouver BC,

April 2022

Of course Lacey had to warn her sister about the surprise visit for Gubby's birthday: Jess would never have forgiven her if half the family had turned up on her doorstep unannounced. She was a micro-manager, planning the kids' activities and meals for the family with military precision. Lacey texted Chris first to ask his advice and within the hour, Jess had called.

'You have to act like you had no idea,' Lacey said, 'otherwise I'll be in big trouble.'

'Thank heavens you told me,' Jess replied. 'We were going to be out of town that weekend. What was Mom thinking? We won't say anything to the kids so at least it'll be a surprise for them. They're going to be so happy to see you.'

'Me, too.' Lacey hesitated. 'But look, there's just an outside chance I won't make it. I have a crazy deadline with a new client that I can't afford to lose.'

'Lacey, come on!' The disappointment in Jess's voice was

palpable. 'Are you kidding me? We haven't seen you for three years.'

'I'm sure it'll be OK,' Lacey said quickly. 'I'm going to try my hardest, anyway.'

She ended the call knowing she'd hurt her sister and hating herself for it. What was wrong with her? All she had to do was get to the airport and sit on a plane, yet her anxiety was going through the roof. She was waking up three or four times a night, her heart racing and her nightshirt soaked with sweat.

'Just go to the doctor and get some Xanax,' advised hot Rick from the apartment opposite. 'It's no big deal. In fact, I can probably spare you a couple of tabs.'

He was the last person she would ever have imagined confiding in, but he'd asked her to feed his cat again and when she told him she couldn't because she was going on vacation, they'd started a conversation about where and who with, and somehow she'd ended up blurting out the fact she was dreading the flight. She hadn't wanted to take medication before then for a number of reasons, but now it seemed the only alternative. Easier than therapy, at any rate. Rick convinced her Xanax was perfectly safe – against her better judgement, she had to admit, but if that's what it took to reach Jess, she was prepared to take the risk.

'We'll look after each other,' Gubby had said, the night before they were due to fly. Lacey had stayed overnight in Bethlehem so she and her grandmother could travel to the airport together. Popping a couple of Xanax, listening to a meditation app on her phone and practising deep breathing were enough to get her through – feeling like a zombie, perhaps, but at least not freaking out. She floated through the airport as though she were underwater, separated from the world by a sheet of gauze, letting Cedric shepherd Gubby through security, find her a seat and ask twenty times whether she'd like him to call for a buggy. There was no point all of them fussing over her. Adele was busy scrolling through her phone for the Airbnb check-in details yet again, continuing the seemingly endless debate about whether they should go there by bus or take a cab.

'I don't know, Mom.' Lacey stifled a yawn. 'Whatever's easier.'

She fell asleep on the plane and it didn't seem long before the four of them were in a cab, then checking into their rented apartment and finally standing on Jess's doorstep, being choreographed by Adele before the big reveal. Lacey's head was pounding by then and her mouth was dry, and filming the moment when Jess opened her door and pretended to be surprised seemed like the stupidest idea in the world. She felt tired and muddled, and for some reason the sight of her sister made her want to cry. Luckily the moment was so chaotic and noisy – especially when Pauly and Emma appeared and threw themselves into Gubby's arms, almost knocking her over – that no one was paying her much attention.

She and Jess didn't have a moment to themselves that night, and the morning after was spent entertaining the kids, giving Gubby her gifts and preparing the birthday lunch.

'I can't believe you just threw this amazing meal together,' Gubby said, when they'd demolished a selection of her favourite food: prawns with cocktail sauce, steaks from the outdoor grill, nut roast for Cedric, and baby potatoes roasted with onions and garlic.

'Well, you know me,' Jess told her. 'The freezer's always full, and it just so happened Chris made your favourite chocolate cake yesterday. Wasn't that a coincidence?'

'So here's to you, Mom,' Adele said, raising her champagne glass. 'Happy ninety-third birthday, and may there be many more.'

'I'm not so sure about that,' Gubby replied. 'I'm about ready to go, if you want the God's honest truth.'

'But we're not ready to let you.' Jess reached forward to squeeze her grandmother's hand. 'So you'd better hang on for a while longer.'

'Now you girls sit and talk,' Cedric said, stacking their bowls. 'We'll be in charge of clearing up.'

'Coffee and cake to follow,' Chris added.

'My, you have got him well trained,' Adele said to Jess, with an edge to her voice that Lacey knew would infuriate her sister. But mellowed by the wine and good company, Jess merely pulled a face at her mother.

When the men had gone through to the kitchen, Gubby folded her serviette and said, 'And now, my darlings, I've got something to tell you all.'

Lacey's stomach turned over; she knew what was coming, and she knew how nervous Gubby would be feeling. It had taken a lot of persuading for her grandmother even to consider sharing her story – with Adele, in particular. In the end, however, she had conceded that it wasn't fair on Lacey, expecting her to keep such a huge secret to herself.

'You look very serious,' Adele said, smiling. 'Have you decided to leave all your money to a cats' home?'

'Hush, Mom,' Lacey told her. 'Listen.'

'Yes, Lacey knows about this already,' Gubby said. Jess glanced at Lacey, raising her eyebrows, and Lacey looked down at her plate.

'You may be shocked, I'm afraid,' their grandmother went on, 'and perhaps even a little angry with me for not having confided in you before. I'm sorry about that, but better late than never.' She cleared her throat. 'The fact of the matter is, I was adopted as a child.'

A stunned silence hung over the table for a few seconds. 'Adopted?' Adele repeated, leaning forward. 'Are you kidding?'

'Obviously not,' Gubby replied. 'It isn't the sort of thing you joke about.'

'Go on, Grandma,' Jess said, frowning at her mother. 'Tell us more.'

Gubby twisted her glass around by its stem. 'I was born in Vienna,' she began, 'in 1929.'

'Vienna, as in Austria?' Adele interrupted. 'How on earth—?'

'Mom, will you shut up for five seconds?' Lacey cried. 'Let Gubby speak!'

'Yes, Vienna, as in Austria,' Gubby went on. She spoke formally, as though reading from a script. 'I lived with my parents in a beautiful apartment in the middle of the city. The first eight years of my life were blissfully happy. My mother and father adored each other: he had an important job at the National Library and she ran a patisserie not far from our home. She was a beautiful woman and the most wonderful cook; people came from miles around to buy her Sachertorte. You know my chocolate cake? That's her recipe, as far as I recall.'

Adele stared around the table at each of them in turn, slowly shaking her head.

'But then in 1938, Hitler invaded Austria and claimed the country as part of the German Reich,' Gubby continued in her story-telling voice. 'The Anschluss, it was called. And that was not good news for us because my father was Jewish.'

'Jewish?' Adele said, her voice rising. 'I'm sorry, you all, but I'm having trouble taking this in. It's like a story Crazy Sue would make up.'

'Whether you believe it or not, it's the truth,' Gubby said calmly. 'I wouldn't lie about such a thing. My mother was a Catholic but I wasn't brought up in either faith; my parents weren't religious. That didn't make any difference, though. I had two Jewish grandparents, so I was classed as a Mischling: mixed blood. My father lost his job, and then things got worse.'

She took a sip of water and blotted her mouth with a napkin.

'Take your time,' Lacey said, rubbing her back. 'You're doing great.'

'It was eighty-four years ago today.' Gubby's voice petered out; she swallowed and waited a few seconds before continuing. 'On my ninth birthday, soon after the Anschluss, we went to the Prater – it's an amusement park in Vienna. There were some Nazis there, causing trouble, and my father had a heart attack and died. He had a weak heart, you see, and the stress was too much.' Her eyes filled with tears. 'I'm sorry, I still can't bear to remember.'

'Of course,' Jess told her. 'You don't have to tell us everything, not if it's too painful.' She glared a warning at her mother but at last Adele was quiet.

'And then, a few days later, we were evicted from our apartment,' Gubby went on. 'It was given to a Nazi family, so we were homeless. But somehow my mother got to hear of an American couple who were rescuing Jewish children and managed to get them to take me, too. She was a very determined woman.'

'She let you go while she stayed behind?' Adele asked.

Gubby nodded. 'It must have taken such courage. I can

remember saying goodbye to her at the station to this day. She was wearing a blue dress with red flowers all over it, as though she were off to a picnic. Do you know, there was a little girl beside me, waving to her parents from the window as the train left, and her father grabbed her and pulled her off. He couldn't let her go.' Her eyes were misty, faraway. 'I've often wondered what became of that child.' She reached into her purse and took out a knife and fork, which she placed on the table. They all stared at the old-fashioned, unremarkable iron cutlery. 'These are the only things I have from home. There was a photograph and a couple of books, but they were lost; I think my new mother must have thrown them away.'

'What happened to your birth mother?' Jess asked.

'I never saw her again,' Gubby replied. 'She was arrested some time later, I gather, and died in prison. Nobody knows exactly what happened.'

'Oh, Mom!' Adele moved around the table and took Gubby in her arms. 'How have you lived with this for so long without telling anyone? Did Dad know?'

Gubby shook her head. 'I couldn't bear to rake it all up again. My first husband was aware of my background because we'd grown up in the same neighbourhood, but I never told Bernard.' She blew her nose on a napkin. 'I'm one of the lucky ones, though. To have made such a good life and be blessed with my wonderful family. What about the poor children left behind in Austria? We should be crying for them, not me.'

'But how come you don't have an Austrian accent?' Jess asked. 'You don't sound anything like Arnold Schwarzenegger.'

Gubby smiled. 'Well, he was older than me when he came to America, for one thing. And for another, I made sure to lose my accent as soon as I could. I was desperate to fit in, you see. In the back of my mind, there was always a fear the Nazis would come looking for me, so I tried to make myself as American as possible. And that's what my adoptive parents wanted. They weren't exactly antisemitic, but Pop played golf at the country club where Jews weren't allowed, and I always knew not to raise the subject. I didn't want to upset them. They were so kind to me when I first arrived – and afterwards, of course. I just wanted to please them so they wouldn't send me back.'

'So Uncle Jim was only your step-brother?' Adele said. 'That's bizarre, I had no idea. You and Grammie looked so alike.'

'I know, we did,' Gubby told her. 'I think that's why my parents picked me out of the children's home, despite being foreign and all.'

'Foreign!' Adele ran a hand through her hair, bracelets jingling. 'Mom, I always thought you were as American as pumpkin pie. I can't get my head around this new version of your past.'

'I wanted to tell you so many times,' Gubby said, 'but the moment never seemed right. First you were too young, then you were a moody teenager, and after that you were having problems with one awful man after another – I couldn't lay this on your shoulders, too.'

'It's a lot to take in,' Adele said. 'There are implications, you know. I was asked for my family health history the other day so I told them about Grampie's Parkinson's, but I guess that's irrelevant. Am I going to have to worry about heart disease now?'

'Jeez, Mom! Why does everything always end up being about you?' Jess burst out, just as Chris was coming through with the chocolate cake, blazing with candles.

'Everyone OK?' he asked, looking at their flushed, upset faces.

'Fine. Just coming to terms with the fact that everything I've been told about my background is a lie,' Adele replied. 'Nothing I'm allowed to be concerned about, though.'

Jess stood up abruptly. 'I couldn't eat a bite of cake, I'm stuffed. Lacey, why don't you and I take the kids to the beach so Chris and Cedric can clear up and Mom and Gubby can talk?'

Pauly and Emma were playing in the back yard but as soon as they saw there was birthday cake, they wanted to stay and eat it, so Lacey and Jess went off on their own.

'Dear Lord,' Jess groaned, closing the front door. 'One day with Mommie dearest and I end up wanting to kill her.' She put her arm through Lacey's as they walked down the street. 'So, tell me the story behind the story. How did you find out?'

'I knew you'd be mad,' Lacey replied. 'Mom asked me to check Gubby's passport and I found out she was born in Vienna. She told me about her adoption in the end, but she made me swear to keep it a secret.'

'Relax! It's fine, I understand,' Jess told her. 'Of course you couldn't betray a confidence.'

Lacey let out her breath. 'Poor Gubby. She's been crippled with guilt, she said, because she'd insisted on going to the park for her birthday. She thinks her father's death is all her fault.'

A light rain was falling, misting their hair as they stepped on to the beach and walked towards the sea, where sail boats were tacking to and fro. Jess picked up a pebble from the sand and sent it skimming over the surface of the water.

'What a burden to keep from everyone your whole life,'

she said. 'I wish she *had* told us sooner, but can you imagine if we'd only found out after she died? We need to find out more. Maybe it's time you started researching a story closer to home.' They walked on over the wet sand. 'Speaking of which . . . how's the book?'

'Finished, thank goodness. Just waiting for the edits. I think it's the best thing I've ever written but it's worn me out.'

'Is that all?' Jess asked.

Lacey looked at her warily. 'What do you mean?'

'You're not yourself,' Jess said. 'We haven't talked properly for ages and yesterday you were acting like you'd had a lobotomy. What's going on?'

There was no point trying to fool Jess: she was forensic. Yet how could Lacey spill the bucket of poison she'd been carrying so carefully for months? She'd held on to this burden for so long that it had become a part of her.

'I don't want to talk about it,' she said. 'Sorry, but I just can't.'

'Yes, you can. You need to speak to someone and it might as well be me.' They'd reached a covered picnic area and Jess steered Lacey towards one of the benches. 'Take your time, I'm not going anywhere.' She kept a hold on her sister's elbow in case she was tempted to run away.

Lacey tried to marshal her thoughts. She found a tissue in her pocket and blew her nose, playing for time, while Jess gazed into the dripping trees, pointedly not looking at her. Where to begin?

'I was kind of out of it yesterday,' she started hesitantly. 'I took a couple of Xanax because I was stressed about the flight.'

'Has the doctor prescribed you medication?'

'No, the guy from the apartment opposite gave me some.'
Jess's mouth tightened. 'Go on.'

Lacey took a deep breath, and then another. She'd have to go through with this. Secrets are toxic, she'd told Gubby; well, she should know.

'So, before lockdown,' she continued, 'before the world went crazy, I went to this bar with a bunch of people, and something bad happened.' Her stomach twisted into the familiar knot of panic and shame. 'Something so awful that I haven't been able to tell anyone.'

'I'm not anyone, I'm your sister,' Jess said. 'And I'm on your side, remember? Team Lacey. So come on – out with it.'

Chapter Ten

Vienna, May 1938

Sophie watched the train with her sister aboard pull out of Westbahnhof station feeling as though the last remnants of her old life were going with it. The Klein family was finished, dead or in exile, and she the only one left behind. There was some commotion as a man ran along the platform and a woman screamed, but she couldn't make out the cause of the fuss and could only hope Hanna wasn't involved. Her sister was somebody else's responsibility now, and she could hardly bear it.

'No point moping,' Mrs Slater told her briskly. 'Self-pity won't help and there are plans afoot: we have an interesting proposal to put to you. Come back to the embassy with me and we can talk it over.'

She turned and strode out of the station, jumping into a taxi in the street outside that had just delivered a couple of travellers. Sophie followed, numb with misery. What did it matter what happened to her now? She had lost everyone she loved. Luckily there was no need to talk as Mrs Slater spent most of the short journey powdering her nose and reapplying her lipstick with the aid of a compact mirror. Having disembarked, they threaded their way through the usual crowds at the embassy and took the stairs to Mr Sinclair's office.

'Ah, Miss Klein.' He rose to greet her. 'Take a seat. Would you like some coffee?'

'Coming right up,' Mrs Slater said, disappearing.

Mr Sinclair leaned back in his chair, appraising Sophie. She straightened uneasily. 'Before we begin,' he said, 'I must inform you that everything you're about to hear is top secret. You can't discuss the subject with anyone apart from Mrs Slater and myself, or the people we might send to meet you. Is that clear?'

'Perfectly.'

'Jolly good. Later you'll be asked to sign the Official Secrets Act but that's merely a formality – you're bound by it anyway.' He took out a handkerchief and blew his nose with some gusto. 'Well, now we've got that out of the way, tell me what you know about the British Royal Family.'

'Very little,' Sophie replied, nonplussed. She racked her brains, trying to come up with some scrap of information to offer him. 'Wasn't there some scandal recently?'

'I take it you mean the abdication? Not exactly a scandal, but yes – the previous king, Edward VIII, renounced the throne to marry an American, Wallis Simpson, and his younger brother inherited the title. George VI has been on the throne for a year and a half but unfortunately the previous incumbent – the Duke of Windsor, as he's now known – is still very much in evidence. Ah, coffee!' He rubbed his hands. 'Marvellous.'

Sophie helped herself to sugar and declined a cigarette.

If nothing else, she was glad of the chance for a hot, sweet drink with these strange people before deciding what to do next. The English were eccentric, she knew that, but why was she being asked about the Royal Family and why could they possibly want her to sign the Official Secrets Act, whatever that might be?

'The British Royal Family have always had close links with Germany,' Mrs Slater told her, once the coffee had been poured. 'As you might know, Queen Victoria married a German, as did her daughter: another Victoria, who became the mother of Kaiser Wilhelm. Several of the King's cousins are now in Hitler's closest circle.'

'You're probably wondering what all this has to do with you,' said Mr Sinclair. 'Well, besides my work at the embassy, I'm also involved with the British government in a more ad hoc capacity. Intelligence is vital, especially at such a volatile time in Europe. Eyes and ears in strategic places, that's what we need.'

'Have you heard of Windsor Castle?' Mrs Slater asked abruptly.

An image came into Sophie's mind of granite walls sprawling along a hillside, studded with towers, turrets, arched windows and possibly a drawbridge; certainly vast wooden doors, strong enough to withstand any battering ram. She must have seen a picture somewhere, or perhaps her English grandmother had described the building. She tried to focus. 'Is that where the King and Queen live?'

'They spend most weekends there,' Mrs Slater replied, 'but they're based mainly at Buckingham Palace.'

Sophie wanted to laugh; the conversation was so surreal. She had no idea why they should be discussing the whereabouts of the British Royal Family so earnestly.

'Esme has become aware of a position at Windsor for which you seem ideally suited,' Mr Sinclair explained. 'A German speaker of the utmost discretion is required to retrieve and catalogue certain letters and sensitive documents. He or she would be based in the Royal Library, reporting to the Librarian, while also undertaking general duties.'

Sophie sat bolt upright, staring at them both. 'Really? But wouldn't they want a British person?'

'Not necessarily,' Mr Sinclair replied. 'You have relevant experience and we shall make sure your references are impeccable.'

What's in it for you? Sophie couldn't help wondering, although she felt a conflicting impulse to shout, 'Yes, let me try for the job! I'll do whatever you want to get it.' To play for time, she asked, 'And is this correspondence between members of the Royal Family?'

Mr Sinclair nodded. 'They're mainly concerned about letters written to and from the Duke of Windsor. Especially those to his younger brother, the Duke of Kent, and his cousins in Germany.' He lit a cigarette and inhaled deeply, looking out of the window. 'The Duke is a wild card. He feels both he and his wife have been unfairly treated and their links with the Nazi regime are of great concern. You might perhaps have seen newspaper photographs of the couple visiting Germany last year? They visited factories, shook hands with all the high-up officials and were entertained by Hitler in his mountain retreat. In fact, the Duke and the Führer had a private meeting with only an interpreter and secretary in attendance. The Duchess wasn't invited, though one can bet she found out all about it afterwards.'

Sophie nodded to show she was paying attention, although

she found it hard to concentrate and could only hope he wouldn't expect her to remember any of this.

'And for another thing,' Mrs Slater broke in, 'the Duchess was rumoured to have been having an affair with von Ribbentrop when that gentleman was the German ambassador in London. Now he's Hitler's foreign minister. There are concerns that any confidential information the Duke might come across will go straight to the Nazis, by way of his wife.'

'You won't be told any of this, of course,' Mr Sinclair continued, 'but the King must be worried incriminating letters to and from the Duke might end up being made public – he's famously indiscreet – or they could be used for extortion. Naturally, we're also keeping a close eye on him and the Duchess.'

'And who is "we", if you don't mind me asking?' Sophie said.

'The British Secret Service, of course,' Mrs Slater replied.

'The Windsors are currently living in France,' Mr Sinclair went on, 'but have made no secret of their desire to return to Britain sooner rather than later, which is the last thing the King – and frankly, any of us – would like. George VI has only been on the throne for a short while and needs to establish himself without being constantly undermined.' He stubbed out the cigarette, even though it was only half smoked.

'The Duke will do anything to embarrass his brother and doesn't give a fig for the stability of government or the reputation of the monarchy. All the same, we believe he has supporters in high places who might wish to see him back on the throne – for a variety of reasons.' He turned a shrewd gaze on Sophie. 'We need to know who his allies are, and what their plans might be. If there are documents out there that might threaten national security, we have to be aware of them, too. Naturally that aspect of your role must remain top secret: no one should suspect you have any connection with the intelligence services.'

So here was the catch: they were putting her up for this position and in return, she would be spying for the British government. 'How am I supposed to have heard about this job, if that's the case?' she asked.

'Through the British cultural attaché in Vienna, who is currently writing you a glowing letter of recommendation. He's an old friend of your father's, don't you know. The idea of a hidden agenda might seem a little daunting but rest assured, we're acting in the country's best interest. The government has no bias – we only want to keep Britain safe.'

Sophie nodded, digesting the implications of what she'd just been told. Could she rise to this challenge? And what would happen if anyone suspected her story didn't add up?

'So, what do you say?' Mr Sinclair went on. 'Are you prepared to help? There are certain risks involved but you'd be carrying out a role of vital importance.'

Sophie looked down at her hands, knotted in her lap.

'I'm afraid there's no time to think this proposal over,' Mrs Slater added. 'We need your answer here and now.'

'Of course.' Sophie met her gaze. 'I should be honoured to accept.'

What else could she say? She needed a route out of Vienna urgently and there could hardly be a better one than this.

'Marvellous.' Mr Sinclair smoothed his hands along his trouser legs. 'That's settled, then. I have another meeting now, but Esme can fill you in on the details.'

They all stood, and he and Sophie shook hands again. 'Goodbye, Miss Klein, and good luck,' he said. 'I'm sure this will be au revoir, not adieu.'

After he'd gone, Mrs Slater took Sophie through to her office to deal with the paperwork. She asked Sophie to sign a copy of the Official Secrets Act, filled out and stamped her new passport and completed an entry visa to Britain. 'I've made you a little older,' she said, 'for added authority. Twenty-five feels about right, wouldn't you say?'

'Do you honestly think I'm up to this?' Sophie asked.

'Obviously, or we wouldn't have recruited you in the first place,' Mrs Slater replied crisply. 'I suggest you keep any doubts to yourself from now on. Act the part and it'll soon become second nature.'

Within half an hour, everything was settled. Seeing her new credentials, Sophie wondered how it must feel to hold the power of life or death in one's hands.

'An interview has been provisionally arranged for you at the castle on Monday at noon,' Esme Slater said. 'That gives you a couple of days to reach England, and you can stay in London the night before with sponsors we've found through the British Library.' She scribbled something on an index card and passed it across the desk. 'This is the address. They're expecting you at some point on Sunday. Telephone if you're delayed.'

Sophie glanced at the paper. 'Lord and Lady Wilton, 46 Cheyne Walk,' she read, followed by a three-digit Chelsea telephone number. 'I can stay in a hotel,' she said quickly. 'I don't want to be a nuisance.'

'Oh, I'm sure they'll have staff. Besides, you should meet. Lord Wilton has agreed to act as your guarantor.'

'Even though he doesn't know me?'

'The Wiltons are keen patrons of the arts,' Mrs Slater replied. 'And the lure of a connection with the royals, no matter how distant, seems to appeal to Lady Wilton in particular.'

'I assume they don't know about my connection with the intelligence services?'

'Absolutely not. As far as they're concerned, you're simply a librarian from Vienna, over there on a cultural exchange.'

Sophie hesitated. 'Can I ask you something, Mrs Slater?'

'Call me Esme, dear. And yes, of course – whatever you like.'

'This might be a stupid question, but why not pool resources and work together with the royal household? You're on the same side, surely, with the same aim in mind.'

'It isn't quite as simple as that,' Mrs Slater replied. 'The Duke of Windsor is the King's brother, after all, and blood is thicker than water. If any particularly embarrassing information comes to light, the family might want to bury it rather than informing the government. Not a stupid question, but perhaps a naïve one. You must learn the art of subtlety, my dear.'

She took a bottle and a couple of glasses from her desk drawer. 'Lesson over. Care for a congratulatory drink? It's a little early but nobody's watching.'

'I might not get the job, though,' Sophie said. 'What if they think I'm too inexperienced?'

'That's unlikely to happen. Your English is perfect and you'll have references at the very highest level. Absolute discretion is the main requirement here: the King and Queen are terrified of any salacious details being leaked to the press, and your trustworthiness will be beyond question.'

She passed Sophie a sherry with a mirthless smile. 'Besides, there are no other applicants.'

Sophie had gulped half her drink before she thought about it and collected herself. 'I've never moved in royal circles before.'

'Oh, I doubt you'll have a great deal of contact with the family. Not at first, anyway. Don't be overawed: they're a very ordinary couple, thrust into the limelight in a way they never expected. She's short and dowdy and he has an unfortunate stammer – the least charismatic of those four brothers and quite unsuited to be king, but here we are. He's terrifically jealous of the Duke and they both loathe Mrs Simpson, which is fair enough. Funny, I still can't think of her as a duchess. You must be respectful, of course, but go in there with your head high.'

She chinked her glass against Sophie's. 'Here's to our new partnership. I've no doubt you'll do well at the castle, once you've developed a little more guile. You're unobtrusive, which is the perfect qualification in our line of work. I can imagine you sitting in a corner of the library, taking everything in with those sharp eyes of yours. We want to know everything: not just what you read but what you might hear.'

'And how will we keep in touch?' Sophie asked.

'Through our contact, Aunt Jane. She's an old friend of your English grandmother who lives in London. She'll meet you every month for a visit to the V and A or tea somewhere. There'll be a telephone number to call should you need to get in touch more urgently.'

Sophie studied her unexpected mentor. Esme Slater was too bony and angular to be beautiful but she had an undeniable presence. She was immaculately dressed, her make-up a flawless mask and her every movement radiating a languid self-confidence. She gave the impression of being detached, perhaps a little cynical, yet she had saved Hanna and now she was coming to Sophie's rescue.

'How come you speak such perfect German, Mrs Slater?' she asked. 'Esme, I mean.'

'My father was German and I spent much of my childhood in Berlin.' She leaned back in her chair with a cigarette held aloft, watching Sophie like a cat. 'You know, you remind me a lot of myself. I lost my parents when I was about your age so I understand how it feels to be cast adrift, and I was a bookish child, more at home in the library than on the playing field.' She topped up their glasses. 'Now, tell me about your British family. Do you have any relatives still in the country?'

A warm glow of alcohol was coursing through Sophie's veins. 'None,' she replied, taking another sip. 'My grandmother was an orphan, a foundling child. She went into service and left England when she married.'

Sophie and Hanna had heard the stories about Oma Rose so many times they could recite them by heart. She had been abandoned on the steps of an orphanage as a baby but had pulled herself up by her bootstraps, going into domestic service at the age of fourteen and ending up as a lady's maid to one of the country's most eligible debutantes. When her mistress had married, Rose had accompanied the happy couple on a honeymoon in Europe lasting several months, and caught the eye of a handsome violinist in a Viennese hotel orchestra.

'She had green eyes and beautiful chestnut hair with a natural curl,' Ingrid would say as she brushed her daughters' own, less glorious locks, 'so long she could sit on it, and such a tiny waist she hardly needed a corset.' Rose had returned to England with her employers when the honeymoon was over but the violinist, Viktor, had followed her to London.

'Her mistress refused to let her leave so she ran away with him in the middle of the night,' their mother would go on. 'She threw a suitcase out of the window and climbed down a huge oak tree outside her bedroom, and they were married the next day.'

Sophie and her sister had worn the baby clothes Oma Rose had made for their mother – she had become a dressmaker after her marriage, and her hand-smocking was exquisite – and they'd inherited the English custom of taking tea from a china pot at half past four, with a splash of milk added last. Their mother cooked scones from a British recipe which they ate with jam and whipped cream (clotted cream not being available in Vienna), and she instructed the maid to sprinkle damp tea leaves over the rugs before sweeping to prevent the dust flying about, as was done in the finest English country houses. That was as much as Sophie knew of the British way of life; it didn't seem enough to prepare her for Lord and Lady Wilton of Cheyne Walk.

'I wouldn't mention anything about having a grandmother in service,' Mrs Slater advised. 'That won't go down at all well with the Wiltons. In fact, the less you say about your personal circumstances, the better.'

She drained her glass and stood, signalling the meeting was over. There had been no mention of a Mr Slater, Sophie thought, shouldering her rucksack, and Esme wasn't wearing a wedding ring. Perhaps she was also divorced, like the American woman who had lured away the Duke; they were both racy sorts.

In the space of a few hours, Sophie's future had been decided. She was throwing her lot in with the British, and what a strange bunch they were.

Chapter Eleven

Vienna, May 1938

Sophie walked out of the British Embassy for the last time, past the harassed officials with their folders and clipboards and the ringing telephones, out through the courtyard and into the city which no longer felt like home. There was nothing to keep her here, yet she had a sudden feeling she was abandoning her parents – her father hastily buried in an unmarked grave and her mother's body unclaimed in the mortuary – and that if she were to turn in the other direction and run through the streets, she would open the door to their apartment and find her father reading in his chair by the window, looking up at her with a smile, and her mother walking through from the kitchen, wiping her hands on a tea towel. Leaving made their loss irrevocable.

The queue of people trying for visas now extended into the street. Suddenly, someone clutched her arm. 'Sophie?' asked a female voice, and she turned to see Tamara Grossman, her mother's assistant. Usually immaculate, now her dark hair was dishevelled and her blouse wrongly buttoned. They embraced, the tears coming immediately to

Sophie's eyes because Tamara and her mother were so close that she had sometimes been jealous, seeing them working so harmoniously together, and she couldn't bear to explain what had happened to Ingrid.

'The shop is closed,' Tamara said. 'I went to your apartment but there are Germans living there now. Nazis, I suppose. Where is your mother?'

Sophie clasped Tamara's hands in hers, the tears falling now, and simply shook her head.

'Oh, the dear lady.' Tamara dashed her eyes with the back of her hand. 'May her memory be a blessing. And what about your poor father?'

'He is gone, too,' Sophie replied. Perhaps if she spoke those words often enough, she would come to believe them.

Tamara didn't seem surprised; those were the times they were living through. 'So where are you and Hanna staying?' she asked.

'Hanna has gone to America and I'm leaving for England tomorrow,' Sophie replied.

Tamara squeezed her hands so tightly that Sophie gasped. 'Let me come with you, please. I have been like a sister to you. Your mother loved me like a daughter, you know that.' She sank to her knees on the pavement, still clutching Sophie's hand. 'I'll do whatever you ask.'

Sophie helped her up, mortified. 'Tamara, I'm so sorry but I can't take you, not now. I only have a visa for myself. Once I'm in England though, I'll do whatever I can to help you, I promise.'

'I have no one else to ask,' Tamara replied, brushing down her clothes. 'You are my only hope.' She reached into her purse, took out a notebook and scribbled an address with shaking hands on a page which she tore out and passed to

Sophie. 'You can write to me here. I'm staying at a friend's house. Don't forget me, Sophie, I beg you. For dear Ingrid's sake.'

'I won't,' Sophie promised, shaken and guilty. There was nothing she could do for Tamara now; she had to save herself and only then could she help others. Her mother might have tried to persuade Mrs Slater to rescue Tamara with a stroke of her pen, but Sophie couldn't risk jeopardising her own chances. She had to be more Ruth Hoffman than Ingrid Klein, brutal as that sounded. Besides, she knew it wouldn't work.

On the way back to Leopoldstadt, she passed a smartly-dressed man who reminded her of her father, emerging from the men's public toilets with a bucket and mop. A uniformed Nazi was shouting at him and a small appreciative crowd had assembled to watch. '*Saujüdin!*' jeered a boy in Lederhosen. Most people wore swastika armbands or some other sort of Nazi insignia now, and she felt conspicuous and vulnerable in the street without that disguise. It would have killed her to wear the hated emblem, though. Hurrying on, she bought a meat-loaf roll from a street vendor, not daring to look at the woman who served her, and walked as quickly as she dared back to Ruth's room, where she ate it in ravenous mouthfuls.

'I'm alive,' she told herself, sitting on the edge of the couch and staring at her hands as though they belonged to someone else. 'I'll get through this one way or another.'

At last there was time to think. She sat back, closing her eyes, and let her mind drift. The routine that had been so vital to her sense of identity had disappeared, leaving only a void. She'd wanted to establish herself in a career before she married, if she married at all; her boss at the library

113

seemed to have a marvellous time as a single working woman, unburdened by husband or children. In Vienna, of course. Where else in the world would anyone want to live? Yet now these dreams seemed as remote as the fairy stories she used to read Hanna at bedtime. There was no option: she had to get out of the city one way or another, and soon. The Royal Library, at Windsor Castle! What would Vati have said? It was as though he were looking out for her, too – just as Mutti was taking care of Hanna – sending this chance of the perfect job her way.

Finally she allowed herself to remember her father's death and imagine her mother's, trying to absorb the fact they were gone forever. When her moment came, she would be like them: brave, dignified, magnificent. Until then, she would nurse the flame of hatred burning inside her into a rage strong enough to devour the Nazis and all they stood for. One day, the world would know what they had done and God willing, she would be there to see it. A new Sophie Klein would emerge from this ordeal: strong and ruthless, without a shred of pity.

She'd gathered her remaining possessions and was about to leave the room when a hammering on the door sent her rushing the other way, into the kitchen and out on to the metal fire escape. Down in the street, she took to her heels and ran, while the man who must have been Ruth's landlord stuck his head out of the window and shouted at her to stop. Making her way back to the station, she bought a ticket for the night train that would take her out of Austria and spent the afternoon sitting on the same bench that she and Ruth had occupied a few days before. Our turn will come, Ruth had said, and she'd been right.

Ein Volk, ein Reich, ein Führer – one people, one realm, one leader – proclaimed a banner on the wall opposite, and Hitler's stern face in profile gazed out from one of the giant posters that were plastered all over the city. Sophie shivered. To reach the French coast and the night ferry to Dover the next day, she would have to travel through Germany, and her belongings and papers would be inspected at every stage of the journey. Quite apart from the valuables in the lining of her coat, her father's Mauser pocket pistol from the war was digging uncomfortably into her inner thigh. She would be arrested instantly if it were discovered, but the risk was worth it; she'd rather kill herself than end up in prison, and maybe she could take a few Nazis with her.

Around her, travellers passed to and fro: small children asleep in their parents' arms; a group of musicians with instrument cases on their backs; a few single women, like herself. Evening came at last and the train platform was announced, prompting a rush to the ticket barrier. She pushed her way through and stared brazenly at the stormtrooper inspecting her papers and luggage, daring him to challenge her. She would tough it out, as Ruth had advised. Having never felt particularly Jewish before, now she was part of the minority forced to run for their lives – reclaiming her heritage, that fatal bloodline which apparently defined her. She was ashamed of all the times she'd heard a shouted insult in the street or seen antisemitic graffiti being daubed on a wall and looked the other way, too scared or lazy or preoccupied to speak up. Nazis had been skulking in the shadows for years, feeding off people's apathy, until Hitler had lifted the rock and the brownshirts had come scuttling through the city like dung beetles.

When the train pulled out of the station, all she could

feel was relief. Closing her eyes, she tried to sleep, jammed between an elderly priest and a woman with a toddler grizzling on her lap. The atmosphere in the carriage was fraught, uneasy. Travellers watched their neighbours with suspicious eyes and spoke only to those in their party; they ate bread and cheese or meat in snatched mouthfuls, guarding their provisions like jackals. More brownshirts boarded the train at Salzburg, shouting and gesticulating with their guns, and Sophie's courage faltered. There were so many of them, brutish and drunk with power.

As the train approached the German border at dawn, her stomach clenched with fear. The railway tracks ran alongside a river and dusk was falling gently over timbered cottages and fields full of grazing cattle who lifted their heads as the train rattled past. The landscape was beautiful, but the country and its people were dangerous. Sophie's palms were damp and her heart beat erratically. An unexplained delay of several hours at Munich frayed her nerves even further. She wanted to use the lavatory but daren't draw attention to herself by leaving her seat; when at last the engine started up again, she almost wet herself in relief. Eventually they were through Frankfurt and approaching Brussels, and then, what seemed like many hours later, she opened her eyes to find that the posters on hoardings alongside the track were written in French.

She had to change trains in Paris, pacing anxiously up and down the platform as she waited for the train to Calais and the night ferry which would take her to Dover. The cosseted first-class passengers could stay sleeping in their carriages, loaded on to the boat as though travelling in a giant pram, but she would have to spend another night sitting upright. Yet she was glad not to be shut away below, glad to find a space at the rail to watch as the ship finally sailed from Calais, putting mile after mile of churning black water and white spray between her and the people who had killed her parents. Her thoughts turned to Hanna, soon to embark on a longer voyage to America; she hoped her sister had made friends by now and that people were being kind to her. Their lives were heading in different directions, which was another loss. Yet she and Hanna were safe; that was the most important thing. She would miss her sister desperately until they were reunited one day, God willing, but even if she didn't make it through, the knowledge Hanna had escaped was her only consolation. She had done the right thing, even though it had nearly killed her, and her mother would have been pleased.

Letting her hair stream back in the wind, Sophie gave a silent prayer of thanks to whichever gods had brought them both to this point. When the lights of mainland Europe had been swallowed up in the dark, she turned her face in the other direction: towards England, the future, and freedom.

Chapter Twelve

London, May 1938

It took Sophie almost an hour to walk from Victoria Station to the Wiltons' house in Cheyne Walk. She kept having to stop and check she was on the right road or gaze at some unexpected sight: a double decker omnibus, for example, with a curving staircase at the back and a conductor standing on the deck, or a policeman in white gloves directing the traffic. They were the only men in uniform, which came as a welcome relief. There wasn't a swastika to be seen and the hoardings were plastered with advertisements for cigarettes, gin and razor blades rather than the Third Reich. The streets were narrower than those of Vienna and shabbier, too, with litter piling up in the corners, and most of the people she passed appeared down at heel. They regarded her with indifference and for that, she was grateful. A woman with a shopping basket had even pulled her back when she stepped off the kerb into the path of a car. She'd gasped, expecting a blow or an arrest, and the woman had looked at her strangely.

Passing a café on the street corner, she realised she was

ravenously hungry and went inside to spend some of the British currency for which she'd exchanged her Reichsmarks at the station. She ordered a cup of tea and a rock bun, which was one of the cheapest things on the menu, but the cake when it came was almost inedible: dense and claggy, studded with hard, burned currants. Each mouthful took a lot of chewing before she could wash it down with a gulp of tea. Remembering her mother's Buchteln – fluffy yeast buns, soft as clouds – she was suddenly overwhelmed by a wave of homesickness and grief. Tears blurred her eyes as she bit down on a currant, almost cracking a tooth. What was she doing in this strange, dirty country where she knew no one? Taking a fork, she jabbed it so sharply into her thigh that the pain made her gasp. She would not give way to self-pity, she would not. When the waitress, a motherly sort, asked her if she would like a fresh pot of tea and perhaps another pastry, she was able to politely decline and ask for the bill.

I've arrived in England for an interview at Windsor Castle, she told herself, straightening her spine, and I'm a guest of Lord and Lady Wilton. All the same, the face that stared back at her from the mirror in the ladies' lavatory was dishevelled and wary. She'd slept in her clothes for the past two nights and they were covered in smuts from the boat and train. Hastily she washed her face and hands, wetting and smoothing an unruly lock of hair. The splash of cold water cleared her head and for the first time, she allowed herself a shiver of excitement. She had escaped! And now here she was in England, on a secret mission of national importance. Her parents would have been so proud; she imagined them urging her on.

The house on Cheyne Walk was four storeys high, white stucco on the ground floor and pale brick above, wrought-iron balconies in the middle and small dormer windows peering from under the roof. Sophie rang the brass bell and stood back, readying herself. After what seemed a long time, she heard footsteps advancing within the house and the door was yanked open by a furious-looking maid in a black frock, white apron and cap. Sophie gave her name, aware of being inspected from head to toe, and was informed that Lord and Lady Wilton were both out, she hadn't been expected till later and her room wasn't aired.

'I don't mind,' she replied firmly. 'I've been travelling for days and all I want is to lie down. If you could show me to the room, I'd be grateful.'

The girl sniffed, opened her mouth and then closed it again, turned on her heel and set off at a brisk pace. Sophie followed, along the black-and-white-tiled hall and up a wooden staircase with an ornate carved banister. Inside, the house was dark and seemed tremendously tall, with endless flights of stairs looming above her head. A clattering of pans could be heard somewhere in the basement, and a pungent, meaty smell that wasn't entirely pleasant wafted up the stairs.

'Will you be wanting luncheon yourself?' the maid asked over her shoulder, walking along a corridor on the second floor and throwing open a door. She stood back to let Sophie into the bedroom, folding her arms in a manner that suggested wanting luncheon would not be a good idea.

'No, thank you,' Sophie replied, standing in the middle of the room and looking about. 'Well, this is lovely.'

The girl went over to the window and heaved up the sash, sending a draught of fresh air swirling into the room. 'You get a nice view from the front of the house. Have you been to London before?'

'No,' Sophie replied. 'I've never been out of Austria.'

'And I've never been out of London,' the maid replied. She seemed to be softening. 'Can't see the point. When's your luggage arriving?'

Sophie held out her rucksack. 'It's here.'

'That's all you got?' The girl's eyebrows disappeared under her cap. 'Shall I unpack for you, then?'

'That won't be necessary.' Instinctively, Sophie clutched the haversack closer.

'They change for dinner, you know,' the maid went on. 'Have you got a frock in there?'

'Not exactly.' She had left their family home in such a hurry, stuffing whatever came to hand into the rucksack. She glanced down at the clothes she was wearing: a rumpled blouse, filthy at the cuffs, her old gathered skirt that now had a grease stain on the front, and scuffed lace-up shoes. They were the only pair she'd brought.

The girl clucked, shaking her head. 'I'll have a word with her Ladyship. She might be able to fix you up with something. We can't send you in for dinner looking like that, if you'll excuse me for speaking plainly.'

She gave a mischievous grin that softened her words and Sophie could tell they were meant kindly. 'Of course,' she replied. 'It's a relief to have someone telling me how to behave.'

The girl was about her age, thin and pale, with dark circles under her eyes and an habitual frown creasing her brow. When she smiled, though, she became somebody quite different. For the first time in months, Sophie felt as though she'd met a person she could trust, who might even become a friend. She probably didn't have much in common with this girl, but then she had nothing in common with the Wiltons, either.

'Thank you so much . . .' She hesitated. 'What's your name?'

'Gladys, Miss. Well, I'll let you be. There's water in the jug and the bathroom's next door. Drinks in the drawing room at six-thirty and dinner prompt at seven.' She withdrew, closing the door behind her.

Sophie kicked off her shoes and sat on the edge of the bed, examining her room. It was about half the size of their entire apartment in Vienna, furnished with a four-poster bed, a desk in one of the windows, a chest of drawers holding the bowl and ewer, a dressing table with a silvered, ancient mirror and a chair. There were two clocks: one on the wall and a carriage clock on the mantelpiece, so at least she wouldn't be late for drinks that evening. Heavy velvet curtains dressed the tall windows and a picture of peasants building corn stooks in a dreary field hung above the fireplace.

She walked to the window. Only a wide road separated the house from the muddy brown river – the Thames, she assumed – busy with barges, a paddle steamer and several smaller boats, including a police launch zipping past with a blue light revolving on its prow. A bridge with ornate pillars and a spider's web of white struts stood on her left, and beyond that on the other side of the river she could see the vast smoking chimneys of a power station. A few motor cars drove along the road, and then a horse pulling a cart laden with milk crates clip-clopped slowly past. The scene was calm, orderly, utterly alien. Even the dusty air blowing in from the road and the water beyond smelt of the unknown.

Several hours later, she woke from a doze in her chair to find Gladys hovering nearby.

'Beg pardon, Miss,' she said. 'Her Ladyship would like to see you in the drawing room and you might want to freshen up first. I'll wait for you outside.'

Sophie was out of the chair in a matter of seconds and in a few more had brushed her hair, straightened her clothes, splashed her face with water and thrust her feet into her shoes.

'That was quick,' Gladys said approvingly when Sophie joined her in the corridor, still fuddled with sleep. She seemed in a better mood than earlier. Downstairs, she opened a set of double doors, announced, 'Miss Klein, ma'am,' and withdrew.

Lady Constancia Wilton stood by the fireplace, holding a fat Pekinese dog which stared at Sophie with black button eyes. She was in her fifties, Sophie estimated, a melancholy woman with a languid air and long, pale hair drooping out of a bun. She held out her hand that wasn't clasping the dog and said, 'Miss Klein, how d'ye do? So glad you made it and have had a chance to rest. How was the journey? Simply awful, I expect. I find travelling most wearisome.' She spoke in breathy flurries, her words scattered on the air like fallen leaves.

Sophie shook the hand that had been proffered, trying not to squeeze too hard as Lady Wilton's grip was feeble and damp. She wondered whether she should curtsy, but the moment passed. 'The journey was fine, Lady Wilton. I'm so very grateful to you for helping me come here. Honestly, I can't thank you enough.'

'Don't mention it,' her Ladyship replied. 'Esme knows we like to do our duty. *Noblesse oblige*, as Perry likes to say. We sent a missionary to Africa last year. Now, would you like some tea? I'll call for hot water to freshen the pot.' A gleaming silver teapot stood on the side table, along with plates, cups and saucers, milk jug and sugar bowl and a vast slab of cake. Lady Wilton set down the dog, brushed its hair from the bodice of her flowery dress and tugged on the bell pull beside the fireplace.

'Help yourself to some Boodle's cake, Miss Klein, it's Cook's speciality. Or shall I cut you a piece?' She attacked the cake with a knife and, after some effort, managed to hack off a chunk and pass it to Sophie. 'Oh, where is that girl?' She rang the bell again. 'She's even slower than usual today. Do you have problems with staff, Miss Klein? Servants are the bane of my life, believe me.'

An image came into Sophie's head of their maid, Annalise, with her closed, inscrutable face and sullen mouth. She had changed since she first started working for the Kleins five years before, become more stubborn and taciturn, less inclined to work or even to play with Hanna, whom she'd initially seemed to like. It occurred to Sophie now that she might have been the one to give their father away, to have overheard a snatch of conversation at home and whispered confirmation of his Jewish identity around the building.

Luckily, at that moment, Gladys appeared. When asked for hot water to freshen the pot, she informed her mistress that the range had gone out and Cook was having one of her turns. There was a smudge of soot on her forehead.

'Well, really! That's too bad.' Lady Wilton flapped her hands ineffectually. 'And what about dinner?'

'The kidneys were cooked earlier, ma'am,' Gladys replied. 'They can be warmed in a chafing dish.'

'I shall go down to the kitchen and speak to Mrs Lovage,' Lady Wilton declared. 'She really is the laziest creature in Christendom.'

'I wouldn't advise it. She's been at the cooking sherry.'

'That will be enough, Gladys. Pour Miss Klein a cup of tea and then you may leave,' Lady Wilton ordered, with an attempt at dignity.

When Gladys had left the room, she said to Sophie, 'The girl tells me your luggage has been mislaid. You might like to borrow some of my daughter's clothes in the meantime. We can't have you looking like a ragamuffin for your interview at the castle.'

'That's very kind.' Sophie glanced down at her travel-stained garments. 'Please forgive my appearance.'

'You look rather young to be a librarian, if you don't mind me saying,' Lady Wilton observed. 'Still, Esme tells me you have the highest qualifications and impeccable references. You certainly speak English well enough.'

Sophie was once again grateful that the letter of recommendation she'd received had been glowing, and the reference her former employers at the library had provided was similarly complimentary. She was learning to restrain her instinct for self-deprecation; people will take you at your own valuation, her mother used to say. She smiled modestly and bore down with her fork on the Boodle's cake. The whole piece shot off her plate to land on the carpet next to the sleeping Pekinese, which opened one eye and then closed it again; clearly not a fan of the cook's speciality either. Luckily, Lady Wilton had turned aside to pour herself more tea and hadn't noticed – or pretended not to.

'We shall be interested to hear about the royal goings-on,' she went on. 'My husband and I were lucky enough to be invited to the palace when Edward was king – David, as we know him – but his brother isn't nearly as sociable. Of course, they'll all be going to the castle for Royal Ascot next month, so that should be interesting. We bumped into David and Wallis there a couple of years ago and they were most hospitable, although of course Wallis couldn't enter the Royal Enclosure on account of being divorced, which was awkward. Happy days!' She gave a cross little laugh and stood. 'Well, that's enough from me. It's been good getting to know you, Miss Klein – or may I call you Sophie? My husband suggests we have drinks in the library this evening before dinner so you can talk books. Six-thirty sharp. He's particular about punctuality.'

When Sophie returned to her room, she found a selection of clothes laid out on the bed: a day dress in flowered cretonne, two drooping skirts, one tweed and one gabardine, three voluminous blouses and a black evening gown trimmed with jet beads that click-clacked like tiny, angry beetles when she picked it up. Lady Wilton's nameless daughter was shorter and wider than she was but luckily the frocks and skirts were long, and could be gathered in. Gladys put her head around the door to see how she was getting on.

'I'm not sure. What do you think?' Sophie adjusted the shoulders of the gown and squinted at her reflection in the ancient dressing-table mirror. She had no idea what was expected of her.

'You could do with a belt or a couple of safety pins,' the maid said. 'I'll see what I can find downstairs.'

'And what about shoes?' They both looked down at her lace-ups.

'Miss Ottoline has large feet, to go with the rest of her,' Gladys said, 'otherwise I'd have brought you a pair of hers. Are those all you got?' Sophie nodded. 'I could polish 'em, I suppose.'

But when she returned a short while later with a length of ribbon in lieu of a belt, she was also carrying a pair of black shoes: plain but serviceable, with a buttoned strap across the instep. 'Cook's best,' she said. 'She won't be needing them tonight.'

'Are you sure she won't mind?' Sophie tried one on for size.

'What she don't know won't hurt her. Just leave them outside your door later and I'll put 'em back in the morning.'

'Well, thank you. I'm very grateful.' She was glad of this chance for a dress rehearsal in polite society before confronting whatever lay in store for her at Windsor.

'Would you like me to do your hair, Miss Klein?' Gladys asked. 'There are some pins in the dressing-table drawer.'

Sophie was about to refuse when she changed her mind. It would be such a treat to feel herself taken care of, and her hair was currently hanging down in a girlish plait. 'That would be lovely,' she said. 'But you must call me Sophie.'

'I couldn't do that,' Gladys replied, laughing at the idea. 'Well, maybe in private.'

Sophie sat at the dressing table, looking at herself in the mirror and feeling the tension ebb away as Gladys brushed her hair in long, steady strokes. Her face had changed in some indefinable way: the hollows under her cheekbones were sharper, her green eyes more guarded.

'Does Lady Wilton have any other children, apart from Miss Ottoline?' she asked, feeling the need to make conversation.

'There's Miss Maud – Lady Sutherland she is now – married and up in Scotland,' Gladys replied. 'Miss Ottoline's trying to catch a husband in India and won't be back till Christmas.'

So Lady Wilton was probably lonely, Sophie thought. Lonely and looking for another good cause: were those her only motives? 'It's so kind of the Wiltons to let me stay, and be my sponsors,' she went on.

'Well, they like a project,' Gladys replied, mumbling through a mouthful of hair pins. She twisted a final hank of hair deftly around Sophie's head and jammed several pins in place to secure it. 'There. How does that feel?'

'Perfect. Thank you, Gladys.'

They both contemplated her reflection. I could easily be twenty-five, Sophie thought, if not older. She had become elegant and mysterious.

'Don't be nervous,' Gladys said abruptly. 'You're as good as any of them, remember.'

At six-twenty-five precisely, Sophie left her bedroom and went down to the library, following Gladys's directions. She found a tall, thin man pacing up and down in front of the fireplace, hands clasped behind his back.

'Ah, Miss Klein,' he said, taking out a pocket watch and glancing at it before snapping the case shut. 'Jolly good. Come in and have a sherry, if that's your tipple. Or maybe you'd prefer a gin and something?'

'A sherry will be lovely, thank you,' Sophie replied. 'Lord Wilton, thank you so much for—'

'Don't mention it,' he said, striding over to the sideboard. 'That's really my wife's department, anyway – good works, that sort of thing, ha ha – nothing to do with me, though a pleasure, of course. Gather you're a bookish sort of person?' He handed her a crystal glass, the size of a thimble.

'Yes, I—'

'Jolly good,' he said again. 'Chosen a few gems from my

collection to show you. Heard of Audubon? Course you have, any bookish person knows Audubon.' A large illustrated book lay open on a side table. 'See this? First volume of *Birds of America*. Quite a coup, eh?' Lord Wilton took a pair of cotton gloves out of his pocket and inserted his large bony hands into them. 'Notice the detail? Exquisite.' He turned the pages reverently. 'Rum feller, you know. Entirely self-taught and led a rackety life by all accounts but knew a thing or two about birds, I'll say he did. Seen anything like this before? Course you haven't.'

All that seemed to be required from Sophie was the occasional appreciative murmur while Lord Wilton held forth. He lobbed questions at her like tennis balls which he then answered himself, every so often letting out an alarming bark of laughter. She was happy to let him lead the conversation, relieved that he showed no interest in her whatsoever. The room smelt exactly as a library should: of old paper, leather and sweet, sticky glue, overlaid with furniture polish and the smoke from a thousand dead fires. Another wave of homesickness hit her so unexpectedly that she had to put out a hand to steady herself, imagining her father sitting in that chair under the lamp with a book on his lap. She could almost feel his hand on her shoulder. Lord Wilton didn't seem to have noticed but a few seconds later, he closed the Audubon and said, 'Now, come and sit down, drink your sherry and we'll talk about Wodehouse. Come across PG?'

'No, I can't say—' Sophie began.

'What?' Lord Wilton stared at her in mock outrage: the first time he'd actually looked at her directly. 'Don't know Pelham Grenville Wodehouse, the funniest damn feller who ever lived?'

He threw himself into a chair, picked up a book from the side table beside it and proceeded to read out loud, breaking off to explain characters or background details, or to guffaw at particularly hilarious episodes. Sophie found Wodehouse baffling – too many characters and one of them a pig – but Lord Wilton's enthusiasm and the unself-conscious energy of his performance were so endearing that her spirits rallied. Where was Lady Wilton, though? Had the range been revived and was the cook in a fit state to finish cooking the meal?

Lord Wilton suddenly snapped the book shut and took out his pocket watch again. 'Time for dinner.' He sprang to his feet. 'Permit me to escort you, Miss Klein.'

Sophie took the arm he offered and they processed out of the library and into the hall, at the exact moment Lady Wilton was descending the stairs in blue crêpe de chine with a sequinned bodice.

'Very fetching, my dear,' her husband said graciously as they swept past. She fell into step behind them, which seemed wrong to Sophie and also excruciatingly embarrassing. The dining room lay on the other side of the corridor, a chilly room dominated by a long mahogany table with a chair at each end and one in the middle. Lord Wilton escorted her to the central spot and took his seat at the head of the table, with Lady Wilton resplendent at the other end. Gladys appeared with bowls of beige, lukewarm soup on a tray; she avoided Sophie's eye and stood by the wall, looking straight ahead, once her cargo had been delivered and the wine poured.

There followed one of the strangest meals of Sophie's life. The kidneys were horrid, as she'd expected, and Lord and Lady Wilton spoke only to her and not each other, so she was constantly turning her head like the umpire at a tennis match. Lady Wilton talked about various social events in London, notably a private view of the Chelsea Flower Show, which she'd attended a few days before, along with the King and Queen.

'Not that they noticed me,' she said, waving a chunk of kidney on the end of her fork. 'If there is such a thing as the royal orbit these days, I'm well out of it. Old Queen Mary was there, too: the King's mother. You'll get to know them all, I suppose. By sight, at least.'

The prospect still seemed unreal to Sophie. 'Some more wine, please, Gladys,' Lady Wilton snapped. 'Really, I shouldn't have to ask.'

'Vienna, eh?' Lord Wilton boomed from his far corner. 'Went there once on a cycling holiday. Beautiful city. Not much of a one for opera but saw some damn fine horses.'

Sophie tried hard to keep up. 'Do you mean the white ones? The Lipizzaners?'

'No, I most certainly do not!' He gestured for Gladys to bring over the wine bottle. 'Damn it, girl, you must never refer to a horse as "white"; they're always "grey".'

'And yesterday was Empire Day,' Lady Wilton continued, 'the anniversary of Queen Victoria's birthday. We went to a Royal Command concert at the Albert Hall, also attended by the King and Queen. I should imagine there'll be photographs in the newspaper. Have you looked, Peregrine?'

'Even if the coat is white,' Lord Wilton said, 'the skin underneath will be black and the eyes dark. There are a few white horses with pink skin and blue eyes, but that's rare. Just as well, if you ask me. Pretty rum-looking, don't you think?'

And so the meal went on. After a sloppy dessert referred

to as 'Queen of Puddings' and greeted with rapture by Lord Wilton, the ladies retired to the drawing room, leaving his Lordship to brandy and a cigar.

Sophie refused the offer of coffee. 'If you don't mind, Lady Wilton, I'll go to bed soon. It's been a long day and I have to be up early in the morning. In case I don't see you tomorrow, thank you again for your hospitality.'

'Now don't take this amiss,' she replied, 'but in our country it's considered good manners to write a short note to one's host if one has stayed the night. A bread-and-butter letter, some people call it, or a Collins – after a character from a novel, in case you were wondering. Just thought I'd mention it in case things are done differently in Austria. It would be a shame to give the wrong impression through ignorance.'

'Of course.' Sophie was too bewildered to feel offended.

'Jolly good,' Lady Wilton said. 'We all want you to be a success, my dear. And I should like to keep in touch. I shall write to you at the castle and you must come and visit us again. You can think of this house as a home from home.'

'Thank you. You're very kind.'

'You're bound to be a little nervous,' Lady Wilton went on, 'but don't worry. You must understand that in this country, it's *who* you know that matters, rather than *what* you know, and you're lucky enough to know some pretty influential people.'

Am I? thought Sophie. I hope so.

Chapter Thirteen

Point Grey, Vancouver, April 2022

The evening that was seared into Lacey's memory for all the worst reasons had begun in the most ordinary of ways. Another writer she had run into a few times on the circuit had invited her to the launch of his latest book: the biography of a celebrity chef who after a battle with cocaine and a public meltdown had gone into therapy, become sober and established a new restaurant in a cool district of Philly. Disappointingly, the launch was held in a bookstore with only tepid white wine and potato chips on offer. After a couple of hours, five or six of them had gone to a nearby bar in search of cold beer and something more substantial to eat. Lacey didn't know any of the others particularly well: a few writers, a girl who worked in the store, some guy who wrote restaurant reviews and his friend. The bar was noisy and it had been hard to talk, with the conversation depressingly all about how many people were dying from Covid. She was bored, and had just decided to cut her losses and go home when a fresh round of drinks appeared on the table and someone pressed a glass into her hand.

After that, her memories of the evening were disjointed, confused, terrifying. She was holding on to the wall of a corridor that ran with water; somebody howled with laughter that turned into screams; bright lights hurt her eyes and her limbs had become so heavy that she couldn't raise her arm, couldn't shout for help although she knew something was terribly wrong. At one point she was huddled outside in the cold and someone was yelling into her face while cars hurtled past.

She woke up in her apartment, God only knew how many hours later, with no idea how she'd got there. It was daylight, and she was lying on her bed with vomit down the front of her dress and in her hair. Her bag was beside her with her phone and wallet inside it, but her shoes were missing and her tights were in shreds. She sat up, taking inventory. Bloody left knee, broken nails, a scattering of small bruises on her upper arms that looked like fingerprints. Her bra and knickers were intact, thank God. She was shivering, deathly cold and her head thumping. Crawling under the duvet, she lay back down with tears leaking from the corners of her eyes and slept again. Waking in darkness, she staggered to her feet and drank a bottle of water before stripping off and scrubbing herself in a scalding shower until her skin was pink.

'What's happened to me?' she asked herself repeatedly – though, of course, in essence she knew. Her drink had been spiked. She'd been roofied: that was the phrase, wasn't it? She'd only had one glass of wine at the launch and a couple of beers afterwards, not enough to account for the state she'd woken up in or the way she felt now.

It took another couple of days for her body to get back to anything like normal, while imagining what might have been done to her when she was helpless tortured her mind. She didn't think she'd been sexually assaulted but it was hard to know for sure. There had been a man beside her for some of the time, as far as she could recall, and someone must have made those bruises on her arms. A stranger had humiliated and violated her for their own gratification and the thought made her weep with impotent fury. She sat with her phone in her hands but couldn't bring herself to call Jess, her mother or any of her friends, or contact the cops. What would she say? She didn't remember anything significant, couldn't identify anyone, wasn't even sure how she'd got home. The thought of having been seen in such a state made her wince with shame: a shame that was compounded when hot Rick said with a leer when she passed him in the corridor one morning, 'Feeling better? You were a little the worse for wear the other night.'

When she told him she thought her drink had been spiked, he only laughed. 'Sure. That's what they all say.'

'Was there anyone with me?' she asked.

'Yeah, a girl,' he replied. 'Seriously? You don't remember? Long blonde hair, glasses and a stripy sweater.'

The girl from the bookstore. It took a few days to track her down since Kate (that was her name, according to the store's Instagram account) worked irregular shifts, and several more to summon the courage to confront her. Lacey was frightened of what she might find out and wary of exposing herself to ridicule when she still felt so vulnerable. Maybe she should just try chalking the whole thing down to experience, and take more care next time she went out. Yet what had happened was so wrong. How dare anyone treat her like that?

'I was worried about you,' said Kate, the bookstore

137

blonde, when they finally met. 'I didn't want to leave you alone in the apartment, but you said you were fine and wanted me to go. You were very clear about that. I guess I should have checked up on you the next day, so sorry about that.'

Lacey couldn't blame her for not hanging around – or coming back, either. A drunken stranger? Most people would have run a mile. 'It was so kind of you to look after me,' she said. 'The thing is, I'm pretty sure my drink was spiked.'

'Oh my God! Are you kidding?' Kate's eyes widened behind her thick lenses. 'That's awful. I thought you'd just had too much to drink.' She was young, about nineteen or twenty, but full of confidence. The kind of girl I used to be, Lacey thought fleetingly.

'I can't remember what happened that evening.' She suppressed a small internal shudder and pressed on. 'Did you see me with anyone, or notice anything strange?'

'Let me think a minute.' Kate glanced towards the cash till. 'My supervisor's watching. Walk with me to the crime section and I'll pretend to look for something.'

She ran her fingers along a row of spines, selected a book and gave it to Lacey. 'I lost track of you in the bar for a while, and then you were sitting outside on a bench with this guy.'

'What guy?' Lacey's heart beat faster. 'Did you recognise him from the launch?'

'I don't think so.' Kate wrinkled her nose, looking about twelve now. 'He had grey hair but he wasn't that old: in his forties, I'd say. I don't know whether he'd been inside or just walked by in the street. You were looking pretty wasted so I asked if you were OK and he said he was taking care of things. I'm not sure why but he made me feel uncomfortable, so I stuck around for a while, and then you threw up.'

Lacey groaned. 'I haven't been throwing-up drunk since tenth grade.'

'Maybe just as well you did,' Kate said. 'He disappeared pretty fast after that, so I found your driver's licence for your address and walked you home. There was no sign of your shoes, I'm afraid.'

'I'm so grateful,' Lacey told her. 'I dread to think what might have happened if you hadn't been there.'

'That's OK,' Kate replied. 'We have to look out for each other. You should report it to the police – the bar might have CCTV footage. The creep who did this needs to be caught before he tries it again.'

'I will,' Lacey promised, and she really meant to.

She called in at the bar on her way home before she could lose courage but the guy wiping tables said no one had ever reported their drink being spiked there before, not once, and anyway they didn't have CCTV, there was no need for it. This was a respectable venue and she should think carefully before she started throwing accusations around. She'd probably gotten food poisoning or simply had too much to drink, and anyway, what was he supposed to do about it now? She should have come back the next day but in fact there wouldn't even have been much point in doing that, since she said herself she had no idea what had happened and if she didn't know, he sure as hell didn't either.

It was quite the onslaught, and all Lacey could do not to humiliate herself by crying. She left without another word. Soon afterwards, the mayor ordered everyone to stay at home and the police would have other things on their minds than some vague, unsubstantiated accusation – or so Lacey told herself then, and Jess now, sitting on a bench in the damp picnic area.

Wordlessly, her sister leaned in for a hug and at last Lacey let the tears flow. It was such a relief to have found a way to talk, to hear her words spilling into the damp air and evaporating, the story losing a fraction of its power to hurt because she had shared it with someone who loved her.

'You know this isn't your fault?' Jess held Lacey at arm's length and gazed into her face. 'You are absolutely not to blame for what happened.'

Lacey shivered. 'I just keep thinking about what some random guy might have done to me while I was out of it.'

'I'm not surprised. If I could lay my hands on whoever did this to you . . .' Jess shook her head. 'Do you think you should talk to a therapist?'

'Maybe.' Lacey blew her nose. 'I couldn't face it before, but now I've shared the whole thing with you, maybe the telling will be easier.'

'I'm glad you did,' Jess said. 'Better late than never. But listen, while I'm doling out advice: never, ever take pills that haven't been prescribed for you. Promise? Otherwise you could end up in serious trouble.'

'OK, OK.' Lacey held up her hands. 'I just couldn't see how else I was going to make it here.'

Jess shook her head. 'Well, this has been quite the day for revelations: you and Gubby both.' She pulled Lacey to her feet and hugged her again. 'It can't have been easy. We'll talk some more before you leave but maybe now we should get home and see if world war three's broken out.'

They walked back arm in arm, and Lacey felt lighter than air. For the first time since the assault – this is how she would think of the incident now – she could imagine feeling confident and free, able to function normally again. Maybe not immediately, but soon. She turned to look back the way they'd come, the twin tracks of their footprints close together in the sand now already filling with water.

As they approached the house, Jess's daughter Emma ran down the path to meet them. 'Nonna and Gubby are fighting,' she whispered, taking her mother's hand. 'Well, Nonna is.' (Adele liked the cosmopolitan sound of Nonna, refusing point blank to be anyone's grandma.)

'Don't worry, darling,' Jess said, swinging her daughter along the path. 'You know what Nonna's like. She doesn't mean half the things she says. Where's your brother?'

'Watching TV in the den,' Emma said.

'Well, why don't you go and join him,' Jess suggested. 'And try not to worry – I'm sure everything's OK.'

Emma was only six, inclined to take life seriously and not used to raised voices. Jess and Chris were both calm and even-tempered, as a rule, and drama was something to be avoided in their household.

Chris was in the utility room, unloading the washing machine. 'I'm keeping out of the way,' he said in response to Jess's raised eyebrows, and Lacey's heart sank even further.

In the kitchen, they found Gubby sitting in the hanging egg chair by the picture window, her feet barely touching the floor, while Adele paced around her like a caged animal. Cedric sat at the long table, one leg crossed over the other, like a theatre critic watching a play he wasn't at all sure about.

'There you are,' Adele declared as her daughters walked in. 'I'm trying to talk some sense into your stubborn grandmother.'

Gubby seemed agitated, appealing to them with her eyes. 'What is it?' Lacey asked, approaching the chair.

Her grandmother beckoned her closer and whispered in her ear, 'Get me out of this damn thing! I've been stuck in here for half an hour with Delly ranting at me.'

'Sure.' Lacey leaned forward but it was hard to get a purchase on the seat, which swung away wildly as soon as she touched it. In the end, she had to wrap her arms round Gubby and heave her bodily out of the seat, and they were both giggling like naughty children.

'Well, I'm glad you think this is funny,' Adele said, glaring at them with her hands on her hips. She looked amazing, as always, in a teal velvet jumpsuit with a tasselled gold scarf that matched her highlights. Lacey suddenly longed for a different kind of mother, one who would pay as much attention to other people's feelings as she did to her appearance. She guided Gubby towards the table and Cedric jumped up to pull out the chair next to his.

'Why don't you sit down, too,' he told Adele. 'You're making me nervous.'

'No, thank you,' she replied. 'I prefer to stand.' Turning to Jess, she said, 'Come on, surely you'll back me up. We've been cheated out of our family inheritance and I'm not going to lie back and take it.'

'How do you mean?' Jess asked warily.

'Compensation, obviously.' Adele threw herself into a chair, forgetting her preference, and ran her fingers through her hair. She was whipping herself up into an emotional frenzy. 'My mother's home was taken away from her by the Nazis. She lost everything, including all her possessions, and somebody needs to pay.'

Gubby sighed. 'But it happened so long ago. The people

142

who were responsible are dead and I've got one foot in the grave myself. I'm not going to spend my last years reliving so much misery and suffering.'

'I don't believe you!' Adele burst out. 'How can you simply accept what happened? Why aren't you raging?'

'Because that's not how I want to live,' Gubby replied. 'I decided a long time ago that my revenge is to lead the happiest, most productive life I can. I don't want to think of myself as a victim, not when I've been so blessed. Especially compared to the others.'

'We should go to Vienna, all of us,' Adele said. 'Find your old apartment and—'

'Mom!' Jess began, but Cedric interrupted her by pushing back his chair and standing up. (He really was extremely tall.)

'That's enough, Adele,' he said, in a voice none of them had heard him use before. 'You've explained your point of view, but your mother is entitled to hers and we should leave it there. It's a shame to spoil such a happy day by arguing.'

Everybody stared at him for a few seconds, flabbergasted.

'Thank you, dear,' said Gubby at last, patting his hand. 'I couldn't agree more.'

Adele's mouth was hanging open. 'Well,' she said, recovering herself, 'I thought at least I could have counted on your support, but clearly everyone is determined to gang up against me.' She stood, too, picking up a napkin and then throwing it down again. 'I'm going for a walk. By myself, so don't anyone try to follow me.'

Nobody did. They sat awkwardly, not looking at each other, while Adele stalked out of the room and then the house, slamming the front door behind her.

143

Eventually Cedric cleared his throat. 'She loves you all very much, you know.'

'We do,' Gubby replied. 'It can just be a little exhausting at times.'

Chris put his head around the door. 'Everyone OK for drinks? A cup of tea, or maybe something stronger?'

'Tea would be great,' Gubby said. Cedric asked for some more mineral water and Jess a glass of brandy.

'Do you want a lie-down, dear?' Gubby asked her. 'I was thinking of taking a rest myself. It's been quite a day.'

'Actually,' Cedric began, 'I'm glad of the chance to talk to you all alone. It won't take long.' He adjusted the knot of his tie (being formally dressed, as usual). 'The thing is—' He placed both hands on the table, splaying out his long, pale fingers. 'Well, it's just that—'

Oh God, Lacey thought, he's going to tell us he's about to break up with Mom.

Cedric looked down at his hands. 'So the thing is . . .' Now he gazed up at the ceiling for inspiration before continuing, 'The thing is, I'd like to ask Adele to marry me, and it would be nice to have your blessing. Or at least, I thought perhaps you might appreciate fair warning.' He gave a shy, endearing smile.

It was the second time he'd reduced them to silence in less than ten minutes. After a few seconds, Gubby said, 'Good heavens, that is a surprise. Are you absolutely sure?'

'One hundred per cent,' he replied. 'She's an extraordinary woman. That spirit! So bold and fearless. Why wouldn't I want to marry her?'

Because she can be a total pain in the ass, Lacey thought. 'What wonderful news,' she said, reaching over to give Cedric a hug.

'I've been waiting for the right moment to propose and maybe now's the time. It would be good to bring everyone together. Of course she might not accept.' He smoothed his hair self-consciously. 'That's a possibility I have to bear in mind.'

'Mom'll bite your hand off,' Jess said. 'She ought to, anyway.'

'I hope so,' he replied. 'Weddings are such happy occasions, aren't they? Adele seems to have become fixated on the past. I'd like her to look forward and realise she has a lot to be thankful for. Without wishing to sound immodest, naturally.'

'Well, I for one am delighted,' Gubby said. 'Welcome to the family. At least no one can say you don't know what you're letting yourself in for.'

'Cedric, you're a saint,' Lacey said. 'If Mom doesn't marry you, I will.' Which was weird, but he didn't seem to mind.

'This calls for more champagne.' Jess got to her feet. 'But if anyone has any other surprises, they'll have to wait. I don't think I can take much more today.'

Lacey glanced at her grandmother, who caught her eye. They stared at each other for a moment before Lacey looked away. Gubby could always tell what she was thinking.

Adele came back after a couple of hours in a better frame of mind because she'd found a runaway dog on the beach and returned him to his owner, who'd said she looked like Pink and asked her whether she was a model. She wanted to make up with her mother but Gubby was resting, so she changed into jeans and played with Emma and Pauly in the yard instead while Cedric read a book in the treacherous egg chair by the window, occasionally looking out at them with his habitual inscrutable expression. Everyone needed

145

a little down time; Chris had gone to play tennis with a friend.

'Who'd have thought it?' Jess murmured to Lacey as they sat next to each other on the couch, watching TV and talking about inconsequential things. The sun had come out and later they would take the kids for supper at their favourite café by the beach, the adults being too full to consider eating much more. This is what she'd been missing, Lacey realised: simple companionship. By the time Gubby came downstairs, the house was calm and ordered, and Emma was laughing as Adele braided her hair.

We look like any normal happy family, Lacey thought – if such a thing existed – as they set off for the café, the kids walking with their grandma and she and Jess with theirs, while Chris and Cedric brought up the rear, talking about – she strained to listen – ah, glucose spikes. Adele didn't mention Vienna once during the meal and she looked at Cedric with a different expression now: not quite admiring, but certainly appraising. On the way back, Cedric suggested the two of them take a walk along the beach to catch the sunset, which everyone else oh-so-casually agreed was a great idea.

'Why are you looking like that?' Pauly asked, seeing Jess and Lacey exchanging smiles.

'No reason,' Lacey replied, breaking into a run. 'Come on, I'll race you home.'

Back at the house, Chris started getting the kids ready for bed upstairs while Lacey and Jess talked with Gubby about their childhood: what they remembered of their father, and the time they had spent in Bethlehem after running away from Tony.

'Such frightened little things standing on my doorstep,'

Gubby said. 'Jess, you were angry, too, and so was I after finding out how that man had behaved. Your mother should never have brought him into the house but at least you got away from him in the end, and that was down to her.'

'And you,' Lacey said.

'Well, I guess.' Gubby patted her hand. 'It's just a pity that you had to grow up without a decent man in your lives. But you married a good one, Jess, and maybe your mom's about to do the same.'

Which just leaves me, Lacey thought. What chance do I have now? And do I even want to find someone, anyway? Quickly she ran through a list of the kind, funny men she liked – there were several, and not all of them gay. Keith, who wrote sports biographies and coached a wheelchair hockey team; Howard, whom she always recommended for ghostwriting books about music; her college friends, Mike, Lynton and Joe, whom she hadn't seen for far too long; the guy in her local coffee shop with the wonderful smile . . .

'Don't worry, Lacey-Lou,' Gubby told her. 'You have plenty of time.'

And then the door opened and suddenly the house was full of noise as Cedric and Adele burst in, bringing the kids tumbling downstairs to see what all the fuss was about.

'I had no idea,' Adele kept repeating, shaking her head. 'Isn't it exciting? He actually went down on one knee.'

'A mistake in retrospect, perhaps.' Cedric dabbed at the damp, sandy patch on his trouser leg.

'That's such a pretty ring.' Lacey caught her mother's madly flailing hand for a closer look. It was old-fashioned and charming: four large pearls set in gold surrounded a diamond at the centre, with two smaller pearls on each side to form a cross.

'My grandmother's,' Cedric said. 'I've been waiting a long time for the right woman to wear it.'

So he hadn't been married before; Lacey had wondered, and suppressed a twinge of misgiving. She hoped he was up to the challenge. Smiling modestly, Cedric had the air of a man who knew he'd aced a daunting task: pride mixed with relief.

'And you can be flower girl.' Adele scooped up Emma and whirled her around, making her shriek.

'Thanks, Mom,' Jess said. 'Now she'll never get to sleep.'

'Well, I for one am ready for bed,' Gubby said. 'Will the bride- and groom-to-be escort me back to our Airbnb so we can leave these poor folks in peace?'

At last they left, Lacey staying behind to read Emma a bedtime story. It took the kids a while to settle but eventually she and Jess were able to take their tea on to the porch and sit looking up into the vast, unfathomable sky.

'It's good, isn't it, to think Mom is someone else's responsibility now,' Jess said. 'Getting married kind of makes that official.' She glanced at Lacey. 'Are you OK?'

'Sure. Feeling better than I have in a while.'

'You and Gubby both unburdened yourselves today,' Jess commented. 'I wonder if she's relieved, too.'

When Lacey didn't reply, Jess asked sharply, 'What is it? Tell me.'

Was it wrong to share a secret she'd only found out by snooping? And yet, surely Jess had a right to know about her great-aunt. After a moment's hesitation, Lacey said, 'Gubby has a sister.'

'A sister?' Jess repeated, incredulous. 'Are you sure? How do you know?'

'Because I came across a letter from her in the bureau.'

'So have you asked Gubby about it?'

'I daren't,' Lacey replied. 'She was mad enough when I looked at her passport without asking – she'll go crazy if she finds out I've been reading her private mail. I've been giving her a hundred chances to open up but for some reason she won't mention this woman. She actually told me she was an only child.'

'They must have fallen out,' Jess said. 'That doesn't sound like our Gubby though – family's the most important thing in the world to her. I wonder what happened?'

Lacey stared up at the stars. She had no answers, only the same question. What could have made their grandmother disown her sister so completely that she wouldn't even acknowledge her existence?

Chapter Fourteen

Philadelphia, May 2022

There were three sheets of paper, covered in elegant, unmistakeably European handwriting that still hadn't faded, even after eighty-four years. *Dearest Hanna,* the letter had begun, and Lacey had felt a tingle run through her body because she knew that Hanna was Gubby's given name – although she now spelled it with an 'h' at the end – and it felt as though she was hearing her great-aunt's voice, as clear and lively as if she'd been writing the day before. The letter was illustrated with tiny drawings of soldiers in bearskins, flags, crowns, statues and trumpets, and Lacey had fallen a little in love with Sophie as she read.

> *Windsor Castle*
> *27 May 1938*
>
> *Dearest Hanna,*
> *I am writing to you in English because this is what we must both be speaking now, and because we don't want people to think we have secrets by using a language they don't understand. I think of*

you often, my darling sister, and hope that you're happy in America, and that you've settled into the children's home. Perhaps you've already found a foster family? Please write and tell me your news, because now I have an address, and a very special one, too. I'm living in Windsor Castle, which was built in England many hundreds of years ago. And how did I come to be here, I hear you ask? Well, a couple of weeks ago I presented myself for inspection at the castle (nervously) and was interviewed by the Master of the Household (very grand) and the Royal Librarian (almost as grand), and now I am an assistant in the Royal Library! I live on the north terrace of the castle in a small room with a view over the park.

To describe my new home: the castle is right in the town but as soon as you go through the main gate, you find yourself in another world. The place is laid out in two halves called wards, divided by a tower on a small hill, and there are twenty more towers at intervals along a wall round the perimeter. The lower ward contains a splendid chapel and lodgings for retired soldiers, while the castle staff (including me!) live in the upper ward, which contains the Royal Family's state apartments, and where you will also find . . . the Royal Library! Ta daa! (This is the sound of a trumpet blowing.) I've seen the King and Queen from a distance, along with the two princesses: Elizabeth, who is twelve, and Margaret Rose, who is almost eight and makes me think of you. The family have just arrived for the weekend because there is to be a grand dinner here,

attended by Mr Joseph Kennedy, the American
ambassador to Britain, and his wife. Perhaps I might
get the chance to tell them my sister is living in their
country, and that I trust she is being taken good
care of.

I keep thinking of Papa, and how much he would
love to see me now. (We must keep talking about
him, dear Hanna – I know Mutti would want us to
keep his memory alive.) The library was once part of
a gallery where Queen Elizabeth used to walk with
her ladies when the weather was too bad to go
outside. People say she still haunts the place, and
that you can hear her footsteps behind you in the
library when nobody's there, but I haven't come
across her yet. I think this must be the most
beautiful set of rooms in the castle. They contain
hundreds of books, of course, and paintings, and
many other interesting things besides – including the
overshirt that the king who was beheaded, Charles I,
wore at his execution. And a portrait made out of
hair that was cut from his head afterwards! His
body and head are buried (separately) in the chapel,
along with many other British kings and queens. It
is all quite gruesome.

Despite the ghosts, I feel safe here, and I hope the
same is true for you in America. We have seen
terrible things but there is still kindness in the world
and good people who are willing to help us. I pray
for you every night and sometimes think I'll wake in
the morning and find you in your bed under the
window, with your teddy on the pillow and the sun
shining through the curtains. What a lot we'll have

153

*to talk about when we see each other again! Don't
forget me either, my darling. I'll come for you and
we'll be together again one day, I promise.*

A thousand kisses and love always,
Your Sophie

Lacey had photographed the letter on her phone, leaving
the original in Gubby's bureau, and read the text so many
times she could almost recite it by heart. Sophie sounded
so loving and concerned; she couldn't imagine why Gubby
would want to disown her. Maybe she'd been killed during
the war and her memory was too sacred and sad even to
be mentioned? Or perhaps there'd been some terrible
argument about an inheritance, or the question of reparations?
Lacey spent her working day tracing the stories of people's
lives and the thought of investigating this, the most important
one of all, was irresistible. Her grandmother wouldn't need
to know what she discovered – if anything, which was by
no means certain. With the old familiar tingle of anticipation,
she opened her search engine.

Gubby had told Lacey her parents' names and, as luck
would have it, in 1934 there'd been a census in Austria that
she could access online. After a couple of hours' work, Lacey
had tracked the family down. There they were, living in
Josefstädter street in Vienna: Otto Klein, born 1885,
librarian; Ingrid Klein, born 1894, pastry chef; Sophie Klein,
born 1919; Hanna Klein, born 1929. Lacey stared at the
words as though she could conjure up the people behind
them. Soon she was looking at a satellite picture of the
apartment building in which the family had lived, now home
to a high-end fashion label; there would be little point in
Adele marching in there to demand compensation. A second

census had been carried out in 1939, after the start of the Second World War, but by then another family was living at that address. The Kleins had been erased.

Yet Sophie had existed, and now Lacey was on her trail. What could have happened to her during the war? She might have been killed, but Lacey went on to comb through all the usual sources and could find no record of her death. Abandoning that thread, she started on some more general research in various family history websites and eventually – bingo! – found a marriage certificate. Her pulse quickened. Sophie Klein had married Henry Dedham at a church in Windsor on 6 April 1944. Nine years later, they'd had a son: Nicholas.

Lacey sat back in her chair, stunned. Somewhere out there was an actual blood relative (maybe more by now) who probably had no idea of her existence either. Her mother and this guy Nicholas were first cousins! Gubby's brother Jim hadn't had kids and Adele was an only child; she'd always been jealous of people from big families. She ought to be told what Lacey had discovered, surely – although that was bound to mean Gubby getting to hear of it. Lacey had no desire to upset her grandmother all over again; she'd need to arm herself with more information before taking such a drastic step.

It turned out that Sophie had died in 1994 at the age of seventy-five. Of course, there'd been little chance of her still being alive – she'd have been over a hundred by now – but seeing her death spelled out in black and white was a shock. Lacey couldn't bear to think of this vibrant, loving woman forever out of reach. She'd been almost twenty years younger than Gubby when she passed away: a relatively short life, but had it been a happy one? Lacey would have been six then, living in Pittsburgh with her mom and sister. She couldn't remember having much contact with Gubby at that time, and would have had no idea what was going on in her life.

Sophie's husband Henry died three years later, which just left their son. Nicholas Dedham: it wasn't that common a name. There could be no going back now – he was almost within reach.

Less than an hour later, Lacey had tracked him down. Nicholas Dedham was a history lecturer at a branch of the University of London in Berkshire, not far from Windsor. He was an expert in the twentieth-century Jewish diaspora and had published several papers on the subject. She saw a photograph of him on the internet, receiving an award for something or other, and stared at his face with a jolt of recognition. He was smiling, with the same dimples in his cheeks as the ones she had inherited from her mother and Gubby; dimples that Jess was so cross to have missed out on. He had the same oval-shaped face as Adele, too, with a wide forehead, eyes a little too close together for perfection, and full, finely moulded lips. The family resemblance was clear.

Closing her laptop, Lacey went for a walk so she could think. The weather had turned warm and the people she passed were in short sleeves, their legs bare. She headed for Washington Square, where trees rustled in the breeze and jets of sparkling water shot up from a fountain into the bluest of skies. Part of her wished she'd never read that letter; the last thing she wanted was to cause Gubby more pain. She'd thought telling the truth at last would have liberated her grandmother, but Gubby didn't seem relieved to have unburdened herself. She wouldn't answer any of their questions about her life in Vienna or what had happened to

156

her parents, saying it was all a long time ago and raking up the past was too painful. Luckily for her, Adele and Cedric's news had dominated the rest of their visit to Vancouver so the talk was mostly of bridesmaids and wedding venues.

On their last day, Jess had taken Lacey aside and whispered that the two of them should sneak off, though she wouldn't say where: it was going to be a surprise.

'Seriously?' Lacey said when, after walking several blocks, they stopped outside a store front decorated with vivid graphics: an eagle with a rose in its beak; a skull with worms wriggling out of the eye sockets; trees, waves and waterfalls.

'Seriously,' Jess replied, pushing open the door. 'We're going to get matching tattoos. This way there'll always be a link between us, even when we're apart.'

Lacey looked down at hers now: a tiny picture on her ankle of Piglet, dangling by one paw from a balloon. (Jess had a slightly larger Winnie-the-Pooh, also towed by a balloon.) The sight of it made her smile. She liked the image of floating through life, lighter than air, and the thought of her rational, unemotional sister coming up with the idea filled her with gratitude. The tattoo told her she was loved, made her feel safe. And yet – safe enough to fly to England and tell a stranger they were related? She'd mulled over her options and this seemed the only possibility. Either she let the matter drop until after Gubby died or she'd have to meet Nicholas Dedham, if he agreed. The matter was too complicated to explain in an email or a phone call; he'd probably think she was nuts. Besides, if she stayed in Windsor, she'd be able to consult the Royal Archives at the castle in person and maybe find out more about Sophie's time there.

That evening, she called Jess to share her plans. 'Why not wait until the fall and then I can go with you,' her sister suggested, but Lacey wanted to leave soon. Her next book had been delayed because the client was sick so she was unexpectedly free, and her blood was up. She was a thirty-three-year-old woman; of course she should go to England, if that was the right thing to do. Her grandmother had left Europe to start a new life in America at the age of nine, for goodness' sake. Lacey brought Adele to mind, too. She'd have been furious if her drink had been spiked and wouldn't have let some bartender fob her off; she'd have gone to the police and forced them to investigate. She'd raise hell, which was perhaps why Lacey still felt reluctant to talk to her mother about what had happened. Yet maybe anger was a healthier response than fear and shame? The women in her family were fighters; she was letting the side down.

Before she could lose her nerve, Lacey emailed Nicholas Dedham at his college address. She debated for a while about how much to say and in the end, simply wrote that she was coming to England soon and would like to show him a letter she believed had been written by his mother, Sophie Klein, in 1938; could he let her know a convenient time and place for them to meet? It took a few days for him to reply, by which time she was wondering whether to leave for England regardless and turn up unannounced. What an enigmatic message, he wrote. He was extremely busy at work but there was a four-day bank holiday coming up in honour of the Queen's Platinum Jubilee, and perhaps they could meet at his college at the start of the holiday on Thursday, the second of June. It was a brief, business-like message that gave nothing away.

Lacey replied to say any time he cared to choose would be fine and she looked forward to seeing him soon. The thought of meeting Sophie's son and getting to know her great-aunt at last sent waves of excitement and nerves racing through her body. Maybe she was finally within touching distance of some answers. Whatever she found out, surely it was better to know the truth.

She managed to book flights without too much trouble, although short notice made them expensive – luckily, she was able to use Air Miles – but finding accommodation in Windsor was another matter. Every hotel, guest house and rental apartment seemed to be full and she'd almost given up hope when she stumbled across a one-bed in a block within ten minutes' walk of the castle, which you could apparently see from the living-room window. There weren't any reviews because the place was newly converted and had only recently been listed but it looked perfect, and the dates she wanted were available. It was almost as though Sophie wanted to be found, Lacey thought, clicking the reservation button. For better or worse, she was on her way. Jess was the only person who knew exactly where she was going; she told her mother and Gubby and anyone else who asked that she was heading to England for a research trip, and nobody thought to question her further than that.

The journey went more smoothly than Lacey had expected. Flying to Vancouver had been a useful dress rehearsal and this time, she had no need of Xanax: deep breathing, worry beads and the meditation app on her phone were enough to get her to England. After a couple of years in the wilderness, she was finally getting her life back on track. Telling Jess what had happened and hearing confirmation that none of it had been her fault, and that she had no reason to feel ashamed, had lifted the dark cloud that had been twisting her mind into ridiculous knots. She was beginning to like herself again, and that changed everything. The woman in the seat next to hers was a nervous flyer, and Lacey was even able to reassure her.

Windsor was conveniently close to Heathrow and within a couple of hours of leaving the airport, Lacey was gazing at the castle through her train window. She hadn't expected it to be quite such a presence, with those massive granite walls looming over the town. Joining a stream of other travellers, she walked through the station precinct and up the hill for a closer look, imagining how the place might have looked in her great-aunt's time without the fast-food outlets and tourist tat. Union Jack bunting hung everywhere and the store windows were crammed with crowns and flags; at one point Lacey found herself staring at a life-size cardboard cut-out of the Queen. That was a shock. She'd never been especially interested in the British Royal Family but found herself strangely moved, thinking of the twelve-year-old girl Sophie would have glimpsed, now looking back on her seventy-year reign. A diminutive figure with the ever-present handbag, who had lived so long and weathered so much of her country's history. Everyone seemed to be in a good mood, despite the drizzly, grey weather – even the armed police near the castle entrance – thirsty for celebration after a couple of difficult years and full of affection for the woman who had stood beside them and shared their troubles since the Second World War.

Lacey's spirits lifted as she wheeled her suitcase along narrow cobbled streets in search of the apartment she'd rented for the week. Windsor was quaint and somehow manageable: the vast sky uncluttered with skyscrapers and the buildings so old and quirky. There were plenty of planes overhead to remind her of the twenty-first century, but that was inevitable with the airport so close. She passed a tiny crooked house that looked as though it were about to slide into the street, selling pearls, of all things, and felt the urge to run in and buy something pearly. Shopping could wait, though: she had the whole of the next day for exploring and was exhausted from travelling. All she wanted was to kick off her shoes, change out of her damp clothes and take a shower.

She'd messaged the landlord to tell him what time she'd be arriving but when she rang the doorbell of the apartment block in Park Street, there was no reply. She rang again with increasing urgency, several times. There was bound to be some explanation, some silly mix-up over timing that would soon be resolved. Despite her rising alarm, she wouldn't listen to the warning voice in her head saying anything that seemed to be too good to be true usually was. Eventually the intercom crackled into life and a weary-sounding man asked what she wanted.

'To come in, of course,' she said. 'I've rented this place for the week. Are you Michael?'

'Oh God, not this again,' said the man, an edge to his voice now. 'You've been scammed, I'm afraid. I bought this apartment a year ago and I don't rent it out. You'll have to contact the agency to try and get your money back.'

'So what am I meant to do now?' Lacey asked, her voice cracking.

'I don't know and I don't care. Choose more wisely next time.' And with a final buzz, the line went dead.

Lacey gazed down the street. Looking for what, exactly? It wasn't as though a knight on a charger was going to come riding by to rescue her. She was starving, needed a pee and her phone was almost out of battery. This trip couldn't have got off to a worse start.

161

Chapter Fifteen

Windsor, June 2022

The town was completely full, Lacey discovered. Everywhere was booked for the Jubilee weekend, naturally, and there wasn't a hotel room, rental apartment, bed and breakfast or hostel bunk to be had. She must have called most of them. The good news was that she'd found a café with a friendly waitress where she could charge her phone, wash her hands and eat a sandwich. This is not the end of the world, she kept reminding herself, it's just a bump in the road. Eventually she went on to the couch-surfing site she'd joined a few years before – more out of desperation than anything else – and pinged a message to a host in Windsor, explaining what had happened. Anna Speedwell, that was her name (which was cool); she looked friendly and she got great feedback from all her guests. Lacey carried on with her futile search, not expecting a reply any time soon, but amazingly enough, about half an hour later she received one: Anna would be happy to help her out for tonight, at least, and they could see how they got along. She happened to have a cousin in Philadelphia and might ask for a return favour some day.

'You're sorted, then?' said the waitress when Lacey paid her check.

'Let's hope so,' she replied, leaving a generous tip. 'Cross your fingers for me.'

She'd stayed in someone's New York condo, back in the days when she was still travelling, and hosted an Italian girl who'd come for a wedding in Philly, so she knew the score. You weren't expected to pay rent, but it was customary to bring a small present for the host and generally help around the place. She bought a couple of bottles of wine along the way, trying not to get her hopes up.

Anna turned out to be as lovely in person as she was in her photo. She flung open the door of the small mews house with a smile that made Lacey feel instantly welcome.

'Come in! I can't believe you've been scammed, you poor thing. Just as well I happened to be checking my emails. Here, let me take your case.'

She had an open, freckled face with blue eyes and auburn hair, and wore a T-shirt and denim cutoffs; her slim legs were covered in freckles too, and she had a silver chain around her ankle.

'I'm so grateful,' Lacey said, handing over the wine. 'You're really digging me out of a hole.'

She followed Anna down a short hall and into the open-plan ground floor, where light streamed through a large picture window that was probably once a stable door. The room was small but chic, all white walls and blonde wood with a jute rug underfoot. It was also immaculately tidy.

Lacey gazed around. 'This place is gorgeous. How long have you lived here?'

'A couple of years,' Anna said. 'I'm lucky, aren't I? My aunt died and left us some money so I could just afford it.

That's one of the reasons I like to have people staying – helps with the guilt.' She gave an apologetic smile. 'Sorry, too much information. I always overshare.'

She's so nice, Lacey thought; where's the catch?

'You will literally have the couch,' Anna went on, 'as my brother's staying for a few days while the builders are working on his place.' Some alarm must have shown on Lacey's face because she added, 'That's OK, isn't it? He's house trained, more or less.'

'Sure,' Lacey said, adjusting her expression. How could she object?

'Great. Now, do you want a cup of tea or would you sooner get straight into the shower? I guess it's a bit early to start on the wine but I'm game if you are.'

'Shower, please,' Lacey said gratefully. 'If you don't mind.'

'English plumbing, I'm afraid. Don't get too excited.' Anna led the way to the bathroom, which was at the top of the stairs, with a couple more steps up to the two bedrooms.

Lacey stood under the steaming water – more of a trickle than a waterfall, admittedly – sluicing away that particular airport smell and taking stock. She seemed to have landed on her feet; there was only the question of Anna's brother to be reckoned with. Yet even if he were awful, she could put up with him for a few days, surely – or however long Anna let her stay. And if he were half as engaging as his sister, she had nothing to worry about. She was more concerned about making a mess: the house looked like a show home.

'I'm a neat freak, as you've probably noticed,' Anna said over a glass of wine back downstairs. 'Blame the job. I'm a nurse and infection control is my speciality.'

'So how have the past couple of years been for you?' Lacey asked.

165

She shivered. 'Awful. I'm still trying to process what we went through.' She topped up her glass, though Lacey's was still full. 'But come on, this is too heavy to talk about when we've only just met. What brings you to Windsor? Have you come for the Jubilee?'

'Not especially.' Lacey went on to tell the story of her great-aunt fleeing Nazi-occupied Vienna and ending up working at Windsor Castle. 'I have an appointment at the Royal Archives to see if there's any record of her there, and I'm going to meet her son in a couple of days.' She didn't mention finding out about Sophie by accident, or the fact that her great-aunt seemed to be the outcast of the family.

Anna had to be up early for work the next day, so she took the last of the wine up to her bedroom. 'I've eaten already but help yourself to whatever's in the fridge,' she told Lacey. 'I probably won't see you in the morning, and I'll try to be quiet when I leave. Oh, and I've texted Tom to tell him you're staying. Honestly, apart from the fact he leaves wet towels on the floor and his bedroom's a tip, he's fine. He's out tonight, too. Don't worry, based on past performance he'll probably just stagger straight upstairs and pass out.'

All the same, Lacey felt vulnerable, lying on the sofabed that night. She'd made a barricade with her suitcase so that anyone coming in from the hall wouldn't see her head, at least, but that still left the rest of her. Oh, lighten up, she told herself, switching off the lamp when she couldn't keep her eyes open another second. This is an adventure.

She woke with a start, jolted by a thump somewhere near her feet. Sitting up in the pitch black, clutching the duvet to her chest, it took a few seconds to work out where she was. Someone was blundering about in the dark, bumping into things and muttering. She froze, her heart thudding, until a sudden crash made her scream.

'Oh God,' someone said. 'I forgot. The bloody couch surfer.'

She gathered her wits. 'The bloody brother, I assume?'

'Sorry,' he said. 'I need a glass of water. Do you mind if I switch on my phone torch?'

'I guess not.' But she did; it was embarrassing, being caught in her night clothes with her hair all over the place. 'Just don't point it at me,' she added, lying back down and pulling the duvet over her head.

She heard footsteps, a cupboard door opening and closing, a tap running, then the footsteps approaching her swaddled form.

'Nighty night,' said the voice, passing by, and something about its tone made her smile under the duvet. Really, the situation could hardly be more ridiculous.

She lay awake for a couple of hours and fell asleep around dawn, waking again when the front door slammed as Anna left for work. It was still early but jetlag had struck; she decided to get up and buy some provisions. She was on probation, after all, and couldn't see why Anna and her brother should have to put up with a stranger on their living-room couch for nothing in return. Pancakes, that's what she'd make, with bacon or strawberries and maple syrup. She bought eggs, milk and flour, and coffee too, since Anna was running low. There hadn't been much in the fridge apart from wine and a few bottles of tonic water. It was good to have someone else to cook for and she found herself humming as she moved around the tiny kitchen, trying to replace everything exactly where she found it. She'd already had to pick up a trash can that had been knocked over in the night and shovel the garbage back inside. Soon a delicious smell of home was wafting through the house, and her mouth watered. It would be hard to resist eating all the pancakes herself.

The shower was running upstairs but now – clothed, fed and rested – she felt able to take on Anna's brother.

'Morning.' He was rubbing his damp hair sheepishly as he walked into the kitchen. 'Something smells good.'

'I thought you might like a decent breakfast,' she said, getting up to pour him a coffee. 'Fruit or bacon with your pancakes?'

'Now you're talking,' he replied. 'Can I have both or is that weird?'

'A little weird, but I guess it's your house – almost – so your rules.'

'My name's Tom, by the way,' he said, watching as she loaded his plate. 'Sorry I gave you a shock last night. I'm not sure I deserve a breakfast like this but I'm not going to turn it down.'

They were clearly siblings. His hair was a darker chestnut than Anna's and he had fewer freckles, but they shared the same easy smile and frank blue eyes. Although he wasn't movie-star handsome, he had bucketloads of charm and that, Lacey decided, was just as good, if not better. She felt like smiling, too, whenever she looked at him, despite how mad she'd been the night before. It was oddly intimate to be sharing breakfast and, for a second, she allowed herself to imagine waking up beside him, seeing that tousled head on the pillow next to hers. Get a grip, she told herself sternly, and went over to her bed – now restored as a couch – to retrieve her phone.

'That was amazing,' he said, pushing his plate aside. 'You stay there and I'll clear up.'

Now it was her turn to watch him as he loaded plates and mugs into the dishwasher, washed pans and wiped the worktop, whistling tunelessly. He had a great body: long legs, broad shoulders and strong, muscular arms. He was clumsy, though, slopping water on the floor and shoving utensils carelessly into drawers. Anna would not have approved.

'Let me help,' Lacey said, when she'd had enough of the mayhem. 'You wash and I'll dry and put away.'

They worked together companionably and then chatted over coffee. He was fascinated to hear about Sophie, and Lacey even found herself telling him about her grandmother's reluctance to admit she had a sister. 'So maybe I shouldn't be here, trying to find out about her,' she finished. 'Except the amazing thing is, I've tracked down her son: our cousin, an actual real-life British relative. I'm going to meet him in a couple of days.'

'Are you kidding?' he said. 'This is a grade A mystery – of course you should try to solve it. I would. Maybe I can help you.'

'Haven't you got a job to go to?' she asked, laughing at his enthusiasm.

It turned out he was an actuary – something to do with risk management and probability that she didn't fully understand – on gardening leave for a month before starting a new job. 'It's all change: new flat, new job.' He crossed his legs, stretching his arms above his head so his T-shirt lifted, revealing a glimpse of tanned, taut stomach. 'But at the moment, I'm in limbo. Nothing to do but drive my sister mad and spend too long in the pub.'

Lacey looked at her watch. 'Hey, I'd better get going. I'm due to visit Windsor Castle in an hour.'

'Can I come with you?' he asked. 'All the years Anna's lived here and I've never been.'

'Sure, if you want.' She tried to sound casual. 'Yeah, if you can manage to get a ticket, that would be great.'

Windsor Castle was overwhelming: she'd never walked into a place so steeped in history, so richly atmospheric. It was incredible to think kings and queens had been living there for nearly a thousand years; Henry VIII and one of his wives were actually buried in the royal vault. The castle was a fortress, according to her guide book, built on high ground above the River Thames as part of a ring of fortifications around London by William I after he'd won the Battle of Hastings in 1066. It had been designed to repel raiders: the studded doors were several inches thick and the twenty huge towers along the perimeter wall had narrow, arched windows no arrows could penetrate. Swords, axes and pikes were mounted on the interior walls, while faceless knights in armour on ebony horses guarded the grand staircase. Geometric displays of weapons turned them into decorative objects – criss-crossed muskets in a herringbone pattern, concentric circles of revolvers like some tribute to an Indian goddess of destruction.

The state rooms, by contrast, were luxurious and colourful. Every curtain was swagged, fringed and tasselled to within an inch of its life; every wall was painted, papered or gilded on a lavish scale, lit by vast crystal chandeliers suspended high overhead or clusters of lamps on branched candelabra, their glow reflected in endless mirrors. Entering the Crimson Drawing Room felt like falling into a giant box of chocolates.

Lacey's only disappointment came from the fact she couldn't see the Royal Library. It was difficult even to work out where it was, since the first guide she asked only knew that the public weren't allowed access. Eventually another pointed out an unobtrusive door in a corner of the Queen's Drawing Room, which Lacey could only look at longingly, imagining what lay on the other side.

'This isn't the actual Queen's drawing room, is it?' Tom asked. 'Stupid question, but what if she wants to put her feet up with a cup of tea?'

They were told the Queen's private quarters lay on the other side of the castle, near the state entrance: a suite of bedrooms, bathrooms, reception rooms, audience chambers, even a library (another one) and writing room.

'This place feels like a village, a whole little world apart,' Lacey said as they were walking back through the lower ward at the end of the tour. An elderly couple carrying shopping bags walked up their front path and into one of the terraced houses opposite St George's Chapel, where pots of geraniums stood on windowsills and a cat stepped delicately along the garden wall. Four soldiers in khaki uniform marched past, guns over their shoulders and eyes fixed ahead.

'Can you imagine living here?' Tom said. 'Unreal.'

Lacey glanced at him, easily striding along beside her. She was glad he was there but it had to be said that he was a distraction. She was too aware of his presence: his hand on her elbow when he wanted to point something out, his intent expression when studying the display cases, his infectious smile. They had just met and she was only here for a week; this attraction wasn't going to lead anywhere. She knew what Jess would have said.

'My great-aunt did,' she replied. 'Just before the war.' She had hoped to get some sense of her great-aunt here but not even knowing what Sophie looked like kept her remote and unclear.

Tom threw an arm around her shoulder, making her heart lurch. 'This must be emotional for you. Come on, I'll show you the wonders of the Long Walk and then we can have lunch.'

She couldn't work out whether he was coming on to her or whether he acted this way with everybody – but there was no point speculating. They walked down the long, straight avenue she'd glimpsed from inside the castle, bordered by elm trees and pasture where deer were grazing. It felt as though she'd known Tom for years – he was so relaxed and companionable – and the more she talked, the freer she felt: the strain of those anxious months easing with every word. He asked her about the books she'd written and she found herself telling him about Frances, and the years of abuse she'd had to endure from her controlling husband.

Tom had sighed. 'Men are such shits. Some of them, anyway.'

They spoke about their sisters, too: Anna, whose best friend Caroline had died of leukaemia, prompting her to become a nurse, and Jess, becoming a second mother to Lacey during the bleak Tony years. She told him about Adele's wedding plans, and how she'd misjudged Cedric. He described his parents' bitter divorce and his mother's new partner whom nobody liked – not even Anna, who gave everyone the benefit of the doubt.

'It's so kind of her to open up her house the way she does,' Lacey said.

'I know. She still feels guilty that she leads this charmed life while Caroline had to die. I keep telling her it's pointless but she won't listen. And the men she goes for . . .' He shook his head. 'Still, I can't talk. That's really why I'm staying with her: my latest relationship has come to the usual sad end.' He glanced at her. 'How about you?'

'Me?' Perspiration prickled under Lacey's arms.

'Yes. Are you single?' His question fell into the damp, still air and stayed there.

'Um.' Lacey hesitated, her mind racing. She knew suddenly that she couldn't face the emotional upheaval, the investment in a man she was already falling for who would end up breaking her heart one way or another. Better to nip this in the bud right now, concentrate on the reason she'd come to England in the first place and spare herself the inevitable disappointment. 'No, actually,' she said. 'I have a partner.'

'Ah.' She couldn't tell if he were disappointed. They walked on in silence for a moment before he asked, 'Been together long?'

She shrugged. 'A while.'

'But he didn't want to come on this trip with you? Or she? Sorry, shouldn't make assumptions.'

'He couldn't get the time off work.' She tried unsuccessfully to think of a way of changing the subject.

'And what does he do, this anonymous boyfriend?'

'Dermot?' she said wildly. 'He's a marine biologist.'

'Ah. He's Irish, then?'

Dear God! Why was he so interested? 'No, actually,' she replied. 'His parents just liked the name.'

'Dermot,' Tom repeated thoughtfully, rolling the name over on his tongue. 'Dermot. Hmm.'

And then, thank goodness, a Labrador puppy came rushing

towards them with its apologetic owner in hot pursuit and she could change the subject. Afterwards, they had a desultory discussion about this and that – the deer in the park, the Jubilee Lunch that was being held on the Long Walk that Sunday, whether Anna would be happy for Lacey to stay the rest of the week (if she promised to make pancakes every morning, Tom thought that was a no-brainer) – until they were walking out of the park, heading for a pub with tables outside and masses of flowers in pots and hanging baskets, along with the obligatory Union Jack bunting. The front door was propped open and drinkers were lined up at the bar amid a hubbub of chat and laughter.

'I reckon we've earned a beer,' Tom said. 'My shout.'

Lacey turned to him, anguished. 'I'm sorry, I can't do this.'

'What's the matter?' he asked, his expression changing. 'Are you not feeling well?'

She was already backing away. 'Don't worry about me, you go ahead. I can take a cab home.'

He caught up, taking her gently by the shoulders. 'Lacey, what's wrong? Tell me!'

'Nothing,' she said. 'I just need to leave, sorry. This is too much.'

She was being pathetic, irrational, but the thought of accepting a drink from a man she'd only met that morning, no matter how lovely he seemed, brought her out in a cold sweat. She'd been fooling herself, letting her imagination run away with her as usual and assuming she could carry on with life as though the trauma of the past two years had never happened.

So that was the end of their fine romance, over before it had begun.

Chapter Sixteen

Windsor Castle, May 1938

Walking up Castle Hill and approaching the trade entrance to Windsor Castle, Sophie had the strangest feeling of coming home. Every detail of the building seemed familiar: she might have walked through that great stone arch or gazed up at the crenellated battlements in a previous lifetime. Nervously, she gave her name to a policeman at the entrance who consulted a list before handing her over to a servant in red-and-gold livery. The footman led her down a flight of stairs and through a maze of stone-flagged underground passages, low-ceilinged and dimly lit, towards what she would later recognise were the offices of the Master of the Household and the Royal Librarian on the other side of the castle.

'You'll soon find your way around,' he told her. 'Don't worry about getting lost – someone will turn up sooner or later to put you right.'

They happened to be passing a selection of pikes and helmets mounted on the wall and Sophie shivered at the thought of wandering around this catacomb for days, with no one even having noticed she was gone. How many others had gone this way before her, running their hands along the smooth stone wall as she was doing now? The busy life of the castle continued above their heads while down here, all was cool and shadowy and secret, silent except for the sound of their footsteps. Eventually they climbed another flight of steps and emerged via a set of huge doors in one of the twenty or so towers that studded the castle's perimeter wall. The place was a fortress as well as a home and she was glad of that, relieved to hear the great slabs of wood ease into place behind her and know she was safe.

After the briefest of introductions to the Master of the Household – a tall, terrifying man with military bearing and a clipped moustache – she was delivered via a secretary to the Royal Librarian, who proceeded to grill her in the nicest possible way over a cup of tea about her qualifications and experience, her view of the current situation in Vienna, and her attitude towards the country in which she might find a home.

'Absolute loyalty, sir,' she replied. 'If I'm allowed to stay, you have my word on that. I would fight to defend England with the last breath in my body.'

Would she? Her father had fought for Germany in the war and look where it had got him.

The Librarian smiled, and she wondered whether she'd gone too far. 'Let's hope it won't come to that,' he said. 'But I appreciate your sentiment. The monarchy is a sacred chain that connects us to our past and in times of upheaval, more precious than ever. And Windsor is the heart of it, you know. There's been a castle here for nearly a thousand years, ever since the Normans invaded Britain and chose this spot above the Thames to protect London from the west. Buckingham Palace is modern in comparison.'

Sophie had felt a twinge of guilt, knowing there were secrets she would have to keep from this scholarly man. Yet deception would be part of her life from now on and she might as well get used to it.

'Back to business,' the Librarian went on. 'I've been without an assistant for a few months now so we have got a little behind, and the previous king, Edward, was somewhat – how shall I put it? – casual, with regard to state papers. Besides day-to-day work in the library, we're looking for someone to round up any significant items that might have gone astray so they can be added to the archive. Papers, letters, that sort of thing, from his time as Prince of Wales as well as king. He often wrote in German, so you would be ideally qualified for the role.'

'It sounds fascinating,' Sophie said carefully.

The Librarian cleared his throat. 'You may come across more intimate correspondence, which obviously must be kept private and should be set aside for me to deal with. The Duke and his youngest brother, the Duke of Kent, have both led somewhat unconventional lives. Youthful indiscretions, that sort of thing. I hope you're not easily shocked.'

'Not anymore, sir.'

'Jolly good.' He shuffled a few papers on his desk. 'Well, you have glowing references and we're aware of your circumstances. It's in both our interests to have the matter settled quickly, so I'm authorised to offer you a salary of twelve pounds a month, with food and accommodation provided. How does that sound?'

'It sounds marvellous,' Sophie replied, breaking into a smile. 'Thank you, sir.'

'Thank *you*, Miss Klein.' He stretched across the table to shake her hand. 'In that case, welcome to Windsor. I assume you'd like to start work fairly soon? I've alerted the housekeeper to the fact we may have a new recruit.'

'I should like to start immediately,' Sophie said, 'if that's agreeable to you.'

He clapped his hands together. 'I was hoping you'd say that. Now come, let me show you around.'

He'd taken her to the Royal Library then, back on the other side of the castle near the Queen's Drawing Room. Sophie had felt her shoulders drop and her soul expand as soon as she'd walked through the door. After a traumatic journey, she'd sailed into a safe harbour. Leather-bound books filled shelves that stretched from floor to ceiling, the gilt on their spines glowing in the light of a huge chandelier, while chairs upholstered in red velvet waited patiently at windows and side tables. The first two rooms were devoted to books of history and treasures from the past, displayed in octagonal glass-topped tables: Persian manuscripts with the most exquisite illustrations, she saw from a quick glance, and the bloodstained shirt worn by Charles I at his execution.

'We haven't always treated our monarchs with the same respect,' the Librarian said quietly. They were alone yet Sophie felt he was right to have dropped his voice: libraries should be peaceful, private places.

They went on into the gallery, where Queen Elizabeth used to walk with her ladies when the weather was bad, later incorporated into the library. 'They say she still haunts the place,' the Librarian told her, 'and that Anne Boleyn, one of Henry VIII's wives, has been seen running through the Dean's Cloister, screaming and clutching her head. The castle is full of ghosts. Guards marching by saluted George III, standing in his usual spot at the window – two days after he died.'

A chill like a drop of cold water ran down Sophie's spine. Windsor was steeped in an earthier, bloodier history than the sedate and formal palaces of Vienna. The Austrian monarchy had fizzled out, with the Emperor Franz Joseph dying in the middle of the war, twenty years before, and his successor quietly abdicating at the end of it, but the British royals were here for good – or so the castle seemed to declare.

This part of the library was double height, with a mezzanine balcony running around the room and a ceiling decorated with Tudor badges, each panel telling a different story; Sophie soon had a crick in her neck from gazing up at them. The rarest books were displayed here, including several specially bound for Queen Elizabeth, along with her drinking glass. The bulk of the collection was stored in the Royal Archives in the Round Tower, which they entered through another set of massive double doors.

'This tower is the oldest part of the castle,' the Librarian told her as they climbed the wide, shallow steps inside. 'George IV thought it wasn't sufficiently imposing so he doubled the height and added the turret and flagpole. Then around forty years ago, the Muniment Room on the top floor became a home for the letters and diaries left in boxes after Queen Victoria's death. Private collections have been donated to the archive ever since, and now we have royal household records going back to the seventeenth century. It's a treasure trove, if you like that sort of thing.'

'Oh, I do,' Sophie assured him. 'I should love to look through them.' Adding hastily, 'With your permission, of course.'

A simple wooden plaque on a door near the top of the steps proclaimed 'The Royal Archives' and Sophie's heart began to pound. It still seemed extraordinary that only a few days ago she was hiding out in a tenement room in Vienna, frightened for her life, and now here she was: in the heart of the oldest castle in Europe. They walked through to a reception area with lockers and a desk, at which a young woman with glossy black hair and red-painted lips like a Dutch doll was typing briskly.

'And here is my secretary, Miss Preston,' the Librarian said – a little uneasily, Sophie thought. 'May I introduce Miss Klein? She's come to help us in our hour of need.'

'Charmed, I'm sure.' Miss Preston looked Sophie up and down, seemingly anything but.

'Miss Preston is in charge of our filing and appointments system,' he told Sophie, rubbing his hands. 'The library would grind to a halt without her.'

Miss Preston gave a brittle smile, accepting her due. 'A place for everything and everything in its place.'

'Quite,' he agreed. 'We're on our way upstairs to the Muniments Room but I'll deliver Miss Klein into your tender care when we return, if you'd like to take her to lunch.'

Miss Preston glanced at the clock. 'Of course, sir. I'm afraid it will have to be a quick one, though. The ladies from the Needlewomen's Guild are coming at two.'

'Don't let me delay you,' Sophie said, whereupon Miss Preston bared her teeth again and replied, 'Not at all, it would be a pleasure.'

They took another flight of stairs to the top of the tower and entered a large room with lath and plaster walls and a magnificent vaulted ceiling, surprisingly close to their heads. A bank of card indexes lined one wall, flanked by a large table, while columns of floor-to-ceiling wooden shelves with narrow passages in between took up the rest of the space.

'It's a fairly simple system,' the Librarian told her. 'Items are filed according to date and subdivided by subject in the usual way, with an index card giving their shelf location. Any additions to the archive would need my approval, naturally.'

'Of course,' Sophie agreed.

'I suggest you lay aside any significant documents you might find and we can go through them together. As a matter of fact, several boxes have recently arrived from the Duke of Windsor in France that will need assessing. He and the Duchess don't yet have a permanent home so many of his belongings are stored for safekeeping in Frogmore House, just across the park. When you've settled in, I'll show you around. Now come, let's take a turn around the battlements. You won't find a better view in the whole of Windsor.'

A door in a corner of the room led to one final flight of steps leading out into the open.

'One more thing,' the Librarian added as they stepped into the fresh air. 'I'd be grateful if you kept any sensitive information strictly between ourselves. Any gossip about what you might stumble across will result in instant dismissal. Is that clear?'

'Absolutely,' Sophie assured him. 'You can count on my discretion.'

'I hope so.'

When the intensity of his gaze became uncomfortable, Sophie turned to exclaim over the view. The whole castle lay spread out beneath them: the roof of St George's Chapel and the half-timbered cloisters of the lower ward in one direction, the Long Walk and the southern gardens in the other. Above her head, innocent wisps of cloud floated through a blue void. She felt as though she were poised between heaven and earth, one existence and another.

'This is where I'm meant to be,' she murmured, half to herself. 'Fate has brought me here.'

'Let's hope so.' The Librarian sounded a little alarmed. 'Come to my study after lunch and your contract will be ready for signing.'

'So it's all arranged?' Miss Preston asked, pursing her lips. 'My goodness, that was quick. I had to wait a month after my interview to hear I'd got the job. I should have thought they'd spend more time, not less, checking your credentials – what with you being foreign and everything.'

'I've been in contact with the British Embassy in Vienna for a while now,' Sophie replied. 'Long enough for my credentials to be thoroughly checked, I think.' She smiled in what she hoped was a placatory fashion, because there was no point making an enemy – especially not someone she was going to have to work with every day.

'If you say so.' Miss Preston flung open a door and stood back to let Sophie pass through. 'Well, here we are: the dining hall for clerical staff. Come and meet the girls.'

About forty or fifty people – mostly women, with a scattering of men – sat at long tables in a basement room that looked like it might once have been a crypt. Wide stone pillars supported a low vaulted ceiling, from which hung cast-iron lamps with only a few windows to let in natural light. Considering the standard of food she'd eaten in England so far, Sophie hadn't been holding out high hopes for the meal, but a delicious smell of roasting meat hung in the air and she allowed herself to become cautiously optimistic.

'The food here is very good,' Miss Preston said, as they made their way towards one of the tables. 'We often eat the same dishes as the royals. The menu's in French but I don't suppose that'll cause you any problems.'

'We were beginning to wonder what had happened to you,' said a tall, slender woman with her hair in an old-fashioned crop and a deep, melodious voice, turning around as Miss Preston sat down.

'I've been waiting for Miss Klein,' she replied, introducing Sophie to Mrs Johnstone-Burt and then Miss Maguire, her neighbour on the other side of the table: short and plump, with a cloud of pale hair like thistledown and watery, anxious eyes. Both of the older women were somewhere in their forties, Sophie estimated. Miss Maguire was assistant secretary to the Master of the Household, while Mrs Johnstone-Burt acted as secretary to the Queen when she was in residence at Windsor, and secretary to whoever needed one when Her Majesty wasn't.

'Miss Klein has come from Vienna to work in the library,' Miss Preston told them, adding, with a toss of her head, 'Apparently she has the very highest credentials so we're lucky to have her.'

'Vienna, eh?' Mrs Johnstone-Burt gave Sophie a searching look. 'I should imagine things are quite hairy there at the moment.'

'Now then, JB,' Miss Maguire warned, with an anxious frown. 'No politics at the luncheon table.'

'This is more than politics,' Mrs Johnstone-Burt replied. 'Mags, we can't ignore what's happening.'

'What are you talking about?' Miss Preston demanded, unfolding her napkin. 'What is happening in Vienna, and how do you know about it?'

'Hitler's invaded Austria,' Mrs Johnstone-Burt replied. 'And I know about it because I read the newspapers.'

'Oh, him,' Miss Preston said. 'He's mad, isn't he?' She turned to call one of the waiting staff. 'Now we must hurry if I'm to be back at the archive by two. Is that pork chops I smell?'

'I'm sorry to have made you late,' Sophie said. She glanced around the crowded room, aware of standing out from the other women in their neat costumes and smart shoes. Thankfully, nobody paid her much attention and Miss Preston, seemingly mollified by her apology, was a little kinder towards her for the rest of the meal. She had a fiancé, she soon informed Sophie, waving her be-ringed left hand, who worked in the Department of Supply and was responsible for making sure the Royal Family were suitably fed and watered. He would be overseeing the catering for several important events: the American ambassador and his wife were arriving at Windsor for a weekend visit, along with the Prime Minister, and then there was Royal Ascot, when the whole family and several guests stayed at the castle for the week, motoring over to the races each day.

'Poor Cyril's rushed off his feet,' Miss Preston said, 'making sure it all runs like clockwork. I doubt we shall have much time to spend together.'

Mrs Johnstone-Burt gave Sophie a sympathetic look. 'I imagine our social whirl might seem trivial to you in the present circumstances.'

'Not at all,' Sophie assured her, at the same time as Miss Preston exclaimed crossly, 'Trivial? Honestly, JB! Royal Ascot is the highlight of the social season, as you very well know.'

'I'm honoured to be part of the household,' Sophie added.

'Yes, I should think you are.' Miss Preston pushed back her chair. 'Now come along, Miss Klein. We can't keep the Needlewomen waiting.'

Sophie followed her obediently out of the dining hall, her mind busy. She had the measure of Miss Preston, she thought. Miss Maguire seemed harmless but Mrs Johnstone-Burt was a different proposition: kinder but cleverer, too, which made her dangerous. They'd all have to be kept at arm's length if she were to survive at the castle, and survive she would. Somehow she'd fetched up in one of the safest places in Britain, and she'd fight tooth and nail to stay there.

Chapter Seventeen

Sophie shifted on her chair, yawning. Dinner had finished and she could hear the clink of china and glass as footmen cleared remnants of the banquet from the dining room: the remaining crystal glasses, crumpled napkins and gold and silver vases of hothouse roses and sweet peas. She had peeked into the room as the long table was being prepared several hours before, and was dazzled by the quantity of gold cutlery laid out on an endless snowy tablecloth. The servants worked silently and fast, according to a well-established routine, and she'd watched for a while, mesmerised by their deft precision. How did the King and Queen feel, sitting at the head of this table? Did they accept this luxury as their due, or was the constant attention a burden?

'He didn't want to be king, you know,' Mrs Johnstone-Burt – JB – had told her, the other evening over bedtime cocoa. 'He hadn't been trained for it in the way his brother was, and that stammer makes everything more difficult for the poor man. If it weren't for his wife, he'd be lost.' JB clearly had a high regard for the Queen, although she wasn't as effusive as Miss Maguire – Mags – who 'simply adored' Elizabeth and was obviously jealous of JB's closeness to Her Majesty. (Miss Preston had no nickname – or at least not one the other two women chose to share – which made Sophie think they might not like her very much.)

The whine of bagpipes floated above a buzz of conversation from the drawing room next door and Sophie felt the usual pang of melancholy pierce her, like a knife to the heart. When the King and Queen were in residence at Windsor, the piper would play each morning to wake them, walking along the terrace outside Sophie's room, and she would be overwhelmed by emotion: a longing for the life she had left behind, grief for those she had lost, fear for the future. She'd written to Tamara Grossman, saying that although she hadn't found a job for her yet, she would keep trying and not lose hope. And one day she'd found a letter from Hanna resting in her pigeonhole: a hastily written page from the foster home, saying she'd arrived safely in America and was having fun with the other girls.

Alongside the pain of exile, there was beginning to burn in Sophie's heart a small, bright flame of hope that she could make something of her life. The castle had given her a chance to heal. She loved the very bones of the place: the solidity of those massive towers and impregnable doors; the secret maze of dimly lit underground passages, opening out into vast state rooms; the spiritual beauty of St George's Chapel, where she could sit for hours, lost in thought; the backdrop of lush countryside glimpsed through windows, so astonishingly green that it seemed unreal.

Sometimes she would wake at dawn and, impelled by some strange restlessness, slip outside to the Long Walk, heading for the Copper Horse statue of George III with his finger pointing back towards the castle. Herds of deer lying beneath the trees watched her pass, amorphous shapes in the half light. As soon as she made out the ominous figure, she would obey his command and turn to hurry home. The relief of slipping back through the trade gate and feeling the great walls surround her was exquisite. Her identity card, signed by the Master of the Household himself, gave her permission to move freely around the castle and its grounds, and many of the guards and policemen were already beginning to recognise her. She found herself looking out for one tall constable, in particular, who reminded her somehow of Wilhelm and would tease her in a brotherly way about her early starts, and wave if she ever turned back to see if he were watching. She had no desire to flirt but it was reassuring to feel someone was looking out for her.

Approaching footsteps and louder voices alerted Sophie to the royal party's approach. She stood, straightening her frock and tucking a strand of hair behind her ear, checking the arrangement of treasures laid out for guests to inspect. The Librarian had suggested they might like to see jewellery belonging to Mary, Queen of Scots, and the original blue garter after which the Order of the Garter was named – the order of chivalry celebrated on Garter Day at the castle in June. Sophie sometimes despaired at the amount of history she had to learn, but the Librarian had lent her books, and Mags and JB were near by to answer her questions. The three of them had adjoining rooms on the castle's north terrace and shared a sitting room with a couple of the other secretaries along the corridor; Miss Preston was living with her parents in the town while she and Cyril saved for their wedding.

A footman wearing a powdered wig opened the door to the Lantern Room and the King and Queen walked through.

Sophie curtsied before gazing hastily at a point on the opposite wall. Their Majesties didn't like being stared at when at home, Mags had told her, being the object of so much attention the rest of the time. One should be ready to spring forward when needed but otherwise aim to fade into the background, like a familiar but useful piece of furniture. The temptation to glance around was strong – there were other important guests, too, including the British Prime Minister – but Sophie resisted, her arms stiffly by her sides. She was there to answer any questions the guests might have and to make sure the precious relics were safely returned to the archive.

'Far too soon for so much responsibility,' Miss Preston had muttered sourly but JB had pointed out Sophie was the obvious choice, given that she lived above the shop, so to speak.

She could hear the King explaining the Order of the Garter to Mr Kennedy, the American ambassador, and the Queen telling Mrs Kennedy about the rivalry between Mary, Queen of Scots, and Elizabeth I, who imprisoned her and then ordered her execution.

'And now what have we here?' the Queen murmured, moving on to the next exhibit. Sophie's moment had come. It's a letter of condolence from Abraham Lincoln, Your Majesty,' she said, curtsying again. 'Written to Queen Victoria on the death of her husband, Prince Albert. I thought Mr and Mrs Kennedy might be interested to read it.'

'What a nice idea,' the Queen replied, smiling at Sophie with her head tilted. 'An example of the link between our two countries.'

She held herself with great dignity, and her eyes – when Sophie dared meet them – were intensely blue, her complexion dazzlingly clear. 'Don't be overawed,' Esme Slater had advised, yet although the Queen did indeed seem natural and kind, as Mags was always saying, it was impossible to forget her status.

'I haven't seen you before,' she went on, as Mrs Kennedy examined the letter. 'What is your name, my dear?'

'Sophie Klein, Ma'am.' Sophie dropped another curtsy. 'I've just started work in the Royal Library.'

'Well, I hope you'll be happy there,' the Queen said. 'The library is one of our favourite places. By the way,' she added, turning aside and lowering her voice, 'you don't have to curtsy every time you address me. Once is enough.'

'Yes, Ma'am.' In her confusion, Sophie found herself curtsying again and had to apologise, but the Queen only laughed and moved on.

Until then, Sophie had only glimpsed the King and Queen through a window, disembarking from an armoured motor car, but she had already met the princesses. Collecting the precious blue garter from its display case earlier that evening, the sound of children's voices had stopped her in her tracks. Hurrying through the library, she had found one young girl halfway up a tall sliding ladder, and another looking up at her from the ground. The girl on the ladder had been laughing at first but the laughter had died away and she was staring ahead, motionless, gripping the ladder with both hands.

'Margaret Rose, stop being silly and come down this minute!' the older girl called.

'I can't!' she wailed. 'I'm stuck.'

Her sister – for Sophie had worked out by now who the girls were – put her hands on her hips and said crossly, 'Well, you'd better get unstuck. You climbed up there so you can jolly well climb down.'

191

'Please, Lilibet,' Margaret pleaded. 'I'm going to fall.'

The older girl tutted and laid a tentative foot on the bottom rung of the ladder, glancing up uncertainly.

Sophie had visions of both princesses being marooned in mid-air or, worse, tumbling down together. 'Wait!' she cried. 'Hold on tight, Margaret, and I'll climb up to fetch you.'

Elizabeth stood aside, scrutinising Sophie without a word. There was no time to waste in pleasantries: hitching up her skirt, Sophie swarmed up the ladder until she was standing directly behind the little girl and could put an arm around her waist.

'I've got you,' she said cheerfully. 'Down we go, one step at a time.'

They made slow progress at first, but Margaret gradually gained confidence until she was able to jump off the last rung of the ladder and run to take her sister's hand. The two girls stared at Sophie, as though waiting to see how she'd react. They were lovely to look at, with creamy complexions and shining curly hair, dressed in identical print dresses – one blue, one green – with lace collars. Elizabeth wore stockings and Margaret ankle socks.

'Thank you for helping us,' the older girl said in a clear, composed voice. 'I don't believe we've met?'

'No, we haven't.' Was Sophie meant to curtsy? She decided not to, given the circumstances. 'My name is Miss Klein,' she went on, 'and I've recently arrived to work in the library.'

'Well, we're sorry to have disturbed you.' Elizabeth poked her sister's side. 'Aren't we, Margaret?'

'Thank you, Miss Klein,' Margaret said, quite unabashed, 'although I could have climbed down on my own, you know. I was just about to.'

Elizabeth tutted again but before she could speak, they

heard footsteps and turned to see a middle-aged woman with a harassed expression bustling towards them. 'There you are, girls,' she said, with an accent Sophie couldn't identify. 'I've been looking for you everywhere. It's time for tea, as you very well know.' She glanced at Sophie. 'I hope these two aren't getting in your way.'

'Not at all,' Sophie replied. 'It's been a pleasure to meet them.'

She watched as the girls were led off, Margaret breaking away to give the ladder a shove that sent it whizzing down the tracks and the nurse remonstrating with her. As they reached the doorway, Elizabeth turned back with a final, searching look. She was the most extraordinarily self-possessed child Sophie had ever met.

Sophie was to see more of the Royal Family over the coming days. Apart from weekends, they spent the week of Royal Ascot at the castle, along with many guests, and the whole household seemed to be *en fête*. There were strawberry-and-cream teas in the Orangery each afternoon after the races and dinner parties every night, accompanied by music from a military string band in the Minstrels' Gallery. At mid-day, a procession of cars with the King and Queen in the first would drive slowly down the Long Walk and through the park to Ascot, followed by a series of vans containing luncheon, prepared in the castle kitchens, that would be served in the Royal Box by a retinue of staff. Sophie didn't meet the princesses again, but she glimpsed them several times from a distance: playing with a couple of dogs on the lawn, wearing sunhats, or driving through the park in a pony and trap with their governess sitting behind. The Royal Family were closely guarded on trips outside the castle but within its grounds, the girls seemed to have more freedom than might have been expected.

The last evening of Ascot week, after all their guests had left, Sophie saw the King and Queen and their two daughters walking across the quadrangle towards their apartments in the golden evening light. The breath caught in her throat. They looked so ordinary: mother and father arm-in-arm, older daughter beside them and the younger girl running ahead. Margaret's charm and naughtiness reminded Sophie very much of Hanna, and for a moment she had the strange sensation of watching her own family from the outside. The Windsors seemed such a close unit, the four of them, just like the Kleins had once been. Did they know how lucky they were? Not because of all the pomp and pageantry but because they loved and supported each other, and they were safe. She couldn't allow herself to become bitter, yet she was disorientated; the life she had left and the one she led now were so far apart that both felt equally unreal. Whenever she was in company, Sophie was concentrating too hard on the persona she'd created – conventional, dull, dedicated – to think about anything else, but alone at night in her narrow bed, she would wonder who she actually was.

Hanna was the only one who knew the real Sophie Klein. Sophie had written several letters to the children's home in America and finally received another in return, resting in the pigeonhole she checked twice a day in the entrance hall of the north-terrace apartments. Her sister said she was well and happy and that she'd just had a hot dog with fried onions. The hot dog had obviously made a big impression because she drew it too, in a fat bun with lots of red and yellow sauce. The letter made Sophie sob because now she missed Hanna more desperately than ever. She longed for the feel of that warm, sleepy body in her arms, and the scent of Hanna's hair when she buried her face in its softness.

In the morning, Miss Maguire – who slept in the room next door – drew Sophie to one side on their way to breakfast in the dining room and said, 'Would you like to go to the pictures with JB and me this Saturday evening, Miss Klein? *Pygmalion* with Leslie Howard is coming to town and it's meant to be frightfully good.'

'How kind,' Sophie replied, momentarily flustered, 'but I have so much reading to catch up on that I'd better stay home. Thank you for thinking of me, though.'

'Another time, perhaps.' Mags gave her a sympathetic smile. 'Or maybe we could go for a cup of tea one Sunday? We should like to help you settle in and it must be terrifically hard for you, so far from your loved ones.' Her eyes were suspiciously shiny: she was prone to sentimental tears.

'Yet I feel very much at home already,' Sophie said. 'You and Mrs Johnstone-Burt have been so welcoming.'

The two women often invited Sophie for cocoa or tea in the secretaries' sitting room and seemed to take an almost maternal interest in her wellbeing, which had to be handled with care. Mags had a sewing machine and offered to take in Miss Ottoline's clothes. If Sophie was talking to her, she could deflect the conversation away from herself with a well-timed question about the Queen: her likes, for example (fishing, horse racing, gin and Dubonnet) and dislikes (lack of punctuality, slovenliness, highly spiced food). 'And the Duchess of Windsor?' Sophie once dared ask, but Mags shut up like a clam, so she never raised the subject again.

Mrs Johnstone-Burt, however, took a lively interest in Sophie's background and opinions, and was harder to distract. She wanted to know whether Sophie would like to attend a synagogue in town, or whether there were any dietary restrictions she might feel too shy to share with the housekeeper. In the end, Sophie had to assure JB that she was quite content, not particularly religious but loved evensong in St George's Chapel and preferred not to talk about Vienna, if that didn't seem rude, as the memories were too painful.

She knew their curiosity came from a place of kindness. The same could not be said of Miss Preston, unfortunately; the prickliness she had shown towards Sophie on her first day had only intensified. Luckily they didn't have too much to do with each other: Sophie spent most of her day upstairs in the Muniments Room while Miss Preston worked mainly in the office below. There were occasions, however, when the Librarian summoned them both to his study or asked Sophie to supply Miss Preston with documents for a forthcoming research visit, and the secretary was unfailingly brusque and offhand. Sophie toyed with the idea of asking Miss Preston whether she'd done anything to offend her, but decided that would be according her behaviour too much importance. And then one morning, matters came to a head.

Sophie had the use of a desk at the back of the office, underneath a noticeboard displaying various useful pieces of information. For some reason, a narrow table had been placed between the desk and the wall, putting the board out of reach and making the notices hard to read. Squinting at the lists for the umpteenth time, she had lost patience, pulled out the table and placed it at the end of her desk, forming an 'L' shape. Miss Preston happened to be out of the room and hadn't returned by the time Sophie went to lunch. She didn't appear in the dining room later but that

196

wasn't unusual; she'd sometimes spend her meal break in the town. Walking back into the office at two, Sophie found her standing motionless, staring at the new arrangement with her hands on her hips.

'Now at least we can pin things on the board,' she said pleasantly, making her way past Miss Preston to the desk. 'Those notices must be years out of date.'

'How dare you,' the secretary replied, in a low voice fraught with menace.

'I beg your pardon?' Sophie stared at her.

Miss Preston's ruby lips were set in a thin line and two bright spots of colour burned in her pale cheeks. 'This is my office, not yours,' she said, quivering with rage. 'If you want to make any changes, you must ask my permission.'

'But you don't use that desk,' Sophie objected. 'And surely this setup makes much more sense?'

'I have worked in the Royal Archives for five years,' Miss Preston went on. 'My mother worked in the castle kitchens for eight and my grandmother was a housemaid here when Queen Victoria was on the throne. You have been here five minutes and you're German.' She spat out the word.

'Austrian, actually,' Sophie said.

Miss Preston ignored her. 'You must put the table back exactly as it was before. Immediately.'

Sophie considered her options before deciding now was not the moment or the issue on which to take a stand. 'All right,' she said. 'If you insist.'

It took a minute or two for her to return the furniture to its original position, under Miss Preston's furious gaze. 'I'm sorry to have upset you,' Sophie said when the job was done. 'It's just a table.'

'This is Windsor Castle,' Miss Preston replied through

gritted teeth. 'It is *never* just a table, or a chair, or anything else. We are talking tradition, and precedence, and years of history that you can't possibly understand. I don't know exactly what you're doing here but the sooner you go back where you came from, the better.'

It was a ludicrously heated argument over something so trivial and Sophie might have laughed, had she not realised the depth of Miss Preston's animosity towards her. She had inadvertently made an enemy in the household and that was the last thing she needed. Miss Preston might be ridiculous but she could prove to be dangerous, too.

Chapter Eighteen

Windsor Castle, June 1938

Sophie spent her first few weeks at Windsor familiarising herself with the letters, state reports, household accounts and private diaries stored in the Royal Archives, going back hundreds of years. The Librarian also showed her the castle's Royal Bindery, where several men were kept busy repairing and conserving books under the direction of an expert bookbinder from Venice. He asked her to keep track of their progress and identify other volumes needing attention, since this was another area in which the department had fallen behind. Sophie was careful never to imply that his previous assistant had been remiss in any way, because she had (inevitably) been a great friend of Miss Preston, who still visited her now that she was married and living in the town. Sophie and Miss Preston kept each other at arm's length but managed an adequate working relationship, interacting only when strictly necessary and occasionally going so far as to comment on the weather. When she was in the office, as opposed to up in the Muniments Room, Sophie was aware of Miss Preston's simmering resentment on the other side of the room, and it made her nervous. Many of the other staff were suspicious of her accent, she could tell, and opinion could easily be whipped up against her.

At mealtimes, Sophie sat with Mags and JB or on her own with a book, while Miss Preston had taken to eating with the Department of Supply in the basement of the Clarence Tower. Each of the towers had its own function and staff – its own personality, almost – down to the house- and kitchenmaids. The princesses, Mags had told Sophie, slept with their nurses in the Lancaster Tower when they came to visit, some distance from their parents' apartments: a forbidding place with stone staircases and winding passages that must have been freezing in winter.

When Sophie could find her way around the archive and was known to the housekeeper, the Superintendent of the Castle and other senior members of staff, the Librarian took her to Frogmore House, beyond the golf course across the Home Park.

'Miss Klein is to be given access to all parts of the house and its contents,' he told the housekeeper who let them in. 'She's acting on my authority.'

'But these here boxes that have arrived from the Duke are his private things for safekeeping,' the woman replied. 'Not intended for the archive, I believe.'

'Nevertheless, Mrs Bruton, they must all be assessed if they're to be stored here,' he said. 'We've come across state papers among his possessions before.'

'If you say so.' The woman looked Sophie up and down, pursing her lips. She was tall and thin, with sloping shoulders and an expression that would have curdled milk.

Several times in the course of that first morning, Sophie had caught Mrs Bruton watching her from the doorway, her arms folded. 'Thank you,' she'd said eventually, getting up to close the door. 'If I need any help, I shall come and find you.'

She'd surprised herself with her own daring, but the world hadn't come to an end: she'd heard Mrs Bruton's footsteps retreating down the corridor, and the housekeeper hadn't come near her for the rest of the day.

Frogmore House looked imposing from the outside: an elegant white mansion in the Palladian style, set in beautiful grounds overlooking a lake. Inside, however, the rooms were small and cluttered, crammed with ill-assorted furniture and collections of porcelain ornaments, waxed fruits and flowers under glass domes, stuffed birds and small animals. Glassy-eyed stags' heads watched Sophie disapprovingly as she crouched on the dusty carpet in one of the upstairs bedrooms, going through the Duke of Windsor's belongings. She shivered at the thought of his reaction, could he have seen her.

Having read many of the Duke's letters and papers in the archive already, she'd formed an opinion of his character and it wasn't favourable. He came across as vain, self-centred, thoughtless and capricious: prone to changing his mind on a whim at the last minute. About half the crates he'd sent back contained winter clothes and boots, and the rest were filled with books, papers and correspondence. There were endless accounts from his tailor and bootmaker, folders of reports and letters – including some unpleasant anonymous messages from someone claiming to be the Duke's illegitimate child – and several scrapbooks of press cuttings covering his travels as Prince of Wales. A clipping from *Men's Wear* magazine of April 1924 proclaimed, 'The average young man in America is more interested in the clothes of the

Prince of Wales than in any other individual on earth.' Someone had underlined the sentence and added two exclamation marks in the margin.

Sophie opened every crate to see what was inside, reading odd snippets here and there when curiosity got the better of her. They would all have to be numbered, the contents methodically catalogued and any items of historical significance extracted for the Librarian's perusal. The books would have to be examined particularly carefully, for the Duke had a habit of slipping letters between their pages to preserve them.

After supper that evening, she walked back to her room with JB and asked whether she might pick her brains.

'Of course.' JB looked delighted. 'Fire away. Anything you like.'

'There is so much I don't know about the abdication,' Sophie began. 'I don't wish to pry but it would be useful to talk to someone who was here during that time.'

'I understand.' JB opened her door. 'You'd better come in and sit down. We might be a while.'

Sophie took the only chair and looked around the room, identical in size to hers but so much cosier. The overhead light had a pink fringed shade which cast a soft glow, and paintings hung on every inch of the wall. The floor was covered in a mosaic of rag rugs, and framed family photographs jostled for space on the chest of drawers and bedside table.

'I have a lot of nephews and nieces,' JB explained as she made herself comfortable on the bed, settling a cushion behind her back and crossing one leg over the other. 'And this room has been my home for nearly ten years.'

'It's lovely,' Sophie replied, contrasting the homely clutter with her monastic cell next door but one.

'Too many nick-nacks; the housekeeper despairs of me. Now, the abdication.' JB fixed Sophie with a beady look. 'This is strictly between ourselves, you understand? I'm not one to gossip but as part of the household, you should know the state of affairs.'

'Naturally.' Sophie's eyes watered in her attempt to look trustworthy.

And so JB began to talk. It had been an extraordinary time, she said, for the country as well as the Royal Family. Edward had been a handsome and charismatic Prince of Wales and was widely popular, despite reports of his playboy antics and affairs with married women. Sowing his wild oats, people said; he would settle down once he was king. His infatuation with Wallis Simpson had seemed just another flash in the pan, so it was a tremendous shock to discover that he was prepared to renounce the throne for her. Many felt him to be leaving his country in the lurch, valuing personal happiness over duty and putting his brother in the most awful predicament. Queen Mary, the Queen Mother, had been devastated, and of course poor Bertie and Elizabeth's lives were turned upside down, not to mention Lilibet's – and Margaret's, to a lesser degree. They had to leave their family home in Piccadilly and move into Buckingham Palace, for one thing, and swap their beloved weekend retreat, Royal Lodge in the Great Park, for austere Windsor Castle.

'And Edward seemed to have no idea what he'd done!' JB declared. 'After he and his brothers had signed the Intent of Abdication, he just shook hands with them and walked out of Fort Belvedere, cool as a cucumber.'

Sophie hadn't yet visited the Fort, Edward's Windsor retreat when Prince of Wales, where he would entertain his mistresses and hold riotous parties. The Librarian had said most of his belongings had been moved to Frogmore House, although the Fort might be worth a look later.

'And what about after the abdication?' she pressed JB. 'What did he do next?'

'Well, Mrs Simpson was still married – to her second husband, incidentally – so he had to keep away from her until she was divorced. He went to stay with Kitty Rothschild in her castle near Vienna for a few months. Apparently he was a difficult house guest, complaining about being bored, running up huge bills and expecting Kitty to settle them. He and the Duchess are obsessed with money. They have expensive tastes and don't like paying for them.' JB smiled. 'But now I'm straying into the realms of gossip. You must excuse my feelings – I've seen the havoc that pair can cause, always demanding this or that and claiming to be hard done by. The King won't have his brother's phone calls put through anymore, and who can blame him.'

'And where do they live now?' Sophie asked.

'In France. At this precise moment, I believe they're cruising around the Riviera on a yacht, dining in Cannes every evening.' She looked around her room, dappled in the evening sunlight. 'I wouldn't swap my life for theirs, though, not for all the tea in China. They have no real friends, you know, only hangers-on.'

Sophie went back to Frogmore House the next afternoon, letting herself in with the key she'd been given.

'Back again,' the housekeeper observed, emerging from her room beside the kitchen.

'As you see, Mrs Bruton,' she replied pleasantly. 'I'll be here for weeks if not months, I should imagine.'

Upstairs, the room looked much as she'd left it the day before, the crates stacked neatly together, but the hammer and screwdriver she'd used to lever up their lids were missing from the windowsill, where she'd made a point of putting them so they'd be to hand. She eventually found them on the floor, beside the crate containing the scrapbooks. A splinter of wood had been gouged from the lid and when she opened the box again, she could tell instantly that something – or things – had been removed from it. The crate had previously been crammed to the brim; now there were three or four clear inches of space at the top. She sat back on her heels, wondering what to do. Mrs Bruton was the only other person who held keys to this room, which Sophie had definitely locked the night before, but it was pointless to accuse her of interfering without any evidence. She replaced the lid, pushed the box to one side and pulled a ledger from her bag.

'Would you like a cup of tea, Miss?' The housekeeper's voice made her jump.

'No, thank you,' Sophie replied neutrally. 'I've just had one.'

'Well, call me if you need anything. You've quite a job ahead of you.' Mrs Bruton turned to leave. 'Best let you get on with it.'

The housekeeper's husband was a groundsman and they lived in a cottage on the estate, Sophie found out that evening. Chances were, whatever had been removed from that crate – and maybe others – was still in Frogmore House; it would be dangerous to take anything from the premises and risk being accused of theft. She would come back at the weekend when the place was empty and have a thorough search without Mrs Bruton watching her like a hawk. Early

Sunday morning, that would be the best time. On Saturday, she was making her first trip to London to meet Aunt Jane, and that assignation was taking up her mind to the exclusion of almost everything else.

The week before, her heart had leapt at the sight of an envelope in her pigeonhole. She didn't recognise the spidery handwriting, nor the photograph that fell out of the card inside – two kittens in a basket – of a smiling elderly lady with white hair, wearing a feather-trimmed pillbox hat.

Dear Sophie,
   I'm so glad to hear you've arrived safely in England and would like to invite you for tea on Saturday 18 June. I'll meet you at four on the third floor of the Lyons Corner House in Coventry Street, Piccadilly, if that's convenient. If not, please telephone Battersea 4732.

   PS: I've aged a great deal since we last met, and enclose a photograph so you'll recognise me.

Sophie had bought a frame for the photograph from Woolworths in the town, and displayed it next to the snapshot of her family at Lake Achensee. 'My Aunt Jane, an old family friend,' she would tell anyone who cared to ask. Of course, nobody did. She had no visitors and the contents of her room remained a mystery to the outside world – which was probably just as well, since she had removed a loose brick halfway up the chimney breast and hidden her father's Mauser behind it. Only Miss Maguire, walking past her open door one morning, spotted the photograph and exclaimed, 'What a charming lady! Your grandmother, perhaps?'

Sophie put her right, wondering briefly whether Aunt Jane might truly become a friend before dismissing the idea; theirs would be a working relationship and friendship was a luxury she'd have to learn to live without.

This trip to London was the first time she'd left Windsor, and she set off for the station after lunch with some excitement and a dash of trepidation. At least now she looked a little more like everyone else: the housekeeper had given her a couple of skirts and blouses from lost property, and an advance on her wages meant she had been able to buy a smarter pair of shoes and a hat for the outing.

The Corner House café in Piccadilly was an imposing four-storey building with a white-and-gold frontage. Sophie pushed open the brass revolving door and entered a familiar world: tables laden with china and silver teapots, potted palms, and waitresses in black frocks, white aprons and caps hurrying to and fro with stacks of plates balanced halfway up their arms. A string quartet was playing in the lobby and an odour of fried food and cigarette smoke hung in the air, rather than the enticing smell of coffee. Adjusting her expectations, Sophie took the stairs to the third floor, where every table seemed to be occupied by identically dressed women in coats and hats, despite the warmth of the day. She hovered on the threshold, scanning the crowd, until she saw someone wave and recognised the jaunty pillbox hat Aunt Jane had worn in her photograph. Waving back, she hurried towards the table with a thrill of anticipation.

'So lovely to see you,' the old lady said, rising from her seat to kiss Sophie on the cheek. 'How are you, dear? Settling in?'

And Sophie felt her spirits rise, as though Aunt Jane really were an old friend who cared about her. She sat down and let herself be fussed over, the waitress summoned for a menu and a cup of tea poured.

'Thank you but I won't have anything to eat,' she said. 'I had a big lunch. The food at Windsor is really very good.' She glanced around to see who was within earshot but the other customers – mostly women – were deep in conversation and no one seemed to be paying her much attention.

'When we've had our tea, I thought we might go for a walk in Green Park,' said Aunt Jane. 'It might be easier to talk there. This room is a little noisy and my hearing isn't what it was. But tell me about your work in the library. Is it interesting, and have you made friends?'

They chatted for half an hour or so, Sophie describing her duties in general terms, the people she had met and day-to-day life in the castle. 'I still can't get used to having every meal cooked for me or my bedroom cleaned,' she said. 'Of course we had a maid in Vienna, but she never went into my room.'

'Yes, you must make sure not to leave personal items lying about,' Aunt Jane replied. 'That would be careless in the extreme.' And Sophie caught a glimpse of some inner steel that made her think this was not a woman to be crossed, despite her mild demeanour. 'Now let me call for the bill,' she went on, raising her arm, 'and we can take a turn around the park.'

Considering her age, she set a brisk pace; Sophie had to hurry to keep up. They crossed the road by the winged statue pointing his bow down Lower Regent Street and walked along Piccadilly, past the enticing windows of Fortnum and Mason's and a liveried doorman standing outside The Ritz hotel, and turned left into Green Park.

Aunt Jane glanced behind after they'd walked a fair

distance, and Sophie did, too. 'Try not to make it so obvious,' the old lady said, in an entirely different tone of voice. 'You could hardly look more furtive if you tried.'

Sophie began to apologise but Aunt Jane cut her off. 'It's all right, let's not waste time. Do you have anything significant to report?'

Sophie marshalled her thoughts. 'So far I've just been getting to know the archive, but some boxes have arrived from the Duke of Windsor in France. They're being stored in Frogmore House and I'm about to examine them in detail. I believe at least one has been tampered with since I first saw it.'

'By whom?'

'Possibly the housekeeper – she's the only one with a key to the room, as far as I'm aware.'

'We know about those crates,' Aunt Jane told her. 'Do what you can to check the contents and track down whatever's missing. If someone else is after those documents, they must be important. It's vital you find them before they fall into the wrong hands.'

And how was she meant to do that? Sophie wondered, with Miss Preston – and probably half the household besides – already convinced she was a German spy and watching her every move? 'I'll do my best,' she promised. 'Can you give me a rough idea what I'm looking for?'

A middle-aged couple strolled by, arm-in-arm. Aunt Jane took Sophie by the elbow, steering her off the path and across the grass towards the bandstand.

'You'll know it when you find it,' she said. 'Remember the telephone number I sent you?' Sophie nodded. 'Memorise it and destroy the card. If you need to speak to someone urgently, ring that number. Whoever replies, even if it's me, say, "The Sachertorte is delicious," and they'll reply, "It is my grandmother's recipe." If they don't keep to that exact wording, put the receiver down.'

She released Sophie's arm, looked around again as if casually taking the air, and said, 'Well, dear, this has been lovely. We must meet again soon. I'll drop you a line, but in the meantime do telephone me whenever you feel the need.'

'Thank you, Aunt Jane,' Sophie replied. 'I'll be sure to let you know if anything crops up.'

She watched her pretend aunt walk away, shoulders rounded and her gait more uncertain: just another unremarkable elderly lady, enjoying a sunny afternoon in the park. Sophie turned in the other direction, making her way back to The Ritz. She asked the doorman where she might find the bar and once there, bought a brandy and drank it down in one. What had seemed – well, not quite a game, but certainly a distant hypothetical situation, had suddenly become frighteningly real. And she was alone, that much was clear, with nothing but her wits to rely on.

Chapter Nineteen

Windsor Castle, June 1938

'There she is, Little Miss Rise and Shine. Where are you off to so early in the morning?'

The tall policeman, the one who made Sophie's heart beat a little faster, was smiling at her from under his helmet.

'Oh, just library business,' she replied, handing over her identity card. 'Nothing particularly exciting.'

'And what have you got in there?' He gestured towards the basket she was carrying. 'Goodies for your grandmother? You'd better watch out for the big bad wolf.'

The smile faded from her face. 'It's my ledger,' she said, taking the book out and showing it to him. 'Would you like to look through it?'

'It's all right, I trust you.' He nodded. 'Bye for now, Miss Klein.'

'And what is your name, Officer?' she asked.

'PC Dedham. But you can call me Henry.' And he had the nerve to wink at her.

'Well, PC Dedham,' she said, 'if you have any doubts

about my credentials, I suggest you speak to the Royal Librarian, who will vouch for me. Good day.'

She turned to leave without waiting for him to reply, her cheeks burning. What a fool she'd been! He'd only been watching her because he wanted to know what she was up to, coming and going at strange times. And he was condescending, too. Little Miss Rise and Shine, indeed! Still, it was a timely reminder that she should be more careful. She skirted the edge of the golf course and took the lane past Frogmore Cottage to the big house, cutting across fields to approach from the back and stopping for a moment under cover of a group of trees to look around. Frogmore Cottage was uninhabited at the moment, as far as she knew – the Brutons living elsewhere on the estate – but she wanted to make sure no one was following her.

It was shortly after seven on a glorious summer morning and the scene was picture perfect: two swans gliding on the lake, the mansion behind a dazzling white in the sunshine. She stopped for a moment to feel its warmth on her skin, imagining herself and Hanna sitting on the grass for a picnic: their mother's rolls, fresh butter and a hunk of cheese, red-skinned apples. After they ate – no, it would have to be before, for the sake of their digestion – they would plunge into the glassy water for a swim, the mud silky between their toes. One day, she would make this happen.

When she opened her eyes to see the tall arched windows of the house staring loftily back at her, for a moment she felt like taking the biggest rock she could find and hurling it through them. What use was a place of this size and beauty if nobody lived there? The waste of it all suddenly revolted her, along with the ignorance and complacency of the people she lived among.

'Don't you know what is happening?' she would shout, standing on a chair in the vaulted dining room. 'While you fuss about second helpings of pudding and free passes for Ascot, Hitler is taking over Europe!' He had his sights set on Czechoslovakia next, that was common knowledge, claiming Germans were living there who wanted to be reunited with the fatherland.

But this country has given you sanctuary, said a small voice inside her head; you should be grateful. Unclenching her fists, she let out a long, shaky breath and came back to her senses. Now was not the time for histrionics. She walked back along the lane to the front of the house and, glancing briefly around, let herself in.

'Mrs Bruton?' she called, walking across the echoing, high-ceilinged hall. 'It's me, Miss Klein.'

Nobody answered, and there was no reply when she knocked on the door of the housekeeper's room. She called again and listened, putting her ear to the wood, but all was still and quiet on the other side. The door, however, was locked, and so was that of the adjoining kitchen – despite Mrs Bruton having been told Sophie should have access to all parts of the house. She ran lightly up the stairs to see whether any of the crates had been interfered with since she'd left them on Friday – they hadn't, as far as she could tell – and to check the place was indeed deserted. Once reassured, she slipped downstairs and out of a side door to the back of the house, looking for an open window or a door she might force to gain entry. No luck there but, prowling along the terrace, Sophie discovered a chute dropping down two or three feet to what looked like an abandoned coal cellar. She could dimly make out steps at the other end, which should, if she'd calculated correctly, lead up into the kitchen. She peered down and, before she could lose her nerve, bunched up her skirt in one hand and slid down, landing with a thump on the rough stone floor and skinning her knee in the process. Swearing, she rubbed off the dirt and limped towards the stairs – only to find that the door at the top of them was bolted from the other side and wouldn't budge, no matter how hard she shook it.

Worse was to come. The coal chute down which she had so impulsively – and stupidly – slid was completely smooth, without the slightest possibility of a foot- or handhold. It was ridiculous: the rim wasn't far above her head but she couldn't reach it, no matter how hard she tried, leaping up and scrabbling for purchase. The only thing she found that might possibly be used as a step was a pallet covered in green mould that collapsed as soon as she stood on it, and although the cellar floor was covered in rubble, she couldn't scrape enough stones together to raise herself higher than a few inches. She gazed up at the mocking blue circle of sky, imagining being stuck down here until the next day – or maybe even longer, if Mrs Bruton didn't hear or chose not to rescue her – and, throwing caution to the winds, let out a despairing cry.

Nobody answered.

'Help!' she screamed again, her voice reverberating around the dank, dark walls. Silence. She launched herself at the chute for one last try, scrabbling frantically at its slippery surface before dropping to the ground.

And then, to her surprise and joy, she heard the sound of footsteps crunching over gravel and, seconds later, saw the sky darken as a face peered down at her, blocking out the light.

'Well, if it isn't Miss Klein,' said PC Dedham. 'Fancy meeting you here.'

She stared back at him, the excuse she'd been preparing dying on her lips.

'Since when did library business include fossicking about in a coal cellar?' he asked, relishing the moment. 'Looking for overdue books? You won't find any down there.'

'If you'd care to help me out, I can explain,' she said stiffly, hands on her hips.

'With pleasure. I can't wait to hear what you come up with.' He dropped to his knees, taking off his helmet and jacket, then lay flat on his stomach and stretched both arms down towards her. When she reached up, standing on tiptoes, he was able to grab her by the wrists and, grunting with effort, haul her up in one swift motion and deposit her beside him on the ground – as though he were landing a fish.

'Thank you.' She sat up, then got to her feet and scrambled a safe distance away, brushing herself down.

He stood, too, shrugging on his jacket and fastening the buttons. 'I knew you were up to something. Come on, out with it – and the truth this time. I shall find out sooner or later so you might as well tell me now.'

'This is a question of national security,' Sophie began, trying to sound official despite the state of her: cobwebby clothes, bleeding knee, hair all over the place. 'I'm examining some boxes that have arrived from the Duke of Windsor at the request of the Royal Librarian. I have reason to believe at least one of the crates has been tampered with and an item or items removed.'

He looked at her sceptically. 'And hidden in the cellar?'

Sophie blushed. 'No, in the housekeeper's room, which is locked. I was trying to gain access via the coal chute.'

She could see the policeman trying not to smile. 'Not the best idea. I'd advise against a career in burglary, Miss Klein.'

'I wasn't considering one,' she replied, dabbing at a rivulet of blood trickling into her sock.

'Here, use this.' He passed her a pristine, neatly folded handkerchief. She was aware of his eyes on her as she shook it out and tied it around her leg. 'Better give that knee a good wash when you get home.'

'Will you help me, PC Dedham?' she asked. 'I must find out if anything has been taken from those boxes. Can you force a lock? I have a key to the front door of the house but that only gets us so far.'

'I know you do; I watched you use it.' He sighed. 'This isn't the right way of going about things. I should escort you off the premises and return with a search warrant.'

'There's no time!' Sophie could have shaken him. 'And this information is probably top secret – it has to be retrieved immediately and handed over to the Librarian, on the orders of the King. You could end up in serious trouble by involving anyone else.'

PC Dedham gazed at her, and then into the distance. 'Very well,' he said eventually. 'Can't believe I'm saying this, but we could give it a go.'

'Thank you.' Sophie had already turned back towards the house.

'Just a minute, Miss.' She felt his hand heavy on her shoulder. 'You're still under suspicion. Don't even think about bolting off on your own.'

'So I think we can safely say that if any documents *have* been taken from that crate – which I'm beginning to doubt – they haven't been hidden here.'

PC Dedham looked around the housekeeper's room, sparsely furnished with a desk, an easy chair, a standard lamp and a butler's sink in the corner. The desk drawers contained an accounts book from 1927, a pen with a splayed nib and a dried-up bottle of ink, three pencil stubs and a block of blue chalk used for powdering billiard cues. Copies of *Mrs Beeton's Book of Household Management* and *Murder on the Orient Express* by Agatha Christie sat on the leather surface. A pantry behind a beaded curtain to the side was similarly bare, its shelves containing only a meat safe (empty), several milk churns and jugs of various sizes. The only consolation was that it had been the work of a moment for him to force the lock with the aid of a Swiss Army knife.

'So what do I do now?' he asked Sophie. 'Let you off with a caution, I suppose.'

'But I haven't done anything wrong,' she objected.

'I don't know . . . Breaking and entering a cellar? We could probably make it stick.'

She couldn't tell whether he was joking. 'I don't understand it,' she said. 'I'm sure something's been taken and I'm just as sure we'll find it somewhere here.'

She walked through a side door into the great empty kitchen, copper pans hanging from hooks on the wall and bowls that probably hadn't been used for years ranged according to size along the shelves. The atmosphere was even more mournful than anywhere else in the house: as though the room was waiting to be brought back to life, like the kitchen in Sleeping Beauty's castle. She gazed out of the window, rubbing her arms for warmth, and caught sight of a small domed building set into a slope not far from the lake. It was almost hidden in the undergrowth.

'What's that?' she asked PC Dedham, who had come to stand beside her.

He squinted, following her finger. 'Oh yes, I see. An ice house, at a guess. They'll cut ice from the lake in winter and store it there to use through the summer.'

Sophie couldn't take her eyes off the stone igloo, which might have been a home for pixies: it seemed to be calling to her. Who would bother to search a derelict outbuilding, or even notice it? In a matter of seconds, she'd unbolted the kitchen door and run outside, with PC Dedham following in hot pursuit, and took only a few minutes more to reach the little stone house. Somebody had been here recently: a tuft of grass on the threshold had been trampled, and a bramble torn from the bush that arched overhead. The wooden door was unlocked. With a bit of effort, she was able to push it open and bend double to peer inside. The cold, dank air hit her like a slap although there was no ice stored there now, as far as she could tell. In the dim light filtering around her through the doorway, she could just make out discarded sacking and a pile of bricks lying on the floor. PC Dedham asked her to stand aside and produced a torch from his breast pocket, playing its beam around the cavern.

'There!' Sophie cried, grabbing his hand in her excitement and directing the light towards a dark, solid rectangle propped near the back wall, its edges straight and symmetrical. She dropped to all fours and crawled towards it, gasping momentarily from the pain of her injured knee. Reaching forward as the torchlight threw flickering shadows on the wall, her hand met a smooth surface. The object wasn't particularly heavy, she discovered, dragging it towards her and clutching it to her chest as she shuffled out backwards.

'You should have let me go,' he said, when she emerged. 'Look at the state of you!'

Sophie glanced down. 'I'm sorry about your handkerchief.' It was black with dirt, spattered now with fresh blood.

He reached for the booty in her arms. 'I should like to take a look at that first, if you don't mind.'

Reluctantly, Sophie handed over the slim leather satchel. Now she remembered having seen it beneath the scrapbooks a couple of days before; she hadn't been able to open the clasp, which seemed to be locked or stuck. PC Dedham made short work of it now with his magic penknife. He drew out a sheaf of documents, glanced at them and then at Sophie before returning them to the case and passing it back to her.

'You understand I can't let you take these papers away,' he said, 'but you might as well see what they are.'

Sophie thought quickly. 'I need to deliver them to the Royal Librarian. He lives on the estate, I think?' The policeman nodded. 'We could go together. But first I have to see what we're dealing with – there may be letters that need translating. You can watch me, if you like.'

They walked back to the house in silence, bolting the kitchen door from the inside and exiting through the housekeeper's room. 'She might notice her door's been tampered with,' he said, 'but there's nothing to be done about that now.'

How did Mrs Bruton, or somebody working with her, know to extract this particular case? Sophie wondered. Could she have telephoned the Duke and received instructions from him, or had she always been aware of its importance?

They went upstairs to the bedroom where the crates were stored and where Sophie had left her basket and ledger. She showed PC Dedham the damaged crate and, while he inspected that and the other boxes, pulled a chair up to the dressing table at which she'd been working, took out the contents of the leather case and began to read.

All the papers spread out before her related to the Duke and Duchess's visit to Germany in the autumn of the year before. There were several handwritten pages, describing visits to hospitals, housing projects and youth camps in various German cities – even a beer hall in Munich. These accounts were told in the third person, emphasising the rapturous reception that greeted the Windsors everywhere they went and portraying the Duke as the champion of the working classes, both English and German. At last Wallis was greeted with the deference she deserved, noted the reporter, addressed everywhere as 'Her Royal Highness', the title denied her in Britain. There followed a few typewritten accounts of these same tours, with names and other details filled in. Nothing very startling, Sophie thought, leafing through – until she came across a slim sheaf of cream paper, typed in German, and the hairs stood on the back of her neck.

She must have gasped, because PC Dedham turned from the window and asked, 'Everything all right?'

'Fine,' she said, collecting herself. 'I just knocked my knee against the table. But there is a document here that needs translating before I present it to the Librarian.' She held up the pages. 'Do you see? If you can give me half an hour or so, that should be plenty.'

He nodded and she set to work, concentrating only on the report in front of her, her pen scratching across the pages of her ledger. Occasionally she heard the policeman yawn, or turn over the pages of some book he might have taken from the crate, but she didn't turn to look or stop writing. At last she put the cap back on her pen, the ledger in her basket and stood, her head swimming.

'Thank you, I am finished now. Shall we go?' And she passed him the leather satchel. 'You can check that everything is in place.'

They went downstairs, Sophie stopping briefly in the bathroom to bathe her knee which, she was now aware, had begun to throb. She retied the bandage, did what she could to tidy her hair and set off with her police escort.

'The house is a couple of miles away,' PC Dedham told her. 'Will you be all right to walk?'

In the event, however, she didn't have to, because he flagged down a car taking choristers to St George's Chapel and persuaded the driver to make a diversion. Being a policeman had its advantages, Sophie thought, squashed next to Henry Dedham on the front seat. She wasn't sure what he made of her now.

The Librarian lived in a stone house covered with wisteria, a couple of miles from Frogmore. Sophie rang the bell and stood back, realising what a strange pair she and PC Dedham must make. Certainly the smartly dressed woman who came to the door, pulling on her gloves, looked startled to see them.

'May I speak with the Librarian?' Sophie asked. 'It's Miss Klein. I'm sorry to bother you on a Sunday but this is urgent.'

They were shown into a sunny sitting room, with newspapers and empty cups on a side table. The air smelt of coffee and toast, and Sophie's stomach growled; she hadn't had anything to eat since the evening before. She sat on the edge of the sofa while PC Dedham stood by the mantelpiece, looking about. They heard the woman calling, then a muttered conversation somewhere above and footsteps hurrying down the stairs.

'Miss Klein, is everything all right?' the Librarian asked, striding into the room with his collar upturned and a tie in his hand. 'And who is this?'

PC Dedham stepped forward and introduced himself, showing his warrant card. Sophie gave her side of the story while he chipped in to add any relevant (although in her view, mostly unnecessary) details.

'But the long and short of it is, we've found documents that Miss Klein thought should be handed straight to you,' PC Dedham finished.

'Confidential documents,' Sophie added.

'Thank you,' the Librarian said. 'Might I ask you to step outside for a moment while Miss Klein and I have a private conversation?'

When they were alone, Sophie took out the papers and laid them on the coffee table. 'These are reports of the Windsors' trip to Germany last year,' she said, fanning them out. 'Nothing particularly significant. But this,' and she took out the sheaf of cream pages, closely typed in German, 'seems to be a transcript of a private meeting between the Duke and Herr Hitler at Berchtesgaden.'

'Good God.' The Librarian stared at the text in disbelief.

At that moment there was a knock on the door and the woman who had let them in, now wearing a hat, put her head around it. 'Sorry to interrupt, darling,' she said, 'but we'll be late for church if we don't leave now.'

'Something's come up,' he replied, his voice strained. 'You'll have to go on without me, I'm afraid. Ask that young policeman to come back for a moment, would you?' He shuffled the papers back together in a pile and sat looking at them as though they might catch fire.

'You called for me, sir?' PC Dedham came in, taking out his notebook as though ready for action.

'Thank you for your help,' the Librarian replied, 'but you can leave this matter with me. There's no need for an official report. Is that clear? If there are any difficulties, I'll speak to your superior, but Miss Klein has been following my instructions and acted properly. Her work is authorised by the Superintendent of the Castle.'

'Of course.' The policeman tucked the notebook back in his breast pocket. 'Shall I escort you back to the castle, Miss Klein?'

'She'll be staying here with me for the next little while,' the Librarian said firmly. 'Good day, Constable.'

When the two of them were alone in the house, he took Sophie through to a study, its shelves lined with books and a typewriter on the desk. 'I'd be obliged if you could translate this document,' he said, handing her back the transcript. 'There's paper here and a pen, in case you want to make a rough copy before you type it up. Do you need anything else?'

'Might I have a cup of tea?' Sophie asked. 'I didn't have time for breakfast this morning.'

'Good heavens, yes, of course. The least we can do. I'll see if the cook's about.'

He hurried off, reappearing later with a tray laden with a teapot, milk jug, cup and saucer, and a plate piled high with buttered toast. 'Just call me if you need anything else.'

'Thank you, sir.' Sophie wound a sheet of paper into the typewriter. 'How many copies would you like, though? I couldn't find any carbon paper.'

'One will do.'

It took Sophie a couple of hours to finish the translation to her satisfaction. From time to time, the Librarian put his head around the door to see how she was getting on, and finally she was able to hand him a reasonably well-typed document, together with the cream-coloured original.

'Marvellous, Miss Klein,' he said, putting them both in a new manila envelope. 'I'm extremely grateful to you for handling this matter so efficiently.'

Sophie didn't need to ask whether this transcript would end up in the Royal Archives; she had a strong suspicion she'd never see either her translation or the original again. The sentiments expressed were so shocking, they could surely never be made public.

By this time, the Librarian's wife had come back from church and the invisible cook had put Sunday lunch in the oven. Sophie was invited to stay but said she was a little tired and would get back to the castle, if they didn't mind, so the Librarian gave her a lift home.

'Thank you, Miss Klein,' he said as he dropped her off. 'You have done the Royal Family a great service, and the country, too. Perhaps greater than you realise.'

'My pleasure,' she replied, with a faintly puzzled expression she thought he would find reassuring. 'See you tomorrow, sir.'

She went straight to her room without bumping into anyone, luckily, and shut the door. Untucking her blouse, she removed from her liberty bodice the pages she'd torn from her ledger, on which she'd copied out the original document in Frogmore House under PC Dedham's nose. Where could she hide them? Under the mattress? No, that was too obvious. On the wall hung a framed painting of a mountain scene that reminded her of Austria, bought from a junk shop in Windsor. The backing plate was held by tacks which were easy to remove with a pair of nail scissors, and the pages fitted perfectly behind it.

When the picture was back on the wall, she washed her face and changed her clothes, soaping PC Dedham's handkerchief and leaving it to soak in the basin. The Librarian hadn't noticed she'd hurt her knee, and she could tell he and his wife were relieved she didn't want to stay for lunch. She ate a hearty meal in the housemaids' dining room under the Victoria Tower, which the live-in staff used at weekends, and in the afternoon, walked through the town to the riverbank. Stopping at the first red telephone kiosk she came across, she took a pile of coins out of her pocket and laid them on the shelf, then picked up the receiver and gave the operator a number. When her call was answered, the pips sounded their frantic beeping.

'Hello?' she called, too loudly, fumbling in her eagerness to press pennies into the slot. 'Hello? I wanted to say, the Sachertorte is delicious.'

'It is my grandmother's recipe,' came the reply.

Sophie gave her information as succinctly as possible and waited to be told what to do.

'Thank you,' said Aunt Jane, her voice betraying no emotion. 'Could you come to London next Sunday morning at ten? I'll be sitting on the usual bench but don't speak to me. Hide the item in a newspaper and leave it there.'

'Of course.' Sophie replaced the receiver, scooped up her remaining change and walked out to sit on a bench in the sunshine, looking at the brightly coloured narrow boats and thinking about what she'd done. She'd been sent to Windsor Castle to uncover exactly this kind of secret, and Mr Sinclair and Mrs Slater would no doubt be pleased with her work, but she had crossed a line. She had moved from a place of safety to unknown territory, and there could be no turning back.

Chapter Twenty

Lacey and Tom sat on a bench in the train station precinct, of all places, eating pre-packed sandwiches and watching the world go by.

'I'm sorry,' Tom said again, 'I just thought you'd like the whole olde worlde British thing. You know, half a pint of warm beer and a soggy meat pie in the pub. Guess I always come on too strong.'

'You really didn't,' Lacey replied. 'Look, I'm not going to keep telling you this is my fault, not yours. I just . . . Well, I can't explain but you'll have to trust me: you did nothing wrong. It was a lovely thought.'

Tom screwed an empty potato-chip bag into a ball and tossed it into the bin beside them. 'Anna's always telling me I should play it cool. Maybe one day I'll learn.'

Lacey couldn't help smiling. 'What?' he asked, smiling himself.

'That's exactly what my sister Jess says to me.' Now she was laughing. 'I scare guys off because I'm too intense way too soon. Planning my wedding outfit on the second date, introducing him to my friends before he's ready, that kind of thing.'

'Texting the minute I get home, bringing my toothbrush round to hers when we've only just met,' Tom went on, stretching his arm along the bench. 'I know where you're coming from.'

Without thinking, Lacey leaned her head against the sleeve of his jacket. She couldn't believe they were having this conversation. Talking to Tom was so easy and straightforward; he was honest and not afraid to open up. So maybe you should be honest, too, said a little voice in her head that she chose to ignore. A group of Chinese tourists passed by, posing for photographs beside the replica steam engine that had taken Queen Victoria from Windsor to London and back again; she had taken a selfie beside it herself.

'I really like you, Lacey,' Tom said, looking at them rather than her. 'But look, you're only here for a week and there's Dermot to consider.'

'Dermot?'

'You know, the marine biologist with the Irish name who isn't Irish.'

'Oh yes.' She chose her words carefully. 'Well, actually that relationship probably isn't going anywhere.'

He laughed. 'All the same, shall we just be friends and hang out together without any stress? You're good company, for one thing, and for another, I need to know how this story about your great-aunt turns out.'

'I'd love that,' she said.

'Great.' He stood. 'And I should let you know I'm going to move out of Anna's and move back to mine so you can have a room to yourself. My bags are packed and in the car already.'

'Not on my account?' She got to her feet as well. 'That isn't fair! I should be the one to go, not you.'

'It's fine, honestly. I'd been planning to leave soon, anyway – we're getting on each other's nerves and there's going to be an almighty bust-up before long if I don't get out of her hair. You know how families are. I'm sure she'd rather share with a girl who cooks like a dream than her annoying brother.'

'Maybe she'd sooner be on her own,' Lacey said. 'I'll keep looking for somewhere else to stay.'

'Actually, I think it would be good if you stayed,' Tom told her. 'Anna works such long hours and the job is so demanding that she doesn't get much of a chance to socialise. She probably appreciates company at home. Besides, with you around, she might actually eat something. That girl doesn't look after herself properly.'

'Well, I guess it's only a few more days till I leave, anyway.'

'And let's make the most of them.' He reached out his arms. 'Friendly hug, to show we're all good?'

'Sure.' Lacey didn't want to let go: it was such a comfort to feel his arms around her, to lay her head against his chest and smell the shower gel they'd both used that morning.

'Great.' Tom released her. 'So, can I give you a lift to meet this cousin of yours? Day after tomorrow, right?'

'Thanks, that would be awesome.' They agreed on a time and swapped phone numbers.

'Call me whenever you like,' Tom said. 'It won't take long to drive over.'

She watched him walk away, relaxed and unhurried as he shouldered through the crowd, thinking how ridiculous it was that she would count the hours till she saw him again.

Lacey wandered through the town for a while, picking

up a few things from the bakery she thought Anna might like. When she got back to the house, she stowed them away in the empty fridge and packed her suitcase, not liking to assume she could move straight into the bedroom Tom had vacated. He'd stripped the bedsheets so she threw them in the washing machine, found some fresh ones in the linen closet, made the bed and vacuumed the carpet. By the time Anna came home from work, she was sitting in the kitchen with a cup of tea, feeling like a 1950s housewife waiting for her husband.

'Shall I put the kettle on?' she asked. 'Looks like you've had a hard day.'

'You could say that.' Anna dropped her bag on the counter with a weary smile. She was pale under the freckles, her eyes red-rimmed. 'Actually, I might head straight for the wine. Feels like midnight by my body clock.'

She took a bottle from the fridge, poured a glassful of wine and took a sip, closing her eyes for a moment. 'Oh, that's better. So, how are you?'

'Great,' Lacey said. 'I visited Windsor Castle with your brother and then we had a wander down the Long Walk.'

'Tom? Are you kidding?' Anna pulled out a chair and dropped into it. 'Do you know the number of times I've tried to drag him round the castle? He must like you.'

Lacey felt her cheeks grow hot. 'Oh, my God,' Anna crowed, 'you like him, too! Well, how about that?' She reached for another wine glass and filled it, pushing it across the table in Lacey's direction. 'Come on, keep me company.'

'It's a bit early for me,' Lacey said awkwardly. 'I'll stick with my tea for the moment.' Anna was so insistent, though, that eventually she gave in. She didn't have to drink the wine, after all.

'But I see Tom's moving out,' Anna said, after she had checked her phone. 'That's not good timing from your point of view. Still, can't say I'm sorry – we'd have been at each other's throats if he'd stayed much longer.'

'You might want the place to yourself,' Lacey said. 'I was going to call the hotels again, see if there've been any cancellations.'

'Don't do that. We get on pretty well, don't we? It's nice having you around.' Anna topped up her glass.

'Well, let me cook you something,' Lacey said, alarmed at the rate the wine bottle was emptying. 'French toast, maybe?'

'If you like. I'm not super hungry.' Anna rubbed her face, pausing with her hands over her eyes for a moment. 'I'm feeling a bit rough, actually. Somebody passed away on the ward this morning and it always throws me off track. You'd think I'd be used to it by now.'

'I'm so sorry.' Lacey turned around from the fridge, eggs in her hand. 'Are you sure you wouldn't rather be on your own? I can go out for a walk or something.'

'God, no. It's great you're here. I hate coming back to an empty apartment when something like this happens.' She smiled at Lacey. 'So what are we going to do about you and Tom? Seriously, I know we've only just met but you would be perfect for each other. Tom's such a great person and he's always gone for these girls who aren't really interested in him; they're either on the rebound or secretly in love with somebody else and only using him to make the other guy jealous. It's almost like he wants to be rejected.' She reached for the wine again. 'I can totally see you two as a couple, though.'

Lacey dropped a chunk of butter in a pan on the stove, adjusting the heat. 'Before you get carried away, I should remind you that I'm going back to the States in five days. Sure, your brother seems nice, but I don't really know him.'

'You don't need to,' Anna said. 'Go with your gut instinct. Besides, I've known him all my life and I can tell you he's one of the good ones. Why not have a quick shag and see how it goes?'

Lacey laughed, dropping a slice of eggy brioche into the hot fat and listening to it sizzle. She was glad Anna couldn't see her face. 'French toast coming up in two minutes. Do you want blueberries with that?'

No reply. She turned to see Anna with the wine glass pressed to her cheek, her eyes far away. 'Anna? Blueberries with your French toast?'

'Sure.' She shook her head, coming back to herself. 'Whatever. Yeah, that would be great.'

After they'd eaten, Anna went upstairs for a nap because she was going out later and Lacey sat on the couch, reading a book about Austria under German occupation during the Second World War. There were so many questions she wanted to ask her grandmother, though she knew she wouldn't dare. And maybe Gubby couldn't answer anyway, having been so young at the time. Her mind kept wandering, though, and she found herself reading the same page two or three times. There was something desperate about Anna that worried her: an emptiness behind those lovely eyes that no amount of alcohol could fill. For the first time, she could see the advantages of staying in an anonymous hotel.

Yet when Anna reappeared a few hours later, hair washed and face freshly made up, Lacey was reassured. She seemed so young and happy. Who wouldn't want a drink after a tough day at work?

'Why don't you come along?' Anna asked, pulling down her cropped top and adjusting her tiny skirt. 'I'm only going to a bar with some friends, no big deal. This outfit isn't too much, is it?'

'You look amazing,' Lacey said, smiling a little wistfully. There was nothing like that feeling of dressing up and setting off for the evening, full of anticipation; she could just about remember it. 'And thanks, but I'm staying in tonight. I've an appointment at the Royal Archives tomorrow and I want to do some more reading first.'

'Well, if you're sure.' Anna picked up her bag and flicked her hair over her shoulder. 'See you tomorrow. Don't wait up.' She stomped towards the door, the soles of her heavy boots squeaking on the floor.

'Anna?' Lacey called.

She turned around. 'Changed your mind?'

'No, I just wanted to say, be careful. You know, in the bar tonight.'

Anna laughed. 'Come on, I'm a big girl. You don't need to worry about me.' And then she was gone.

Lacey hauled her case up to the second bedroom and unpacked, trying to take up as little space as possible. She lay on the bed and stared at the ceiling, feeling very far from home, and then she called Jess – as she always did when she was anxious and unsettled.

'I've met someone and I really like him,' she wanted to tell her sister. 'I think this might be the real deal, but I can't see how to make it work.'

'I'm going to the Royal Archives tomorrow,' she said instead. 'You can't look through them yourself, you have to request information from the staff there. I asked if they could let me see anything to do with Windsor Castle in the

Second World War, but who knows what they'll come up with.'

'Well, good luck,' Jess replied. 'Listen, Lace, I have to go – the kids are kicking off. We'll speak again soon, OK?'

Lacey scrolled mindlessly through her phone for a while. She couldn't find a Tom Speedwell on Instagram, which was maybe suspicious and maybe not, and the pictures of people on their glamorous vacations were depressing. She hadn't posted any Windsor views or selfies; she didn't want anyone to know where she was in case the expedition turned out to be a wild-goose chase, as she suspected it just might be. Yawning, she turned out the light and closed her eyes.

Some time later, she was woken by a ring on the doorbell. Sitting up with a thumping heart, she gathered her wits, went over to the window and drew back the curtain. A cab stood outside the house with its door open, and two shadowy figures were standing on the garden path. She pushed up the window and asked, 'What is it?' her voice alarmingly loud in the dead of night.

'Can you come down, please?' a man called back. 'She's lost her keys.'

Lacey threw on a sweatshirt and hurried downstairs. The front door had a chain that she fastened before opening it. Through the gap, she could see Anna, head bent and auburn hair falling over her face. Hastily, she unchained the door and opened it fully.

'Thank you.' The man thrust Anna over the threshold and virtually threw her bag in after her. 'She's thrown up in my cab. I've taken seventy pounds from her purse but that hardly covers it. That's half a night's takings I'm going to lose by the time I've cleaned up her mess and aired the car.'

Lacey was doing her best to support Anna in the hall. She couldn't get a look at her face but she smelt awful: cigarette smoke, vomit and something else Lacey didn't like to imagine. 'I'm so sorry,' she told the cab driver. 'Do you need more cash?'

He shook his head, sighing. 'The state of her. She should get a grip.'

Lacey apologised again and thanked him, closing the door and replacing the chain. She propelled Anna down the hall and on to the sitting-room couch, where she sat with her legs splayed, groaning quietly. Her skin was greenish-white under her freckles and her mascara had run, leaving her with panda eyes and weeping black tears down her cheeks.

'Stay there,' Lacey ordered. 'I'm going to fetch a bucket.'

She had to run back with it, and found herself holding Anna's hair out of the way as she threw up again. 'I'm sorry,' Anna whispered, wiping her mouth with the back of her hand. 'Don't hate me.'

When Lacey felt it was safe to leave her, she fetched a washcloth from upstairs and a glass of water from the kitchen. She washed Anna's face and took off her boots, putting them outside the back door when she realised the smell was coming from something trodden into the soles (more joy for the cab driver). When Anna had managed to keep down a few mouthfuls of water, she propped her on her side, tucked a throw over her and put the bucket within easy reach.

'Call me if you need anything,' she said, but Anna was already asleep. Lacey watched her chest rise and fall for a few minutes, then went upstairs to lie awake for what remained of the night. She fell asleep when it was already light, waking with a start to realise she'd have to run if she was going to make her appointment at the archive in time. Anna hadn't moved but she was breathing, she hadn't thrown up again and the glass of water was empty. Lacey refilled it and left, closing the door quietly behind her. She couldn't afford to be distracted. Later, they might talk.

The castle was closed to regular visitors when Lacey arrived for her session in the archive, so there were no queues for her to battle through. After the usual security checks, she was issued with a pass which she showed to a policeman on the gate and, once admitted, walked up the hill towards the Round Tower, then through another archway to a small room opposite to wait for the other researchers who'd be working in the room that day. When the group of three was complete – a novelist, she found out, and a student researching for a PhD about Queen Victoria – they were taken across to the Tower and through the double doors up the wide, shallow stone steps inside, leading to the archive office and reading room. Sophie must have climbed up and down these stairs so many times, Lacey thought, trying to picture her. Was she dark or blonde? Petite like Gubby or tall and striking as Adele?

They left their bags in lockers and went up another flight of steps to allocated desks in the reading room. Lacey had schooled herself not to expect too much, but she couldn't resist a thrill of excitement at the sight of a thick manila folder waiting for her. Heart thumping, she untied the ribbon, opened the cover and began to leaf through the pages inside. At first, there seemed too much haphazard information to take in; the records weren't filed in strict date order but jumped around according to topic. She got a sense of the size and complexity of the household, seeing references to the various towers, each with their housemaids, the footmen and cellarmen, Round Tower clerks and lady clerks, yeomen of the pantry, storemen, upholsterers, fine art gilders and metalsmiths; even a State Invitation Assistant. And then out of the blue, she struck gold: a complete list of staff registered at Windsor Castle in 1939, for the purpose of issuing ration books. And there was Sophie Klein – acting Royal Librarian. Lacey stared again, certain she'd been mistaken, but the title was clear. How was that even possible?

She raced through the file, searching for further references to the Royal Library. There were umpteen requests to save paper and fuel, to keep the inner doors closed to conserve heat, to collect spare pieces of string and restrict baths to five inches of water only – even a poignant letter from a Mrs Johnstone-Burt asking if the clerical staff in the north terrace could keep their wireless sets, despite the ban on electrical items – but her great-aunt's name wasn't mentioned anywhere, and wasn't included among the castle staff at the end of the war in 1945. Sophie Klein had disappeared again. What could have happened to her?

Lacey closed the folder and leaned back in the chair, rubbing her tired eyes. The harder she tried to find out about Sophie, the more elusive she became. She left the folder on the desk, as instructed, and went downstairs to retrieve her purse and coat.

'Did you find that useful?' asked the archivist who'd handled her initial enquiry.

'Well, yes and no,' she replied. 'I only found one reference to my great-aunt, Sophie Klein, and that's raised more questions than answers.'

'Sophie Klein,' repeated the woman, scratching behind her ear with a pencil. 'Now where have I heard that name before?' She frowned, looking out of the window. 'Let me think . . . Yes, I've got it! Somebody researching for a book about the secret intelligence services asked if we had any information about a Sophie Klein. We couldn't find anything, though.'

'The secret intelligence services?' Lacey repeated. 'Seriously?'

'Sure.' The archivist pulled up a screen on her laptop, ran the cursor down a list of names and copied one on to an index card. 'Here's the woman: Camilla Lewis. She's written a couple of books about wartime spies so you should be able to find her details on the internet. Maybe you'll be able to help each other.'

Lacey stared down at the card in her hand without actually seeing it. Her great-aunt, a spy! On the one hand, the idea seemed absurd; on the other, it made perfect sense. Someone leading a double life was more likely to disappear for a while without leaving a trace. Only when she was being escorted out through the great double doors did a thought come to Lacey's mind that made her pause, horrified. Which side had Sophie Klein been working for?

Chapter Twenty-One

Windsor, June 2022

Lacey let herself into the mews house with some trepidation, not knowing what she might find. The place was quiet and smelt of bleach. She hung her raincoat on the coat stand and headed upstairs.

'Lacey? Is that you?' Anna was sitting up in bed, cradling a mug in both hands.

She put her head around the door. 'How are you feeling?'

'No better than I deserve.' Anna gave a rueful smile. She was pale but in control of herself. 'I'm sorry you had to deal with me last night.'

Lacey sat on the edge of the bed. 'That's OK.' She smoothed out the quilt, a starburst design in various shades of blue patterned cotton. 'This is beautiful.'

Anna ran her hand over the quilt too. 'It is, isn't it? My granny made it. Most of these scraps come from dresses she sewed for me when I was a kid.' She didn't look much older now.

'Can I fix you some lunch?' Lacey asked.

She groaned. 'I'm not up to eating yet.'

'OK.' Lacey hesitated, folding her hands in her lap.

'What is it?' Anna asked, her expression hardening. 'Am I in for a lecture?'

'I was going to tell you about myself. Something that happened a couple of years ago.' It was easier to speak the words the second time around: Lacey could describe what had happened without crying or feeling ashamed. Maybe each time she told the story, it would become more bearable. 'Not knowing what might have been done to me was the worst part,' she finished. 'Coming round and realising I'd been so vulnerable, so exposed. I still haven't come to terms with it yet.'

Anna sipped her tea, looking at Lacey over the rim of the mug. 'Must have been awful. That wasn't the case with me, though. I just had one too many glasses of wine. No one to blame but my own stupid self.'

'I'm not trying to blame anyone, but—' Lacey searched for the right words. 'You were lucky. The cab driver last night might not have been such a decent guy. Look, of course it shouldn't be up to us women alone to keep safe, but there are some evil people around and when you're completely out of it, you have no defences against them.'

'So this is a lecture, just a subtle one.' Anna put her mug on the bedside table. 'Well, thanks for your concern but you're not my mother. If you're going to turn all disapproving on me, you can find somewhere else to stay. And now if you don't mind, I'd like to get some sleep.'

'Sure.' Lacey stood, stung. 'I'm sorry, I didn't mean—'

But Anna had turned over, pulling the quilt around her ears. Lacey left the room, shutting the door quietly behind her, and took a deep, shaky breath. It had taken a lot of courage for her to open up like that, and she was both relieved and disappointed by Anna's reaction – or lack of it. Anna treating the incident as just one of those things, although admittedly horrible at the time, made Lacey look forward to a time when she might feel the same. Yet she wanted Anna to realise the trauma she'd gone through so she'd make sure nothing like that could ever happen to her. At the end of the day, though, Anna was still virtually a stranger and responsible for her own life. She held all the cards, too: if she wanted Lacey to leave, of course she would have to go.

To put off the endless task of calling around the hotels, she distracted herself by trying to find Camilla Lewis. It took all of five minutes for her details to pop up on the screen, along with the title of her latest book, *Written Out of History: A Short History of Wartime Espionage*. A couple of minutes later, Lacey was texting her a message, explaining her connection to Sophie Klein and wondering whether they could talk. She was sitting on the couch, mind wandering down all sorts of rabbit holes, when her phone pinged with a message from Tom. 'Free for lunch? Non-threatening sandwiches by the river?'

'Sure,' she texted back. They'd be seeing each other the next day when he gave her a lift to the college, but she wanted to talk to him and there wasn't much point playing it cool. Grabbing her coat, she headed for the pin on the map he'd sent her.

Twenty minutes later, she spotted him across a bridge on the other side of the water. He waved and her spirits rose, but she made herself stroll towards him, rather than run.

'This bench gives the best view of the castle,' he said, greeting her with a cautious hug.

She sat beside him, unwinding her scarf and gazing at the grey ramparts looming above the trees. 'It's the perfect spot.' There was nowhere else she'd rather be.

He passed her a tuna sandwich – homemade this time. 'So how did it go at the archive this morning?'

She paused, deciding how much she wanted to share. 'Well, it was interesting, but I didn't find out much about Sophie. How are things at your place?'

'Fine. It's full of dust but just about manageable.'

'You might be able to move back in with Anna,' she told him. 'Looks like I've outstayed my welcome.'

'Really?' He raised his eyebrows. 'That's a shame. I thought she liked having you around.'

'Tom, there's something I need to ask.' She laid down her sandwich (which, incidentally, was delicious). 'Is there anything about Anna that concerns you?'

'How do you mean?' He was instantly wary – though not apparently surprised.

'Are you worried about her for any reason?'

Lacey met his eyes and they looked at each other for a long time. Don't let me down, she begged him silently.

'I suppose you're talking about the amount she drinks,' he said eventually.

Lacey nodded, relieved. 'She came home last night completely wasted. It's none of my business but I think she needs help. She's a nurse – she must know the harm it's doing to her body. Tell me honestly, were you staying with your sister to keep an eye on her? And did you expect me to do the same? You should have warned me what I'd be letting myself in for.'

'It wasn't like that, I promise,' he replied. 'My flat isn't ready so I've truly needed somewhere to crash. I hadn't realised the amount Anna was drinking and I've tried to talk to her about it, but she freezes me out. I'm sorry, maybe I should have spoken to you, but I didn't want to go behind her back. I was hoping she might restrain herself if you were around – maybe even open up a little.'

'I'm a stranger, though,' Lacey said. 'She's hardly going to confide in me.'

He sighed. 'And I'm her brother, you don't have to rub it in. Look, I'll have another try soon, I promise.' He threw a crust into the water and they watched a bunch of ducks squabble for it, tails upturned. 'You don't feel like a stranger,' he said abruptly. 'It's like I've known you for ever.'

'Same here,' she wanted to say, but something stopped her. When he took her hand, though, she didn't pull away. He rubbed his thumb over her palm and her stomach flipped. They had so much to talk about; how could she leave when this conversation was just beginning?

'Lacey,' he said, 'correct me if I'm wrong, but I'm kind of assuming Dermot doesn't—'

And at that moment, her phone began to ring, shrill and insistent. 'I'm sorry,' she said, detaching her hand, 'but I'd better answer this.'

She took a few steps away from him and tried to compose herself. 'This is Lacey Jones. How may I help you?' She hardly knew what she was saying.

A brisk, no-nonsense voice announced itself as Camilla Lewis, and eventually Lacey remembered who that was.

'I had no idea Sophie Klein had a sister,' Camilla kept repeating. 'Living in America, you say? Are you sure?'

'Absolutely. I've seen a letter from Sophie to my grandmother, written when she'd recently arrived at Windsor Castle.' Lacey had regained control of herself. 'I visited the

Royal Archives earlier today and they told me you'd been asking about her. I wondered why.'

'You won't get much joy there,' Camilla said, dodging the question.

'Would you like to see this letter?' Lacey offered. 'I think you might find it interesting.'

'Exactly how much do you know about your great-aunt, Miss Jones?'

'Hardly anything. My grandma never even told us she had a sister.'

'Well, that's not surprising.'

'What do you mean?' Lacey asked sharply.

'I think we should talk face to face,' Camilla replied, after a short pause. 'You're in Windsor and I'm west London – it's not impossible. I'm not very mobile, though. Could you come to my house sometime this Saturday? If you can tear yourself away from the Jubilee celebrations, that is. And if you really want to find out more about Sophie Klein.'

'Oh, I do,' Lacey assured her.

'Fine. But I have to warn you, you might not like what you hear.'

Which made Lacey more uneasy than ever, afraid now to ask for further details. After they'd made arrangements to meet, she ended the call and turned to Tom. 'Sorry, I have to go. Are we still on for tomorrow? I can easily take a cab if you'd rather.' She couldn't meet his eye.

'No, it's fine. See you then.' He didn't look at her either.

Gathering her things, she more or less fled back over the bridge, unsettled by the conversation with Camilla and her complete inability to handle the situation with Tom like a grownup. If he had ever really liked her, which she still found hard to believe, he wouldn't anymore, and who could blame him. She asked about vacancies at every hotel and guest house she passed, and the last bed-and-breakfast gave her the number of a place out of town that would probably have a room.

Back at the house, Anna was sitting at the kitchen table. 'I'll be out of your hair soon, I promise,' Lacey told her straight away.

'Please don't go,' Anna said, pulling out a chair. 'I'm sorry for being so vile when all you did was look after me and actually give a shit.'

Lacey sat opposite her. 'I do. Give a shit, I mean.'

'I know, and thank you for that.' Anna patted her hand. 'But you have to understand, this is how I cope when things are tough. Every so often I have an epic night out, drink too much and make a fool of myself, and then things go back to normal. There are healthier ways to deal with stress, I admit, but yoga doesn't do it for me. And it's only booze – I never touch drugs.'

'Is there anyone at work you could talk to about taking a break?' Lacey asked. 'Sounds like you're burned out.'

'I can't do that,' Anna replied. 'They wouldn't manage without me.'

'Well, it's up to you.' Lacey felt suddenly exhausted by other people's complications and demands. 'But you don't have to justify your existence, you know. You can just be. Hang out in your lovely house for a while and take stock.'

She went upstairs to lie on the bed, feeling about a hundred, and slept for a couple of hours. In the evening they ate takeaway pizza and drank soda, chatting about nothing in particular. Anna would have to find her own salvation, Lacey decided, tossing and turning in bed that night, and in a few days' time she'd be hundreds of miles away from Tom so there was no point working herself up over him. In the morning she would be meeting her mother's cousin and taking a huge leap forward in solving the mystery of her family. That had to be her priority.

'Jeez.' Lacey stared at the spectacular red-brick building confronting them. 'I wasn't expecting this.'

Circular towers and tall chimney stacks dressed in stone crowded each corner of the massive structure, with a clock tower behind that showed they were ten minutes early. The campus looked like a deserted film set: its car park was virtually empty and only a few students sat on the lawn in front of the main entrance.

'Quite something, isn't it?' Tom switched off the car engine. 'Victorian architecture at its most extravagant. I had a girlfriend who studied here so I know the place quite well. If we had more time, I could show you around.'

'Then maybe I'll just have to come back.' Lacey threw open the car door and climbed out before he could answer. She wouldn't, obviously; that was the sort of meaningless phrase people came out with when they had to say something.

The short journey from Windsor had been punctuated by awkward silences but all the same, she was glad of Tom's company. Now the moment had come, the thought of introducing herself to Nicholas Dedham made her sick with nerves; if she'd been on her own, she might well have turned tail and run.

'Are you sure you want me along?' Tom asked. 'I'm happy to wait in the car.'

Lacey took out her phone to find the directions she'd been given to her cousin's office. 'Please come. I need the moral support.'

'He can't eat you.' Tom gave her shoulder a reassuring squeeze.

They walked up a flight of steps and through a huge arch to a quadrangle dominated by a statue of Queen Victoria, looking grumpy. 'She never made it to a Platinum Jubilee,' Tom said. 'Diamond, that was as far as she got: sixty years on the throne.'

Across the quadrangle, they entered the building by a side door, walked down a corridor, then up a flight of steps and along another corridor in the opposite direction, back the way they'd come. Lacey was beginning to think her cousin had been playing an elaborate joke at their expense by the time they arrived at a door with his name on it. She knocked and waited, pulling a face at Tom as they hovered like two anxious students arriving for a tutorial. Nicholas Dedham was on home turf; it might have been easier to have met him in a coffee shop.

The door opened so suddenly that she took a step back, and a balding man with black-rimmed glasses stood on the threshold. He looked about a decade older than the photograph she'd seen, and it was a decade that had not treated him kindly.

'Miss Jones? Do come in.' He showed no desire to shake her hand, so she stuck it in her pocket.

'Thank you,' she said, the butterflies in her stomach fluttering more violently at the coldness of his tone and his suspicious expression. 'And this is my friend, Tom Speedwell.'

Dedham nodded, retreating behind his desk as though it were a barricade and gesturing towards two fold-up chairs for them to sit on. His office was bare and modern, contrasting with the college's ornate exterior, furnished only with the chairs and desk, flatpack bookshelves and a couple of metal filing cabinets. A framed print of a mountain lake hung on the wall. 'You mentioned a letter from my mother in your initial email,' he said, crossing one leg over the other. 'May I ask how you came by it?'

'I found it in my grandmother's bureau,' Lacey replied, matching him for plain speaking. 'We discovered only recently that she'd escaped to the States from Vienna after the Anschluss at the age of nine and been adopted by an American family. Her birth name was Hanna Klein and I believe she's your aunt: the younger sister of your mother, Sophie. She recently turned ninety-three.'

Nicholas Dedham put his elbows on the desk, interlaced his fingers and rested his chin on them, scrutinising Lacey. You have nothing to be ashamed of, she reminded herself; don't let this man intimidate you. Her fingers found the tattoo on her ankle and she let them rest there, strengthened by the thought of Jess's presence beside her.

'We had no idea our grandma even had an older sister,' she went on. 'Maybe you didn't know about Hanna, either, so I'm sorry if this news comes as a shock.'

'I did learn about your grandmother,' he said, weighing every word, 'but only after my mother had died. Her sister was mentioned in the will. My father and I made every attempt to find her but with no success: the trail came to a dead end.'

'Gubby's first husband died young,' Lacey told him. 'She moved east and married again.' She glanced at Tom, wondering what he thought of this convoluted family history, and the sight of his calm face was reassuring.

'May I see this letter?' Dedham asked.

'The original is still in my grandmother's possession, but I have a copy on my phone.' Lacey passed it over.

Nicholas Dedham smiled for the first time as he read it, scrolling down the screen.

'Your mother sounds so lovely,' Lacey said when he'd finished.

His smile faded immediately. 'She was.' He passed back the phone. 'An extraordinary woman. It's just a pity her sister never got to know her as an adult.'

'I don't understand it either,' Lacey told him. 'My grandma's so loving, as a rule.'

'And does she know you're here?'

Lacey shook her head. 'I haven't even told her I found Sophie's letter.'

'And so the charade goes on,' Dedham said. 'May I ask what you hope to achieve by this visit? Are you dreaming of some touching reunion where we all cry and hug each other like they do on TV? If that's the case, I'm afraid you'll be disappointed.'

'Of course not,' Lacey replied, surprised by the bitterness of his tone. 'I want to find out about your mother, that's all. She's a part of my family and I don't even know what she looks like.'

Mr Dedham sighed, folding his arms. 'I can see why you might be curious, but you have to understand, it's too late to play happy families. According to Dad, my mother was deeply wounded by her sister's behaviour, cutting her off in the way she did. Mum had a traumatic time during the war but went on to make a good life with my father and me, just the three of us. We didn't need anyone else then and I don't appreciate you digging up the past now. Nothing good can come of it.'

Lacey's fingers had twisted together; she made a conscious effort to relax them. 'I'm sorry to upset you, Mr Dedham.

Your mother was obviously a remarkable person, coming to England as a refugee and ending up in Windsor Castle. I found a reference to her in the Royal Archives yesterday. Is it true that—'

'I'm not upset, Miss Jones,' he interrupted, getting to his feet, 'but there seems little point in continuing this conversation. Thank you for letting me read my mother's letter. If at some stage you were able to retrieve the original, I'd be grateful to have it back. You can send it to me at the college.' This time, he extended his hand. 'Goodbye. Enjoy the rest of your stay.'

Lacey grasped his cold palm. 'Thank you for your time. You can't stop me trying to learn about Sophie Klein, though. I'm meeting a writer called Camilla Lewis on the weekend who knows more about her.'

He glared at her, suddenly furious rather than frosty. 'That woman is a crackpot. I'm warning you: if you repeat anything she says in a public arena, I'll sue you for slander. Is that clear?'

'Look, I'm not about to go spreading rumours about your mother. I'm only interested in the truth, and obviously I'll keep it to myself.' Lacey was beginning to feel cross too. She'd come a long way to meet this guy and he couldn't even bring himself to be polite, let alone friendly.

'Before we leave, could I ask a question?' Tom put in. 'You said your mother's sister was mentioned in the will: has she been left some bequest? If so, Lacey could take it back with her. However you might feel, surely your mother's wishes should still be carried out.'

Dedham looked uncomfortable. 'There was a small token: a book, as far as I remember. If you leave me your address, I can put it in the post.'

'That seems a hassle,' Tom said easily. 'We can drop by and pick it up.'

'But I'm not coming into college for a week or so.'

'Then we can swing by your house,' Tom replied. 'It's OK, we don't have to come in.'

'Fine, if you insist,' Dedham said, with an awkward laugh. 'I'm not trying to cheat you out of your inheritance, Lacey.' He took out his phone. 'Shall we say Monday morning? Give me your number, and I'll text you my address and a convenient time to meet.'

Out in the corridor, safely on the other side of the door, she realised her legs were shaking. 'At least he called me Lacey by the end,' she whispered to Tom as they walked away. 'And thanks for pinning him down about the bequest. Sorry you had to sit through that.'

'Are you kidding?' He was invigorated. 'Lacey, you can't let this drop. Why is that man so defensive? His mother's clearly been involved in some sort of scandal and he's worried you're going to uncover it. You have to do some more digging.'

'Do I?' She was beginning to have second thoughts. 'Maybe I'd rather not know.'

Chapter Twenty-Two

Windsor Castle, June 1938

When Sophie returned to Frogmore House on Monday, there was no sign of Mrs Bruton, the housekeeper, and PC Dedham was on guard at the door. A bicycle stood propped against the wall near by.

He nodded at her. 'Morning, Miss. I'm to keep you company for a couple of hours until the new housekeeper arrives this afternoon.'

'It will be rather dull for you, I'm afraid,' Sophie replied.

'Oh, I'm used to that,' he said, smiling. 'The policeman's lot is not a happy one.'

He seemed rooted to the spot. 'Excuse me,' she said, shifting her basket from one arm to the other.

'Have you recovered from all the excitement yesterday?' he asked. 'How's the knee?'

Sophie could feel herself blushing. 'Much better, thank you. I've washed your handkerchief but not ironed it yet. And thank you for yesterday, I appreciated your help.'

'So it turned out you were right,' he said. 'About those

papers, whatever they were. I'd say you were wasted in the library – you ought to try my line of work.'

'Oh no, I want a quiet life.' Sophie made an effort to smile back at him. In that moment, she could think of nothing better: losing peaceful hours in the archive, reading about history rather than living through it.

'You could have fooled me. I've been told not to ask questions, but a man can't help being curious.'

Sophie made no reply. They looked at each other for a while before the policeman said, 'Well, I'll let you get on. I've brought provisions – perhaps we might have tea together later?'

'That's a kind thought but I'll be far too busy to make tea,' Sophie told him hastily.

'You don't have to.' He stood aside at last. 'I'm a dab hand in the kitchen. I'll bring you a cup.'

She thanked him again, pushed past and hurried upstairs, berating herself for the pleasure she'd felt at his idea. She was only human, though, and couldn't cut herself off from other people entirely. And mightn't it be useful to have an ally in the police? Yet he would want to know everything, and she couldn't afford to let him find out a fraction of what she'd been up to. She thought about the innocuous painting on her bedroom wall and the explosive papers hidden behind it; the picture seemed to pulse whenever she looked at it. There in black and white were Hitler and the Duke of Windsor, sharing a vision of the future that horrified her.

When PC Dedham knocked on the door at eleven, she said she couldn't afford to take a break and was concerned, anyway, about spilling tea over important documents. And she closed the door firmly, hardening her heart against the disappointment on his face.

She'd formed some idea of the task ahead by the end of that week, and told the Librarian it would probably take her six weeks or so to examine and catalogue the contents of all the crates, given her other duties. He was treating her with more elaborate courtesy than ever, reiterating what a marvellous job she was doing, and she might have felt guilty, had she not told herself this sort of mission was the reason she'd come to Windsor – or rather, been sent there. She slept with the transcript under her pillow on the Saturday night and tucked it into her liberty bodice in the morning before leaving for the station, only transferring it to a copy of yesterday's *Daily Mirror* in the train lavatory. She'd been looking out for Aunt Jane's familiar pillbox hat but the woman on the bench was wearing a headscarf, pulled low over her forehead. Sophie recognised her shoes, though. She laid the newspaper on the bench between them and rose to leave.

Passing on the transcript left Sophie light-headed with relief but there would be no brandy at The Ritz this time: that was a habit she couldn't afford to develop. She caught the next train to Windsor and rushed back to her room like an animal returning to its lair.

'Back so soon?' said Mags, coming out of hers as Sophie opened the door. 'Is everything all right?'

'Fine, thanks,' Sophie replied breathlessly, 'but London seems awfully noisy and I have a headache coming on.'

'You'll feel better after a lie-down,' Mags said. 'Would you like me to bring you some lunch on a tray?'

'Thanks, but I'm not hungry,' Sophie said – although she was in fact ravenous.

When the coast was clear, she went for a long walk, stopping at a pub for a meat pie, which she ate in the garden with a glass of stout. She would save up for a bicycle, she decided, remembering PC Dedham's, and explore the countryside. Work would keep her busy and in time she'd become more used to living alone: free as one of those birds overhead, wheeling through an empty sky. Maybe one day she could accept not hearing from Hanna and let her sister go, free to lead her own life without any burden of expectation. For now, she had enough to contend with, maintaining a low profile at the castle in the face of Miss Preston's hostility, while carrying out both her official and unofficial duties. She couldn't let herself become too cosy within the Windsor family, like Mags and JB, whom she couldn't imagine being able to cope in the outside world. They were all cosseted within the castle, looked after but kept in their place by tradition and a rigid chain of command.

These are not your people, she told herself when the Queen's mother died in London at the end of June and the whole household went into mourning. The Countess of Strathmore had passed away peacefully, and Sophie would not be moved by the Queen's dignified sorrow – unlike Mags, who crept about red-eyed for days, and JB, uncharacteristically quiet. Nor could she take pleasure in the royals' triumphant state visit to France, where the Queen was radiant in a wardrobe of mourning white designed by Norman Hartnell. Sophie's family had gone, and she could not find comfort in another. She had to keep herself apart, the memory of Vienna fierce in her heart and her hatred of the Nazis still burning.

She often thought of Tamara Grossman and had appealed to the housekeeper at Windsor on her behalf, to be told there were no vacancies at present, and if any should arise, priority would be given to British girls – particularly at a time like this, with so much unpleasantness abroad. Sophie had also spent hours trudging around the town's bakeries and hotels but nobody there wanted to employ a foreigner either. Don't give up, she begged Tamara silently: I haven't forgotten you.

Time passed and the gentle heat of early summer gave way to a blazing August, growling with thunder. Sophie spent her mornings in the Royal Archives, keeping out of Miss Preston's way as she explored the collection, and her afternoons at Frogmore House or Fort Belvedere, the Duke of Windsor's weekend hideaway, becoming more closely acquainted with him than she might have chosen. She found nothing of any great political significance but came across several letters to him from the Duke of Kent: Prince George, the youngest of the four brothers.

'Even more of a rake than Edward,' JB informed her. 'Clever but wild, although he's settled down since marrying Marina – Princess Marina of Greece, that is – and having children. He and Edward are still close, I believe, though Marina and Wallis apparently don't get on.'

The brothers shared a tailor so there was plenty of chat about double-breasted versus single-breasted suits and the precise width of trouser cuffs. Sophie also came across a scribbled note stuck into a copy of Sassoon's *Memoirs of a Fox-Hunting Man*, referring to intimate correspondence between Prince George and a man named 'R' in Paris who had turned out to be a blackmailing bastard of the first order and could make life awkward for everyone. Edward had obviously helped his brother because later she found an effusive letter of thanks for sorting out the 'Paris affair'.

She extracted both messages to give the Librarian at what had become their regular weekly meeting on Friday afternoons. He received them with a look of embarrassed distaste and a muttered apology that she should have to witness such sordid goings on.

Sophie could have told him she'd seen far worse, but she was keen to preserve the image of herself as an innocent, possibly prudish young woman, more interested in books than affairs of the heart. PC Dedham seemed to have disappeared, which helped in that regard; she hadn't seen him since the morning in Frogmore House when she'd refused his offer of tea, and she couldn't think of an excuse to ask where he'd gone. Out of sight, out of mind – although unfortunately that wasn't turning out to be the case.

Thunder rumbled across the English summer skies and the weather in Europe was ominous too. Hitler's demands that Germans in the Sudetenland area of northern Czechoslovakia should be reunited with their homeland were becoming increasingly urgent, according to the newspapers. JB subscribed to *The Times* and let Sophie read it when she'd finished; she'd also successfully petitioned for the live-in clerical staff to have wirelesses in their rooms, given the current situation. Mags couldn't see any need for a wireless, the news being so alarming, but was persuaded by the thought of light music and entertainment – especially fast-talking Tommy Handley. Sophie could hear her tittering on the other side of the wall when 'Mr Murgatroyd and Mr Winterbottom' was playing ('two minds with not a single thought').

By September, the fields around Windsor were shorn and dotted with hay stooks, the traffic slowed by tractors and horse-drawn carts as the harvest was gathered. What should have been a time of peace and plenty became fraught with tension as wrangling over the Sudetenland area, bordering Germany, intensified. JB read *The Times* with a serious expression and Mags was increasingly prone to tears, forbidding any sort of political discussion.

'I simply can't bear the thought of another war,' she'd say. 'Young folk have no idea what it's like, but we lost so many of our friends, our husbands and brothers. The waste of all those lives!'

Sophie, whose father had fought on the German side, had no desire for a debate either. Her English was good and getting even better day by day, but she still spoke with an accent and was often met with suspicious looks in the town, and sometimes around the castle.

After some negotiation between the British, French and German governments, a proposal was drawn up announcing that the Sudetenland should be annexed by Germany; the Czechs were not consulted but forced to reluctantly accept Hitler's terms. As if he would be satisfied by this concession, Sophie thought, waiting anxiously for her turn with JB's newspaper. When she finally managed to fall asleep in the early hours, the idea of cheering crowds greeting the Führer in London gave her nightmares. Posters appeared on hoardings and leaflets were posted through letterboxes, appealing for volunteers to join the Air Raid Precautions service, and gas masks were issued to everyone in the country – even babies, who were encased in what looked like an incubator. She drew a picture of herself in a gas mask in her letter to Hanna, not wanting to alarm her sister but casting around for news in the face of silence from America.

Miss Preston's friend, the previous library assistant, was now in the family way and appalled by the contraption.

However Miss Preston's fiancé, Cyril, recently enrolled as a volunteer ARP warden, had assured her of its efficacy, using a doll to demonstrate how the mask should be fitted.

'He's proud to be doing his bit for the country,' Miss Preston said. 'Soon we may all be called upon to serve one way or another. Even you, Miss Klein.'

Sophie had her doubts about Cyril Jenkins. He would occasionally collect Miss Preston after work – Pamela, though Sophie couldn't imagine ever calling her that – taking off his hat and holding open the door for his lady love with an elaborate flourish. She seemed cowed in his presence, though: reluctant to express an opinion of her own when she was usually so forthright. Cyril was the one to decide whether they went dancing or to the pictures, and which film they should see. Miss Preston fell in with his plans surprisingly readily, because she wasn't shy of voicing her opinion when he wasn't around. The couple had been engaged for three years, according to Mags, but Mr Jenkins was the only son of a widowed mother who wasn't prepared to let him go in a hurry.

Hitler's territorial demands became ever more outrageous: now the evacuation of all Czechs from the Sudetenland and its occupation by the German army. The Czech army was ready to fight but would need allies; Britain and France readied themselves. And then, at the very last minute, Prime Minister Neville Chamberlain proposed a conference between Germany, Italy, Britain and France to settle the dispute – and Hitler agreed!

'Can you believe it?' Mags cried, promptly bursting into tears.

She cried again when Chamberlain returned from Munich on the last day of September, announcing that he and Hitler had signed an agreement to resolve their differences by negotiation. 'Peace with honour,' he said, waving a piece of paper. 'Peace for our time.' Such a dignified, handsome man whom Sophie had had the honour of seeing in the flesh; how she longed to believe him!

'Why the long face?' Miss Preston asked her, clack-clacking away at the typewriter. 'Aren't you pleased we've avoided another war?'

'If that were true, I would be,' she replied. 'But anyone who believes Hitler will keep his word is a fool.'

She should perhaps have been more diplomatic; Miss Preston practically burst with indignation. 'I should remind you, Miss Klein,' she snapped, her colour rising, 'that you are a guest in this country and have no business insulting its elected government.'

She bristled for the rest of the afternoon and when Cyril arrived to collect her (they were having an impromptu supper in town) she told him loudly, 'According to Miss Klein, we shouldn't be relieved the crisis has been averted. Apparently she knows more about world affairs than our Prime Minister. Aren't I lucky to have the benefit of her opinion?'

'On the contrary, Pamela,' huffed Cyril, 'I think you're extremely unfortunate. You have my very greatest sympathy.'

And they both glared at Sophie, united in outrage. Mr Jenkins was in casual attire: a blazer with brass buttons and a cravat, which only emphasised the shortness of his neck, making his head look as though it were served up on a paisley ruff. Sophie might have laughed if she hadn't been so anxious.

At least there was one politician with a clearer grasp of the situation. 'You were given the choice between war and dishonour,' Winston Churchill told the Prime Minister in parliament. 'You chose dishonour, and you will have war.' Mags thought Churchill a warmonger and wouldn't hear any mention of his name, but Sophie agreed with him wholeheartedly.

Since her discovery of the Hitler meeting transcript and the tact with which she'd handled it, the Librarian was increasingly ready to confide in her. That week, at their regular Friday afternoon meeting to discuss library business and other more confidential matters, he was in no mood for celebration either.

'I fear this is only a temporary reprieve,' he said, gazing out of the window. 'I've been having discussions with the King about storing some treasures from Buckingham Palace here at the castle, which is more secure though by no means impregnable. And to complicate matters, the Duke of Windsor wants to meet Hitler again and sue for peace. He'd like to act as a sort of unofficial ambassador.' He sighed. 'Any news from Fort Belvedere?'

'A couple of letters, sir,' she replied, passing them over. 'From the Duke's cousins, Prince Philipp of Hesse and his brother, Christoph. I've attached my translation.' She'd stumbled across them in the pocket of a shooting jacket in the loft, along with a couple of spent shells.

The Librarian took a brief look, raising his eyebrows. 'Good heavens. Definitely not for public consumption. Thank you, Miss Klein – leave them with me.'

Philipp and his younger brother Christoph were German grandsons of Queen Victoria and now high-up members of the Nazi party, JB had told her. There must be an alternative archive somewhere, Sophie had decided, bursting with letters from embarrassing relatives and lovers both male and female, protestations of admiration for the Führer's ideals, claims of illegitimate children and extortion demands for a whole host of misdemeanours. She had a strong suspicion most of the documents she came across would never be filed in the Muniments Room, and that made her feel justified in handing over transcripts to Aunt Jane each month. She kept the purely salacious material to herself but copied anything of the slightest political significance.

'And what is the mood of the household?' Jane would ask. 'Still loyal to the King?'

'As far as I know,' Sophie replied. The trouble was, she wasn't on chatting terms with any of its key members, apart from the Librarian. JB was too discreet to pass on any snippets from the Queen, while any vaguely political or controversial news sent Mags into such a spiral of anxiety that she was incapable of coherent speech. Sophie wondered whether Mr Sinclair and Mrs Slater felt they were getting good value out of her, although finding the Hitler meeting minutes had been such a coup that surely she could rest on her laurels for a while. Aunt Jane certainly seemed to regard her with new respect.

The Librarian sipped his tea in silence and Sophie was about to make her excuses to leave when he said, 'If war does come, which I fear is inevitable, everyone's role at the castle will change.'

Oh Lord, Sophie thought, he's about to tell me I won't have a job. Yet she managed to say only, 'Of course, sir,' her voice steady.

'You've become a valuable asset in the short time you've been here,' he continued. 'I've been most impressed by your dedication and discretion.'

'Thank you.' Sophie waited for the 'But . . .' that was bound to follow.

'And now I'd like to prepare you for greater things, train you up so that I can concentrate on safeguarding the precious items in our collection: items we cannot allow to fall into enemy hands. Are you willing to take on extra responsibility, Miss Klein? I need a safe pair of hands in the library, and I'd like them to be yours.'

Sophie was stunned for a moment, then weak with relief. 'Thank you for your trust in me, sir.' She bent her head modestly. 'I should be honoured.'

'Good.' He shuffled some papers on the desk, continuing in his usual businesslike tone, 'Well, we can discuss this further as the need arises. Thank you, that will be all.'

So my position at the castle is secure for the time being, Sophie thought, closing the door behind her, but what happens when the Nazis come? Will these walls be strong enough to protect me then?

Chapter Twenty-Three

London, November 1938

Sophie had noticed the face of London changing on her monthly visits to meet Aunt Jane. Through the train window, she saw turfed mounds springing up like green mushrooms in people's back gardens – air raid shelters, she discovered from the gentleman beside her – allotments being dug in parks and rosebeds uprooted to make way for vegetable patches. The roads were clogged with unusual traffic: men on bicycles in unfamiliar uniforms, lorries crammed with rowdy teenage boys, pairs of women with clipboards knocking on doors. 'If the cloud that overhangs Europe should burst, it won't be rain but bombs that will fall, and God help us if we are caught unprepared,' read the latest ARP recruiting leaflet.

Sophie's gas mask stood in its case on her chest of drawers and her father's Mauser lay waiting in the chimney breast. She would volunteer for whichever service would have her, once she'd decided where she would be most useful. These preparations filled her with hope, alongside the dread. Britain was small compared to Germany, but its people seemed ready to resist and she loved them for that – although maybe not Cyril Jenkins, whose duties as warden apparently gave him licence to march into their quarters, unannounced, and ask whatever questions popped into his head.

On this particular Saturday in November, Sophie was travelling to London at the invitation of Lady Wilton, with whom she'd been corresponding on a regular basis. Miss Ottoline was back from India and Lady Wilton was arranging a small dinner party for her; if Sophie were able to stay in Chelsea overnight and take a day's holiday, she might also like to attend the Armistice Day service at the Cenotaph with them the next morning. Sophie had been looking forward to the event but the recent news from Europe had been so shocking, she could think of little else. A Polish Jew had shot and killed a German diplomat in Paris, unleashing a wave of the most savage reprisals against Jews in all the German territories. Sophie pored over eye-witness accounts in the papers, sickened by what she read. The violence she'd witnessed in Vienna was nothing compared to this orgy of destruction: across Germany, Austria and the Sudetenland, Jewish homes and businesses were set on fire, their windows smashed. Women were raped and men beaten up and arrested while the police stood by. Many suicides were also reported: people threw themselves from windows or took cyanide pills, saved for the worst of times that had now come. At least her parents were spared this fresh horror, Sophie thought, walking through the chilly London streets, and Hanna was hundreds of miles away in America. The knowledge her sister was safe helped soothe the pain of hearing so little from her.

Sophie had arrived at Chelsea in the afternoon and was dreading the thought of more Boodle's cake (or even worse, perhaps the *same one*) but to her relief, only a plate of stale Garibaldi biscuits accompanied tea in the drawing room.

'Shop-bought,' Lady Wilton announced dolefully, biting into one. 'What would my mother have said? And I suppose we ought to stop eating Garibaldis now Italy's gone Fascist.'

She'd finally had to dismiss Mrs Lovage, the cook, for gross insubordination and the theft of some silver plate, she told Sophie, and they had been managing with agency staff for the past couple of months.

'Could be worse,' Miss Ottoline said cheerfully. 'I got used to eating the most extraordinary things in India.' She was a robust girl with rosy cheeks and small, friendly eyes: as energetic as her mother was listless.

'Well, it hasn't done you any harm,' her mother observed. 'You're positively sylph-like.' She turned to Sophie. 'We've had to have a whole new wardrobe made. Are you still short of things to wear, my dear?'

'Mother! If my clothes don't fit me, they certainly won't do for Miss Klein,' Ottoline exclaimed. She squeezed Sophie's hand, an unexpectedly moving gesture. 'Such terrible news from Germany. You must be so anxious.'

'Thank you,' Sophie replied. 'Yes, it is awful. My parents are dead but I still have friends in Vienna.' Tamara of course, who was never far from her thoughts, but she also wondered briefly whether Ruth had managed to escape, and if Wilhelm were still alive. 'I'm so grateful to this country for taking me in and yet I feel guilty, thinking of those left behind.'

'I can imagine,' Ottoline said.

'As a matter of fact, I wanted to talk to you about something.' Sophie laid down her plate. 'My mother ran a pastry shop in Vienna and her assistant, the most wonderful cook, is looking for a position in this country. Would you consider employing her?'

Lady Wilton turned over the idea, chewing her biscuit thoughtfully like a cow with its cud. 'No, I don't think so,' she said eventually. 'Peregrine doesn't like foreign food and Gladys would never accept her.'

'Really? Sounds like a good idea to me,' Ottoline said. 'Papa's done nothing but complain about the cooking since I've come home and Gladys could hardly get on worse with anyone than she did with Mrs Lovage, short of actually killing them.'

'You've been so kind to me, Lady Wilton,' Sophie told her. 'Tamara is desperate. I don't even know if she's still alive.'

'But my digestion is delicate,' Lady Wilton replied (at which Ottoline raised her eyebrows). 'I couldn't eat food that's greasy and full of garlic.'

'It wouldn't be,' Sophie assured her. 'I know, why don't you let me prepare dinner tonight so you can taste some Viennese specialities?'

'You can cook?' Lady Wilton stared at her. 'Extraordinary! But we have guests this evening. What would they think?'

'They don't have to know,' Sophie said. 'Perhaps your cook can help me. We'll make everything in advance and Gladys can serve the dishes.'

'I think that's a marvellous idea.' Ottoline jumped up. 'Let's go down to the kitchen, you and I, tell Mrs Whatsername the plan and see what provisions she has. Mother, dinner last night was inedible – we have nothing to lose.'

The agency cook didn't like the idea of acting as sous-chef but was prepared to take half her wages and the evening off. Sophie found a bowl of stewing beef in the cold larder, eggs and cream on another shelf, and flour and sugar in the pantry. There were apples, tomatoes and onions stored in an outhouse, and Miss Ottoline was happy to run to the shops for the paprika, cinnamon and caraway seeds she needed. There was no time to lose if the goulash was going to cook long enough for the tough meat to melt into a rich gravy. When the stew was simmering nicely, Sophie turned her mind to pudding.

'I'd like to cook apple strudel,' she told Ottoline, 'but it's quite ambitious. Would you be able to help me?'

How many times had she and her mother made strudel together, one on either side of the kitchen table as she and Ottoline were standing now, stretching the pastry until it was thin enough to read a letter through. Sophie wasn't merely cooking a meal, she was honouring her mother and grandmother and the traditions that had shaped them. Maybe one day she would teach her own daughter how to make Apfelstrudel – but there were a good many hurdles to be jumped before then.

'I never realised cooking was such fun,' Ottoline said, taking off her apron at the end of their marathon session. 'But goodness, it's hard work. We'll only just have time to change before dinner.'

Gladys had been watching the proceedings with some suspicion, hands on hips. 'You've left the kitchen tidy, I'll say that for you,' she admitted grudgingly.

'Lobster soup's in this pan,' Sophie told her (from a tin, but livened with a splash of brandy). 'To be served with melba toast, which I'll prepare when the guests are having drinks. We'll have to manage without a fish course. Goulash to follow with egg noodles; I'll finish those off when you're clearing away the soup dishes. Apple strudel's keeping warm in the bottom oven.'

The meal was a triumph. Nobody seemed to notice Sophie's occasional absences to powder her nose and the goulash was delicious, the noodles light as feathers, and the apple strudel quite unlike anything the guests had ever eaten before. They were a party of eight: the Wiltons, Sophie, a nervous young curate and a retired colonel who'd lost a leg in the war, plus a painter and his wife who lived further along the road. Chelsea was a bohemian area, Lady Wilton told Sophie, bursting with artists and writers. Conversation was lively, focusing largely on Miss Ottoline's application to join the Fanys: the First Aid Nursing Yeomanry, who were currently recruiting women to train as drivers and mechanics. Ottoline had already been interviewed and was on tenterhooks, waiting to hear if she'd been successful.

'Splendid idea,' said the colonel. 'My sister was a Fany in the last show and tore all over France in an ambulance. It was the making of her.'

'It sounds rather dangerous,' the curate observed with a wan smile.

'And definitely unladylike,' added Lady Wilton.

'Thank goodness,' Ottoline said. 'I've always been a tomboy, Mother – might as well put my rough-and-tumble skills to good use. We shall all be caught up in the storm that's coming, even you.'

Lady Wilton sighed and turned to Sophie. 'Regale us with tales from Windsor, Miss Klein. Have you seen any more of the King and Queen? He seems to be making a fist of things, but I can't help thinking if David – sorry, Edward

– were still on the throne, he'd have been able to appeal to Hitler and sort this mess out.'

Luckily, before Sophie had to answer, the painter's wife asked, 'Is it true their house in France has a gold-plated bathtub in the shape of a swan?' and she was able to change the subject. The letters she'd read and the rumours she'd heard across the staff dinner table (from those less discreet than Mags and JB) led her to think the Windsors still regarded Hitler with admiration rather than horror. The Duke seemed desperate to regain the power he'd once had, and willing to go to any lengths in pursuit of it – even, though she could scarcely believe it, to betray his own family.

'Marvellous dinner,' Lord Wilton said when all the guests had gone. 'Can this friend of yours cook like that, Miss Klein? Course she can, or you wouldn't have recommended her. Think we should give her a try, Constancia? I'd say so. No doubt Gladys will come around in due course.'

'I believe you've been in contact with Mr Sinclair and Esme Slater at the British Passport Office in Vienna?' Sophie replied, seized with dread they might already be too late. 'I'll send a telegram to Miss Grossman tomorrow. Thank you!' She could have kissed him, though no doubt he'd have been mortified. 'You won't regret this, I promise.'

She went down to the kitchen before bed to see what Gladys thought about an Austrian cook.

'Doesn't much matter to me, Miss,' Gladys replied. 'Don't tell them upstairs but I'm thinking of training to be a nurse. Reckon we shall need them before long. My dad was gassed in the war and I looked after him towards the end. Seems more useful than making beds and dusting.'

'That's an excellent idea,' Sophie told her. Gladys was far

too clever and resourceful to spend the rest of her life looking after the Wiltons.

Everyone was hoping for the best and preparing for the worst, and Sophie found the Armistice Day ceremony the next morning particularly poignant. She remembered her father in the silence which followed Big Ben's chimes at eleven o'clock. He'd never talked about his time in the war, but always gave money to the wounded veterans who begged on street corners in Vienna: sad, broken men, their minds damaged as much as their bodies. Sophie could see old soldiers in the crowd around her, standing a little straighter as the military bands played. Ordinary people like these paid the price for wars started by tyrants, and her heart broke at the thought of the thousands more who would have to die, along with those already lost. No doubt she should have been contemplating higher things, but she could only burn with hatred in the bitter cold for Hitler and the misery he'd unleashed. Britain was her country now, and the sight of the King bending to lay a wreath at the Cenotaph filled her with pride. He carried himself with such dignity on these occasions that one could overlook his speech impediment and flashes of temper, his slight stature and the occasional awkwardness of his manner.

Sophie was getting to know the Royal Family little by little from their weekend visits to the castle. She would see them arriving from London in an armoured car, the princesses usually travelling separately with their nurses and the Scottish governess, who always seemed to be running after one or both of them. Margaret Rose, in particular, led her a merry dance, although one day Mags reported that it was Elizabeth who'd fallen into the pond, apparently looking for a duck's nest, and emerged dripping with green slime. Mags adored the girls and was always craning for a glimpse of them through any nearby window. The princesses were often to be seen driving a small pony cart around the Home Park with Elizabeth at the reins – usually their governess or nurse beside them but sometimes alone – and they were allowed to roam where they liked within the castle walls, which were guarded by soldiers as well as the police.

One morning, the Librarian informed Sophie that the King and Princess Elizabeth would be visiting the library that afternoon and she might like to be on hand. She wondered whether the King wanted to meet her, but he merely nodded when she curtsied and didn't ask to be introduced; perhaps he preferred to keep her at arm's length, given what she'd learned about his brother. He wanted to show his daughter some of Queen Victoria's diaries, which Sophie had retrieved from the archive and laid out ready on a table. She watched them discreetly from a distance, touched by the obvious closeness of their relationship: the patience with which he answered his daughter's questions; her hand resting easily on his shoulder; their mutual pleasure in each other's company. After a while, the King went off to speak with the Librarian and Elizabeth wandered over to the table where Sophie was cataloguing some recent acquisitions.

'Hello, Miss Klein,' she said. 'How are you settling in?'

'Very well, thank you, Your Royal Highness,' Sophie replied, surprised the girl should have remembered her name.

The princess smiled. 'You don't have to call me that, it's quite a mouthful. Elizabeth will do.'

'Then you must call me Sophie. Agreed?'

'Agreed.' And the two of them shook hands.

'What are you doing?' Elizabeth asked, pulling out a chair.

'Seeing where these books should be placed in our collection, and which of them need repairing at the bindery,' Sophie told her. 'See here? The middle section will need to be resewn and the leather cover is weak.'

'I've never been to the bindery,' the princess said. 'Will you show me around one day?'

'With pleasure,' Sophie said, smiling.

Elizabeth regarded her gravely. 'Papa tells me you've escaped from Austria. Were things very difficult there?'

'Yes, they were,' Sophie replied. There seemed little point in sugar coating the truth. 'Germany has annexed the country and is making life impossible for Jews, among others.'

'And is there a royal family in Austria? What's happened to them?'

'Not anymore,' Sophie said. 'We only had a government and that is German now.' Of course, even a girl as young as Elizabeth must be aware of the risks that ran alongside her privilege; after all, it was only twenty years since the entire Russian Royal Family had been murdered by revolutionaries.

'Don't worry,' she added. 'We're safe in a castle and Hitler's far away.'

'But getting closer,' the princess said. 'Do you think he'll try to take the whole of Czechoslovakia?'

Sophie met her eyes. 'Yes, I'm afraid he will.'

Elizabeth nodded. 'Thank you for telling me the truth – everyone else tries to fob me off. I need to know these things, you see. Goodbye, Sophie. I hope we can talk again.'

From that moment on, the princess would occasionally seek Sophie out in the Muniments Room or the archive office, much to Miss Preston's consternation, to chat to her about some book she'd enjoyed or Hitler's latest speech in the Reichstag. And once when Sophie was walking back through the Home Park on a Sunday afternoon in the pouring rain, the princesses stopped to give her a lift in their pony cart. It was a wild ride. 'Faster!' Margaret shouted, reaching over to slap the reins her sister was holding, while their governess shrieked and Sophie clung on for dear life.

Christmas came in a flurry of snow, clothing the park in a frozen white blanket against which the castle walls stood out in even starker relief. The Royal Family was staying at Sandringham, as usual, so the atmosphere at Windsor was relaxed. A meal for the whole household was held in St George's Hall and each member of staff was given a large mince pie and a Christmas pudding (dark, heavy, indigestible – Sophie passed hers on to Mags). She was homesick for old Vienna and her childhood Christmases: her mother baking Vanillekipferl cookies and her father lighting a candle on the Advent wreath every Sunday. She'd sent her sister a rag doll, a book about a chimney sweep who turned into a water baby and a jigsaw puzzle – to her new address, because Hanna had written to tell her she'd been taken in by an American family, the Millers, who lived in a town called Santa Barbara and were very nice. They had a baby boy whom Hanna was helping to look after, so now she was a big sister, too.

'Taken in': what did that mean? Sophie wondered. She'd sent a Christmas card to Mr and Mrs Miller, introducing herself, but had no reply. The only cards in her pigeonhole were from the Wiltons, inviting her to a New Year's Eve party, and Tamara Grossman, who'd safely arrived from Vienna the month before and would be cooking for the event. Tamara said she was finding English people very strange and missing Vienna desperately, but at least she was safe – for the time being. Sophie sat holding the card in her hands, thinking how pleased her mother would have been to hear of Tamara's escape. She missed her parents terribly and held long conversations with both of them in her head, imagining their responses, but they seemed to be slipping further out of reach. Those happy people in the photograph by Lake Achensee belonged to another world.

That winter, Sophie was colder than she could ever remember. Windsor Castle became a giant ice house, draughts swirling down the stone corridors and up the winding staircases. Her toes and fingers were swollen with chilblains and she went to bed every night fully dressed, spare clothes piled on top of her blankets. The small electric stove in her room could only be switched on for a couple of hours each morning and evening and most of the heat disappeared up the chimney, warming the Mauser pistol; thankfully she'd made sure to store the ammunition separately in case of accidents.

Yet gradually the dark evenings receded and yellow daffodils dotted the grassy mound beneath the Round Tower. Sophie spent long hours in the Muniments Room, having completed her search of Frogmore House and Fort Belvedere, and became a familiar figure in the bindery: a place where she felt particularly close to her father. It would be fair to say Signor Agnelli put up with her visits, rather than encouraging them. He was an uncommunicative man, as far from the stereotypical demonstrative Italian as one could get, although Mags (who liked to see the best in everyone) said he was only grumpy because he missed his family in Venice. Sophie liked seeing the men at work, folding, stitching or gilding leather, and it was a relief not to be the only foreigner for once: besides Signor Agnelli, an apprentice from Leipzig had recently been employed. He and Sophie had exchanged a few words – but in English, by common consent. Anti-German feeling was growing and she was becoming used to hostile looks from shopkeepers in town. She spent most of her time inside the castle walls, or on long solitary bike rides across country at the weekend.

Returning to the castle from one of these outings, she was overtaken by a man on a motorcycle who waved and pulled in beside her. It was PC Dedham – only not a PC any longer.

'Detective Sergeant now,' he said. 'So if there's any sleuthing to be done, Miss Klein, I'll take care of it.'

'I'll bear that in mind,' Sophie replied drily. She was delighted to see him, though; happier than she had any reason to be. His cheerful face lifted her spirits and reassured her. If she were ever in the worst trouble, she had a feeling he would try to help.

On a particularly beautiful spring day in the middle of March, German troops marched into Czechoslovakia and Hitler took control of the entire country. The assurances he'd given the British Prime Minister at Munich were shown to be worthless, as Sophie had predicted.

'So you were right,' Miss Preston told her at lunch the next day. 'I suppose you're very pleased with yourself.'

'Really, Miss Preston,' JB murmured.

'How could I be?' Sophie was so angry, she forgot to be discreet. 'The day Hitler invaded Austria was one of the worst in my life. The Nazis murdered my parents – how do you think I feel about seeing them occupy Czechoslovakia?'

Miss Preston pursed her red lips. 'Sorry, I'm sure. I always seem to be saying the wrong thing.'

'In this case, certainly,' JB said. 'There are dark times ahead. We must show a united front instead of sniping at each other.'

A couple of days later, Chamberlain made the threat clear, declaring in a speech to the country that he couldn't trust Hitler not to occupy other countries. At the end of the month, he announced that Britain would defend Poland if that country were invaded by Germany. The stage was set; now all anyone could do was wait. Following Gladys's example, Sophie enrolled on a first-aid evening class where she learned to bandage broken limbs and treat burns, and everyone was encouraged to plant potatoes, runner beans and tomato seeds for the year ahead. The Royal Family came less frequently to Windsor at weekends, and when they did, the King was shorter-tempered than ever, the Queen clearly anxious beneath her customary smile. A teacher from nearby Eton College gave Elizabeth history lessons so she was too busy to see much of Sophie. Only Margaret Rose was as high-spirited and naughty as ever, shielded from any disturbing news.

In April, when Sophie had been at the castle for nearly a year, Hanna's tenth birthday rolled around: the anniversary of undoubtedly the worst day in their lives. Sophie sent her a copy of *Emil and the Detectives*, the story of a crime-solving twelve-year-old boy in Berlin, and a jumper she'd knitted, hoping it was the right size. By then she'd received a couple of letters from her sister which she reread countless times and kept under her pillow, but the world Hanna described was alien: full of cookouts and outings to baseball games. Still no word from Hanna's foster parents, the Millers. Still, her sister seemed to be happy, and would have had no idea Europe was teetering on the brink of disaster.

The following month, the King and Queen set off for a six-week tour of Canada and America while the princesses stayed at home in Buckingham Palace. If they came to Windsor at all, it was to stay in Royal Lodge, their former country home in the park. Sophie received a handwritten invitation from Princess Elizabeth to tea there one Sunday, much to Miss Preston's annoyance. Elizabeth showed her the miniature cottage in the grounds, presented to her by the people of Wales, and when they were sitting on the floor in the tiny drawing room, she told Sophie, 'Papa says we can't avoid war any longer. Do you agree?'

'Yes, I'm afraid so,' she replied.

'He's hoping America and Canada will take our side,' Elizabeth continued. 'That's the main reason he and Mummie have gone over there, but I can't help worrying while they're away. What if war's declared while they're still abroad and they can't come back?'

'I don't think that will happen,' Sophie said. 'But if it does, maybe you and Margaret will join them overseas.'

'We wouldn't dream of it,' the princess said. 'Papa belongs here – he'd find some way of getting home, and Mummie would never leave him. We'll stay together in our own country, come what may.'

The King and Queen returned safely from their successful tour, much to everyone's relief. Four days into their visit, the Duke of Windsor had broadcast a plea for world peace on NBC America but the BBC refused to air it and even the Duke of Kent was cross with his brother for trying to upstage the King. Sophie was able to tell Aunt Jane that, as far as she knew, no one at the castle approved of the Duke's behaviour.

Two months later, Hitler's army assembled on the border

with Poland. Countries were taking sides: Germany and the Soviet Union had signed a pact promising not to attack each other, while France had also agreed with Britain to defend Poland if necessary. Tension rose in the sweltering August heat: Londoners were ordered to black out their windows, and sleep was hard to come by on those suffocating, anxious nights. On 1 September, Nazi troops marched into Poland; two days later, the British ambassador in Berlin handed the German government a note stating that unless an immediate withdrawal was agreed by eleven a.m., Britain would declare war on Germany. The country held its breath. As church bells rang out on a glorious Sunday morning, JB, Sophie and Mags clustered around the wireless to hear Prime Minister Chamberlain announce that no such undertaking had been received. They stared at each other, ashen-faced.

'So that's that, then,' JB said, her voice flat. Mags was too stunned even to cry.

A couple of hours later, air-raid sirens sounded across the country, sending people rushing into whatever shelter they'd managed to improvise – or, losing their heads completely, screaming down the street. Thankfully, it turned out to be a false alarm.

That afternoon, Sophie moved her father's pistol and ammunition from its hiding place in the chimney to a loose floorboard directly beneath her bed. She wouldn't let the Nazis take her alive.

Chapter Twenty-Four

Windsor Castle, September 1939

In some ways it was a relief the period of waiting was over; so said JB, and nearly everyone agreed (apart from Mags, who'd fallen into a state of nervous collapse and had to spend two days in bed). At least now they had some idea of what lay ahead and could begin preparations in earnest. All over Britain, thousands of children were shepherded on to trains and buses that would take them away from cities and into the safety of the countryside. The princesses were up in Scotland, where they'd been spending the summer at Birkhall, so it seemed sensible for them to stay there, leaving the King and Queen to carry on with their duties at Buckingham Palace. At Windsor Castle, the housekeeping team swung into action immediately, shrouding the State Apartments in dust sheets, taking down paintings, turning glass-fronted cupboards to the walls and unhooking the great crystal chandeliers. There would be no more visitors or grand state dinners – and the Royal Library would be closed for business, too. The Librarian summoned Sophie and Miss Preston to the weekly Friday meeting, where he stunned them both by announcing that since he would have to spend so much time away from the castle, arranging safekeeping of various treasures from the royal collection, Miss Klein would become acting Royal Librarian for the duration of the war.

'And I trust you will do everything in your power to assist her, Miss Preston,' he added. 'Miss Klein will oversee library business on a day-to-day basis and liaise with the bindery, and you will report primarily to her. I've already informed Signor Agnelli of the appointment.'

Closing her mouth with a snap, Miss Preston muttered, 'Yes, sir.'

Sophie hardly took in a word of what else was discussed: something about sandbags, possibly, and research requests that would have to be cancelled. She avoided Miss Preston's eye for the rest of the meeting but when it was over and they were out in the corridor, the secretary let her have it with both barrels.

'Acting Royal Librarian, indeed!' she hissed. 'You're a foreigner! You have no idea how things are done in this country. I'll report to you because I've been told to, but you'll never have my respect.'

'I can probably live without it,' Sophie replied, with icy dignity. 'We'll have to work together, Miss Preston, so we might as well try to get on. If you find that impossible, perhaps you should consider joining another department.'

She was following Mrs Slater's advice – 'Act the part and it'll become second nature' – and was surprised to find how easy that was.

The Muniments Room at the top of the Round Tower was now truly Sophie's domain, and she spent longer hours there than ever, overseeing her treasures. Some particularly precious items were to be moved for safekeeping to the vaults beneath the castle – cavernous spaces carved out of the chalk foundations. The Tower of London was also being cleared, the Librarian informed Sophie, including the Jewel House. The damage to morale if the Crown Jewels were to fall into enemy hands would be incalculable – as Sophie knew only too well. Her father had been appalled when Hitler ordered the removal of Charlemagne's imperial crown and regalia from the Hofburg Palace to an underground vault in Nuremberg Castle.

Walking around the battlements, Sophie imagined Nazi troops goose-stepping down the Long Walk while she – maybe the castle's only survivor – crouched behind a wall to pick them off with her Mauser, one by one. She didn't know how to shoot, and the Germans would be out of range, but that didn't stop her picturing the scene. By now, she had company on the roof: the ARP team had been installing a system of bells and alarms connecting every tower and the rooms below. As dusk fell, the castle became a hive of activity as housemaids and groundsmen attended to the blackout, closely followed by wardens and firemen inspecting it. All night long, footsteps echoed down shadowy corridors lit only by the dimmest bulbs, and weapons mounted on the wall appeared more sinister than ever.

Sophie had arranged to meet Aunt Jane at the usual spot in Green Park soon after war was declared. Victoria Station was busy with the last few groups of evacuees, excited or forlorn children with labels around their necks, clutching suitcases, gas masks and teddy bears. She thought of Hanna – probably so at home in America by now that she no longer felt like a refugee – and for the first time, could allow herself to be glad her sister was happy somewhere else and spared yet more upheaval. What did it matter whether the Millers kept in touch with her, as long as they were kind to Hanna? They'd thrown her a birthday party at a swimming pool, she'd written, with balloons and sausages cooked outside on a grill.

Sandbags were already appearing in doorways along Piccadilly, and Sophie spotted signs to a public air-raid shelter. She couldn't help glancing up at the sky. It seemed inconceivable that German bombers might soon be on their way, as inconceivable as actually wearing the gas mask slung in a case over her shoulder. More trenches had been dug in Green Park and areas of grass were being levelled – for gun emplacements, maybe? Sophie didn't like to ask; these days her accent was usually greeted with hostility. She'd been looking for Aunt Jane's familiar pillbox hat and so was surprised to see Esme Slater sitting on the usual bench by the bandstand. Mrs Slater rose as she approached and Sophie followed her at a discreet distance deeper into the park, where they sat to talk in a more secluded spot behind some rosebushes.

Apparently she and Mr Sinclair had been having a 'pretty hairy' time since Sophie had last seen them: he had been arrested by the Nazis on suspicion of spying but released a few months later, while she had been questioned and roughed up a little on several occasions, hiding out with friends and eventually escaping from Vienna in the nick of time a week before war was declared. She didn't look her usual elegant self: her hair was drooping and the toes of her sensible walking shoes were scuffed.

'I hear you're a great success at the castle,' she said, lighting another cigarette from the stub of the last. 'Congratulations. I knew you could do it.'

'I've been appointed acting Royal Librarian, actually,' Sophie told her casually. 'For the duration of the war.'

'Bully for you.' Mrs Slater gave her customary dry smile. 'But now listen, our friend the Duke of Windsor's back in the country and angling for some sort of glamorous position abroad. He's meeting the King at Buckingham Palace – without Wallis, since neither the Queen or his mother will receive her – but we think the pair of them might come your way, maybe drop in at Frogmore or Fort Belvedere and chat to a few people. Could you keep an eye on them?'

She said that so casually, as though it would be the easiest thing in the world. 'I'll try,' Sophie replied, rather than refuse outright. 'I can't follow them everywhere, though.'

'Do your best.' Mrs Slater blew out a plume of smoke, gazing into the distance. 'They seem to know more about the royal household than we do. Somebody's feeding them information and you can be sure anything Wallis hears will go straight to the Germans, courtesy of that swine von Ribbentrop.' She ground out the cigarette stub with her clumpy shoe. 'Well, best be off. Toodle-oo, dear. Keep up the good work. You can relay any news to Aunt Jane in the usual way.'

She turned back. 'Oh, by the way, your friend Ruth Hoffman sends her regards. We've found her a job in Paris. Quite a bright spark, isn't she?'

'She is indeed.' An image of Ruth flashed into Sophie's head, her face absorbed as she sawed away on the violin. Of course the intelligence services would want to make use of her cunning and determination. Ruth was a survivor, and good for her.

After getting to know the Duke at one remove, it would be interesting to finally see him – and Wallis, of course, who was such a controversial figure – yet there were areas of the castle where Sophie couldn't lurk without attracting attention. The King and Queen's private apartments were above the bindery workshop in the basement of the Victoria Tower, but the workshop was accessed by an underground passage and she had no business venturing above stairs. Mrs Slater was asking too much, Sophie felt, especially at the present time. Everyone in the castle had been on edge since war was declared, vying with each other to do the right thing as conspicuously as possible. Mags's sewing machine was constantly whirring as she helped the housekeeper run up endless blackout blinds, JB had joined the Women's Voluntary Service and Miss Preston was furiously knitting scarves and gloves for the soldiers, whether they wanted them or not. An advance guard of British troops was already training in France, ready to repel the German invasion that would no doubt soon come. Waiting and watching the inexorable advance of the Nazis through Poland – that was all they could do, and it was driving them all slowly mad.

After she'd met Mrs Slater, Sophie called in at the Wiltons' to see how Tamara was getting on and say goodbye to Gladys, who was about to begin her nurse's training. They hadn't had much chance to talk at the New Year's Eve party since Tamara was so busy in the kitchen, but that evening the Wiltons were out, so there was to be a small party below stairs. The three women drank coffee with a nip of brandy and ate Vanillekipferl and Sachertorte, and Sophie could almost imagine she was back in Vienna – apart from the fact they were speaking English, for Gladys's benefit.

'There are guests here for supper three, four times a week,' Tamara complained. 'Always I am to be cooking, and for

luncheon and tea as well. These English people eat like—'
She puffed out her cheeks.

'Cheer up, Tammy,' Gladys told her. 'At least you're over
here and not stuck in Vienna.'

'*Oh, mein geliebtes Wien!*' Tamara felt in her sleeve for
a handkerchief. 'Every night I dream of home.'

Gladys pulled a face at Sophie. 'You just missed Miss
Ottoline,' she said, changing the subject. 'She's passed her
tests and now she's having a whale of a time driving the
top brass around. She's meeting all these suitable young men
so her Ladyship's delighted, but Miss Ottoline says she's
having far too much fun to look for a husband.'

'Every woman wants a husband.' Tamara blew her nose
loudly. 'And I will never find one because I am down in this
kitchen all day long.'

'Gordon Bennett!' Gladys poured another slosh of brandy
into Tamara's cup. 'You're wetter than a wet weekend in
Whitby. Still, I shall miss your biscuits.' She popped the last
one into her mouth.

'And what will we do when you are gone?' Tamara asked
dolefully. 'If there is a new maid who is lazy and Lady
Wilton does not like?'

'It's just as well that girl can cook,' Gladys told Sophie
when Tamara had gone up the back stairs to bed, 'otherwise
I'd have tipped her into the Thames long ago. You'd think
she'd be grateful, coming to a nice house like this. And
the Wiltons aren't so bad. His Lordship might be a bit
peculiar but there's no harm in him – not like some I
could mention.'

'I know,' Sophie said, sighing. 'She's grateful, of course,
and so am I. It's hard, though. We can't expect people to
understand the things we've gone through, but we can't

forget them either.' She squeezed Gladys's hand. 'Soon you'll be off! Are you excited?'

'I can't wait.' Gladys's eyes shone and her unremarkable, pinched little face was suddenly transformed. 'I want to see the world outside of London – go abroad, maybe. If Miss Ottoline can do it, so can I.'

'Of course you can,' Sophie said. 'Will you write and let me know how you get on?'

Gladys was the nearest thing she had to a friend, she realised, and she didn't want to lose touch with her. She daren't look too far ahead but perhaps one day, when the war was over and Gladys was no longer in service, they would get to know each other properly.

The war would test everyone in ways they couldn't anticipate, Sophie thought, fumbling her way through the pitch-black town of Windsor towards home that night. It might liberate some, as well as destroying others, and who was to say which camp she would be in by the end of it all.

Peering ahead, she caught sight of a dark shape and heard voices above the footsteps: a man's, low and angry, and a woman's, alternately soothing and pleading. The pair were walking with a torch trained on the ground and she hurried to take advantage of the light – at a safe distance, because this sounded like a conversation they'd want to keep private. Suddenly the couple stopped abruptly so she did, too, not wanting to get too close. The man swore viciously, the woman gave a small cry and the torch beam swung wildly for a second – revealing Miss Preston, shrinking away with her arm twisted behind her back, and Cyril Jenkins towering over her. There was some sort of wordless scuffle and then a pause before the footsteps resumed in silence.

Before she could think about it, Sophie quickened her pace. 'Yoo hoo,' she called. 'May I tag along with you?' It had already become common practice to join up with strangers in the blackout, especially if they had a torch.

'My goodness, if it isn't Miss Preston and Mr Jenkins,' she said breathlessly, once she'd reached them. 'May I walk with you up the hill? I've been meeting my aunt in London and stayed far later than I should have.'

'And was that journey necessary, Miss Klein?' Mr Jenkins asked. 'You know the trains are meant to be kept free for the movement of troops and evacuees.'

Miss Preston said nothing.

'Maybe not, strictly speaking,' Sophie replied, 'but poor Aunt Jane's so nervous these days that it seemed a kindness.'

'Then perhaps you should encourage her to move to the country, as the government advises.' He was always so quick to tell other people what to do.

Sophie kept up a stream of undemanding conversation for the next ten minutes or so before peeling off to make her way to the castle, leaving the couple free to carry on to Miss Preston's house unaccompanied. She had no idea whether her intervention had helped, but at least it might remind Cyril Jenkins the blackout couldn't hide him completely.

The next day, JB came back to Windsor after spending a week at Buckingham Palace, helping the Queen with her correspondence.

'Did you see the Duke of Windsor?' Sophie asked casually over lunch. 'I gather he's in the country.'

'Indeed I did.' JB laid her knife and fork neatly together. 'Dickie Mountbatten brought him and Wallis back from

289

France in a destroyer. The Duke was saying he wouldn't leave unless the King sent a private plane to collect them, but he saw sense at last, thank goodness.'

'Do you think they'll visit the castle?' Sophie went on. 'I should like to see if the Duchess is as chic as everyone says.'

'I doubt it,' JB told her. 'I heard a rumour they might drop in at Fort Belvedere but they're not staying long in the country. Wallis hates it here. I wouldn't be surprised if they ended up in America for good.'

'Ladies, we shouldn't be talking about this sort of thing,' Mags said, glancing around. 'You never know who might be listening.'

'But it's only the three of us,' Sophie protested. 'And no one else within earshot.'

The dining room was virtually deserted. Day by day, the household dwindled as temporary staff weren't replaced, servants on reserve with the forces were called up for duty and a significant number of women left to get married.

'You're right, though, Mags,' JB said. 'I shouldn't be so indiscreet.'

'Anyway, I must go.' Sophie looked at her watch. 'I've volunteered for the fire-watching team and it's my first training session this afternoon.'

They all dispersed to carry out various good works: JB collecting jumble for a sale the next week and Mags sewing a siren suit that she proposed to wear during bombing raids. Fire-watching would suit Sophie perfectly. She loved looking down at the park from on high, the river glinting in the moonlight like a black satin ribbon and the Long Walk a ghost track for travellers from long ago. Besides, she wasn't sleeping much so it was no hardship to spend part of the night doing something useful, and even if there was no immediate threat from German bombers, it was best to be prepared.

The wardens and engineers had devised a system of warning bells and a telephone network to connect watchers on the roofs with those sleeping below. The most urgent bell meant they should proceed to the nearest shelter immediately. If the alarm sounded during the day and anyone was out in the grounds, they were to make their way to a tunnel in the hillside that led to a vast evil-smelling cave, its walls studded with pebbles.

Luckily, Cyril Jenkins' ARP duties mainly concerned the blackout so there was no danger of Sophie running in to him up on the roof. Miss Preston was subdued that Monday, her eyes downcast. It might have been wiser not to have got involved in their argument, Sophie reflected, but too late now. And then as she handed over a file, the sleeve of Miss Preston's blouse fell back to reveal an angry red welt on her wrist.

Sophie couldn't pretend she hadn't noticed – their eyes had met – and it seemed callous not to say something. 'That looks sore.'

Miss Preston flushed. 'I burned my arm on the oven shelf. Such a silly! Cyril's always telling me to take more care.'

For the first time, Sophie felt the tiniest pang of sympathy. The two of them had managed to establish some sort of working relationship and Miss Preston was certainly efficient. She was an organised and methodical secretary, and her typing was extraordinarily fast. Yet she was no friend of Sophie's – she'd never tried to make her feel welcome – and no one had forced her to become Cyril Jenkins' fiancée. Soon-to-be wife, in fact. A few days later, Miss Preston informed the lunching ladies that she and Mr Jenkins had finally fixed the date and would be married next June.

'So you'll be rid of me at last,' she told Sophie with a tight smile. 'Naturally, I shall be giving up work. Cyril wants me at home, looking after him and the house.'

'I never thought she'd go through with it,' JB said in their north-terrace sitting room that evening. 'Or maybe he was the one who needed pinning down.'

'She doesn't seem very happy, though,' Mags observed, and Sophie had to agree: Miss Preston was glassy-eyed and twitchy, like a rabbit mesmerised by a stoat.

'By the way,' JB said quietly, once Mags had gone to bed, 'I shouldn't gossip but a little bird told me the Windsors are dropping by tomorrow morning, so you might get your look at the Duchess. They'll be going to Fort Belvedere but they may call in at the castle, too.'

She would try to catch a glimpse of the couple, Sophie decided, but that was the most Mrs Slater could reasonably expect – after all, she could hardly follow the Windsors around on her bicycle, hoping to eavesdrop on their conversations. The risk was too great, and these anxious days were making her more aware of her vulnerability. If she lost her position at the castle, what would happen then? Apart from the Wiltons, she had no allies in Britain; Aunt Jane or her colleagues might choose not to answer the telephone and she'd have no way of contacting them for help in an emergency. She'd once tried to follow the old lady at least part of the way home but had lost her in the crowd around Piccadilly Circus. She knew virtually nothing about Mrs Slater and Mr Sinclair, either.

A terrible thought occurred to her in the middle of the night: what if Mrs Slater were a double agent, working for the Germans, too? She spoke the language perfectly, with hardly any trace of an accent. Sophie had heard rumours the

Duke of Windsor had taken a mistress in Austria while he was staying at the Rothschilds' castle, waiting for Wallis's divorce to come through so he could marry her. Could that mistress have been Esme Slater? She was just his type, from what Sophie had learned, and everyone said how handsome and charming the Duke could be when he put his mind to it.

Yet Sophie's imagination was running away with her. In the morning, she resolved to be sensible, keep her head below the radar and stop worrying about things beyond her control.

Rumours of the Windsors' arrival had spread around the castle and an electric current seemed to run through the corridors when their car was spotted, driving at a great lick down the Long Walk with their security staff trying to keep up behind. One of the housemaids put her head around the door of the archive office to alert Miss Preston, and all three of them ran up to the battlements for the best view of the Duchess's outfit.

'So chic,' Miss Preston sighed in delight, though it was hard to make out the small figure below in a black-and-white houndstooth coat.

'Apparently the Duke wants to show her the room where he broadcast to the nation after the abdication,' the housemaid said.

'And where's that?' Sophie asked.

'Top of the Augusta Tower,' Miss Preston said, in a tone that implied, 'Don't you know anything?'

'Well, this isn't getting the job done,' Sophie said. 'I'll be in the bindery if anyone needs me.'

'Getting a closer view?' asked the housemaid, and Miss Preston laughed.

'Well, maybe.' Sophie was smiling, too. There was no shame

in admitting that, along with everyone else, she was intrigued by this woman people either loved or loved to hate: the American who had stolen the heart of their king. What was the secret of her hold over him? The Augusta Tower was en route to the bindery if she walked across the quadrangle and maybe she could pick up some innocuous piece of information to show Mrs Slater she'd made an effort.

By the time she'd hurried downstairs, however, the Windsors had disappeared from sight. Sophie entered the building by a side door and took a flight of stairs down to the bookbinder's workshop. It had taken several months but finally she could find her way around the maze of corridors, dungeons and vaults beneath the castle. Maybe if the worst came to the worst, she could hide away in some forgotten corner, raiding the kitchens at night for food.

In the bindery, Signor Agnelli was his usual taciturn self. Sophie asked how they were getting on with a particularly tricky repair: a book published soon after the execution of Charles I, reputed to have been written partly by him and incorporating silk bookmarks that might have been part of the original garter ribbons. The ribbons had had to be removed while the book was resewn but had just been returned from the specialist textile conservator, the German apprentice was able to tell her.

'Marvellous. That is a lovely job,' Sophie said, inspecting them. She was about to leave when she noticed a couple of books on his worktable that seemed out of place: two volumes of what looked like fashion drawings. She leafed quickly through pages of designs by Schiaparelli and Chanel.

'A private job,' Kurt told her in German. Did he not want Signor Agnelli to hear? 'The Duchess's maid asked us to do it. Apparently it's a surprise for her birthday.'

'And when was this decided?' Sophie asked in her frostiest tone. 'I should have been informed.'

Kurt shrugged. 'A while ago, by the Librarian himself.' Everyone in the bindery was reluctant to accept Sophie's authority, she was aware of that.

'I've seen no mention of these books in the ledger,' she said. 'At the very least, the job should be recorded.' She tucked both books under her arm.

'There's no time.' Kurt got up from the bench as if to take them back. 'She's coming any minute now.'

'I won't be long,' Sophie told him, already walking away. She felt his eyes boring into her back and it was all she could do not to break into a run. Something was very odd here: the Librarian would never authorise a private commission, and why would the Duchess's maid be approaching the castle bindery in the first place?

She couldn't risk being spotted above ground so took a zig-zag route along various corridors to an out-of-the-way cloakroom. Locking the door behind her, she laid both books on the floor and examined them inch by inch: looking down the spines, shaking out the pages, running her fingers over the marbled endpapers. They were handsome coffee-table books with no text that might have included a coded message, only exquisite illustrations on thick paper, and nothing out of the ordinary at first glance. Yet was it her imagination, or did the back board of one volume seem a fraction thicker than the front? She felt both covers again to make sure and, her heart in her mouth, worked a corner of the marbled paper free with her fingernail. The paper tore, sending her into a momentary panic; there could be no going back now but, then again, no reason to be careful.

Seconds later, she had drawn out a thin sheet of paper

that had been slipped between the board and the endpaper. It took her only a second more to realise she was looking at a diagram of the air-raid warning system on the roof of Windsor Castle.

Chapter Twenty-Five

London, September 1939

'I took the book straight to the Superintendent of the Castle,' Sophie told Aunt Jane. 'There was no time to waste. The German lad was taken away – for interrogation, I suppose – and we haven't seen him since, but I don't know what happened to the maid or what the Windsors were told, or asked. They might not have been aware the book was being used to carry information, I suppose. And Signor Agnelli's still running the bindery so he must have convinced the police he knew nothing about the matter. Maybe he didn't.' She sighed, sticking her hands in her pockets. 'I have a hundred questions but don't like to seem too interested. Everyone's watching their back in the household these days.'

'Thank you, dear,' Aunt Jane said. 'I'll pass on the information.' She never reacted to anything Sophie told her, only stared ahead with her usual impassive expression. Sometimes Sophie would repeat herself, thinking Aunt Jane couldn't have heard, and would be rewarded with a sharp rebuke.

'I'll have to be a lot more careful from now on,' Sophie

told her. 'The castle's full of police and soldiers and I'm worried about drawing attention to myself.'

'I can understand that,' Aunt Jane replied. 'Perhaps you should lie low for a while.'

'Yes, I will.' Sophie stood, although usually Jane was the one to determine when their meetings ended. It might have been childish, but she'd wanted to be told she'd done well, and going over what had happened made her feel nervous and disgruntled. The Superintendent had thanked her for bringing the matter to his attention, saying what a great service she had performed for everyone in the castle, yet there had been questions, too: why had she gone to the bindery at that specific time, and what had made her suspicious about those particular books? When had she first met Kurt, the apprentice, and had she spent any time with him outside work? DS Dedham had been called into the office and he was listening to all of this, too. It was as though they suspected her of being part of the plot. If she were English, it would never have occurred to them.

'Are you sure you're not after my job, Miss Klein?' DS Dedham had asked as he escorted her out of the office. 'I'd have thought you were busy enough with your own. Seems like we're both going up in the world.'

'The Librarian has every confidence in me,' Sophie replied stiffly. 'I should hope you feel the same.'

'Of course,' he'd said. 'You have a handy knack of being in the right place at the right time. If that map had reached its destination, we should all have been in trouble. So thank you – we're grateful for your help.'

The weeks dragged by. At home, another harvest was gathered in; abroad, the Soviet Union followed Hitler into

Poland, and the country finally fell under German and Soviet control in October. Closer to home, there was a dreadful blow to British morale when the battleship HMS *Royal Oak* was sunk by a German submarine while anchored at Scapa Floe in Scotland, with the loss of over 800 lives. Sophie didn't mention the war when she wrote to Hanna: she only said how cold it was in the castle already, and hoped she was enjoying the sunshine in California. America felt as remote as the moon. The Millers had still not contacted her, and now the letters from her sister were becoming infrequent. You can't expect too much, Sophie told herself: Hanna must be busy and happy, and that's as it should be.

The Duke and Duchess of Windsor were back in France: they were staying in Paris while he took up a post with the British Military Mission and Wallis volunteered for the French Red Cross. According to JB, Chamberlain and the King had warned the generals not to show the Duke anything secret. Sophie hadn't told anyone about the breach of security she'd uncovered; the Superintendent had warned her not to, but she wouldn't have dreamt of doing so anyway. The Royal Librarian ('the real one', she imagined him thinking) had apparently been informed of the matter, but he didn't raise it with Sophie. They met rarely these days, and he no longer seemed inclined to confide in her. He has other things on his mind, she told herself, yet she couldn't help wondering whether he no longer trusted her either.

The castle that had once been Sophie's sanctuary now seemed gloomy and oppressive in the blackout, with few diversions now the princesses were still up in Scotland and the King and Queen stayed mainly in London at weekends. She escaped for long bicycle rides before the weather became too severe. Sometimes DS Dedham would pass her on his motorcycle but she kept him at arm's length, even though she was lonely; Mags and JB were kind, but she longed for a friend nearer her own age. She would often see Cyril Jenkins, too, driving about in a blue Morris van. Petrol was rationed towards the end of the year yet no doubt he was on official business and not troubled by these petty restrictions. She and Miss Preston only spoke to each other when it was strictly necessary. Once she bumped into her with her mother in the town and was introduced to Mrs Preston: a short, stout woman with a loud voice and a bristly chin. They were shopping for towels, and Miss Preston looked more miserable than ever. Sophie hardened her heart.

On a raw day in November, Sophie received a message asking her to report to the Superintendent's office. She was instantly alarmed but he welcomed her politely, inviting her to take a seat. DS Dedham was there too; he closed the door behind her. It was a trivial matter, the Superintendent said, but he felt obliged to let her know they'd received an anonymous letter, claiming she was a spy.

'A spy?' Sophie felt her cheeks grow hot. Did she look guilty? Of course: it must have been written all over her face. 'But that's ridiculous!'

'I know,' the Superintendent assured her. 'Especially given your outstanding service record. The Librarian holds you in the highest regard; he tells me you've handled sensitive matters with absolute discretion. Can you think of anyone who might hold a grudge against you?'

Miss Preston sprang instantly to Sophie's mind. She was jealous, granted, but would she really go to the trouble of sending an anonymous letter? 'There may be some people who resent my position,' she began, 'but I can't think of anyone who'd allege this sort of thing. What makes them think so?'

'It might merely be the fact you're German.'

'I'm Austrian,' she replied, through gritted teeth, 'and I hate the Nazis because they murdered my parents.' How many times would she have to keep saying it?

The Superintendent flipped open a folder. 'Apparently you're also to be seen coming and going at strange hours, and you've contravened blackout regulations.'

Ah, Cyril Jenkins. 'I once fell asleep without drawing the blind,' Sophie said. 'It was an honest mistake and my light was off.'

'Of course. These things happen.' He closed the folder and laid it back on his desk. 'All the same, it would be a good idea if you were to take a break from fire-watching duties for a while.'

Sophie stared at him for a second. So she was under suspicion, in spite of everything she'd done to keep the castle safe! She swallowed hard. 'Of course. If you think that's best.'

'I do. Thank you for your time, Miss Klein.' He stood. 'And try not to worry. We're seeing quite a few of these poison pen letters nowadays.'

DS Dedham showed Sophie out but she didn't look at him. Rumours were dangerous, no matter who started them, and if someone were watching her, she'd have to take more care. Besides being worried, she felt hurt that her loyalty should be questioned. Signor Agnelli from the bindery took his turn on the ramparts, and he was Italian. Why shouldn't she do her bit? She'd miss her sessions on the roof, scanning the empty horizon for bombers that would one day come, and feeling part of a team in the meantime.

Volunteers were drawn from all over the castle: gardeners, kitchen porters and increasingly, kitchen- and housemaids. More of the younger men were leaving the household each week, called up for military service, and the place was becoming far more feminine – not that one could immediately tell whether a man or woman was wearing the overalls.

'My Cyril won't be going anywhere,' Miss Preston said. 'He has a weak heart.' Mr Jenkins didn't look like a man with a heart condition, but you could never tell.

In some ways, the shrinking household was drawing closer together. The staff ate together in the same dining room now, and people from different towers and departments were mingling in a way they hadn't when the focus was on the King and Queen and their important visitors. Windsor Castle felt more than ever like a world apart, which made it all the more upsetting that someone within that community should want Sophie thrown out of it. This was a serious attempt to besmirch her name, and she knew whoever was behind it wouldn't stop there.

Overseas, the war continued with ghastly inevitability. The Soviet Union invaded Finland at the end of November, while troop ships carried on ferrying British soldiers across the Channel to support the French army when the Germans attacked, as they were bound to do. At home, it was turning bitterly cold and staff in the castle were constantly reminded to keep inner doors closed to conserve what little heat their bodies and stoves could generate. A line was painted at five inches around every bathtub to keep hot water at a minimum level and, week by week, the use of bedroom fires was further restricted. Eventually there came a directive from the Master of the Household that all non-essential electrical items were to be banned. JB wrote him a letter asking that the north-terrace clerical staff be allowed to gather around one wireless set for the nine o'clock news, and permission was eventually granted – for the duration of that programme only. What sort of Christmas would it be that year?

One gloomy Sunday morning when Sophie had to escape from the castle or explode, she found herself cycling further than she'd intended, her hair whipped into her eyes by the biting wind. There was a relief in exhausting herself so she had some chance of sleeping at night, but now sleet was driving into her face so ferociously that she couldn't make out the road ahead. When she stopped to look around, she was shocked to realise how far she'd come. The sleet was turning to hail that pounded her body, making her wince with pain, and there were no trees under which she could shelter, only a scrappy hedge on the other side of the ditch. Her sodden skirt flapped against her legs and her hands in woollen gloves were blocks of ice. Turning the bicycle around, she found herself heading into the wind, making progress virtually impossible. Just as she was debating whether to huddle in the ditch and wait for the storm to pass, she caught sight of a single headlamp approaching and called for help. Her voice was snatched away by the gale, but the motorcycle pulled in anyway. It was DS Dedham, of course, and never had she been so glad to see him.

'Hop on the back,' he shouted. 'Leave your bike in the ditch and we'll fetch it later.'

There was no alternative. She held on to his back and kept her head down as they set off into the deluge. He could have taken her anywhere; she had no idea where they were going and couldn't have cared less. After twenty minutes of slow but steady progress, he pulled into the driveway of a cottage surrounded by fields, stopped his motorcycle and gestured for Sophie to run inside while he parked it in the barn. The hail had turned back into sleet, but Sophie couldn't have got any wetter, so she didn't hurry.

'Where are we?' she asked, when Sergeant Dedham joined her in the porch.

'My parents' house,' he told her. 'I was on my way here for lunch. Don't worry, there'll be enough to go round.'

'But I can't turn up looking like this!' Sophie said, mortified.

He laughed. 'It's not an audience with the Queen. Mum and Dad won't care what you look like.'

'Oh, dear Lord!' Mrs Dedham exclaimed when she saw them. 'Two drowned rats.'

'This is Miss Klein, from the castle,' he said. 'She didn't pick the best time for a bicycle ride.'

'Indeed not,' his mother said, inspecting Sophie. Mrs Dedham was a tall, rangy woman with a lined, weatherbeaten face and kind eyes. 'Upstairs with you, young lady, and I'll fetch some dry things. Henry, you can change in the outhouse.'

It was such a treat to be taken care of and let somebody else tell her what to do. Sophie peeled off her saturated clothes and sat on the edge of the bed, wrapped in the towel Mrs Dedham had given her. The bedroom was low-ceilinged and simply furnished, with only a rag rug on the floor, a double bed, an oak wardrobe and a brass-handled chest of drawers, but it was warm. Heat rose from the kitchen below, along with the enticing smell of Sunday lunch, and Sophie luxuriated in it; she would have liked nothing better than to creep under the bedcover and fall asleep, like Goldilocks.

That would have given the Dedhams something to think about, though, so she waited patiently for whatever clothes Mrs Dedham might bring, feeling the tension ebb out of her body and a sensation that reminded her of happiness take its place.

'That's better,' Mrs Dedham said, when Sophie reappeared downstairs in a skirt and jumper with towel-dried hair. 'Now come and sit by the Aga, dear, and we'll hang your wet things on the rail.'

'I'm sorry to invade you like this,' Sophie said. Not the best choice of phrase, perhaps. 'I mean, to turn up uninvited.'

'The more the merrier,' Mrs Dedham replied, lifting the lid of a saucepan bubbling on the stove and releasing a cloud of fragrant steam. 'We've been waiting for Henry to bring a nice girl home.'

'Oh, it's not like that,' Sophie blurted, hot with embarrassment.

DS Dedham was blushing, too. 'Now then, Mother, don't get carried away. Miss Klein is a very important person: she's the Royal Librarian at Windsor Castle, I'll have you know.'

'Well, we are honoured.' Mrs Dedham gave Sophie an appraising look.

'Please, Mrs Dedham, the honour is all mine. I can't tell you what it means to be welcomed into a house like this.' Sophie stopped, afraid she might cry. Luckily, Mr Dedham senior appeared in the kitchen just then, followed shortly afterwards by Henry's younger sister, Joan. Sophie had to be introduced all over again and it seemed only natural to agree that they should call each other by their Christian names – apart from Mr and Mrs Dedham, of course.

They ate at a scrubbed pine table: steak-and-kidney

305

pudding, which Sophie approached with some trepidation because she'd come across suet pastry before. Mrs Dedham's was a revelation, though: robust enough to hold the savoury filling but light and toothsome. Outside, rain pelted against the cottage windows, making the room feel even cosier. The Dedhams were tenant farmers so there was plenty to eat: carrots, peas and potatoes from the kitchen garden and a jug of yellow cream to go with plum tart for afters. Everyone expected food to be rationed before long, like petrol, and the larder was full of bottled fruit and tomatoes, runner-bean chutney and strawberry jam.

'Do you think the King and Queen will have ration books?' Joan asked, and Mrs Dedham said she hoped so, because everyone in the country would have to abide by the rules and the Royal Family should set an example.

Mr Dedham asked Sophie about her family but in a kindly way, and nobody pressed her for details when she said her parents were dead; Mrs Dedham merely slapped another slice of plum tart on her plate, even though Sophie protested she was full to bursting. She told them about her mother's pastry shop in Vienna, and her father's job at the National Library, which had inspired her own career. Henry didn't say much but she was aware of his gaze on her face as he listened intently.

Once they had finished eating, Mrs Dedham went to read the newspaper in the next room and Mr Dedham to check a fence he'd been worried about now the storm had died down. Henry, Joan and Sophie did the washing-up together. Joan told them about her job in the Land Army, working on a nearby farm to replace the men who'd been called up. There were four girls in the team, and she said they were an odd bunch: besides herself, there were two Cockneys who were as tough as nails but hated the countryside, and a debutante who'd never made her own bed, let alone mucked out a cowshed. Henry talked about counterfeit ration books that were already being printed on the illegal market.

'We'd better be off, I suppose,' he said when the dishes were done, looking out of the window at the darkening sky.

Sophie went to thank Mrs Dedham but she was asleep in the armchair so she took her own clothes – by now almost dry – from the kitchen, said goodbye to Joan and ran upstairs to change. Outside, Henry was wheeling his motorcycle out of the barn. The spell was broken and she became suddenly tongue-tied.

'Perhaps I should swap my bicycle for one of those—' Already it felt wrong to say 'Henry'. She added quickly, 'Do you think I could handle a machine like that?'

'I don't see why not.' He brought the motorcycle over. 'Plenty of women ride them. Why don't you take her for a spin around the yard?'

He showed Sophie how to change gear, running along beside her until she felt reasonably confident. How much of England she could discover on a motorcycle! She imagined the miles disappearing under her wheels – although there would always be the problem of petrol. Reluctantly, she brought the machine to a jerky halt and let DS Dedham take the driver's seat. If only they could stay like that, she thought on the drive home with her arms around his waist: together but not needing to speak, not even having to look at each other.

Yet all too soon they were back in Windsor. 'Thank you for rescuing me,' Sophie said, sliding off the motorcycle. 'And for letting me meet your lovely family.' She would treasure the memory of this perfect day, keep it safe and bring it out whenever she felt especially sad.

'Wait,' he said, putting a hand on her arm. 'Don't rush off. I was thinking maybe we might go to the pictures sometime, or maybe for another ride out when the weather improves. What do you say?'

She couldn't look at him. 'I can't, I'm sorry. Thank you for your kindness but please don't ask me again.'

If her circumstances had been different, she would have accepted his invitation in a split second, and the thought of what might have been was unbearable. She hurried through the gate without looking back.

A cold front had set in and the winter was turning out to be even harsher than the one before – the coldest one for forty-five years, so people were saying. The castle was again blanketed in snow, and again Sophie was tortured by chilblains. This year, her clothes froze over the back of the chair until she took to heaping them in bed with her every night, as she'd done the year before. There was still no sign of enemy aircraft in British skies and a good number of the children who'd been evacuated in September were back home with their families in time for Christmas. Nobody knew what lay ahead but there was a general sense the future looked bleak.

The King included a verse from the poem *God Knows*, by Minnie Louise Haskins, in his Christmas Day broadcast: 'And I said to the man who stood at the gate of the year, "Give me a light that I may tread safely into the unknown." And he replied, "Go out into the darkness and put your hand into the hand of God. That shall be to you better than light and safer than a known way."' It was as good a plan as any, Sophie thought. Mags had the text framed and hung it on the wall above her bed.

In January, everyone working at the castle was issued with ration books: those living-in had to hand theirs over to housekeeping so the appropriate stamps could be deducted. Supplies of bacon, butter and sugar were severely restricted, although the two farms on the Windsor estate could provide extra for the kitchens at the castle and Buckingham Palace; vegetables, fruit and flowers were sent from Windsor to London by train every week. The size of writing paper was restricted, and even the shortest piece of string had to be saved for salvage.

Miss Preston was becoming increasingly withdrawn. Sophie would look at her sometimes, slamming the carriage return on her typewriter when the bell made its annoying little ping, and wonder whether Miss Preston could dislike her enough to risk sending an anonymous letter. She thought they'd been getting on better these days – or at least become more adept at hiding their hostility. Could Cyril Jenkins have put her up to it?

Sophie was working quietly in the Muniments Room one day when Detective Sergeant Dedham appeared. Her heart jumped, as usual, but they were always scrupulously formal whenever they bumped into each other around the castle. That morning, he was looking particularly severe.

'Would you come with me?' he asked. 'The Superintendent has requested to see you.'

She followed him without question; something in his tone made her too afraid to ask why. The Superintendent was equally grave.

'I'll come straight to the point, Miss Klein,' he said. 'In response to information we've received, a search of your room has been carried out and a firearm has been found, hidden beneath a floorboard: a German Mauser pistol. What do you have to say about that?'

For a second, Sophie wondered whether to protest her innocence before rejecting the idea. Lying now would be disastrous. 'The gun belonged to my father. I brought it with me from Austria.'

'And do you have a firearm certificate?'

'No. I didn't know one was required.'

The Superintendent leaned back in his chair, folding his arms and frowning. 'Now why would you feel the need to keep a weapon in Windsor Castle?'

'Because I've seen what the Nazis can do,' she replied, 'and I couldn't get hold of a cyanide pill.' She glanced at DS Dedham and then quickly away.

'This is a serious matter,' the Superintendent told her. 'I shall have to inform the Master of the Household and the Governor of the Castle. You should have gone through the proper channels, Miss Klein.'

'I'm sorry, sir. I realise that now.'

'That will be all for the moment,' he went on. 'The weapon has been confiscated, naturally, and I'll come back to you in due course with our decision on the appropriate course of action. Please confine yourself to the castle grounds for the time being.'

'I will.' She rose to leave. 'Might I ask, did you find the gun because of another of those anonymous letters?'

He nodded. 'As a matter of fact, we did.'

'Someone's got it in for me,' she burst out. 'You can't believe them! I've found sanctuary here. Why would I risk losing everything? I'd never do anything to hurt the Royal Family, I swear.'

It was a mistake. The Superintendent drew back with a look of distaste. 'We shall come to our own conclusions. That will be all. Good day to you, Miss Klein.'

Sophie walked back to the Round Tower with her mind whirling and a rising sense of panic. Miss Preston looked up briefly as she entered the office, then carried on typing.

Sophie walked over to her desk. 'May I ask you a question?'

'Well, I can't stop you,' Miss Preston replied, with her usual hoity-toity air.

'Have you been sending anonymous letters about me to the Superintendent? I won't be angry, I just want to know.'

Miss Preston gave a scornful laugh. 'Why on earth would I stoop so low? Don't flatter yourself, Miss Klein. I have better things to do with my time than spread rumours about you. I'm getting married shortly, in case you'd forgotten.'

She was clearly telling the truth; she was a hopeless actor and anyway, she never went anywhere near the north terrace and would have had no chance to look for a gun or anything else in Sophie's room.

If she wasn't writing those letters, though, who was behind them? And how much more did they know? Somebody was determined to get rid of Sophie, and it looked like they might have succeeded.

Chapter Twenty-Six

Windsor Castle, February 1940

Sophie had a week to wait before she was called to see the Superintendent again – a week in which she could hardly sleep or eat. She would wake every morning not knowing whether it would be her last in the castle. The only consolation was that no one seemed to have heard about what the police had found in their search of her bedroom; Mags and JB had both been at work and the housemaid who cleaned along their corridor, Betty, had finished for the day. Miss Preston knew Sophie was on edge but not exactly why.

'These anonymous letters, then,' she began late one afternoon, putting the cover on her typewriter to send it to sleep for the night, like a parrot in a cage. 'Do you think someone's sending them just because you've come from Austria?'

She had finally got the right country. 'I can't think of any other reason,' Sophie replied.

'And you have no idea who's behind it all?'

Sophie shrugged. 'I wondered about Signor Agnelli. He's never liked me much.'

'It can't be a nice feeling,' Miss Preston went on, 'knowing someone's saying horrible things behind your back.'

'It isn't,' Sophie agreed. 'I'm worried people are going to end up believing them, or think I'm too much trouble and tell me to leave anyway.'

'But then what would happen to the archive?' Miss Preston asked. 'They'd have to get somebody from outside to run it, I suppose. The Librarian's far too busy to come back.'

He visited the castle occasionally and would sometimes put his head around the door of the office and ask how they were getting on, always with a distracted air. It must have been quite a responsibility, everyone agreed, safeguarding so many priceless, irreplaceable treasures.

Miss Preston reached for her coat on the stand. 'It would be a shame if you had to leave,' she said, avoiding Sophie's eye. 'I had my doubts about you to begin with, but there's no denying the department's ship-shape and Bristol fashion these days.'

'Thank you.' Sophie was touched. 'That's down to you as much as me, though. Look, do you have to stop working here once you're married? They probably won't replace you and I'm not sure I can manage alone.'

'Cyril doesn't want me to spend all day in an office,' Miss Preston replied, putting on her hat. 'And I shall be busy looking after the house.'

What a waste. 'I can imagine you working for some high-flying general,' Sophie told her. 'Organising his life so he has nothing to worry about but winning the war.'

Miss Preston laughed. 'You are a dreamer, Miss Klein.'

Eventually Sophie found a note in her pigeonhole, summoning her to a meeting with the Superintendent that afternoon.

She was both terrified and relieved the waiting was over, and glad to find that DS Dedham wasn't present to witness what might follow.

'We've decided to take no further action,' the Superintendent told her straight away. 'I've discussed the matter with the Master of the Household and the Librarian, and they feel that, given your personal circumstances and the value of your service here, a line can be drawn under the incident. It seems clear you never intended to use the weapon on anybody else. You are free to go wherever you wish.'

Sophie let out her breath. 'Thank you, sir.'

'But I have to warn you, Miss Klein, there will be a note on your file and any other transgressions may have a different outcome. Is that clear?'

'Absolutely.' She shook his hand and left the office, her legs shaky. From now on, she would take no more risks and feed only the most anodyne information to Aunt Jane: she had to protect herself.

'Everything all right?' Miss Preston asked on her return to the office.

'More than all right,' she replied. 'Very good, in fact.' A wild idea occurred to her. 'Miss Preston, would you be free to come for a drink in the Six Bells this evening? I might ask Miss Maguire and Mrs Johnstone-Burt, too. It's my birthday in a few days so we could have an early celebration.'

'Is that a pub?' Miss Preston asked warily. 'I'm not sure what people would think.' By 'people', she clearly meant Mr Jenkins.

'But the two ladies often go out together,' Sophie assured her. 'Apparently the saloon bar is extremely respectable.'

JB had WVS duties but Mags accepted the invitation with pleasure. There might be a fire in the saloon, she told Sophie, and a certain amount of body heat from people gathered together.

They walked down the slushy hill. 'Such a relief the weather's turning a little warmer,' Mags said, putting her arm through Sophie's. 'By the way, have you heard? The princesses have arrived at Royal Lodge with their nurses and the governess, so I expect we shall see them out and about in the park presently. I do hope they'll be safe, the dear little things. That nice policeman I've seen you talking to has been sent to guard them.'

Sophie digested the information. 'I'm glad they're back from Scotland,' she said. 'It didn't seem right they should be so far away from their parents.'

'Although plenty of children are,' Mags observed. 'It wouldn't surprise me if those girls were sent to America or Canada one day soon.' She squeezed Sophie's arm. 'Listen to me chattering on! Tell me about yourself, dear. Are you stepping out with the policeman? He's terribly handsome.'

Mags was a great reader of romance novels and always on the lookout for new affairs of the heart. She had lost her fiancé in the last war, she'd told Sophie – which perhaps explained why she'd been dreading another so intensely – and now lived her romantic dreams through other people. She was certainly up to date on all the latest gossip.

'So tell me your plans for the big day,' Mags asked Miss Preston, when the three women were settled with their drinks. 'Not long to go now! Is everything in order?'

Miss Preston didn't want to go into detail. They were planning a small wedding, she said, with a reception in a room above a pub that Cyril had chosen. Naturally he was in charge of refreshments, given his contacts, and her mother was saving the family's sugar ration for a wedding cake.

She, Pamela, would probably wear her best frock with a new hat.

'Wouldn't you like me to run you up something special on my machine?' Mags asked.

Miss Preston refused politely and changed the subject. They talked about the rumours clothes might soon be rationed, and how lovely the Duchess of Gloucester looked in her WAAF uniform, which she wore with high heels. The Duke of Windsor had been spotted visiting Cartier in Paris to commission a new piece of jewellery for Wallis. 'Perhaps she needs cheering up,' Mags suggested. 'I imagine working for the Red Cross can be depressing.'

'Pamela?' A loud voice suddenly interrupted their conversation, and they looked up to see Cyril Jenkins staring at them through the hatch from the public bar.

'Cyril.' Miss Preston looked terrified.

In the space of a few seconds, he was beside them. 'I thought you were going to a WI meeting?' he said to his fiancée, ignoring the other two women.

'It finished early,' Mags said chattily, since Miss Preston had been struck dumb. 'Would you like to join us, Mr Jenkins?'

'No, thank you, Miss Maguire,' he replied. 'I should like to take Pamela home. Come along, my love.'

Miss Preston rose obediently and took his arm with a muttered goodnight to the others, allowing herself to be swept away.

'Oh dear,' Mags said, watching them go. 'Still, I suppose it's asking too much for all marriages to be made in heaven.'

It was another few weeks before Sophie caught a glimpse of the princesses. One fine morning in early March, she

317

cycled over to Royal Lodge, left her bicycle by a gate and went for a stroll down the lane. Primroses speckled the verge, a soft breeze was blowing and she decided there was nowhere so beautiful as England in the spring. Rounding a corner, she caught sight of a small group further ahead and recognised them instantly: Margaret riding the pony, the governess leading it, and Elizabeth and DS Dedham walking side by side behind. She watched them for a moment, her heart aching, then turned back before she could be spotted.

Later that month, the King and Queen came to spend Easter with the children at Windsor, and both girls could be seen riding with their father in the Great Park. After Easter, however, events overseas seemed suddenly to accelerate with frightening speed. Mags, JB and Sophie gathered around their wireless every evening to listen to the news, hanging on every word. German forces occupied Norway in April, and in May their troops attacked the Netherlands and Belgium across land and from the air. French and British troops marched north to defend Belgium and the war moved to a different level. Chamberlain resigned immediately, having lost the confidence of the house and – thank goodness, Sophie thought – the King asked Winston Churchill to lead the government. Churchill was not King George's first choice, people said, given that he'd been a particular ally of King Edward VIII. Yet now even he was fed up with the Duke's antics and it was clear he would be loyal to the King. Shortly after that, the staff at Windsor Castle were informed the princesses would be arriving with their staff. Royal Lodge was far too conspicuous from the air and not adequately defended. Nobody knew how long they'd be staying but it was generally agreed to be a good thing for them to be safely inside the castle walls.

Windsor Castle seemed to come alive once the girls were in residence: there was laughter in the corridors, the sound of singing and dogs running around the gardens once again. A second governess accompanied the Scottish one, and four Grenadier Guards had been appointed for the girls' protection, besides DS Dedham and the regular troops guarding the castle. The princesses were to sleep with their nurses within easy reach of the air-raid shelter in one of the middle dungeons, where black beetles scuttled out of cracks in the walls. And two days after their arrival, the early-warning system was tested when a German bomber was spotted on the horizon. Sophie, Mags and JB threw jumpers and coats over their pyjamas and hurried with the other women on their corridor to their nearest underground shelter at the corner of the East Terrace.

'A hole in the ground,' Mags called it, although the place was well-equipped with mattresses, a Red Cross centre and a hot plate to make tea. The Nazis had finally come for her, Sophie thought, huddled in the dark while the aeroplane whined overhead. She had fled across the sea, but they had followed and surely they would hunt her down.

And so began a new routine. The castle was run with minimum staff and everyone had their assigned wartime duties besides their regular jobs. Sophie joined the fire-watching rota again and, thanks to her training course, was one of the shelter first-aid volunteers. The King and Queen came to join their daughters whenever they had a spare weekend, and everyone agreed it was wonderful to see the family back together. They brought their own dogs with them and there was always a noisy reunion with the princesses' corgis. Security was strengthened during these visits, with police and soldiers everywhere; a shooting range was also set up in the gardens and both the King and Queen could be seen practising with a variety of weapons. Sophie thought longingly of the Mauser, no doubt languishing in somebody's desk drawer.

The castle would have been a burglar's paradise. A great quantity of gold plate had been stored in the dungeons and one day, a housemaid who cleaned the princesses' apartment overheard Margaret and Lilibet talking about a trip they'd made to the vault. Apparently the Librarian had taken them and their governess down there one rainy afternoon and shown them the Crown Jewels, wrapped in rags and stored in a biscuit tin. Sophie thought that sounded like one of Margaret's made-up stories.

The Grenadier Guards soon became popular, eating breakfast with the household and attending lunch and tea parties with the princesses. They dug slit trenches all over the park for some mysterious reason, which Margaret loved jumping in and out of and other people fell into at regular intervals. An artist who was painting portraits of the King and Queen installed himself at Windsor to complete them. 'And with a three-course meal every night and the very best accommodation, why wouldn't he?' JB remarked. Like Scheherazade's never-ending stories, the portraits would probably never be finished.

During the week, the girls spent time with their governesses in the schoolroom, took riding and dancing lessons nearby and drove their pony cart through the park – often unaccompanied, Sophie was surprised to see. Yet they had to have some freedom, and surely they were safe within the estate.

One Friday afternoon when the King and Queen were

about to arrive from London, the princesses climbed to the Round Tower battlements to spot their car, accompanied by Detective Sergeant Dedham.

'Why don't you come, too?' Princess Elizabeth invited Sophie. 'I'm sorry not to have seen you before now.' She'd grown up noticeably in the intervening, stressful months; that thoughtful air was even more apparent.

They stood together, looking out over the park. Deer were grazing on the lush grass of early summer and the trees were newly clothed in sharp, fresh green. It was the first time Sophie had seen DS Dedham face-to-face since the gun incident and she felt awkward, but he nodded at her pleasantly enough and said, 'Glad to see you're still with us, Miss Klein.'

'You weren't thinking of leaving, were you?' Princess Elizabeth asked. 'Who should I talk to then?'

'I'm sure you have plenty of friends, ma'am,' Sophie replied.

'But you are my particular book friend,' the princess said. 'I'll come and seek you out again soon, I promise.' She had the most beautiful smile: it lit up her face.

And then the King's car came into view, the Royal Standard flag was hoisted up the flagpole to show he was in residence and the two girls went running downstairs to meet their parents, with Detective Sergeant Dedham following at a distance behind. Sophie stayed where she was a little longer to watch the scene; long enough to notice Cyril Jenkins' blue van in the distance, driving in the direction of the estate farm.

She leaned her elbows on the parapet, thinking about the impending marriage that was now only weeks away. A couple of days before, Miss Preston had come in late to work. She'd

321

fallen down some steps in the blackout, she claimed, wincing with every sudden movement, but Sophie had an idea what might have happened and resolved to do something – anything – to stop Miss Preston making the biggest mistake of her life. She'd been paying particular attention to Mr Jenkins' comings and goings whenever she happened to spot them, so the next Sunday, she cycled along the route he'd taken. He'd parked the van beside a clump of trees near an uninhabited cottage that was slowly falling into disrepair. Sophie walked around it, wondering why anyone would want to stop there. Around the back, she found her answer: a sturdy-looking shed, fastened with a chain and a large, gleaming padlock.

Bad news for the Allies came thick and fast. The Netherlands had fallen in the middle of May, with Queen Wilhelmina fleeing the country and ending up in London; the King met her in person at Liverpool Street Station and gave her a home at Buckingham Palace. Belgium was next to surrender to Germany at the end of May, while German troops had pushed the British, French and Belgian troops back to the port of Dunkirk. To avoid an utterly humiliating defeat, the Royal Navy organised a fleet of every kind of sailing ship to take men off the beaches and home across the Channel. Even Princess Margaret was noticeably subdued.

Miss Preston was staying later in the office each evening. 'Just getting everything in order,' she told Sophie. 'I shan't know what to do with myself when I'm not coming to work.'

She looked miserable and time was running out. 'You don't have to go through with the wedding,' Sophie said. 'You can always tell him you've changed your mind.'

Miss Preston didn't pretend not to understand. 'Can you

imagine how that would go down? Mother's made the cake and my aunt's given us a soup tureen.'

Sophie walked over to sit on the edge of her desk. 'Pamela, this is the rest of your life we're talking about. To hell with the soup tureen.'

'But what am I going to do if I don't marry Cyril? I couldn't carry on working at the castle, not with him here.'

'You don't need to,' Sophie told her. 'You could get a job tomorrow with the Navy or the ATS – they're crying out for girls with your skills. They'd send you away for more training and give you somewhere to live. It would be fun! You don't want to shut yourself away in a house when the world is opening up.' She added a final thrust. 'In fact, it would be unpatriotic.'

Miss Preston lit a cigarette. 'It would, wouldn't it? All the training I've had. I can write two hundred words a minute shorthand.' She sighed. 'But it's pointless. Cyril would never let me go. And Mother loves him – he brought her a tinned ham last week.' She gave a nervous giggle. 'Oops. I wasn't meant to tell anyone that.'

'Does he often give her things?' Sophie asked.

'Only now and then.' Miss Preston tapped a cylinder of ash into the wastepaper bin. 'Christmas and birthdays, times like that.'

A couple of days later, Sophie approached DS Dedham when he was coming off afternoon duty at the Lancaster Tower. He greeted her cautiously and agreed to have a private word with her in the duty office. She told him her suspicions about Cyril Jenkins and described the location of the lockup, while he listened with his head on one side.

'I seem to remember telling you to leave the detective work to me,' he said when she'd finished.

'But this concerns my friend, Miss Preston,' she told him. 'I can't shut my eyes and ears to what's happening.'

'Well, thank you for bringing the matter to my attention. I'll look into it in due course.'

'We need to hurry, though. This man has to be investigated and held to account. If he's—'

DS Dedham held up his hand, interrupting her. 'Enough, Sophie. Let's level with each other. You clearly have a watching brief, but I have no idea who you're working for or what you're trying to find out, and I'm worried you'll end up in serious trouble if you carry on like this.'

'I don't know what you mean,' she said stiffly. 'I'm merely putting together what Miss Preston told me and what I happened to have noticed by chance.'

'There are serious issues at stake here,' he told her. 'Do you realise how much danger the Royal Family's facing? Queen Wilhelmina only escaped by the skin of her teeth and the Nazis bombed the Norwegian royals three times. The King and Queen should be our priority, not some suspect quartermaster.'

He looked at her gravely. 'I want to believe you're on the side of the angels but these are perilous times. Please, think carefully before you meddle in things you don't understand.'

Chapter Twenty-Seven

Windsor Castle, July 1940

On a sunny Monday in the middle of June, Nazi troops marched into Paris. Beautiful Paris, the city of light, now hung about with swastikas. At least the French hadn't cheered as the tanks rolled through their streets, unlike the Austrians. Sophie asked JB if anyone knew what had happened to the Duke of Windsor. Apparently he wasn't in Paris or with Wallis in Biarritz; in fact, nobody could find either of them.

'Let's hope he hasn't gone and got himself captured,' JB said. 'That would be embarrassing.'

A couple of days later, the French Prime Minister resigned rather than sign an armistice and a new government was formed under Marshal Pétain, a hero of the last war, in collaboration with the Germans. Now Britain stood alone. Coils of barbed wire stretched around her coastline that summer and concrete pillboxes with slits for windows had appeared at vantage points. Men who were too old to enlist joined the Home Guard, barricading roads with bags full of earth as sand was in short supply. Road signs had long since disappeared to foil the enemy, who were expected by boat or parachute at any moment.

Churchill rallied everyone's spirits. 'We shall go on to the end,' he declared in Parliament. 'We shall defend our island, whatever the cost may be.'

'Although I can't help worrying about all those young men being wounded and killed,' Mags said hesitantly, glancing around to check no one was listening as they sat in the dining room after supper that evening. 'Don't you think it might be wiser to sue for peace?'

'Absolutely not!' JB was outraged. 'How can we let a man like Hitler rule our country? We have to stand up for democracy. The Queen says she'll die fighting if necessary and I'll be next to her.'

'I suppose you're right.' Mags stood up. 'Well, I'm for bed. I hardly slept a wink last night.'

'Honestly, she should know better,' JB said, when she was out of earshot. 'Once we start talking like that, we're finished.'

'I couldn't agree more,' Sophie replied. She'd learned to keep her political opinions to herself, and it had been a relief to hear JB say exactly what she'd been thinking. 'Oh, she's left her mackintosh behind. I'll take it back for her.'

Mags insisted on carrying a coat if there was the slightest chance of rain. Sophie picked up the shapeless beige garment draped over a nearby chair, noticing as she did so the corner of a piece of paper sticking out of one pocket. It was printed with the word 'WAR!' in block capitals. She drew it out and unfolded it, to find herself reading a propaganda leaflet from the British Union of Fascists. 'Stop the war!' it screamed. 'Remember 1914? Unite with Mosley for peace and prosperity.' There was more text in a smaller typeface, something about Jews being responsible for everything wrong with the world that she scanned quickly. Along the margin of the leaflet, someone had scribbled in pencil, *The Crown Jewels will be collected tomorrow – both of them.*

Sophie stuffed the paper back deep in the pocket and held the raincoat out to JB. 'Actually, I need to call by the office. Would you mind delivering the coat?'

It was impossible. Mags, who didn't have a political bone in her body, who was silly and sentimental and everyone's friend? Sophie walked along the quadrangle to the Round Tower, trying to come up with a rational explanation for what she'd just stumbled across. Yet only the most chilling theory presented itself. Mags slept in the room next to hers. She would have found it easy to slip in while Betty was doing the cleaning – maybe sending her out on some fictitious errand while she searched the place. She could have found the gun and written those anonymous letters. She was always watching, never missing a thing, and encouraging people to confide in her. She'd been working at the castle for years, JB had said; certainly during Edward VIII's reign. What if her love for the current king and queen was a sham and she was still loyal to the previous regime?

Sophie sat in the archive office, wondering what to do. One minute she decided to report what she'd seen to the Superintendent; the next, she thought better of it. She had no real evidence apart from that one leaflet with its cryptic message. What if Mags had taken the paper by mistake and intended to throw it away? What if someone else had borrowed her coat and left it there? Instinctively, though, she knew those excuses didn't ring true. She couldn't talk to DS Dedham, not after the ticking-off he'd given her, and she was wary of approaching the Superintendent on such a

327

minor pretext. She would telephone Aunt Jane right away from a telephone box in town and, in the meantime, watch and wait.

Sophie did her best to seem normal the next day, though it was an effort. She congratulated Miss Preston on her visit to the naval recruiting office and said she had no idea why a police officer should have visited their house and asked to look in the larder. When JB told them the Duke of Windsor had surfaced in Spain, she was as surprised as anyone.

'Apparently Churchill's ordered him back to Britain, but he won't come,' JB said at lunch. 'Honestly, what will that man do next?'

'Are you all right, Sophie, dear?' Mags asked. 'You seem rather quiet today.'

Sophie assured her she was fine, just a little tired. Every nerve in her body prickled; something was about to happen, she knew it. What could that cryptic message mean: 'The Crown Jewels will be collected tomorrow'? Should she tell DS Dedham about it? Should she in fact have taken the leaflet straight to him? Well, it was too late now. She'd spoken to Aunt Jane directly on the telephone the night before and for the first time, had succeeded in shocking her.

In the afternoon, she went upstairs to the Muniments Room and looked out of the window. Her imagination was running away with her, that was all. She had a bird's-eye view of the panorama below: women digging up potatoes in the kitchen garden, soldiers marching by, two abreast – and there were the princesses, waiting by the gate in the pony cart with their governess on the back seat. Detective Sergeant Dedham sat beside them on his motorcycle, a couple of other policemen standing by. Elizabeth flicked the reins and Margaret waved as they moved off at a smart trot, heading down the Long Walk. DS Dedham might have been going to follow but two of the Grenadier Guards were approaching and called out to him. Sophie could see them gesticulating towards the park, but she was too far away to hear what was obviously an animated discussion between the three men. She watched as the trap receded into the distance. For some reason, the phrase 'The Crown Jewels, both of them' flashed into her head.

'No!' she cried, frozen with horror. And then she was off, flying down the stairs two at a time. By the time she'd reached the ground, the air-raid siren was wailing, as she'd known it would be. A red warning: the most urgent. Around her, everyone was rushing for the nearest shelter, but she ran the other way.

'Sophie? What are you doing?' DS Dedham dismounted and hurried towards her, but she didn't slow down. Her eyes were fixed on the motorcycle, its engine still running. She swerved around him to reach the machine, leapt on board and kicked up the stand.

'Hey!' he bellowed. 'Stop!'

But she had already opened up the throttle. 'Come and get me!' she shouted above the siren's blare as the machine roared into life. And then she was off, through the gate and down the Long Walk in pursuit of the pony trap. She knew where the princesses would be heading in response to the alert: to the left through the park and towards the tunnel in the hillside. The wind whipped hair into her eyes, and behind her, though she daren't turn around, she could hear the ringing of bells and a voice through a megaphone, shouting some indecipherable instruction. Good: the more noise, the better. The more people following her, the greater their chances of saving Elizabeth and Margaret from rushing headlong into danger.

Cresting a dip in the road, she suddenly caught sight of the little Norwegian pony, trotting confidently across the grass. She was close enough to see the trap lurching, Margaret laughing and the governess clutching on to her hat. The tunnel entrance loomed maybe fifty feet away – too close.

'Get back!' Sophie screamed, frantically waving her arm as the motorcycle bucketed over the field. They didn't seem to hear, though how could anyone be oblivious of the commotion heading their way?

'Turn around,' she yelled, and at last saw all three faces swivel in her direction. She threw out her arm again. 'Go the other way!'

Elizabeth pulled the reins to slow the pony down just as the first dark figure was emerging from a slit trench near the tunnel entrance: a man in black, wearing a balaclava helmet with a gun in his hand. He was followed by another, both of them running towards the trap, with a third appearing from the tunnel itself. By this time, the princess had wheeled it around, urging the pony into a canter and then a gallop. Sophie gunned the motorcycle towards the trench in an attempt to head the men off, shouting at the top of her voice. The engine protested while the wheels bucked and slid over the bumpy grass, and then she heard a crack as a bullet whined horribly close to her head. More shots came from somewhere behind her, the motorcycle hit a tussock and she was suddenly flying through the air, landing with a thud that knocked the air out of her body. She had just enough wit to curl into a ball and lie there while the fight raged over her head, praying she hadn't been too late.

When she'd recovered sufficiently to look up, the scene

was too confused to make much sense at first. There were police and soldiers everywhere and only one of the men in black was still standing, brawling with several of the guardsmen. He must have lost his gun because he was laying about with his fists, hopelessly outnumbered. The guards overpowered him as she watched, cuffing his wrists behind his back and pushing him towards an armoured van drawn up nearby. Sophie could see the bodies of his two companions lying motionless on the ground, and an ambulance driving towards them. The pony trap stood some way off but there was no sign of the princesses or their governess inside it; a policeman now held the reins. And there on the grass not far away from her sat Detective Sergeant Dedham, clutching his leg.

'Henry!' she cried, staggering to her feet. 'Are you all right?' He looked up, his expression unreadable.

Before she could reach him, she was hauled roughly back and felt her own arms pinioned. 'What are you doing?' she asked the red-faced policeman who was restraining her.

'Taking you into custody,' he replied tersely. 'For stealing a motorcycle, and plenty more besides.'

'But I was trying to warn them!' she said. 'The princesses, I had to reach them. Surely you don't think—?'

He didn't reply, merely pushed her towards one of the waiting police cars. 'Save your explanations for later,' was all he'd say, no matter how loudly she protested her innocence.

She was driven back to the castle in silence and taken directly before the Superintendent.

'Here we are again, Miss Klein,' he said, his voice colder than she'd ever heard it.

'I'm sorry I took the motorcycle,' she began. 'I'd realised

what was about to happen, you see, and there was no time to waste. I found—'

He held up a hand to stop her. 'That's enough. A matter has come to my attention that casts a whole new light on your activities. This morning we received a document that I should like you to look at.'

He passed several sheets of paper across the desk. Sophie stared at them, her heart seeming to stop and then lurch forward at double speed. She recognised the pages instantly.

'That is your handwriting, is it not?'

She nodded; a denial would be pointless.

'The Master of the Household informs me this is a confidential account of a meeting between the Duke of Windsor and Adolf Hitler in 1937, located by you and the Royal Librarian two years ago. May I ask what you were doing, copying a top-secret document and sharing it with persons unknown?'

Sophie's palms were sweating; she wiped them along her skirt. 'I've been working for the British government,' she said. What other option was there? 'If you contact Esme Slater and George Sinclair, formerly of the British Embassy in Vienna, they'll vouch for me.'

They had to, otherwise she was finished.

Chapter Twenty-Eight

Windsor, June 2022

Of course, if Sophie Klein had been spying for the Nazis, that would explain why Gubby wouldn't want to acknowledge her. Lacey tried to imagine how she'd feel if Jess were accused of some terrible crime, and failed. She'd never abandon her sister – but then again, Jess would never do anything that would make her want to.

'You might not like what you hear,' this author Camilla Lewis had said. Still, as Tom had told Lacey, she couldn't stop now: it was better to know the truth one way or another. He'd offered to give her a lift to Camilla's house the next day as it wasn't far from his own, and he could show her the place on their way back. 'Are you sure you don't mind acting like my personal chauffeur?' she'd asked, but he'd assured her he had nothing better to do.

She would put Tom out of her mind until tomorrow, she decided, though she could still feel the delicious longing that had spread through her body at the touch of his hand. Was Anna right? Should she be brave, throw caution to the winds and go for it? To distract herself, she went shopping. She bought Platinum Jubilee T-shirts for Pauly and Emma, souvenir tea-towels for Adele and Cedric and commemorative Queen Elizabeth mugs for Jess and Chris. 'Steadfast and true' read the writing on the side, and how accurate that was. Lacey had seen a photograph of eighteen-year-old Princess Elizabeth in uniform, having joined the ATS in the last year of the war. There couldn't have been many people left who'd fought for their country; this jubilee was a celebration of their courage and service, too. Lacey suddenly wanted to be home, sitting on the porch with Gubby while she still had the chance.

At that precise moment, Jess called. 'Well, I've met Mom's cousin,' Lacey told her, 'but he doesn't want to have anything to do with us. He's not that great, actually, so it's no loss. I'll tell you all about him when I see you. He said his mom left Gubby something in her will but don't get too excited – it's only a book.'

'And are you having a good time?' Jess asked, when Lacey had paused for breath. 'Met any hot English guys yet?'

Lacey groaned. 'Oh God, I have. One, anyway. But what's the point of it, Jess? I'm coming back in four days' time.'

'The point is to enjoy yourself and have some fun for a change,' Jess told her. 'You've been living in solitary confinement for the past two years. It's time to get back into the world, sis. If you trust this guy and he's kind, why not? Just don't get carried away. Keep something in reserve.'

That was the trouble, Lacey thought, hanging up: it was all or nothing with her. Anna was out at work and the house was quiet. Glad of the solitude, she grabbed a sandwich at her favourite coffee shop and went for a long walk through Windsor Great Park. Maybe one day, she would come back; she'd miss the beauty and tranquillity of this place. By the time she got home, Anna was sitting at the kitchen table.

'Do you want a cup of tea?' she asked. 'The kettle's just boiled.'

'Great, thanks.' Lacey fetched a mug from the cupboard and joined her. 'Tell me, do you hang out with all your couch surfers like this?'

Anna laughed. 'No. For some unimaginable reason, I've taken to you.'

'Well, I appreciate it,' Lacey said. 'And the feeling's mutual.'

They drank their tea in companionable silence. 'I've been thinking about what you said,' Anna began. 'You know, about protecting myself. This has been a wake-up call for me, letting myself down in public like that. I've decided to stop drinking for a while. Not for ever – just a month or so to get back on track.'

'That's great,' Lacey said. 'Good for you.'

'Watch this space.' Anna laughed, a little self-consciously. 'Anyway, I want to see if I can go to a bar this evening and drink apple juice. Will you come with me? I think it would be helpful for us both.'

'How do you mean?' Lacey asked, already wary.

'Tom mentioned that you got a bit freaked out when he invited you to the pub.' Anna glanced at her. 'Don't worry, I didn't say anything about what you'd told me, but I guessed that was maybe the reason. Let's go out tonight, just the three of us. I know somewhere quiet in town.'

Lacey thought the matter over. 'OK,' she said. 'Thanks. I'd like that.'

She took particular trouble with her hair and make-up that evening, like a teenager going on a first date. Anna had dressed down but she would look lovely no matter what. I'll just try to relax and see how things go, Lacey decided; no great expectations.

Tom was late because he'd had to wait for the plumber and the traffic was awful. 'Still, at least now I have hot water,' he told them. 'Maybe in another few weeks I can start moving in furniture.'

'I feel bad,' Lacey said. 'Are you sure you don't want to move back in with your sister? I can always take the couch again.'

'No! Anything but that,' Anna protested, but the look she gave her brother was affectionate. They were getting along just fine; Lacey ordered the drinks and watched the bartender like a hawk, but she felt comfortable drinking her beer and Anna was managing with her apple juice. And then a girl Anna knew from work – Shelley, a physio, skinny and blonde – came into the bar.

'Mind if I join you till my friends turn up?' she asked, dumping her jacket on a chair. 'I'll get the next round. What's everyone having? Oh come on, Anna – you can't seriously want an apple juice. This is Friday evening, we all have to get rat-arsed. It's compulsory.'

'I'm on antibiotics,' Anna told her. 'Sorry.'

Tom wasn't drinking because he was driving and Lacey had made her pint last. 'Well, you lot are no fun,' Shelley said, taking a gulp of her gin and tonic. Yet soon she was flirting outrageously with Tom, once she'd discovered he was Anna's brother and that he and Lacey weren't a couple. At first it was funny but then it became tiresome, and the whole dynamic of the evening changed. Shelley had a loud voice and it was difficult to hold a separate conversation while she monopolised Tom. Anna caught Lacey's eye and pulled a face.

'I guess we should get going,' Anna said eventually. 'I'm on an early shift tomorrow. Do you mind if we love you and leave you, Shelley?'

'Wait, I'll come with you,' she replied, quickly swallowing the last of her drink. 'Looks like my lot have changed their minds.'

Lacey's heart sank; she couldn't bear to watch Shelley trying to get Tom to walk her home or take her for another drink somewhere else. Thank heavens, though, in the nick of time, the door swung open and a couple of girls walked through.

'Shell! There you are,' one of them said. 'We've been waiting for you at the Six Bells. Didn't you get my text?'

'Lovely to meet you, Shelley,' Tom said, holding the door for Lacey and Anna. 'Have a great evening.'

The three of them fled into the night. 'That was a narrow escape,' Tom said, letting out his breath. 'I'm sure she's a nice girl, but really.'

'I don't think she is a nice girl, actually.' Anna took his arm, and he held out the other for Lacey so they could walk three abreast. 'As soon as she finds a boyfriend, she cheats on him. I'm glad you were able to resist her charms, Tom. Makes a change.'

'Maybe I'm breaking the pattern at last,' he said. 'Besides, I'm only interested in Lacey, and she's not interested in me, so I'm just going to stay single and die of a broken heart.' He smiled at Lacey to show he wasn't serious.

'Who says I'm not interested in you?' she replied.

Tom stopped. 'Wait a minute. You are?' He was standing under a streetlamp, throwing his face into sharp relief: thick hair, dimples, eyes that were looking into hers with an expression that made her heart melt.

'I might be,' she said, and couldn't help smiling.

'OK, guys. Three's a crowd,' Anna said. 'I'm just going to hurry on home and guess I'll see you tomorrow.' And she walked off at a brisk pace.

Lacey was still smiling as Tom took her hands in his. 'Are you sure about this?' he asked.

She nodded. 'But there's something I need to get off my chest first, which might explain why I've been a bit weird.'

'You don't have to go there,' he said, 'not if you don't feel ready.'

'No, I want to,' she replied. She had told Jess, and Anna, and now she told Tom. Each time, the story became a little easier to bear. That's what it was: a story, a thread in the narrative of her life that she had to accept would always be there.

When she'd finished, he wrapped his arms around her and buried his face in her hair. 'Oh, Lacey,' he said in a muffled voice. 'My poor love.'

She drew back her head and kissed him. 'You don't have to feel sorry for me,' she said, when at last she could speak. 'I'm going to be just fine.'

Tom drove her back to his place and they spent the night on a blow-up mattress in his empty bedroom. 'If I'd known this was going to happen, I'd have put a few candles around the place,' he said, kicking a path through piles of clothing on the floor.

It turned out, however, that the lack of candles wasn't a problem. They fell asleep with their arms wrapped round each other and woke early, light streaming through the curtainless windows, to make love again. There was an unspoken acknowledgement that the time they had together was short, so they might as well make the most of it.

'Maybe I should cancel meeting Camilla Lewis,' Lacey said, when they were eating brunch around the corner from Tom's apartment. 'Spend the whole day with you instead.'

'You can't do that,' Tom replied, calling the waitress for more coffee. 'We need to solve the mystery of Sophie Klein, remember? That's why you're here. Do you realise, if it wasn't for her, we would never have met? I love her, even though she's a spy.'

'We don't know that,' Lacey said. 'But yes, then I guess I love her, too.'

'Anyway, Notting Hill's a cool place,' Tom said. 'You should see it.'

Lacey felt as though she were in a dream, or a movie, wandering hand-in-hand with Tom down streets lined with pastel-coloured houses. They'd parked a few blocks away from Camilla's address: a ground-floor apartment in a tall white stucco building. She rang the bell and stood back, butterflies leaping in her stomach.

The door was opened by a young guy in jeans who introduced himself as Jacob, Ms Lewis's assistant, and took them through to a large, light-filled sitting room lined with books. Camilla Lewis was sitting in a wheelchair at a table by the window, also covered with books aside from a small area cleared for a laptop. She was in her early fifties, Lacey estimated, with spiky red hair, wearing a bright green sweater and lots of silver jewellery: long earrings and bracelets that jangled with every movement.

'Ah, Lacey. Do come in,' she hailed them, with a wave that set the bracelets clashing. 'Excuse me for not getting

339

up to greet you but as you can see, I can't.' And she laughed, as though it were a great joke.

She's mad, Lacey decided; nice, but mad. She introduced Tom and they sat at the table, too.

'Let me get a good look at you,' Camilla said to Lacey, scrutinising her. 'Yes, I can see a definite family resemblance.'

'So you know what Sophie Klein looked like?' Lacey asked, hardly able to believe it.

'Of course. I have a photograph.' Camilla reached for the laptop, clicked a few times and brought it up on the screen. 'There we are.'

Lacey craned forward. Sophie was probably in her early twenties at the time. The picture was in black and white but she seemed to have mid-brown or dark-blonde hair framing an attractive, fine-featured face. Lacey wasn't sure about her own similarity to her great-aunt, but Sophie definitely reminded her of Adele: the curve of their lips was identical. She was gazing straight at the camera with an expression both defiant and wary.

'Wait a minute,' Lacey said. 'Is that—'

'A mug shot?' Camilla finished the sentence for her. 'Yes, I'm afraid so.'

Lacey sat back in her chair. 'So, tell me the whole story. I want to know the worst.'

Camilla folded her hands in her lap. 'I can't do that, I'm afraid. There are significant gaps I haven't been able to fill, but I'll certainly share what I've managed to find out. It's a tangled narrative, so bear with me.'

Apparently Sophie Klein had been arrested in July 1940 under the Emergency Powers Act, which allowed criminals to be imprisoned without trial. She was suspected of sharing confidential information – and of involvement in a foiled

340

plot to kidnap the young princesses, Elizabeth and Margaret, from Windsor Castle, where they had spent most of the war.

Lacey was too stunned to speak. She glanced at Tom, who looked back at her gravely.

'That summer was a terrible time for the Allies,' Camilla went on. 'The Germans were rampaging through Europe, we were humiliated at Dunkirk, and no one thought Britain had much of a hope against Germany. The United States hadn't entered the war by then, of course, and everyone expected the UK to be invaded at any moment. The whole country was on the lookout for spies and fifth columnists, and of course your great-aunt coming from Vienna would have attracted some attention.'

'But that wouldn't have been enough to get her arrested, surely?' Lacey said.

'No, there must have been some sort of evidence,' Camilla agreed. 'Another woman was involved in this kidnap plot: Mary Maguire, who disappeared shortly afterwards, only to turn up years later in America under an assumed name. It turned out she'd been a secret member of the British Union of Fascists for years. Their idea was that Britain would cave in to Hitler without a fight and George VI and Elizabeth would abdicate, leaving the Duke of Windsor to be reinstated on the throne.'

'Wait a minute.' Lacey shook her head. 'The Duke of Windsor?'

'The King's older brother, who reigned for a short time but abdicated to marry Wallis Simpson,' Tom said.

'Well done!' Camilla clapped. 'I do love a young man who knows his history. Wallis and the Duke were hand-in-hand with the Germans, you see; she'd been having an affair with von Ribbentrop, the German ambassador in Britain.

Ghastly man, but that's another story. Edward and Wallis fled to Spain when France fell in June – that was where they'd been living in exile – and he was hanging about there, I believe, just waiting to be called back to Britain and take over. Plenty of Fascists in Spain at the time.' She broke off to ask Lacey, 'Shall I ask Jacob to fetch you a glass of water? You look a little dazed.'

'No, carry on,' she replied. 'I'm just trying to keep track, that's all.'

'Well, the trouble for Hitler was that King George and Queen Elizabeth had no intention of abdicating, and Winston Churchill was also determined to resist. "We shall fight them on the beaches, we shall fight in the fields and in the streets", that sort of stirring stuff. So I suppose the Fascists thought if they could kidnap the princesses and fly them off to Jersey, or another of the occupied territories, the King and Queen would be bound to fall into line.' Camilla paused. 'I fancy a drink myself. Jacob, would you mind?'

'I just can't believe my great-aunt would be involved in something like that,' Lacey said. 'I mean, her father was Jewish and she had to flee Austria. Why would she work with Fascists?'

'Quite. It doesn't make sense,' Camilla agreed. 'I have another theory. When I found out Sophie had come from Vienna, my ears immediately pricked up. The British passport officer at the time of the Anschluss was a certain George Sinclair, who also happened to be working for the intelligence services. He was responsible for helping hundreds of Jews escape the city and only just managed to get out himself before continuing to work for MI5 in this country. Oh, the things I could tell you about him! Remarkable man. He ran a highly successful bugging operation, you know, extracting information from German prisoners. But here are the drinks. Choose your poison!'

Jacob had wheeled through a trolley laden with bottles and glasses. Tom opted for beer while Lacey had a soft drink, wanting to keep a clear head. Camilla talked ten to the dozen and her information was so concentrated, it was hard to keep up.

When Jacob passed Camilla a large gin and tonic, she raised her glass. 'Here's to our wonderful queen, God bless her. Seventy years on the throne, and may there be many more.'

When they'd all drunk a toast, she went on, 'I have a theory that George Sinclair might have been using Sophie Klein to feed him information about the Duke of Windsor. Perhaps instead of working in cahoots with Mary Maguire, she'd actually discovered the truth about her. She'd have had to be discredited before she gave the game away.'

'You mean, Sophie might have been framed?' Tom asked.

'Perfectly possible.' Camilla took a saucer of peanuts from the drinks trolley. 'Help yourself to snacks, by the way. There was a third woman in the triangle, you see: Jane Frobisher. She was one of MI5's most trusted agents. Aunt Jane, they used to call her. She looked like a little old lady who wouldn't say boo to a goose but she was passing most of what she heard straight to the Nazis. She was Mary Maguire's godmother. Rumour has it that she and Miss Maguire's mother had been lovers in Berlin in the 1920s – but that's another story.'

'I feel as though my head is about to explode,' Lacey said.

Camilla laughed. 'Sorry, I do tend to get carried away. Now, you said you had a letter from your great-aunt. Might I be allowed to see it?'

'Of course.' Lacey found the picture on her phone and passed it over.

'She sounds a nice woman,' Camilla said, when she'd finished reading. 'They made her acting Royal Librarian, you know, so they must have trusted her at some point. Not that you'll find anything about her in the archives. The whole thing was hushed up.' She helped herself to nuts and crunched reflectively. 'But you see, what I don't understand is why she was released from prison in 1943, when the war was still raging. I mean, she was accused of treason. At the very worst, she was facing the death penalty and at best, long years locked up. Why did they let her out so soon?' She shook her head. 'Strangely enough, she was in Holloway at almost exactly the same time as Diana Mosley. You know, the wife of Oswald, who led the British Union of Fascists. I wonder whether they came across each other? I must look into that.' She scribbled a note on a pad beside the computer.

'I've spoken to Sophie's son,' Lacey said, 'and we're seeing him again on Monday. I suppose he might know something.'

Camilla laughed. 'You won't get much joy there. He hates me, that's for sure. He said his mother would never talk about the past and just wanted to draw a line under the whole thing, and so does he.'

'How much of all this does he know?' Tom asked.

'He's aware she spent some time in prison during the war but nothing about the kidnap plot,' Camilla replied. 'I've tried to tell him my suspicions but he won't listen. He and his father had some trouble with journalists digging up the story when Sophie died, and I think it's made him paranoid about talking to anyone.' She glanced at the clock. 'Would you both care to join me for lunch? There's a nice little café around the corner.'

344

'That's very kind,' Lacey said hastily, 'but I'm afraid we've made other plans.'

'Of course. Well, you have my number. Drop me a line if you have any questions – and if you find anything out. I should love to learn the truth about Sophie Klein, though I doubt we ever shall.'

Chapter Twenty-Nine

Holloway Prison, London,

December 1940

Sophie sat opposite Henry Dedham in the visitors' room. She had a cold sore on her lip and was aware how awful she must look – it was a blessing, perhaps, not to have had access to a mirror for five months – but he still seemed pleased to see her.

'Thank you for coming. You don't have to, you know.' That's what she always said, although she sometimes thought that if he were to stop, she would give up; simply crawl into a corner of her filthy cell and wait to die. He'd started visiting once the bullet wound on his leg had healed and now came weekly if his shifts and the raids allowed. London was being bombed relentlessly by the Germans every night. If she stood on a chair pushed against the window, she could watch the flash of incendiary bombs and the orange glow of fire, hear the clamour of anti-aircraft fire above the roar of the aeroplane engines. All the women in Holloway were sitting ducks while the war raged around them. They were a mixed bunch: mostly Fascists, with a few unfortunate

Germans and Italians and some East End prostitutes thrown in for good measure. These prisoners found the bombing raids the hardest, because they were desperately worried about their children being killed as the slums were destroyed. Some women became hysterical and the wardens had taken to leaving all the cell doors unlocked so everyone could roam about at night.

Sophie steered clear of the Fascists – especially Diana Mosley, the undoubted leader of their pack, with her cut-glass voice and immaculate blonde hair. She slept under a fur coat, people said, drank port from Harrods and ate a slice of cheese each day from the whole Stilton her husband had sent. Sophie couldn't bear to look at her. She'd made one friend: a German girl who'd been held in Dachau concentration camp before the war because of her communist views but had managed to escape to England. She said Dachau was cleaner than Holloway. Amazingly enough, she'd heard that Sophie's old friend Wilhelm Fischer had been sent to Dachau, too, though of course she hadn't come across him as he was in the men's wing, and didn't know if he was still being held there – or whether he were still alive.

Henry would bring presents for Sophie from his mother: hand-knitted gloves, a jar of jam, once even a precious tin of Vaseline. He'd tell her stories about Joan, who'd become fed up with the Land Army and joined the Wrens, and relay snippets of information from the castle. Cyril Jenkins had been dismissed for stealing goods from household supplies and selling them on the underground market, and then fined for having got someone with an actual heart condition to stand in for his call-up medical in 1939. Miss Preston had broken off their engagement, naturally. There was no mention of her joining the Navy, but then again, no reason for that now Mr Jenkins was out of the way.

Sophie had told Henry that Miss Maguire was a Fascist the very first time he'd come to see her, but Mags had disappeared in the days following the 'commotion', as they referred to it, and nobody had any idea where she was. Signor Agnelli had gone, too: he was the one who'd sounded the alarm on the roof that had sent the princesses heading for the tunnel. The men who'd been trying to kidnap them were members of a rogue Fascist cell, it turned out, hoping to reinstate the Duke of Windsor on the throne. As far as anyone could tell, the Duke had had no knowledge of the plot.

'Do you ever talk to the princesses about me?' she asked Henry once, but he told her they'd all been forbidden to mention her name or breathe a word about the kidnap attempt. The princesses had been told it was a training exercise, so they wouldn't be unduly alarmed.

Sophie would always say at some point during the visit, 'You know I was only trying to warn them, don't you? That's why I took your motorcycle.'

'Of course,' he'd reply, though she was never entirely sure he believed her.

She couldn't tell him about the transcript but she never stopped asking whether there'd been any word from George Sinclair or Esme Slater. 'They could get me out of here,' she'd say, without explaining why.

One day, she received a visit from a dark-haired young woman she didn't immediately recognise. It was Ruth Hoffman, now fluent in a rather slangy English and working in London on some 'boring job for the Ministry of Ag and Fish'.

'I heard you were in here,' she said, glancing around. 'What's that all about?'

'A misunderstanding,' Sophie replied. 'I need George Sinclair or Esme Slater to sort it out. Do you know how to get hold of either of them?'

'Mr Sinclair's incommunicado,' Ruth replied, 'occupied with some hush-hush mission, and sadly Mrs Slater's dead. She was killed by a parachute mine in Shaftesbury Avenue two months ago.'

Sophie lowered her voice. 'You don't think she was working for the Germans, do you? It's just that . . . somebody betrayed me, and I can't help wondering if it was her.'

Ruth shrugged. 'Haven't a clue. Wouldn't have thought so, but you never know.' She passed Sophie a pack of cigarettes under the table. 'Chin up, old girl. You can get through this. I'll come back when I can.'

Ruth would always land on her feet, Sophie thought, but was touched she had taken the time to visit: besides Tamara, Ruth was the only person who had any idea of her former life in Vienna.

'Just try to find Mr Sinclair for me, would you?' she begged.

Whoever had received the transcript of the Hitler meeting from Aunt Jane had kept it to use as a weapon against Sophie; she supposed they would have typed up a copy and didn't need the original anymore. Could it have been Esme Slater? Yet Sophie wondered what sort of person she had become, as news of Mrs Slater's death sank in. She couldn't grieve for anyone, not even her parents. Her heart was frozen.

'Don't waste your time with me,' she told Henry Dedham on his next visit. 'I mean it. I could be stuck in here for years.'

He wouldn't listen. She should have told the wardens she refused to see him, but couldn't bring herself to do without the one good thing in her life. She had stopped writing to Hanna. What was there to say? And she couldn't bear to think of Hanna ever finding out where she was.

The days passed, the seasons changed and the war raged on. Oswald Mosley came to join his wife in Holloway and they lived together in a house in the prison grounds. The women heard snatches of information from visitors and the wardens' conversations but they were isolated from the world, suspended in limbo. Sometimes Sophie wished a bomb would fall on the prison, just to break the monotony.

On an ordinary day in March 1943, she was taken to a small room off the prison governor's office and told to sit there and wait. Two wardens stood in attendance, one on each side of her. They wouldn't answer her questions but she could tell something was up; they kept craning to look down the corridor with an air of great anticipation. Eventually the door opened and in walked the last person in the world Sophie had been expecting to see.

'Your Royal Highness,' she said, standing to curtsy. Princess Elizabeth was accompanied by two policemen. She wore a tweed skirt and blue twinset with a string of pearls, and looked as self-assured as usual – especially for a sixteen-year-old – despite her surroundings.

'Miss Klein,' she said, shaking Sophie's hand. 'I'm sorry to see you here.'

'Yes.' Sophie looked about the room in a stupor. 'It's not very nice, is it?'

The princess laughed and sat down, gesturing for Sophie to sit, too. 'There has been a terrible misunderstanding,' she said. 'We had no idea what had happened to you. I kept asking but nobody would tell me, as usual. They said you'd been moved to another department and I only found out the truth of the matter a couple of weeks ago. DS Dedham let something slip so, of course, I had to follow it up, and then George Sinclair came to talk to my father about you.'

'Thank you, ma'am.' Sophie couldn't allow herself to hope but her heart was beginning to beat a little faster. Had Ruth managed to pull off a miracle?

'You saved our lives that day, with no thought for your own,' Elizabeth told her. 'If you hadn't raised the alarm, we would have driven straight into a trap. Training exercises aren't usually conducted with live ammunition, I believe. You should have been rewarded but instead you were thrown in here. Well, my father has discussed the other issue of national security with Mr Sinclair, the Master of the Household and the Royal Librarian, and the matter has been resolved. I'm pleased to say that you've been granted a royal pardon, with immediate effect. I'm only sorry it's taken so long.'

Sophie stared at her, lost for words. 'Thank you, ma'am,' she whispered eventually.

The princess stood up. 'And now I must be off. I hope to see you at Windsor again sometime soon – you must have a word with the Librarian. By the way,' she added, 'DS Dedham has come to escort you home. He's waiting at the prison gates.' She smiled. 'We offered to give you a lift ourselves but he was most insistent.'

When she reached the door, she turned back. 'I shan't forget what you did for us – never, as long as I live.'

Chapter Thirty

Windsor, June 2022

'Lacey! Good to see you – and Tom, isn't it? Do come in.'

The Nicholas Dedham who opened the door to them was a very different man from the one they'd met at his college. He was in shirtsleeves and carpet slippers, his whole demeanour relaxed. Boy, Lacey thought, he really doesn't enjoy being at work. Maybe it's time to retire.

'You have a lovely home,' she said, glancing around the cottage, its ceilings low and beamed with oak.

'Thank you.' He led them into the kitchen. 'Shall we sit in the warm? Still not very summery weather for you, I'm afraid.'

A book lay on the table with an envelope on top; Lacey tried not to stare at it too obviously. Mrs Dedham – Barbara – came in from upstairs. She was pleasant and friendly, at least ten years younger than her husband. She made them coffee and put out some cookies on a plate before tactfully retiring. Maybe she was the key to her husband's change of mood? In that case, he should take her everywhere, Lacey thought, like an emotional support animal.

They sat with their mugs, each waiting for the other to speak.

'I must—' said Nicholas, at the same time as Lacey began, 'I'm sorry—'

She laughed. 'No, you go first.'

'OK. Well, I must apologise for being somewhat brusque when we last met,' he said. 'I'm a little defensive when it comes to my mother, and I wasn't sure of your motives in contacting me.'

'Don't worry,' Lacey told him. 'I quite understand.'

'I've found the book my mother left your grandmother,' he said, resting a hand on it, 'and something else besides, which has given me food for thought. But first, may I ask how you got on with Camilla Lewis?'

'I thought you said she was a crackpot?' Tom asked pleasantly.

Dedham shifted uneasily in his chair. 'I may have been too quick to judge.'

Lacey relayed the gist of what Camilla had told her, leaving out the inessentials, with Tom adding a few salient details she'd forgotten. 'The long and short of it is, she believes your mother was working for the intelligence services and that she might have been framed to get her out of the way,' she ended. 'You know she was in prison for three years, don't you?'

'Yes. A reporter came to our house soon after my mother died and shouted questions through the letterbox. My father was terribly upset. We never spoke of it again.'

Dedham stood, staring out of the window while jingling some change in his pocket. That was a habit of Cedric's; Lacey had known Dedham reminded her of someone. 'My father suffered from Alzheimer's,' he said. 'Before he died, he told me some rambling story about how my mother had foiled a plot to kidnap Princess Elizabeth and Princess Margaret from Windsor Castle during the war. Apparently she stole his motorbike, rode across the park and raised the alarm. Of course, I didn't believe a word of it. I knew she was working at the castle but the tale sounded like something from a comic book.'

'She was acting Royal Librarian,' Lacey reminded him.

'I thought that was wishful thinking, too,' he admitted.

'Do you know what happened to your mother when she was released from Holloway?' Tom asked.

'She married my father fairly soon afterwards,' Dedham said. 'He was a policeman, a reserved occupation, so he was never called up. He and my mother lived on my grandparents' farm for years, and that's where I was born. My father's sister, Joan, was killed in the war, so I suppose my mother became a sort of surrogate daughter to them. And they must have been surrogate parents for her, having lost her own so traumatically.' He sighed. 'My mother struggled with depression for the rest of her life. She did her best, but Dad and I were always aware of a terrible sadness hanging over her.'

He sat down. 'I'm sorry I spoke harshly about your grandmother. What right do I have to judge her? She suffered in her own way. Has she been happy?'

'Remarkably, considering what she went through,' Lacey replied. 'We all love her; everybody does. She says living a good life is her best revenge on the Nazis.'

'She's a wise woman. Well, here's her book.' He passed it across the table. 'There's a sealed letter inside addressed to her, which naturally I haven't opened.'

Our Island Story, read the title, and the cover showed a

knight on a charger, ships sailing across the sea, and castle battlements in the background.

'Rather old-fashioned,' Dedham said, 'but it gives an idea of British history. I've no idea what your grandmother will make of it.' He picked up the envelope. 'And this is what I found in my father's desk besides. Take a look.'

Lacey shook out an enamel badge, pinned on to a red-and-blue striped ribbon. The words 'For merit' were inscribed on the heart of the cross, which was surmounted by a tiny gold crown inlaid with pearls.

'It's the Order of Merit,' Dedham told her. 'One of the highest honours in the country, the personal gift of the monarch. I believe we should have returned it to the Queen once my mother died, but I had no idea she had it in the first place.' He scratched his chin anxiously. 'I'd better get in touch with the palace once the Jubilee fuss has died down.'

There was a photograph in the envelope, too: a picture of the young queen, smiling radiantly next to another young woman with an even wider grin.

'My mother, with Her Majesty,' Dedham said. 'I still can't quite believe it. She must have rewarded my mother soon after she acceded to the throne in 1952. And have a look at the inscription in that book.'

Lacey opened the front cover. 'To Sophie Klein, with grateful thanks for extraordinary services rendered. Elizabeth, March 1943.'

'Not just any old Elizabeth,' Dedham told them. 'Princess Elizabeth. I've looked up her signature on the internet. So it looks like that cock-and-bull story might have been true, after all.'

Chapter Thirty-One

Bethlehem, July 2022

Lacey had been rehearsing her meeting with Gubby for days, almost from the moment she managed to tear herself away from Tom and go through the boarding gate at Heathrow. At last, she could put it off no longer. She sat in the swing seat on the porch beside her grandmother, the book and envelope burning a hole in her tote bag.

'OK, so there's no easy way to say this,' she began. 'You know I've been away on a research trip to England?'

'Yes, dear,' Gubby replied. 'You told me several times. I'm not senile yet.'

'Well, I stayed in Windsor,' Lacey went on. 'I visited the castle and I found out about Sophie.'

There was a pause. 'Sophie,' Gubby repeated, her voice flat.

'Yes, Sophie. Your sister.'

The seat stopped rocking and an unnatural silence fell. Lacey could hear birds chirping and the distant hum of a lawnmower in someone's back yard. 'I know she went to England and ended up at Windsor Castle because I read her letter in your bureau,' Lacey went on. 'I'm sorry about that but not sorry, too, since it led me to the truth. Sophie was a heroine, Grandma! She probably saved the Queen's life when she was a girl. They actually gave her a medal.'

At last, Lacey dared look at her grandmother. Gubby held her gaze for a long time. 'My parents told me she was thrown in jail for being a spy,' she said eventually. 'They said she was working for the Nazis – some journalist had tracked them down through my foster home and told them the whole story. She went to prison with a load of Fascists.'

'But she was framed!' Lacey said. 'The whole thing was a terrible miscarriage of justice.'

'Oh, my Lord.' Gubby put her hands over her eyes. When she took them away, her face was ashen. 'You have to understand,' she said, 'I had two sets of parents and they both loved me, but in different ways. My adoptive parents were terrified of losing me. I discovered after they passed away that they'd been keeping all the letters my sister had written from England, after reading that first one. I couldn't understand why Sophie never replied to mine, never sent me any Christmas or birthday presents. She didn't even tell me that our mother was dead. Gradually I just put her out of my mind. I was so young at the time, I could hardly remember her – or maybe I didn't want to, because it was too painful. When my parents told me she'd been working for the Germans, it was the final straw. Of course, I felt terrible, discovering all those unopened letters and parcels in my mother's closet years later, but by then it was too late. I couldn't think how to get in touch again, or even find out where Sophie was. In those days, we didn't have the internet; people just disappeared and that was that. And I was ashamed, too, of having believed such a terrible thing about my own sister.'

'I found her son,' Lacey said. 'He's told me all about her.'

'Her son!' Gubby seized Lacey's hand, her eyes suddenly filled with tears. 'When did she pass away, dear? I know she can't still be alive.'

'Nearly thirty years ago. I laid some flowers from us on her grave.' Lacey reached for her phone. 'I can show you a picture.'

'Maybe later,' Gubby said, reaching for a handkerchief. 'You met her son, you say? Do you think he'll ever forgive me?'

'I think he might.' Lacey brought out *Our Island Story*. 'She left you this book in her will, and there's a letter for you inside.' She passed them over and scrambled to her feet, sending the chair rocking. 'I'll go make us a pot of tea.'

'Don't go yet,' Gubby told her. 'Stay with me while I read it.' Her fingers were trembling as she eased open the envelope.

What seemed like an age later, Gubby handed her the letter without a word.

13 February 1994

Dearest Hanna

I have no idea whether you will ever read this letter but I'm writing it anyway. I've been unwell for some time and now it seems my illness has entered a more serious phase, so I wanted to tell you that I have never stopped thinking about you since that day we parted at Westbahnhof station. The

knowledge you were safe was sometimes the only
thing that kept me going through those dark days of
the war.

I hope you've had a happy life, my darling sister:
our golden girl. You were a beloved child and all I
can pray is that you found a family in America to
carry on loving you, and that perhaps now you have
children of your own to love in turn. I have a son,
Nicholas, who along with my husband is my greatest
consolation. I'm sorry that life has led us along such
different paths, but I shared the first nine years of
your life and those memories will never leave me.
There will always be a bond between us that nothing
can break.

Please don't waste a moment in regret, dear
Hanna: we may never be able to forget the terrible
things that were done to us, but at least we can
forgive ourselves.

A thousand kisses and love always,
Your Sophie

'Heavens.' Lacey took a deep breath. 'What an amazing woman.'

'Oh, Lacey.' Gubby reached for her hand and held it tight. 'What have I done? How could I have turned my back on her?'

'Because you were young,' Lacey said, 'and doing what was necessary to survive. If you never heard from her and were told she was working for the Nazis, it's understandable.'

'But I should have tried to find her later.' Gubby turned away, her eyes filling with tears. 'All that time I wasted! I've felt guilty for so long.'

'Stop it, Gubby,' Lacey said firmly. 'You're a kind, loving person and there's no point beating yourself up now. You're not the villain here.' She squeezed her grandmother's fingers. 'Listen to your sister and forgive yourself.'

Epilogue

Manhattan, September 2022

Adele and Cedric's wedding was held in a rooftop garden in the middle of downtown Manhattan, with a fountain in the centre and tables laid out on fake grass amid huge potted palms. Adele wore a white tuxedo and looked incredible, and Cedric made a speech that no one could quite hear as the sound system wasn't working, but it didn't matter. It was one of the most joyful celebrations anyone had ever attended, they all agreed – no fuss, plenty of champagne and love in abundance. Lacey was floating on a cloud because Tom had come over for the occasion. They'd spoken every day since she'd left England, making tentative plans for the future. Tom's new company had a branch in Manhattan which he'd visit while he was over, and Lacey could write from anywhere, pretty much; maybe they could split their time between two countries and see how things went.

'We can make this work,' Tom had said. 'I'm not going to lose you, Miss Jones. Anna would kill me, for one thing.'

For now, Lacey was just thankful to have Tom in her life, to know that whatever the future held, they would share it together. His loving support made her feel strong enough to lay the past to rest. Kate, the girl from the bookstore, had contacted her to say that she'd heard about a guy who'd been accused of spiking women's drinks in the city, and had recognised him from a photo as the man she'd seen with Lacey that night outside the bar. She'd spoken to the police already and wanted to give them Lacey's details, if that was OK.

'More than OK,' Lacey had told her; she'd taken the name of the investigating officer and contacted him herself. Tom had been with her when the cop came to her apartment to take her statement, and she'd been glad of his presence when she looked at the picture of this stranger: sleek grey hair, stubble, a curl to his lip that suggested such allegations were beyond ridiculous. She didn't recognise the guy, but he looked somehow familiar, and then she felt suddenly sick as a scene flashed into her head. How could she have forgotten?

She's turning around from the bar with a drink in her hand to find a man standing behind her, so close she nearly treads on his feet and spills some of her beer on the floor. 'Steady on there,' he says, laying his hand on her arm with a smile, and she apologises, laughing as she transfers the glass to her other hand and shakes droplets from her wrist. She senses him watching as she sits down with her friends and for a moment she's flattered, before she forgets about him completely.

It would be months if not years before the case came to trial, the officer warned, but with Tom beside her, Lacey was prepared to wait.

'What do you think?' she had whispered to Jess in the Ladies' bathroom at the rehearsal dinner. 'Do you like him?'

364

'Ten out of ten,' Jess had replied. 'This one's a keeper.'

'He is, isn't he?' Lacey had sighed. 'I've never felt this way about anyone – not even Matt Crawley in ninth grade.'

'Do you love him enough to move countries?' Jess had asked, but Lacey had only shrugged. One day at a time, that was what they'd agreed.

Tom wasn't the only guest from England: Nick and Barbara Dedham had been invited, too. Gubby had been more nervous about meeting her nephew than Lacey could ever remember. The Dedhams had visited Bethlehem and stayed with Gubby for a couple of days, bringing her to the wedding in their rental car. They were firm friends by then. In fact, Lacey was a little jealous of Nick monopolising her grandmother. He had made copies of the photograph showing his mother with the Queen when she received her Order of Merit and had them framed for each of them.

'And we're having a new headstone made for her grave,' Gubby told Lacey. 'It's going to say, "Beloved daughter, *sister*, wife and mother".'

The most extraordinary thing was, Nick had been invited to return Sophie's Order of Merit to Buckingham Palace in person, and had had a private audience with the Queen. 'It was wonderful,' he told them. 'She was so gracious and natural, not stuffy at all. She remembered my mother clearly. Of course, I can't repeat everything she said because a lot of what went on in the war still has to be kept secret.'

Gubby watched him as he spoke, her eyes glowing with pride. Everyone was terribly worried about the Queen because there'd been reports that her health was failing; that was the only shadow over the occasion. An hour or so after the speeches had finally finished (Adele made one, too, of course, as did Jess, and then Cedric's sister who was clearly so astonished by this marriage that she could hardly find the words), somebody's phone pinged and gradually a ripple of consternation spread through the party.

Tom got to his feet. God, he looked handsome in a tux; Lacey wanted to rip it off right there and then.

'Forgive me for bringing a sad note to the proceedings,' he said, 'but for those who haven't heard, it's just been announced that Queen Elizabeth has passed away. Maybe we should raise our glasses to her in another toast.'

It was a tremendous shock. People had suspected the worst when the Royal Family was summoned to Balmoral, but to have the death confirmed was momentous. 'I can't believe it,' Nick Dedham kept repeating. 'She seems to have been part of our lives forever.'

'Isn't it just like her, though,' his wife said, 'doing her duty right till the end and then slipping away with no fuss. Thank heavens she managed to get through the Jubilee.'

'Although I wish she'd managed to last a bit longer,' Adele said, topping up her champagne glass. 'She's only gone and upstaged me on my wedding day.'

'Mom!' Jess hissed. 'Do you really want me to throw you off this rooftop?'

Gubby looked suddenly exhausted. It couldn't be easy, being reminded of your own mortality. 'Do you want to leave, Grandma?' Lacey asked. The bridal party was staying in the hotel so there was a room she could rest in.

'Maybe I will go downstairs,' she said. 'It's been quite a day. Give me your arm, dear. I'm a little unsteady these days. Let's just slip away quietly.'

They took the elevator. Once in the room, Gubby kicked off her shoes and lay on the bed. She patted the counterpane.

'Sit next to me.' Lacey did as she was told, stroking her grandmother's hand.

'I wanted to thank you, Lacey Lou,' Gubby went on, 'from the bottom of my heart. You found my sister and brought her home to me.'

'I'm sorry I went behind your back,' Lacey said.

'No, you were right. I was being a stupid old woman. Imagine if I'd died without ever knowing the truth!'

'Don't talk like that.' Not today, of all days. Lacey's heart was full and she couldn't bear anything spoiling that.

Gubby sat up, her eyes suddenly bright. 'I'm going to die sometime, and it probably won't be long. We need to be prepared. You'll find instructions for my funeral service in the bureau, along with my will. I want my wake at the Hotel Bethlehem, in the Mural Ballroom. There's money set aside. And a closed casket, for heaven's sake. I don't want the whole town gawping at me.'

'OK, whatever you say.' Lacey blinked back tears.

Gubby held her close for a moment. 'Don't you realise, I'm not afraid to die anymore? I'll see her again, my dearest Sophie, and then I can tell her that I never stopped loving her either.'

'Oh, Gubby,' Lacey sighed, 'how can we manage without you?'

Her grandmother lay back on the bed once more, closing her eyes. 'You will. You'll be sad at first but then I hope you'll remember me and be happy. That's the wonderful thing about life, my darling – it goes on. If we're lucky, that is.'

Lacey would remember those words many years later, when she and Tom had children of their own, and realise how true they were, and exactly how lucky she was.

Acknowledgements

Many thanks to my lovely agent, Sallyanne Sweeney at MMB Creative, and to the incredible Avon team, especially my original editor, Molly Walker-Sharp, whose idea this story was, and Amy Baxter, who saw the project through with such enthusiasm and skill. Thanks also to copy editor Laura McCallen, proofreader Jane Selley and to the design team for such a glorious cover (possibly my favourite so far). I'm also grateful to Julie Crocker and the staff of the Royal Archives at Windsor Castle (surely the best research spot in the world), to Karen Davies, for her encouragement and information about Vienna, to Lucy and Simon Everett in Windsor, and to the Serratelli/Latimer family from Bethlehem PA, that lovely city which is even more special to me because they live there. And huge thanks to my husband for digging me out of the deepest plot hole; this book would never have been finished without him.

The world is at war.
And time is running out . . .

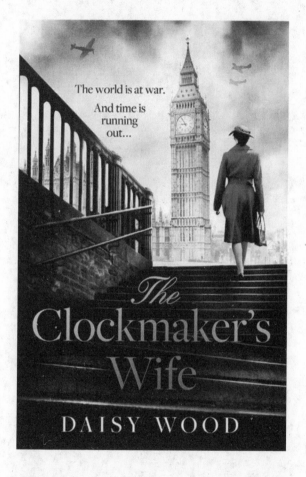

The world is at war.
And time is
running
out...

The
Clockmaker's
Wife

DAISY WOOD

A powerful and unforgettable tale of fierce love,
impossible choices and a moment that changes
the world forever.

A war-torn city.
A dangerous secret.
A shocking betrayal.

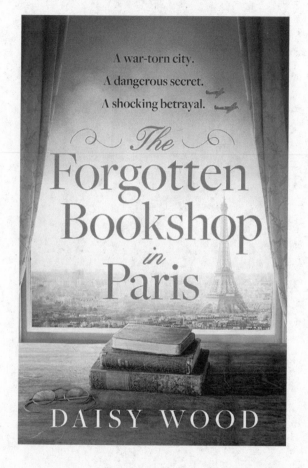

A heartbreaking tale of love and loss in war, perfect for
fans of Kate Quinn and Jennifer Chiaverini.